## "I don't suppose y... her."

Logan chuckled. "Charlie and Duster will never be sold."

"How about if I throw in my house? My car? Oh, wait. It doesn't run. Just the house, then. I don't have much else of value."

"Sorry. Not even your house." Laughing, he brushed an errant strand of hair away from Darcy's face. "But you and Emma are welcome to come out anytime to ride them."

"Tomorrow! Can we come tomorrow?" Emma begged. "Please?"

"Probably not, sweetie. But maybe another time."

Emma didn't speak a word on the way home and trudged silently from Logan's truck to the front door.

"Looks like we're going to have a quiet evening," Darcy said as she watched Emma go to the house. "Thanks so much for the wonderful day."

She impulsively gave him a quick hug and stepped back, suddenly feeling a little flustered and awkward at unexpectedly crossing that invisible line between friends and something more.

Yet how could she regret something that felt so right?

A *USA TODAY* bestselling and award-winning author of over thirty-five novels, **Roxanne Rustand** lives in the country with her husband and a menagerie of pets, including three horses, rescue dogs and cats. She has a master's in nutrition and is a clinical dietitian. *RT Book Reviews* nominated her for a Career Achievement Award, two of her books won their annual Reviewers' Choice Award and two others were nominees.

**Arlene James** has been publishing steadily for nearly four decades and is a charter member of RWA. She is married to an acclaimed artist, and together they have traveled extensively. After growing up in Oklahoma, Arlene lived thirty-four years in Texas and now abides in beautiful northwest Arkansas, near two of the world's three loveliest, smartest, most talented granddaughters. She is heavily involved in her family, church and community.

# Falling for the Rancher

Roxanne Rustand

&

# Her Single Dad Hero

Arlene James

 LOVE INSPIRED BOOKS

Recycling programs for this product may not exist in your area.

ISBN-13: 978-1-335-14612-0

Falling for the Rancher & Her Single Dad Hero

Copyright © 2019 by Harlequin Books S.A.

Falling for the Rancher
First published in 2017. This edition published in 2019.
Copyright © 2017 by Roxanne Rustand

Her Single Dad Hero
First published in 2017. This edition published in 2019.
Copyright © 2017 by Deborah Rather

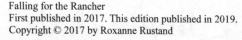

www.Harlequin.com

**Printed in U.S.A.**

# CONTENTS

# FALLING FOR THE RANCHER

Roxanne Rustand

With many thanks to my husband and our children
for their unfailing support, and also to the
wonderful editors at Love Inspired,
who make this all possible.

Love is patient, love is kind. It does not envy, it does not boast, it is not proud. It does not dishonor others, it is not self-seeking, it is not easily angered, it keeps no record of wrongs. Love does not delight in evil but rejoices in truth. It always protects, always trusts, always hopes, always perseveres. Love never fails.
—*1 Corinthians* 13:4–8

# Chapter One

After working at the Aspen Creek Veterinary Clinic for the past thirteen months, Dr. Darcy Leighton had encountered a lot of interesting situations. But walking into the clinic on Friday morning to find a tall, dark and muscular cowboy rifling through the file cabinets was certainly a surprise.

It wouldn't be the first time someone had broken in, searching for drugs or money, but this guy looked like he'd never touched an illicit drug in his life. Why on earth was he here, and how had he disabled the new burglar alarm? She and the other staff had inadvertently set it off more times than she could count, to the point that now someone from the alarm company just called her cell to ask if they'd tripped it again.

But there'd been no such call on her cell phone today.

The intruder had tossed an ivory Resistol hat on the desk, and from his pewter fleece vest and long-sleeve shirt to his well-worn jeans and ostrich Western boots, he appeared more suited to a ranch out West than this little resort town in Wisconsin. Not at all like the jittery, tattoo-covered thief she'd inadvertently confronted late one night while returning to check on a surgery case.

"Excuse me," she said sharply, pulling her cell phone from a jacket pocket. She took a single cautious step back and pressed the speed dial numeral for 911. "I think you'd better leave right now, mister. The sheriff will be here any second."

He shot a brief glance at her over his shoulder, then frowned and gave her a much longer second look. With a dismissive shake of his head, he turned back to the files and continued thumbing through them. "Explaining this filing system would be useful. Are you the receptionist?"

*Receptionist?* Three months ago, the attorney handling Dr. Boyd's estate had sent out a team of accountants who had pored over every last document and computer file for days, then recorded an inventory down to the last paperclip. But this guy sure wasn't wearing a suit and shiny loafers.

"No, I'm not. How did you get in here?"

"A key and the alarm code." He shoved the drawer shut and turned to face her with a sigh. "I'm serious about this filing. Someone here has just a passing acquaintance with the alphabet."

Her gaze landed on the discreet veterinary caduceus logo on the front of his vest. Realization dawned as she stared at a man who had the potential to ruin completely the future she'd so carefully planned. "So…y-you are…"

"The new owner as of last week." He reached forward to shake her hand. "Logan Maxwell."

Still wary, she held back. "We haven't been notified of any sale. Surely the attorney would have let us know."

"That doesn't surprise me. The firm doesn't seem all that competent." He snagged his billfold from his back jeans pocket, withdrew a business card and tossed it on the receptionist's desk. "Call them."

She swallowed back the knot rising in her throat as she eyed the familiar card with the scales of justice symbol in the center and flowing script, but she went ahead and made the brief call to the attorneys' office anyway. Sure enough, this guy was the new owner. Logan Maxwell, DVM.

The news made her heart sink.

She'd been praying that the practice wouldn't sell until she'd saved enough for a solid down payment and finally found a bank that would grant her a long-term loan. She'd also been praying that if that didn't happen in time, the new owner would want to continue business as usual with her on board.

Maybe a younger version of Dr. Boyd, rest his soul.

Not over six feet of toned cowboy with thick, dark lashes shading startling blue eyes, and a grim, suspicious expression on his way-too-handsome face. What was with that narrow-eyed, penetrating stare, anyway?

*He* was the one who'd looked like he might be robbing the clinic when she first walked in, while she'd just been coming in to continue working in the career she loved.

She bit back the wave of disappointment settling in her chest with the weight of an anvil as she called to cancel the 911 request. "I'm Darcy Leighton. Dr. Boyd started slowing down, and he needed an associate vet to keep the clinic running."

"So I heard."

She managed a faint rueful smile. "He'd promised to let me start buying into the practice after I'd been here for a year."

He directed a level look at her. "But according to the

attorneys, no contract was ever signed, and no money was paid."

The anvil pressing down on her heart grew heavier, obliterating her long-held dreams. It took her a moment to respond. "Correct. He died six months after I started, but the attorneys wanted the practice kept running until it could be sold, to maintain its value. So we're all still here."

He glanced at the clock on the wall. "Do the other employees come in by seven thirty?"

Darcy nodded.

He tipped his head toward the hallway leading from the waiting room to the lab, two exam rooms, the surgery room and two offices. "Instead of standing here, let's go back to Boyd's office. We have a few things to discuss."

He stepped aside and followed her to the back office, where she hesitated for a split second before dropping into one of the leather club chairs facing the massive old mahogany desk. He settled behind the desk as if it had been his for decades, and she felt a flare of sorrow.

"It doesn't seem right, seeing someone else in his chair. Doc was an institution here in town for more years than anyone can remember."

"And probably well loved, though from what I see in this clinic, he was behind the times."

"He was a good vet," she shot back, defending her old boss though she knew Maxwell was right. "Even if… some of the equipment here is out of date."

The man had the audacity to roll his eyes. "Show me something that isn't. The list is staggering, but I knew that before buying the place."

She looked at him in surprise. "When were you here?"

"Over a month ago, on a Sunday. I flew in from Montana, and two of the attorneys from Madison met me here. Then I went back to their office and spent a couple days going through the clinic's old financial records."

That explained why she hadn't seen him, then. He'd chosen to delve into the situation when the clinic was closed. "So you've seen that, despite a lack of the latest technology, this practice is busy."

"I hope it continues to be. The horse population in this county is growing rapidly, and there's a real need for an equine practice around here."

"Just equine?" she asked faintly. "What about our small-animal clients?"

A brief grin lifted a corner of his mouth, and she felt momentarily dazzled by the flash of a deep, slashing dimple in his left cheek. If he ever offered a genuine smile, the clinic's circuits just might blow.

"That's all I do, ma'am. Horses."

"Then that's perfect," she exclaimed with a rush of relief. "If you want to focus on horses, I can handle everything else. You've already got an excellent vet tech and receptionist in place."

His gaze veered to the wall of bookshelves. "Actually," he said carefully, as if walking cautiously through a minefield, "I want to have a fresh start. So—"

At a sharp, indrawn breath, he and Darcy looked at the open doorway, where Kaycee, the vet tech, now stood with a hand at her mouth and tears welling in her eyes. Marilyn, the office manager, stood behind her, her face pale with obvious shock.

"You're already firing us—without even giving us a chance?" Kaycee's voice trembled with outrage. "Is that fair?"

"I didn't say that," he said mildly.

"Y-you have no idea how hard we work or how dedicated we are," she retorted. "Doc Boyd always said—"

"Kaycee," Darcy said quietly, though she knew how much the girl needed her job. At just twenty-three, she was supporting her younger brother and sister, while Marilyn had a disabled husband at home.

Knowing their difficult situations, Dr. Boyd had given both of them generous annual raises. There wasn't another job in town that would pay either of them as much for their specialized skills. This practice was the only one for forty miles.

But starting an argument on the new owner's first day wouldn't help anyone's cause.

Darcy looked up at Marilyn. "Are my first clients here?"

The receptionist nodded stiffly.

"Then please get them settled in the exam rooms, Kaycee. I'll be out in a minute." Darcy stood to shut the office door quietly and turned back to the desk with a frown. "They're excellent employees. I can promise you that. I've worked with them for a year. They're both highly professional."

He drummed his long, tanned fingers on the desk. "As I started to say, I feel it's important to have a fresh start here. This is going to be an equine clinic in the future, with far less—if any—small-animal. So I have to assess the kind of staff I really need. And honestly…"

His voice trailed off as he seemed to consider his words, but at the regret and sympathy in his eyes, Darcy suddenly knew exactly what he was going to say. This wasn't just about Marilyn and Kaycee. It was also about her. And given the muscle ticking along the side of his jaw, those changes weren't going to be in the distant future.

What was he going to do—boot her out the door right now? Would he be that callous?

After all she and her little girl had been through during the past two years, she'd thought they were finally secure in their new lives here in Aspen Creek.

Even two weeks' notice wouldn't be enough to get her finances and her future in order. What if she needed to leave town to find employment? How would Emma handle yet another wrenching change?

Blindsided, Darcy felt her heart falter as her thoughts raced through a dozen possibilities. "Even if you're developing an equine practice, you'll find the small-animal side busy and well worth keeping."

"I'm sorry. That's not part of my plan," he said gently.

Time. She needed much more time, and it didn't sound like she was going to get it.

"But it's still going to take a while for you to get up to speed and build up a different clientele, and in the meantime, it sure couldn't hurt to enjoy a solid income." She said a silent prayer and took a steadying breath as she considered just how far she could push him.

"I'll stay on for just the next two months," she continued firmly. "So you can get your feet on the ground here. I'll take care of the clinic appointments while you get settled in and start your horse practice, and then we can reassess. If you realize it's worth keeping the small-animal side going, we can discuss my salary and contract. If not, no hard feelings. I'll just start my own large and small-animal mixed practice here in town. A little competition never hurt anyone, right?"

He stared at her reluctantly for a long moment, then laughed—probably at her sheer audacity—and accepted her handshake. "I guess we have a deal."

\* \* \*

A few hours later, Logan settled into a booth at a cafe at the far end of town and sighed heavily. His goal had been simple and should have been easily met, but his first morning at the clinic certainly hadn't gone as well as he'd planned.

Finding the right veterinary practice to buy had occupied his thoughts for months. Finding one within a reasonable distance to horse breeding farms and also the active horse show circuits in Wisconsin and Minnesota had been high on his list.

The Aspen Creek Vet Clinic and associated property had ticked every box. It had once been a mixed practice, so it included a good clinic building with a corral and small stable out back, which made it perfect for conversion into an equine practice. And a few miles out in the country, Dr. Boyd's house sat on twenty fenced acres with another stable. The house and all of the buildings needed updating, but at least he hadn't needed to hunt for a place to live.

The fact that this little Wisconsin town was far from Montana made it even better.

But all of those thoughts about the property and his future here had instantly fled the moment he'd come face-to-face with Darcy Leighton this morning. Warning bells had clanged in his head. His jaw had almost dropped to the floor. He'd had to force himself to stand his ground.

Curvy, with brown hair and sparkling hazel eyes, she could easily have been the much prettier sister of his former fiancée back in Montana, though for just a moment he'd imagined he was staring into Cathy's deceitful eyes and his stomach had plummeted.

His business plan aside, seeing Darcy on a day-to-day basis would be an intolerable reminder of the past. A time when a pretty face and calculated charm had blinded him to clues so obvious that in retrospect he could not believe his stupidity. Two months. He could manage two months. *Maybe.*

Why hadn't he just said no, offered Darcy a nice severance bonus and sent her on her way? And what on earth was that rush of sensation when he'd accepted her handshake? He'd felt his arm tingle and his blood warm, and when his eyes locked on hers he couldn't look away.

It was only when she'd smiled a little and stepped back that he realized he'd held her hand a little too long.

He certainly hadn't felt this instant connection with Cathy…which made those warning bells clang all over again. He could not afford a second mistake.

He ordered a cheeseburger and Coke when the waitress—Marge, given the name embroidered on her uniform—stopped by his booth. Then he pensively stared out the large plate glass window overlooking Aspen Creek's Main Street.

For a chilly Monday morning in mid-April, there was a surprising amount of activity in town. Most of the parking spaces were filled. Pedestrians were window-shopping as they passed the various boutiques and upscale shops probably meant to lure tourists from Minneapolis-St. Paul and Chicago.

Farther down the street, he'd spied some high-end outfitters displaying kayaks, canoes and pricey backpacks in their windows. A quaint two-story bookstore. Cozy-looking tea shops. Bed-and-breakfast signs in front of grand old Victorians.

The town hardly looked like it could be in horse country, but his research had proved otherwise, and so he had started making his plans. Remodeling. Equipment purchases. Supplies. Promotion, to let horse owners know about him.

Under Dr. Boyd's ownership the clinic had been focused on small animals, so he'd figured he would let the current staff go and then hire people with the equine expertise he needed. People he would carefully interview, and then he'd follow up with background checks on. Thorough background checks.

He felt a shudder work down his spine, wishing with every beat of his heart that there'd been more careful scrutiny of staff at the multi-vet clinic where he'd worked back in Montana. But that was over, done with, and now he had a chance to start his own clinic and do things right.

The waitress returned, gave him a narrow look and set his Coke down with a thud. A few drops splattered onto the table, but she wheeled around for the kitchen without a second look.

Curious, he watched her go and realized that every eye in the place was fixed on him. None of them looked friendly. Feeling as if he'd slipped into some sort of time warp, he eyed the Coke but didn't try it.

A stooped, gray-haired man in a bright plaid shirt, khakis and purple tennis shoes appeared next to his booth. "I figure you must be the new vet," he muttered. He leaned closer to peer at the veterinary emblem on Logan's vest. "Yep. Figured so. Lucky man, buying Doc Boyd's place. He was the best. Best gals working for him, too. Couldn't find any better. You can count your blessings, sonny."

He stalked away, muttering under his breath.

Three elderly women seated at a round table a dozen

feet away craned their necks to watch the old guy leave. As one, their heads swiveled toward Logan. If glares could kill, he'd have been turning cold on the floor. Still, he nodded and smiled back at them. "Ladies."

The oldest one harrumphed and turned away. The one with short silver hair fixed him with her beady eyes. "Paul is right. Everyone loved Dr. Boyd, you know. He wouldn't *ever* have treated his staff badly." "People care about each other in a small town." The third woman lifted her chin with a haughty sniff.

He politely tipped his head in acknowledgment, then startled a bit when a thirtysomething woman slipped into his booth and propped her folded hands on the table.

Judging from the blinding sparkles on her wedding ring, she surely hadn't stopped by to flirt, and given the decidedly unfriendly mood in the café, he hoped she didn't plan to whack him with her heavy leather purse.

"Beth Stone. I own the bookstore in town," she said briskly. "It looked like you might need a bodyguard, so I figured I'd stop by for a minute. Thought I might need to warn you."

He glanced at the other customers in the café, who were all pushing eighty if they were a day. "I think I can handle them. At least, so far."

Her long chestnut hair swung against her cheek as she slowly shook her head. "Your business affairs are your own, of course. I don't mean to pry, and whatever you decide to do is totally up to you. But as you can see, word spreads fast in a small town. Gossip is a bad thing, but people really do care about each other here, just as Mabel told you. No one wants to see a friend hurt."

Clearly eavesdropping from her seat at the round table, Mabel gave him a smug smile.

"I just wanted to offer a little friendly advice," Beth continued. "If you can, take things a bit slow. Settle in. Get to know people. And if you're going to fire everyone at the vet clinic right off the bat—"

"I haven't," Logan said quietly. *Yet.*

"But that's the word on the street, as they say. Not because your employees are blasting the news all over town," Beth added quickly. "There might have been… uh…a client who overheard something while in the waiting room…who happened to stop here at the café, where no secret is ever kept. Ever."

The waitress scuttled up to the booth and delivered his hamburger, then fled back to the kitchen. "Sounds like my hometown in Montana," Logan said.

"Businesses have failed here over far less, and you don't want to drive every last client to some other vet practice in the next town. Just be prepared."

"Thanks."

"People *care* about each other here. And they are as friendly as can be."

He eyed the other customers in the café, who definitely didn't appear friendly at all. "I'll have to take your word on that."

"I promise you, this really is a wonderful town. There are all sorts of seasonal celebrations that draw crowds of tourists. And I can't think of anyone who doesn't have at least one pet, so you'll be plenty busy." She gathered her purse and stood. "And I know you'll really like the staff at the clinic when you get to know them. I've been taking our pets there all of my adult life, and they provide excellent care."

"Good to hear." He poked at his hamburger, which appeared to be very well done, and cold to boot.

"Dr. Leighton in particular—did you know she completed some sort of special residency after vet school? I don't recall, exactly. Surgery, maybe. Or was it medicine? I know that she received some pretty big honors. There was an article on her in the local newspaper when she first came to town. Dr. Boyd was really thrilled when he was able to hire her."

So here was yet another pitch, though delivered more skillfully than most. "I'll be sure to ask her about it."

Beth nodded with satisfaction. "I've got to get back to my store, but it's been nice to meet you. God bless."

He waited until she left, then cautiously lifted the top bun on the burger. Though nothing unexpected appeared inside, the patty was charred to the point of being inedible—yet another message from the good people of Aspen Creek.

So maybe it was for the best that Darcy had railroaded him into keeping her on for a few months, he realized with chagrin.

He could now become acquainted around town, try to avoid alienating any more of the residents and thus improve the chances that his vet practice would succeed. With a new clinic website, a Facebook page and announcements in the regional horse magazines, word would spread, and maybe he could start his life over again, away from the shadow of his past.

All he needed was time.

## Chapter Two

After the Easter service at the Aspen Creek Community Church, Darcy drove up the long lane winding through a heavy pine forest to Dr. Boyd's house, knowing this was probably a big mistake.

Logan certainly hadn't been friendly when he'd first arrived at the clinic on Friday. He'd been gruff and completely lacking in empathy toward her and the clinic staff. He was clearly looking forward to firing them all.

And he probably wouldn't accept her invitation anyway. So why had she even bothered to come?

Because, she muttered under her breath, she should treat him as kindly as she would any other newcomer, even if she had yet to find anything likable about him whatsoever.

"What, Mommy?" Emma chirped from her new booster seat in back.

"Just talking to myself, sweetie." Darcy's mood brightened. Maybe Logan had a wife and kids, and they were all celebrating Easter by themselves, though something about him made her guess that he was probably alone. That would be no surprise, if he was cold to everyone.

She looked up at Emma in the rearview mirror. "I'm guessing that Dr. Maxwell might not want to join us for dinner, but we'll see."

Emma sat up a little straighter to look around and squealed with delight at her surroundings as the house and barn came into view. "Will Barney be here?"

*I wish. I wish everything was still the same—that the old sheepdog would come romping out of the barn to meet us, and that Dr. Boyd would be here, too.*

He'd been more than a mentor during the seven months she'd worked with him. He'd been kind and perceptive and caring, like the grandfathers she'd never known but had pictured. He'd helped her get through the bleakest time of her life.

But now he was gone, and nothing would ever be the same again.

"Barney lives with Marilyn now, sweetie. Remember? And Dr. Boyd is up in heaven."

"Can we go see Barney?" Emma asked somberly.

"Of course we can. Maybe tomorrow." Darcy pulled to a stop in front of the sprawling, rustic log home with river rock pillars and rock siding at the front porch. Set in the shade of towering pines, the house blended into its surroundings and matched the hip-roofed barn and wood-fenced corrals.

It had been the home of her dreams, but the house and clinic had been far beyond her financial reach.

A gleaming black crew cab Dodge pickup with Montana plates was parked in front of the garage, so apparently Logan was home. She stepped out of her SUV, smoothed her peach linen skirt and helped Emma out of her booster seat.

Twisting a strand of her blond hair around her finger, the four-year-old frowned and looked around. "Will there be Easter baskets here?"

"At home," Darcy promised. She bent down to fluff the layers of pink ruffles cascading from the waist of her daughter's dress. "We won't be here long."

A spiral-sliced ham was waiting in the oven back at the cottage, and creamy mashed potatoes were staying warm in a Crock-Pot. Several colorful salads were finished and in the fridge. But the day seemed strange again this year, with just the two of them to celebrate the joy of Easter.

It had to be different for Logan, as well, assuming he had observed the usual Easter traditions back in Montana. Then again, was he even a believer? Beyond the fact that he'd arrived intending to fire her, she knew nothing about him.

At the sound of hammering out past the barn, she took Emma's hand and headed that way, taking in the contrast of the many new boards that now replaced the broken ones.

As they rounded the barn, he came into view. He eyed the three-plank oak fence line stretching toward the heavy timber to the west. Tapped a top board upward into perfect alignment and nailed it in place.

"Hello there," Darcy called out. "Happy Easter."

He spun around, clearly startled, and frowned as he dropped the hammer into a loop on his low-slung tool belt. He gave them a short nod.

It wasn't much of a greeting, but she resolutely strode forward with Emma in tow. "Looks like you've been working hard since you got here."

"Yesterday and today." He tipped his head toward the

corral. "I need at least one safe corral finished before I can go back for my horses and the rest of my things."

Emma had shyly hung back behind Darcy, but now she took a tentative step forward. "You have horses?"

His cool demeanor softened as he looked down at her. "Just two. Drifter is a pretty palomino mare just about the color of your hair, and Charlie is a bay gelding with four white socks and a blaze. I've had him since I was twelve."

She looked up at him in awe. "I want a pony but Mommy says not 'til I'm bigger. That's too long."

Darcy cleared her throat, knowing all too well where *that* conversation was heading. "We actually stopped by because I figured you don't know anyone in town yet, and thought you might like to join us for Easter dinner this afternoon. I didn't think to ask you when we first met on Friday."

"Well, I..."

"It's just the two of us here in town, so we won't have a big family gathering or anything."

Emma's eyes sparkled. "Could you bring a horse?"

He looked down at her and chuckled. "That would be fun, but I'm heading back to Montana as soon as I put away my tools."

Emma's face fell. "Mommy even made my favorite pink fluffy Jell-O. And then I get to hunt for Easter baskets. What if there's one for you?"

That deep slash of a dimple appeared when he smiled at her. "I think I'm too old for that, darlin'. But I know you'll have a great time."

"We'd better go home and let Dr. Maxwell finish up so he can get on his way." Darcy reached for her hand. "I hope you have a safe trip. Let Marilyn know when you'll be back, in case someone asks."

When he looked up at Darcy, his warmth faded as quickly as if he'd turned it off with a switch, and he was back to his aloof business persona. "Probably Thursday or Friday."

"Uh… I'll let her know. Safe travels." She turned away and headed back to the car with Emma.

How awkward was that? He'd shown kindness to Emma, but if he was this cool and distant with his clients, he wasn't going to fare well.

Though if he didn't connect well with them, maybe he'd eventually put the practice up for sale, and perhaps by then she'd be able to find favorable financing. A little flare of hope settled in her heart.

Maybe her dreams could still come true.

"We're down to only fourteen volunteers now," Beth said on Friday afternoon as she studied the list on her iPad. She drummed her fingers on the vet clinic receptionist's counter. "I never expected six would cancel. All of our posters promised there would be twenty, and the handyman fundraiser auction is tonight. Guess I was too optimistic."

"There should still be enough money for the church youth group trip, though," Darcy said.

"For the kids, probably. But not enough to cover the chaperones' expenses, and some of those parents just can't afford it otherwise. Without enough chaperones, the trip is off. Have you asked Logan to participate? I'll bet he would be willing."

"Ask him? I barely know him." Darcy shuddered. "He doesn't seem like the benevolent type. And this would be an awfully big favor."

"Wouldn't it be a great introduction for him in the

community, though? Participating for such a good cause would surely cast him in a more favorable light. He didn't exactly have an auspicious start in town."

"Thanks to Paul Miller, who had no business starting those rumors at the cafe." And mostly thanks to Logan himself, but she tried to rein in that uncharitable thought. "For all I know, Logan doesn't even have the skills for this sort of thing. I've seen him wield a hammer, but that was only on a fence board."

"Call him and find out," Beth insisted. "You have his cell number, right? Tell him the auction is for just twenty hours of labor. Surely he could manage to do something useful for someone."

"Maybe. But I haven't even seen him all week—not since he showed up and announced that my career, my whole life, is being turned upside down. Marilyn's and Kaycee's, too, and you know how much they need their jobs." Darcy thought for a minute. "Oh, and I also saw him briefly last Sunday, when he refused my invitation for Easter dinner and was pretty much cold as ice when we talked. A very brief conversation, I might add."

Beth grinned. "And here I thought he might just be the perfect match for you. Handsome, same career, lots to talk about…"

Darcy snorted. "No way. Sounds like fairy-tale stuff to me. Been there, done that, and I'm not going down *that* road again. Ever."

"If he's been gone all week, maybe he's changed his mind about buying the clinic and is scouting out other possibilities."

"I wish," Darcy retorted dryly. "But I think the purchase of the clinic is a done deal. Signed contracts and all of that. He called the clinic this morning and told

Marilyn he'd be back sometime late today with his two horses and the rest of his things. That sounds permanent to me."

"So, will you make that call?" Beth fixed Darcy with an expectant look. "Please? We could bend the rules so he wouldn't even need to appear onstage."

Darcy laughed, remembering Logan's narrow-eyed glower when they'd first run into each other at the clinic. "That actually might be for the best no matter when he shows up back in town."

"Just be sure to let my assistant know as soon as you have an answer, because Janet will be printing the final version of the program at six thirty, and the auction starts at eight."

There were reasons Beth had made such a success of her bookstore, and sheer determination topped the list. Darcy sighed heavily as she glanced at the clock on the wall. "I'll send him a text. I need to take Emma to her dental appointment at four, and I'll be busy with clients all afternoon. If he doesn't respond by then, Kaycee can ask him when he stops in."

Beth beamed. "Perfect."

"Well, hang on to that thought, but I doubt he'll agree. Anyway, I suspect most bidders have already set their sights on the handyman they prefer, so Logan might not generate much for the fundraiser."

"Are you still planning to bid on Edgar Larson?"

"Absolutely." Darcy fervently clapped a hand against her upper chest. "He is the man of my dreams."

Beth laughed. "But just a bit old for you, sweetie—by forty years at least. And don't forget about Agnes."

"All the better. I understand Ed is the best craftsman in the bunch, and my late aunt's cottage is in serious need of repairs. And I hear his wife sends along her incredible caramel rolls whenever he starts a new job."

"So I've heard. Those rolls alone should double his worth during the bidding."

"I sure hope not. But I suspect every single, divorced or widowed woman in town wants to win him as much as I do."

"As do all of the women whose husbands can barely change a lightbulb. Edgar is our biggest draw every year, bless his heart. Last year he was first on the program, and a third of the audience left as soon as his work was auctioned. This year, we've got him last."

"I'll sure be hoping. Last month I did a lot of calling around, trying to find someone to start doing repairs and updating. The reputable firms are booked at least six months out, and I may no longer have that kind of time to wait."

Beth rested a comforting hand over Darcy's. "Our whole book club is praying you'll be able to stay in town one way or another, believe me."

"I'm praying, too. But I still need to be prepared." Darcy tapped a brief text to Logan and held up her phone for Beth to see, then hit Send. "There, it's done."

"Thanks a million." Beth leaned in for a quick hug. "Now we're all set."

Probably not, Darcy thought as she headed into an exam room, where a cocker spaniel was awaiting a health exam and vaccinations. Would Logan even consider the request?

There was no answer to her text by the time she'd finished with the spaniel.

Nothing by the time she finished with her other appointments and gathered her purse and car keys to go pick up Emma. Of course not. She hadn't expected him to agree, but at least he could've been thoughtful enough to respond.

She stopped in the kennel room, where Kaycee was checking on the IV running for a beagle recovering from surgery. "I still haven't heard back from Dr. Maxwell. Can you keep trying to reach him? Or tell him about the auction if he stops by the clinic?"

"No problem."

"Oh, and let Janet or Beth know about his answer, in case they need to add his name to the program."

"Will do." Kaycee shut the cage door, turned around and grinned. "Did I hear you say that you're pinning your hopes on Edgar? He's my uncle, you know. Crotchety as can be."

"So I hear, but I'm praying he'll agree to continue working for me after the twenty hours are up."

"Best wishes on the bidding, 'cause it's probably your only chance of getting him to do any work for you. Outside of the annual youth group auction, he's superfussy about who he works for. Says he's semiretired."

"So…if I don't have the winning bid, you could put in a good word for me later on?" Darcy said. "Please?"

"I'll ask, but it probably won't make any difference. His own niece tried to hire him for a project last winter and he flat-out said no. Then again, the whole family knows she's high-maintenance, and he probably didn't want the bother."

"I promise you that I'm not," Darcy said with a smile as she headed for the door. "I'm desperate, not difficult."

As she drove to the babysitter's home to pick up Emma, the truth of her own words weighed heavily on her heart.

The cottage needed a lot of work, as dear old Aunt Tina hadn't been able to keep up with repairs and updates during her final years. But now there was a ticking clock to consider.

If Logan Maxwell did let her go at the end of two months, her options would be to establish a new practice here—a financial impossibility right now—or to find a practice elsewhere, looking for an associate. But how would the cottage ever pass the mortgage home inspection for a buyer if she suddenly had to sell it and move on?

As she waited at the only stoplight on Main Street, she looked heavenward and briefly closed her eyes. *Please Lord, help me win the bidding for Edgar—and give me more time to work things out.*

A large crowd had already gathered in the church reception hall when Darcy arrived with Emma in tow just minutes before Pastor Mark began his opening remarks at a podium.

Two long bake sale tables displayed delectable treats, while several other tables offered arts and crafts items. At the far end of the room, two women were offering hot chocolate and coffee from the kitchen serving window.

"I know you just had supper at home, but would you like some hot chocolate or a treat?" Darcy asked. "I see some pretty frosted cookies on that table."

Emma nodded somberly. "A cookie. Can we go home?"

"Um… I need to stay, sweetie." The daytime babysitter who took care of Emma after morning preschool every day was rarely available for evenings, and Darcy hadn't been able to find anyone else.

She settled Emma on a chair with her cookie and took the chair next to her. "One of the nursery ladies and some teenagers from the youth group are watching kids in the nursery. Would you like to go play with them?"

"I wanna go *home*."

Emma's mood didn't bode well for the evening, but Darcy could hardly blame her. It had already been a long day for her, and this was now Emma's usual bath time, to be followed by a bedtime snack and a stack of books to read. In the hope that Edgar had been moved to an earlier time slot, Darcy opened her program and looked down the list.

It was up to fifteen names now, each followed by a brief description of the types of handyman jobs they preferred. Some were members of the church with other careers but willing to mow, rake or help paint. A few offered to help with household repairs or a specific auto maintenance task rather than the twenty hours. A couple said "negotiable."

Edgar was still at the end of the list and… Oh, my. Darcy drew a sharp breath in surprise. There was Dr. Logan Maxwell's name, second to last. No skills listed. She glanced at it again in disbelief. He'd actually volunteered?

Surprised, she glanced around the crowded room trying to find Beth or Janet…or even Kaycee, who had planned to take a shift at the bake sale table. Glimpsing Kaycee in the crowd milling at the back of the room, she dropped her jacket on her chair. "I'll be right back, sweetie. You'll be able to see me just right over there."

Emma looked up from nibbling the edge of her cookie and yawned. "Then can we go home?"

"In a little while. Once it gets started, the auction shouldn't take long." She strode toward the crowd as Pastor Mark yielded the microphone to Lewis Thomas, a short, spare man with thinning hair and a booming voice, who encouraged vigorous bidding for the sake of the youth group, then began describing the terms of the auction.

He abruptly launched into a rapid-fire auctioneer's patter, and one after another, the handyman volunteers were auctioned off. Fifty dollars. A hundred. Several went for one fifty.

A woman with a gleam in her eye shouted, "One seventy-five! That one's my husband, and now he'll *have* to take care of my honey-do list!"

The audience erupted in laughter.

"Hey, Kaycee," Darcy called out as she edged through the people pressing forward toward the podium and made her way to Kaycee's side. "I'm dying to know what Dr. Maxwell said—and how you convinced him to volunteer. Will he be here tonight?"

A faint blush bloomed on Kaycee's cheeks. "I'm really sorry, Doc. I never saw him at the clinic. I left two messages on his cell, but he never called back."

Darcy felt the blood drain from her face. "B-but he's on the program."

The younger woman's eyes widened. "Maybe he talked to someone else?"

"He wouldn't have known anyone else on the committee." Darcy bit her lower lip. "I'll find Beth or Janet. No worries."

"If he's listed and his work commitment is auctioned, he's *got* to follow through, it's like a *contract*," Kaycee said darkly.

"Surely not if the listing is a mistake," Darcy retorted. "Try calling him right now. Find out if he knew about this and get him over here right away. He doesn't need any more bad press in town. I'll try to find Janet and get his name removed."

But as she turned to scan the crowd, her gaze landed on Emma. The little girl was still dutifully sitting in her chair a dozen feet away, the cookie barely touched, and tears were trailing down her cheeks. Darcy's heart lurched as she hurried over, slipped into the chair next to Emma's and gave her a hug. "I'm so sorry, honey— but you did see where I was, right?"

Emma gave an almost imperceptible nod.

"And did you see your Sunday school teacher just over there? And you know Beth, and Sophie—" Darcy glanced around. "I even see Hannah in the next row. You were safe, I promise."

Emma nodded tearfully, her lower lip trembling.

"Stay right with me while I find someone, all right?" Darcy scooped the child up into her arms, and Emma sagged against her shoulder, too tired to answer.

Darcy tried to make her way through the crowd, but now everyone was out of their chairs, craning their necks to see who was up next as another five handyman volunteers were auctioned in quick succession.

"Dr. Logan Maxwell," the auctioneer shouted above the hubbub. "New guy in town, and already helping the community. Gotta give the guy credit. Doesn't say what kind of work he can do, but let's go. Starting at two hundred, folks—who is ready to go?"

Darcy froze in horror as the auctioneer's voice slipped into an almost indecipherable sales patter and the crowd fell silent.

People exchanged glances.

A few snickered.

A stage whisper filtered through the room.

"Who'd want to bid for the likes of him? My poor cousin works at the clinic and said she'd soon be out on her ear…"

Time seemed to stop as more whispers spread through the room. Then the room fell silent once again when the auctioneer dropped the starting bid to a hundred seventy-five. A hundred fifty. "C'mon folks…he's a real bargain at that. You'll be helping the kids, and maybe he can even spay your cat."

Uneasy laughter rippled through the audience. "How 'bout a hundred twenty-five, then…"

Darcy desperately scanned the crowd. Surely someone would be glad to grab such a bargain…or maybe just have mercy on him. Right now he was like an outcast, a pariah who would be the talk around town for a long, long time. And from the hard expressions she saw, that wasn't going to change. *Please, Lord, encourage someone to bid.*

Kaycee appeared at Darcy's side. "This is awful. But on the other hand, he's mean and he kinda deserves it."

"No one ever deserves ridicule, and that's what will happen," Darcy said quietly. "He'll be the only guy who failed to receive a single bid. Ever."

"He's still mean," Kaycee retorted.

"To him, the clinic is business, not personal. He's not changing things out of spite."

"He doesn't know any of us, really," Kaycee said with a stubborn pout. "And he doesn't care. Anyway, there's nothing we can do about it. The rules say no one can win more than one handyman each year. You want Edgar and I have an apartment, so I don't need a handyman at all."

Darcy needed Edgar desperately. It might take all of

what little she had in savings to win him—and even that might not be enough.

Potentially losing her job and trying to move away two months from now would be hard enough. Without his skills, it might be impossible to fix up the cottage enough to sell it in a few months.

But now empathy for Logan burned through her, taking a hard, painful hold of her heart. Could she stand by and let him become the humiliated laughingstock of the auction if no one bid even a few dollars?

She elbowed Kaycee sharply. "*Bid*," she whispered. "Now."

Startled, Kaycee stared at her. "What? I don't have the money."

"I'll pay. Bid against me just to bring it up to a decent amount so it isn't embarrassing for him, and then I'll take over. Seventy-five dollars max."

"Isn't this dishonest?"

"We'll be increasing the youth fund profits, not trying to get a deal," Darcy whispered back. "And I'll certainly honor my bid if I do win."

Kaycee weakly raised a hand to bid.

"We've got fifty, folks," the auctioneer cried out jubilantly. "Now, do we have seventy-five…"

Darcy nodded.

From across the room, she saw Gladys Rexworth eye her speculatively, and her heart sank.

"Eighty," the older woman barked. Her mouth twisted into a malevolent, superior smirk, and now Darcy realized this was personal.

Darcy closed her eyes briefly, remembering the run-ins she'd had with the woman in the past.

She hadn't wanted Logan to lose face in front of the

community. But now this—this would be even worse. Gladys was a wealthy, spiteful woman who seemed to take pleasure in causing others grief with her wicked tongue.

Darcy didn't even want to imagine how Gladys might enjoy having the new vet under her thumb, and then spread her vicious comments after setting impossible standards for his work.

Darcy held Emma a little tighter and swallowed hard. "Eighty-five."

Gladys lifted her chin triumphantly. "Two hundred."

*Please, God, tell me what to do here.* Edgar stood next to the podium, awaiting his turn. The man who could swiftly, expertly deal with the most serious projects at the cottage...

Her shoulders sagged. "Two twenty-five."

Gladys's eyes widened and mouth narrowed. Then she shook her head.

"The vet is the bestseller so far tonight, folks," the auctioneer crowed. "And our lady vet is the winner! Could this mean there's a little romance in the air?"

Darcy groaned and ran a palm down her face at the titter of laughter in the audience.

"Now for the last opportunity of the night, we have..." The auctioneer droned on.

A sudden gasp spread through the crowd, and every head turned toward the back entrance.

Dr. Maxwell stood in the open doorway—windblown, disheveled and breathing hard, as if he'd run all the way from the clinic. His incredulous gaze shifted from the auctioneer to Darcy. "What on earth is going on here? I never—"

With Emma still in her arms, Darcy hurried to his side, looped an arm through his, and hauled him back outside. "Everything is fine, folks," she called over her shoulder. "He's just surprised to find he's worth that much. I sure am."

As she shut the door behind them, the auctioneer's delighted voice followed her outside. "Back to the highlight of the evening, folks. We have Edgar Larson, your last chance to bid. He's a fine carpenter who tops our auction every single year…"

She cringed inwardly. What in the world had she done?

## Chapter Three

Her face pale, Darcy put her daughter down, leaned against the exterior wall of the church and closed her eyes. She looked as if she were on the verge of collapsing.

Her little girl gave Logan a wary look and hid behind her mom's legs, as if she thought he was the big bad wolf.

He moved a step closer in case Darcy crumpled to the ground. "Are you all right?"

"I can't believe I just did that," she moaned. She shot a sidelong glance at him. "I didn't plan to go that high, but then Gladys…"

"And I can't believe someone put my name on an auction block—and for what, I have no idea," Logan bit out. "I don't even know those people."

"*Those people* are members of this church, some of whom generously offered handyman skills, babysitting or hours of yard work to be sold at the annual handyman auction. The others are the generous folks in town who often pay far more than a deal is worth, because every dollar helps the youth group attend an annual faith rally in the Twin Cities," she retorted wearily. "If you'd answered my text messages on your cell, it wouldn't be at all confusing."

"I don't check my phone while driving."

"Not even at a gas station?" Now she sounded exasperated. "Or when you stop to eat?"

"I drove for several hours without good reception, and there *were* no messages."

"Then you need to switch cell companies."

The loud clang of metal against metal rang out from down the street. He glanced toward the sound. "That would be one of the horses in my trailer. I stopped at the clinic before going home and found a brief note on my desk that said, 'Auction at the church—be there at eight tonight,' so I came straight over here. Why am I involved in this?"

Her shoulders slumped. "My friend Beth is the committee chair, and she was desperate to have a few more names on the list. She also…um…thought it might give you some good PR in the community."

Beth, of course. He'd worked for days sorting and packing possessions to bring back to Wisconsin, hauling things to Goodwill and wrapping up the details of his old life in Montana.

Now, after fifteen hours in his truck, plus three long stops to unload the horses for a break from travel, all he wanted right now was to get them into the barn and collapse on his sofa. The coming week was going to be even more hectic…but now what had Beth gotten him into?

"So she just went ahead and added my name?"

"No. I told her I would ask you, but apparently her assistant added you at the last minute before running off the programs." Darcy shot a dark glance at him. "I suppose she figured that you—like all the others who volunteered—would be more than happy to help out the kids."

"And what does this involve, exactly?"

"The winning bidder gets twenty hours of your time—but it can be just a few hours here and there. Carpentry, home repairs, lawn care…whatever."

"So if I simply decline, you can save your money and I can save my time. Easy enough—"

A young woman with a long curly blond ponytail burst out of the building, headed straight for Darcy and pulled her into a brief hug. "I'm so sorry, honey. I was helping in the nursery, but heard about what happened in there—that you bid on someone no one else wanted. That was the kindest thing ever. I know how much you wanted Edgar instead."

*No one else wanted?* Logan didn't want to be in this situation at all, but hearing he didn't compare to some guy named Edgar didn't sit right, either. "Who's Edgar?"

Darcy ignored him. "Please—tell me Ed went for some impossible amount so I couldn't have won his bid anyway."

The woman bit her lower lip. "Two seventy-five."

Darcy's face fell. "Nooo."

"But remember, you'll never know how much higher the winner would have gone to beat you—it could have ended far, far above your budget."

Darcy scooped Emma up into her arms. "I'll keep that thought when I go back to trying to hire someone."

"Who knows? Maybe your guy has some great skills, too." The woman's speculative gaze swept over Logan. "I don't think we've met. I'm Hannah Dorchester, one of the physician's assistants in town. And you are…"

"Logan Maxwell."

"So *you're* the one Darcy just bailed out, in front of all those people?"

Bewildered, he looked between the two of them. She'd bailed him out? "This was all a mistake. I'll go inside and straighten this out right away."

"Please don't make a scene." Hannah sidestepped to block the door. "The kids are all excited and celebrating. Anyway, it's all over now, so there's no rush. Go home. Think about it. Do you have any idea what Darcy just did for you?"

Darcy rested a hand on Hannah's forearm. "It's okay. He never agreed to this in the first place."

"I need to get back inside to help Beth wrap things up for the night." Hannah glanced at her watch, then tilted her head and gave Logan a brilliant smile. "Can I stop by the clinic for a few minutes first thing tomorrow? You can give me your decision then."

He gave a noncommittal nod, though he already knew what his answer would be.

Once she'd gone back into the building, he turned to Darcy, but at the sound of a horse delivering a another solid kick to the horse trailer, he reached for the keys he'd shoved in the back pocket of his jeans. "I'm being paged, so I'd better get those horses home."

She smiled at that. "Of course."

He would be free of this crazy situation tomorrow, no doubt about that. But all the way back to his new home, he couldn't escape the vision of Darcy's expression.

She'd been clearly embarrassed, but he'd also caught a hint of desperation and bitter disappointment. So what was going on with her, for this auction to matter so much?

And who in the world was Edgar?

\* \* \*

Hefting another bale of fragrant alfalfa that the farmer had just tossed down from the hay wagon, Logan looked over his shoulder at the approach of an unfamiliar car.

A moment later, the woman he'd met after the auction last night stepped out of the vehicle and approached him with a hand shading her eyes from the morning sun. Hannah, if he remembered correctly, though last night he'd been so tired he didn't know for sure.

"I called the clinic, but Marilyn said you were taking care of a hay delivery. So I decided I'd just bop out here. Beautiful drive, anyway, with all of this timber and those rocky bluffs. I always loved coming out to Doc's place for his annual barbecues."

"I could've saved you the trip if I'd had your number."

"That's why I wanted to see you in person." She laughed softly. "Beth and I are hoping you won't get off that easy."

"I'm sorry, but—"

"Honestly, I think you'd be better off if you just let it stand. Good PR and all that."

He tipped his head toward the house. "Even if I wanted to help y'all out, I just don't have the time. I can barely get in the door with all of the moving boxes stacked inside. It'll take days to finish fencing the pasture and longer to take care of repairs in the barn."

"But—"

"And then there's going to be extensive remodeling at the vet clinic. A lot of time just getting the new practice going, and we're still in foaling and breeding season, which means long days and even longer nights when I start seeing clients."

"Last year a guy backed out," Hannah said darkly,

as if she hadn't heard a word about his complicated life. "It was the talk of the town for months when the winning bidder demanded her money back from the youth group, and that started a big flap about the future of the auction—liability, worries about lawsuits—but without this big fundraiser, too many deserving kids will miss a wonderful opportunity. This year we'd been praying there wouldn't be a single glitch to jeopardize the auction concept. But now there is. You."

"This reminds me of a conversation I had with Beth at the cafe." He stifled a laugh. "Darcy has some pretty convincing friends."

"My fiancé likes to say I'm forthright." Hannah rolled her eyes. "Others just say stubborn. But if it's for a good cause, why not?"

There were now a good twenty bales waiting for him on the ground. The man on top of the stack was holding another and eyeing him impatiently. "If that's it, then…"

He turned to get back to work, but she touched his arm. "Please."

"Look, I—"

"If you don't care about the kids, well…"

"It isn't that I don't care—I just don't have time."

"Then think about Darcy and what she gave up for you."

"What do you mean?"

"She's single, you know, with no family around to help. Her little cottage is a wreck, and she's been trying to hire a good handyman for months. But the good ones are booked 'til after the end of the year. And now, with her job in jeopardy since you showed up, she might have to sell and move. The cottage needs a *lot* of work before it can be listed."

Baffled, he shook his head slowly. "How could just twenty hours of labor make enough difference, then?"

"She wanted to win Edgar. She'd been saving for months, hoping he would get the work started and then be willing to keep working for her. He's a wonderful craftsman, but takes very few new clients."

"Then she shouldn't have bid on me."

"That's what I say. But she has a soft heart. She felt bad for you when no one else would bid. I'm sure she didn't want you to face any ridicule."

"I'm sure I could've handled it," he said dryly.

"Maybe so…but with half the town angry over you threatening to fire the entire vet clinic staff, why add more fuel to the fire? And—" Hannah bit her lower lip, as if deciding how much more to say "—the other woman who drove the bidding up is…well, I think Darcy went so high 'cause she was trying to save you from a potentially bad situation. Very bad."

The man on the hay wagon cleared his throat. "Hey, Doc, I need to get back to the farm. You want me to just keep pitching these off or what?"

Now there were a good fifty bales tossed into a jumbled pile on the ground, and at last one had landed wrong and broken. The farmer was muttering under his breath.

"I'll be with you in just a second."

He turned back to Hannah. "What if I made a donation to cover Darcy's bid instead of doing the work?"

Hannah folded her arms over her chest. "Fine, donate the two twenty-five. Except Darcy is still left high and dry. No Edgar, and no other skilled craftsmen are available until January…at least. Like I said, this is a small community."

"Fine. I'll do it, then," he said on a long sigh as he lifted a bale and started into the barn.

But long after Hannah left, questions kept spinning through his thoughts as he stacked bales into one of the box stalls he was using to store hay.

So Darcy had been struggling to save up for this auction? He knew what she was being paid at the clinic, and saving up a few hundred bucks for her beloved Edgar shouldn't have been any big deal.

Yet apparently she was strapped for cash.

So what was her problem? Credit card debt? A gambling problem? Sheer irresponsibility? She didn't seem like the type, but then, his own sister had mired herself in debt from online shopping, and he'd had to bail her out more than once so she and her kids wouldn't lose their condo.

And then there was his ex-fiancée—who had been far worse. He knew all too well how a person could be caught up in a web of embezzlement.

So maybe this unexpected situation wasn't so bad after all. If he completed the auction obligation to her, he'd have a chance to observe her situation and see if he even dared keep her around for the next two months.

Desperate people could end up doing desperate, illegal things, and he wasn't going through *that* situation ever again.

Logan logged onto the computer at the clinic on Monday morning and continued the search he'd started at home late last night.

"Marilyn, can you come in here, please?" he called out.

Darcy came in instead, wearing the new clinic uniform—maroon scrubs—plus her white lab coat with the Aspen Creek Vet Clinic logo on the front pocket, and a stethoscope around her neck. "She's out in the parking lot helping Mildred McConaughy bring her dog in. Can I help you?"

"I need to order some equipment, and I'd like an opinion on the vet supply distributor reps around here." He flipped through the battered Rolodex on the desk. "Who do you prefer to deal with?"

"Doc Boyd usually gave his orders to Harold Bailey—the two were old friends who went way back."

He looked up at her, momentarily taken aback. She stood in a shaft of morning sunlight streaming through the windows of his office. He'd first thought she had nondescript brown hair, but now he was struck by its rich, molten gold-and-amber highlights.

It took a moment to gather his scattered thoughts. "And…uh…you don't call him anymore?"

"His branch warehouse is clear down in the Quad Cities, and the company takes too long for deliveries. After Doc passed away, we started using ABC Vet Supply because it has a warehouse over in St. Paul. Next-day delivery, usually, because it's so close."

"So that sales rep is…" He thumbed back through the Rolodex. "Vicki Irwin?"

"She's young and fairly new, but sharp as can be and really follows through. She stops in twice a month. Sooner if we have any issues." Darcy lifted a shoulder in a faint shrug. "But of course, you'll need to decide for yourself which companies you want to use. What kind of equipment are you looking for?"

"The most outdated pieces of equipment are the blood chemistry machine and CBC cell counter—which should run around twenty grand. A new anesthesia machine would be at least four grand more."

"With Doc gone, I didn't feel right making any major purchases, but both are long overdue, for sure. What else?"

"Most everything else can wait a while." He shifted his gaze to the computer screen. "But a new equine ultrasound is imperative for reproductive issues and evaluating injuries."

She whistled under her breath. "Not cheap."

He nodded. "It could run over fifty grand if I duplicate what we used in Montana."

"It'll be fun watching you bring this clinic up to date."

She turned to leave, but he cleared his throat. "Your friend Hannah came out to see me on Saturday. I imagine she told you about it."

"What?" Her mystified expression cleared. "You mean about the auction? I knew she planned to talk to you, but I haven't heard from her since Friday night."

"She and I got everything squared away."

"Good to hear. I told Beth that the committee shouldn't try to push you into something you never intended to do, so you're off the hook."

"But is that what you want? Your friend says you've been saving money for this for a long time." He eyed her closely. "That you really need the help and can't find anyone to do it."

"Yes, well…that's my concern, not yours." A weary smile briefly lit up her face, and she looked like someone who had the weight of the world on her shoulders. "Honestly, I just want to apologize for what happened."

"I understand your bidding saved me from the clutches of a difficult woman."

At that, she laughed aloud. "You do owe me a favor for that. You have no idea."

"I'm going to follow through. Will that just about cover it?"

Her eyes widened with surprise and a touch of wariness. "You don't need to. Really."

"I called Beth just a few minutes ago. It's a done deal."

"Um…" Her gaze veered away, and she swallowed hard. "I don't mean to seem ungrateful, but I…um… need someone who is really skilled as a handyman. Experienced."

"You're worried about getting your money's worth." He heard the unintentionally hard edge in his tone and instantly regretted it when he saw her flinch.

"I must sound so crass." Rosy color washed up into her cheeks. "It's just that whether my daughter and I stay or need to leave town, I… I need the work to be done well and up to code."

"Tell you what. You've got twenty hours of my time, so make a list of what needs to be done. Then let me come over some evening this week so I can see if I have the skill set for what you need. Tonight would be fine, if you're eager to get started."

"That I am." She bit her lower lip. "But if you don't feel it's something you want to tackle?"

"Then I'll donate the full amount of your bid to the youth group, and you can save your money to pay someone else." He offered his hand across the desk. "Deal?"

She hesitated, her expression still filled with doubt, but she finally accepted his brief handshake. "This is beyond generous. I think you're being too kind."

*Not kind*, he thought as he watched her head out of his office. *Just careful.*

Since asking about her around town would only start rumors, he needed to take this into his own hands.

Because absolute trust was a rare and fragile thing, and he couldn't afford to make the same mistake twice.

## Chapter Four

Darcy had given Logan a list of projects and the directions to her house before leaving work at the end of the day. She'd blushed a little, saying she knew there were far more than twenty hours of labor on the list, but she'd thought he might want to choose what he wanted to do.

A tactful expectation that he'd need to select the easier tasks, he supposed.

From that long, long list he'd figured she was living in shabby house worthy of a wrecking ball in a seedy part of town. Probably around the taverns, trailer park and mechanic's shop on the south end.

But he'd followed her directions down several winding, tree-shaded streets into an area of well-kept homes from the early 1900s. Now he stood on the sidewalk in front of 56 Cranberry Lane and just stared.

The surrounding houses were two-story brick, with sweeping covered porches on the front, leaded glass and manicured lawns. Darcy's place was brick as well, but just a single story, with a brick-paved driveway leading past the side of the house to a matching one-stall garage.

It reminded him of a dollhouse in comparison. A neglected one, at that. If Darcy was blowing her money, it hadn't been spent on the place she lived.

Lace curtains in the front window fluttered. Then the door opened and Darcy came across the porch and down the steps and let him through the gate at edge of the sidewalk.

"I'm sure you can already see some of the projects here," she said with a self-conscious laugh, gesturing at the ornate white picket fence surrounding the front yard. "The backyard is fenced as well, and there must be dozens of pickets that have broken or rotted away."

He eyed the intricately cut upright pieces. "These were custom-made."

"My sweet old aunt loved detail. There are lots and lots of gingerbread trim pieces on the cottage, and she echoed that theme in the fence." Darcy smiled fondly. "I loved visiting her, because the place was rather like a little fairyland theme park. Lots of animal and elf statues tucked away in unexpected places, some little goldfish ponds. But now I can't just go to a lumberyard and pick up replacements. She wanted everything to be unique."

He glanced up at the house. "Your aunt…"

"She passed away almost two years ago and left everything to my brother and me. He essentially got her liquid assets, and I got the cottage. So when I was able to find a job in town, I was thrilled."

"Did you grow up here?"

"North of Minneapolis, actually. But after…" Her voice trailed off. "Well. Let's take a quick look around, okay? I put Emma to bed a few minutes ago, and I need to get back inside."

She took him around the house, pointing out broken

gingerbread trim along the eaves and a sagging rear porch, then took him through the back door into the kitchen.

The cupboards and countertops were dated and worn, with a circular burn mark on the counter next to the stove. The vinyl flooring was yellowed and scarred with age. The room was small.

But a row of four sash windows looked out on the backyard, giving it an airy, quaint feel, and the burnished oak woodwork glowed in the light of a stained-glass chandelier that hung over the oak claw-foot table.

"As you can see, there is no end to the projects around here. I can't afford to remodel the kitchen fully, but the sink and faucet need replacing, and the lighting in here is impossible. It's like working in a cave." She led him through an archway leading into a small living room and gestured to the left. "That door leads to two bedrooms and a bathroom. The first priority inside is the carpet, because of Emma's asthma. Fortunately there's beautiful old oak flooring throughout the house, but it needs to be refinished, and there's quite a bit of work in the bathroom, too."

"Your other priorities?"

"Everything," she said simply. "I'd love to remodel the entire place if I could, but anything you want to tackle and have time to finish would be wonderful. I don't expect even a minute extra. I'm just grateful, given all that you have on your own plate."

He turned slowly, taking in the faded floral wallpaper, the lacy curtains and the worn leather furniture that made him think of soft marshmallows. A small television sat in one corner with a DVD player and stack of children's DVDs on top. No high-end electronics here.

"So if you'd won the bid on your friend, you might have gotten everything done?"

"Edgar isn't a friend, but I did hope to convince him to stay on longer for his usual rate. Whether he would've agreed or not, I've no idea."

"Well, I'll do everything I can. You can decide where to start."

"Really—you can do this?"

At the renewed doubt in her voice, he stifled a chuckle. "I'm sure I can't compare to Edgar, but I grew up on an isolated ranch where we dealt with most everything on our own. And then I put myself through college working summers for a contractor."

"Really?" The worried look in her eyes faded. "Perfect. I'd like to start with the picket fence, because it would really improve the curb appeal. Maybe that isn't possible, though. Those swirly edges and the heart cutouts at the top of the pickets must be tricky."

"No problem. I've got a band saw and a jigsaw, and I can use an old picket as a template."

"I realize the fence might take a good part of your hours, but with whatever time is left, can you start work on the kitchen?"

"No problem."

From one of the bedrooms came the faint sound of Emma whimpering.

"Sounds like you're needed, and I'd better get home to do my horse chores." Logan pulled his truck keys from his back jeans pocket as he headed for the door. "Just figure out where you want to start, and I'll come back after work tomorrow to do some measuring. I'll write up a list of materials, and once you have them, I can get to work."

The enormity of the work to be done here and her concern about it were more than clear. He felt a twinge of guilt as he walked out to his pickup.

He'd been in seminars at vet conferences where business consultants recommended making a clean sweep of things, bringing in new staff unencumbered with prior loyalties and stubborn adherence to old routines.

So when he made an offer on the clinic, he hadn't thought too deeply about what his plans would mean to the current staff. His focus had been on new beginnings—financing and building a successful new practice.

If he'd been empathetic enough to consider the collateral effect on the people involved, would he have turned down this chance to start his life over?

And would he now change his plans for the focused vet practice he'd always wanted—what he had specialized in through an extended equine medicine residency and then pursued in the Montana group practice for the past eight years?

That was another question.

"Thanks, Logan—have a good night," Darcy called softly from the door as she closed it.

He stared at the door after she turned off the front light, sorting out his thoughts. She was certainly an enigma.

She was a single mom, which had to be tough. Yet she did have a good career, she'd inherited this house and he'd seen no evidence of profligate spending. If she was as strapped for cash as Hannah had implied on Saturday, where was her money going? Was she a risk as an employee?

He hadn't known her for very long, but while his heart told him no, the logical, analytical side of his brain said yes.

She was the spitting image of the associate vet who had so easily ruined his life in Montana, the one who had so quickly captured his heart. Was that why he felt an inexplicable tug of emotion whenever he ran into her? A physical awareness tinged with a persistent niggle of doubt?

Whatever he felt about her, it had no place in his life. Not now, not ever.

The humiliating interrogations, legal fees and defamation of his character back in Montana were too fresh in his mind to take any chances.

Darcy finished her exam of the Chihuahua and smiled. "Scooter is doing really well. The X-rays show excellent healing."

Mrs. Johnson picked her dog up and cuddled him against her chest. "I was so worried—I don't know what I'd do without my little boy for company."

"You made the right choice when you let me go ahead with the plating and bone graft. Splinting of radius-ulna fractures in these small dogs doesn't always succeed."

"Worth every penny to do things right, I always say." She gave the little dog a kiss on its head.

Darcy handed her a list of going-home instructions. "You said that he always wants to be on the sofa and bed with you. Have you set up some ramps for him? He shouldn't be jumping to the floor."

"I ordered two from a catalog, and they were delivered yesterday." The elderly woman moved toward the door, then turned back with a wink and a smile. "I heard about you winning the new vet at the handyman auction, and I just think it's so sweet. Smart, too, keeping all of the other young ladies at bay like that. Keep him to yourself."

Darcy swallowed hard. "Believe me, that really isn't it at all—"

"Your secret is safe with me." Mrs. Johnson waggled her eyebrows and gave her a knowing look. "Can we assume romance is already in the air?"

"No." Darcy briefly closed her eyes against *that* unwanted vision. "Not at all. Really."

But judging by her smug little smile and the teasing sparkle in her eyes as she left the exam room, Mrs. Johnson didn't believe a word of that denial and wasn't planning to keep her thoughts to herself, either.

Darcy braced her hands on the exam table. Word would spread. People would believe she'd made a pathetic effort to snare the new vet. Maybe Logan would believe it, too, which would be beyond embarrassing.

Marilyn rapped lightly on the door frame. "I've got your next two charts, and—oh, my. Is everything all right? You look a bit pale."

"I'm fine." Darcy straightened. "Just reminding myself that small-town gossip doesn't mean a thing."

Marilyn flicked a hand dismissively. "You mean about you and Dr. Maxwell?"

Darcy groaned. "You do know it's completely false conjecture, no matter where you've heard it?"

"I guessed that already, given that he's probably planning to let us all go during the next few months," Marilyn retorted dryly. "But when you won that bid at the auction, there were lots of whispers going through the crowd. That was bound to happen anyway, with both of you being single and all. People like to talk."

Darcy glanced at the clock on the wall. "Wednesday afternoons usually aren't this busy, but I've been swamped all day. Has he come in?"

"He's been out back working on that old stable and corral all day, far as I know." She handed Darcy the charts. "Kaycee has your next client in the other exam room, but if you need to talk to him, I can go out and let him know."

"No, I'll catch him later. He came over after work yesterday to take measurements for my fence, and I just wanted to let him know that I bought the materials at the lumberyard."

Marilyn's eyebrows rose with sudden hope. "Sooo… are you two getting along a little better?"

Darcy snorted.

"Seriously," Marilyn said. "Maybe if we're all really professional and helpful, he'll decide that we're worth keeping around. *All* of us," she added pointedly.

"I don't think being friendly will change his business plans, but go for it and see what happens. As far as I know, he still doesn't plan to make his final decisions until around June 14—at the end of two months."

"When I think of all the accessibility issues Bob had at our house, and all we've done to make it better for him…" Marilyn bit her lower lip and looked away. "I'm just praying I can keep this job and our house, because Bob's Parkinson's is not going away."

Over the past year, Marilyn had been the motherly one at the office, giving Darcy comfort and advice during her darkest days. Now the tables had turned and Darcy was the one comforting the older woman.

Darcy set aside the charts and gave the older woman a quick hug. "I can't believe there could be any issue with keeping you and Kaycee on board, honestly. If anyone will be packing her bags, it will be me."

"Oh, honey. That would be so wrong."

Darcy stepped back and sighed. "If that happens, then I figure the Lord has better plans for me. I've been thinking harder about starting my own practice here in town. But right now, I'd better get back to work."

At the sound of a nearby footstep, Marilyn turned and paled. "D-Dr. Maxwell," she stammered. "I didn't see you coming."

"Just taking a quick break." If he'd overheard their conversation, there was no sign of it in his voice. "Have you had any calls or emails about the new website?

Flustered, Marilyn fiddled with her bracelet. "Three calls, just this afternoon. I left the messages on your desk. There have been some emails, as well."

Darcy stepped into the hallway to head for the other exam room, but faltered to a stop.

The days and nights were still cool in Wisconsin, and she'd seen him wear just jeans and sweaters or sweatshirts so far. But now he was in a ragged T-shirt and well-worn jeans, dusted with sawdust.

The T-shirt stretched across his powerful chest. The short sleeves clung to his powerful biceps. His tool belt was once again slung low around his hips.

The man could work as a model if he ever wanted an easier profession.

She forced her gaze up to his face. "Sounds like good news for you, then. The potential clients, I mean."

"I updated the new website to show the equine practice will be open starting on Monday, but in the meantime I'd be happy to take calls from anyone curious about available services. Feel free to give them my cell number."

Marilyn nodded and fled back to the receptionist's desk, leaving Darcy facing Logan alone.

"She sure is jumpy," he said mildly.

"She's terribly worried about her job, and Kaycee is, as well," Darcy said in a low voice. "They both have heavy responsibilities at home. It would be a kindness if you could let them know your plans and get the news over with."

He assessed her with a frank, open gaze. "And what about you?"

She shrugged, locked her gaze on his. "I'll either be working here or move down the road and become your toughest competition. The choice is yours."

## Chapter Five

"Is he coming today?" Emma ran to the front door for the fourth time in the past ten minutes, her blond ponytail flying. "With his horse? The one that's blonde like me? Maybe it could stay overnight, or even live with us!"

Darcy had left the vet clinic when it closed at noon, picked up Emma at the sitter and had been trying to settle the little girl down for lunch, to no avail. "No horses, not in town. Not even briefly, because horses need a very good fence, and ours needs lots of work. That's why Dr. Maxwell is coming."

Emma's face fell. "Could we go see it, then? And ride it?"

"Um…maybe someday. Two more bites of your sandwich. Then we'll go outside and get things ready for him. All right?"

Emma dutifully clambered up onto her chair and took two miniscule bites, then raced for the back door. "Then can we get a puppy? You promised, after Elsie died."

Keeping up with Emma sometimes made Darcy's head spin. "Yes, I did. But not until our fence is completely done. We always had to take Elsie for walks, but a nice safe yard would be much better than taking those walks after dark."

"Can you ask Hannah? She has lots and lots of puppies. Cats, too. And a *pony*." Emma's face brightened with excitement. "A pony could stay in our yard!"

Emma asked about horses and ponies every day, from morning 'til night. "When you turn five, we'll look for a pony and a place to keep it. Right now, let's think about a puppy. One thing at a time."

She grabbed a hammer from the utility closet by the back door and followed the little girl out into the yard. She breathed in deeply, savoring the scents of the neighbor's fresh-cut grass and the spring perennials Aunt Tina had planted along the borders of the yard years ago.

Yellow crocuses, grape hyacinths and daffodils nodded cheerfully in the light breeze. Soon the sweet scent of lilacs—her favorite—would fill the air, followed later by the heady scents of the heirloom roses planted on three sides of the tiny brick gardening shed.

All of them brought back bittersweet memories of her aunt and those carefree days of childhood when everything seemed possible and nothing bad had ever happened. Yet.

"Can I help you, Mommy?"

"Why don't you play on your swing set for a while? I'm going to start taking down the broken pickets, and nails are very sharp."

She'd just pried off the first splintered picket when Emma shrieked. "He came—he really came!"

Her heart in her throat, Darcy spun around…and saw Logan saunter through the backyard gate with a stack of boards in his arms and his tool belt slung around his hips once again.

Every time she saw him, she felt a little frisson of awareness, and her traitorous heart seemed to skip a beat. It had to be the jeans and cowboy boots, and that casual cowboy grace suggesting he could drawl *yes, ma'am* and then vanquish her foes with no effort at all.

If only he'd met her late husband, Dean, she would have loved to see him try.

Emma raced to the gate. "Are you a real cowboy?" she asked, looking up at him with adoration she rarely showed to anyone except Darcy anymore. "Did you bring your horse? Mommy says no, but maybe you did anyway."

He chuckled and grinned down at her, the corners of his eyes crinkling and that dimple deepening in his cheek. "Your mom is right, but someday you can come out to my place and we'll see about letting you ride. Would that be okay?"

Darcy strolled over. If only the man knew what he had just started with that little offer.

"Thanks for coming," she called out. "I'm sure you had other ways you wanted to spend your Saturday afternoon."

"No problem." He stacked the pickets on the wrought iron table under a shady oak. "I have more in my truck, but what do you think so far?"

She ran her hand over the smooth, one-by-four pressure-treated slats that the lumberyard guy had promised would hold up for years. Each swoop and curlicue along the edges was exactly right; the little heart cut-outs near the top of each pointed tip were a perfect match to the originals.

"They're beautiful," she said with awe. "How in the world did you do them so fast?"

He shrugged. "Having the right equipment helped."

Emma looked up at him, her eyes hopeful. "Could you make a playhouse, like Sienna has?" she breathed. "Her daddy made it. It's pink and white and has a purple roof. But I don't got a daddy."

"Dr. Maxwell only has enough time to help with the fencing and fix some things in the house, Emma. We need the fence before we can think about your puppy. Remember?"

"But—"

"Let's help him fetch the rest of his things. He and I need to get to work. Okay?"

Emma dutifully followed them out to the black pickup parked in front of the garage, where Logan gave her a single picket to carry. Then Darcy and Logan took the remaining pickets and his tools to the backyard.

Emma watched for a while, then wandered back to her outdoor slide and swing set and played on the upper deck with her dolls.

With Darcy removing damaged pickets and Logan using an electric drill to set the new ones, they were finished with the front yard and backyard a couple of hours later.

"I could've painted them before bringing them over," he said, stepping back to assess the overall job. "But I figured it would be better to do the entire fence all at once, after the peeling paint is scraped. Do you want me to do that or start something else?"

"This is just beautiful," she said fervently. She bit her lower lip, thinking about all of the work he'd done back at his shop. "I can do the painting later on. I'm not even sure how much of your time I have left, though, given what you've done already."

"Eighteen hours would be fair enough." He shrugged. "Does that work for you?"

"But you spent more than two hours just putting it up today. And what about all of the time you spent making the pickets? That isn't fair to you."

"It was simple, and I like woodworking. It was a nice break from working on the barn at home and the one at the clinic. Gave me an excuse to avoid unpacking boxes in the house, too," he added with a grin. "Just forget about it."

He'd been gruff and cold when he'd arrived two weeks ago. She'd been prepared to dislike him completely after that first awkward encounter. But she'd started to see a different side of him now, and it was getting harder to keep up her defenses. Especially when he was so sweet to Emma and being such a good sport about this whole arrangement.

"Thank you," she said quietly. "This means a lot to me."

He glanced at his watch. "Let's go inside and figure out the next project before I head back home."

He and Emma followed her into the kitchen, where he leaned a hip against the counter and surveyed the room. "Not sure how far you want to go with this. The material costs will add up. Do you have a budget in mind?"

"Not really. I can't afford a lot right now, though."

"Are you planning to take out any walls?"

"No. I want a separation between the living room and kitchen. And the layout is fine."

"Do you want to replace the cabinets?"

She laughed at that. "I've spent a lot of time pricing cabinets. No way."

"You could just install updated cabinet fronts at a fraction of the cost." He ran a hand over a cabinet door and opened several of them. "You could add new veneer over the exposed sides and then add new doors. Or you paint or stain the ones you have. These are outdated, but they're well made. You could add nicer hardware, too. Once you decide that, you could consider new countertops."

"They definitely need updating. These are nicked and faded—and that big burn mark by the stove drives me crazy."

"Granite would be nice."

"In my dreams," she said ruefully.

"Sometimes you can find nice pieces of granite that were ordered for a larger kitchen and didn't work out but would fit in a small space, and that could save you a lot of money. You could call some suppliers to see if there's anything you like. Then we'd measure carefully, and it would be cut and delivered. I could install a new sink and faucet."

Excitement over the possibilities started bubbling up in her chest. "Or should I do the lighting instead?

He studied the ceiling. "You have an attic up there, so there should be good access into the ceiling for can lighting. If this were my place, I'd go ahead and do it myself, but I'm not a licensed electrician. That's who you need to call. A wild guess is that it would cost between five hundred and a thousand, depending on how many lights you want and where you buy them. Then again, I have no idea what the going rates are around here."

"What about the floor?" she asked.

"Are you sure there's hardwood underneath the vinyl?"

"I've pulled up some corners of the carpeting in all of the other rooms and also pried up a corner of the vinyl," she said. "It's all narrow-plank oak."

"It wouldn't be hard to rip out the carpet and vinyl and refinish the floors. That needs to be a priority, given Emma's asthma. But if you help, we could get that done and maybe do the counters and sink, as well."

Incredulous, she looked up at him. "Really? Wow. So many options."

She closed her eyes for a moment, envisioning what these changes would mean. How pretty the cottage could become, inside and out. She took another look around, and the possibilities nearly took her breath away.

A smile twitched at his lips as he watched her consider. "No rush if you want to think it over. But if you can decide fairly soon, we can tackle the work before I start getting busy with clients."

"Okay—the floor. Definitely the floor." She grinned up at him. "I think you've just made me the happiest woman in Aspen Creek, bar none. When do you want to start?"

"Tomorrow is okay, or some night after work."

"We have church, and Sunday school for Emma tomorrow morning." She gave him a tentative smile. "Aspen Creek Community Church, if you're interested. The service is at nine."

"No." He drew back a little. "Maybe another time."

"Of course," she murmured. "We'll be home all afternoon and evening if you want to stop by. Lunch is around noon if you want to join us."

\* \* \*

Logan spent Sunday morning finishing up his work on the small horse barn behind the vet clinic and regretting his surly response to Darcy's invitation.

He'd been raised in the church. His parents had made sure of that.

And he was a believer, even if he and God had gone through a major falling-out a few years back when Dad passed away from a heart attack and Mom died shortly after. Two of the best people he'd ever known, gone in the blink of an eye. Logan had prayed night and day that they might survive, but God hadn't seen fit to answer those prayers.

Where was the justice in that, when truly evil people could spend their entire lives loose in society?

His prayers sure hadn't helped with the situation in Montana, either. Since God didn't seem to find his prayers worth answering, Logan had simply…stopped praying.

He stepped back and studied his handiwork. The barn had originally been divided into four fourteen-by-fourteen box stalls, with an exam area with stocks to restrain horses during certain procedures, and a space for hay, bedding and feed storage. He'd repaired and replaced boards, painted the interior white, and installed long banks of fluorescent lights over the stalls and exam area. In time he would add a surgical room with a hydraulic table and more stalls, but this would be a good start.

He glanced at his watch. Grabbed his truck keys and headed out the door. His work commitment at Darcy's place was just that—a business agreement and nothing more. Once he finished those eighteen hours, he would be back to concentrating on his career and the work he was doing on his place in the country. Back to enjoying his life alone.

So why did he find himself whistling as he drove off toward Cranberry Lane? Or fidgeting with his keys like some nervous teenage boy after he knocked on her door?

It made absolutely no sense at all.

# Chapter Six

The last time he'd seen her, Darcy had proclaimed she was the happiest woman in Aspen Creek. On Sunday afternoon she looked a little worse for wear.

Her long hair was caught up into a straggly knot on the top of her head, with long tendrils dangling down her back. Her ragged T-shirt and torn jeans were covered with dust. There was a smudge on her nose. A mask hung from its elastic cord around her neck.

He'd never seen her look so…so vulnerable and pretty and, well, so utterly appealing. But then he looked a little closer. A number of wounds on her hands were haphazardly covered with adhesive bandages.

"What on earth happened to you?"

"I followed your advice. Sort of." She waved a hand toward the living room behind her.

He took a closer look at her hands. "Whatever advice it was, I had to be wrong."

She stepped aside to let him in, and he nearly tripped over a heap of musty carpeting and shreds of carpet pad.

"I figured you could get more of the technical stuff done if I did all of the demolition. So I looked up the process on YouTube, and I've been pulling up carpet. I figured that the sooner I got rid of that dusty, musty stuff, the better it would be for Emma." She abruptly turned away to sneeze. "I had some run-ins with tack strips around the borders, though. The video didn't give any warning about that. And it didn't say that some people might take it upon themselves to fasten the padding down with an ocean of glue. That was an unpleasant surprise."

He glimpsed a pile of furniture in the kitchen. "I could have done this. You should have let me."

Speechless now, he moved farther into the room. She'd managed to pull up all of the carpet and most of the padding, but random patches of padding were still stuck to the floor, and she held a scraper in her hand as if ready to go back to war.

"Someone—not my aunt—did a sloppy job of painting the walls before laying the carpet. There are big splotches all over the hardwood." She gave him an impish smile, her eyes twinkling. "But I also learned about drum sanders and edging sanders on the video, and I got both rented last night just before the lumberyard closed."

His jaw dropped. "When did you do all of this?"

"I took Emma to Hannah's for an overnight because there was so much dust and mold in the air. Then I worked until around three this morning and after I got home from church."

"I'm impressed."

"I've got to finish all of the bits of padding stuck to the floor, but I shifted furniture around so I could at least get all of the carpeting out." She blew at a strand of hair drooping over one eye. "So, what do you think?"

He angled an amused smile at her. "If anyone ever

doubted your work ethic, that thought would be laid to rest. Where do you want me to start?"

"I can keep pulling carpet tacks and scraping the floors in here, but if you want to start on the vinyl flooring in the kitchen, that would be super. This house is so small that I think I can get all of the floors sanded and return the sanders tomorrow morning if I just keep at it."

"No problem."

"Are you sure you don't mind? I feel kinda bad asking you to take on a job like that. I'm guessing the floor is nasty under the vinyl. Then again, maybe this will be a good coworker bonding experience. Right?"

There'd been an invisible wall between them since he first arrived—mutual wariness, at the very least. How could there not be, when he'd initially planned to let her go, and she'd finagled another two months at her job? But working on her house together was slowly easing those tensions, and this was becoming almost…fun.

He grabbed an armload of carpet and carried it out to the pile she'd started by the garage, then kept taking loads of it outside until it was gone.

He started for the kitchen, then headed for the back hallway and bedrooms where Darcy was still pulling stray carpet tacks along the baseboards and prying off ancient bits of rubber carpet pad.

In here, evidence of garish yellow and pink paint splotches trailed across the floor. "Must have been sort of psychedelic," he observed. "But the woodwork is beautiful."

"My aunt moved here in 1978 and had it all redone in vintage wallpaper, as you can see. She loved flowers and calico. And lace. Lots and lots of lace." Darcy sat back on her heels. "So I'll be doing a lot of wallpaper stripping, which I hear is as much fun as this carpet."

He turned to head for the kitchen but spied a white cord dangling just a few inches above his head and looked up. "There must be access to the attic through that trap door. Have you ever been up there?"

She shook her head. "Just once as a kid. I remember there were lots of trunks and boxes crammed in every corner. But I assumed there were lots of spiders and bats, so I didn't linger."

"Want me to check to see how easy it would be to install the can lights for the kitchen?"

Still crouched along the baseboards, she looked over her shoulder. "Be my guest. The bathroom is just to your left, and I've got a flashlight charging in the outlet near the sink. Be careful, though—I don't know how long it's been since anyone went up there. I hope the ladder is still safe."

He grabbed the flashlight, jammed it into his back pocket and studied the dangling cord. "This has got to be one of those folding staircases. Right?"

"Yep."

He reached up and gently tugged the cord. Nothing moved. Reaching up with his other hand in case the ladder apparatus came down too quickly, he gave the cord another tug. Nothing.

"It's jammed. I need to get a stepladder and check this out—"

A deceptively lazy swirl of dust drifted downward like the flakes in a snow globe.

Metal squealed.

The screech of twisting, splintering wood filled the air.

Logan pivoted to get out of the way, but the mass of metal framework and heavy oak above him lurched downward, then crashed to the floor, knocking him flat.

Stars exploded behind his eyelids, and then the room went black.

"This really wasn't necessary," Logan grumbled as Dr. McClaren left the room. "I told you he would let me go home."

In his jeans and a hospital gown that barely stretched across his chest, he seemed to overwhelm the cramped ER cubicle. Darcy had been prepared to stop him if he tried to leave before the doctor showed up. She'd already tucked his boots under her chair and out of sight.

"But you were knocked out."

"For just a minute. No big deal."

"Except that you do have a mild concussion, and that *is* a big deal. And then there's that arm."

"It's fine." He started to stretch but suddenly winced and grabbed for his injured right shoulder.

"I can see it's perfectly fine," she retorted dryly. "No pain at all."

He glowered at her. "It'll be good by tomorrow. It has to be."

After a physical exam, an X-ray and a range-of-motion evaluation, Dr. McClaren had said there were no fractures, but he suspected a partially torn rotator cuff. He'd recommended a sling and minimal use of the arm, and if the shoulder pain wasn't alleviated by NSAIDs or a prescription pain med, an MRI and surgical repair might be next on the list.

"You know the doc is right about taking it easy for a

while. And if you think you'll be seeing equine patients tomorrow, that's a no."

When he eased off the gurney, she helped him shove his feet into his boots. He turned away and awkwardly attempted to put on his T-shirt, but the complexity of doing it with one good arm and a painful shoulder on the other side clearly confounded him. For just a moment, he seemed to sway on his feet.

"Here, let me." Darcy briskly stepped forward and helped him get it on, trying to ignore the intimacy of this moment as she smoothed it down over his broad shoulders. "Are you going to be all right at home?"

He snorted. "Of course."

"Too bad it's your right shoulder. Do you have anyone to stay with you tonight? And what about your horse chores?"

"No problem," he said wearily, rubbing a hand down his face. "I can manage."

"Right. Can you even drive?"

"He'd better not." One of the nurses bustled in, a clipboard in hand. "And yes, he should have someone with him tonight because he had a pretty good rap on the head."

She demonstrated the use of a sling, but he waved it away. Then she ran through his going-home instructions and handed over the printed copy along with a script for a prescription pain med. "No refills on this one. It has to be filled with a physical prescription in hand. I can't call it in to the pharmacy. Do you need a wheelchair to the ER entrance?"

Logan gave her an appalled look. "No, ma'am."

"I can drive you home," Darcy offered when the nurse gave him a last disgruntled look and left the room. "We can run out to do your chores and pick up Emma on the way back to my house." Darcy frowned, thinking about the disaster that was now her home, with furniture still piled in corners. "It'll take me just a few minutes to set up the bedrooms again. Emma can sleep in my room, and you can have hers for the night."

He shook his head. "That's too much trouble. In fact, I could take a taxi home and save you the trip."

"There are no taxis here. And the doctor said—"

"Patients do have rights, and it's my decision. I'm going home."

"You know, my friend Keeley's fiancé had a similar head injury once, and I remember him being a lot more agreeable." Darcy rolled her eyes. "But it's your brain, so go ahead and ignore my offer and my greater wisdom. Good luck."

Out at Logan's place in the country an hour later, Darcy brought his two horses into the barn, grained them and waited in the cool, dark aisle while they ate.

Logan leaned a hip against a stall door and breathed in the clean, familiar scents of alfalfa, leather and horse, his gaze on Darcy. "Thanks for helping me out."

"There was no question at all. I owe you this and more." She turned to look at him. "I'm so sorry that you got hurt. You were only being kind by helping me, and the accident was my fault. I expect you to file a claim with my homeowner's insurance for bills, by the way. I'll call them first thing tomorrow morning."

"You couldn't have known about that ladder apparatus. If it had fallen on you, you might have been killed."

"Because you have a harder head?" she teased.

"I'm a lot taller, and I was already reaching upward. I was able to deflect some of the impact."

"I'm just praying that you heal quickly so your shoulder doesn't hold you back for very long. I...called Marilyn, by the way."

He felt himself tense. "And?"

"You have some appointments tomorrow morning. Two families with 4-H kids needing health papers for their horses, so they can attend a horse project workshop next weekend. Both horses already have current, negative Coggins test results and vaccination records, So now they just need the exams."

"I can handle that."

"As can I, if your shoulder is even more painful tomorrow. It probably will be. And you have a presale soundness exam in the afternoon."

He smiled wryly. "Not exactly land office business."

"For your first day? It's a good start. I'm impressed. I understand there's been a strong response on the website, too. What else are you doing?"

"Two of the local saddle clubs have asked me to speak at their monthly meetings, and I'll be writing an article for the state quarter horse association newsletter next month. I also started a Twitter account as Aspen Creek Equine Clinic, so I figure word will start spreading."

Even in the shady gloom of the barn, he saw her stiffen. "Have you already changed the name?"

"Not yet. I think I found the right vet box to put on my truck for farm calls. Guess I'll need to decide on the name so it can be painted on the side."

She fell silent, and the temperature in the barn seemed to drop thirty degrees.

"I see," she said finally as she looked into the two stalls where the horses had finishing eating and were now heads-down, snuffling around in the cedar shaving bedding. She snapped a lead rope on the palomino's halter and led her back to the pasture, then took the gelding outside. "I've got to pick up Emma and head for home. Do you need anything else?"

"No, but thanks." He straightened and followed her out to her car. "I'll get back to finishing up my hours at your place soon as I can."

"After discovering the wonders of YouTube educational videos, I now realize I can do the floors just fine by myself, which will keep my nights busy for a while." She waved a hand dismissively. "And I'll call around to ask some electricians for estimates on the lighting. Everything else can wait. Don't worry about it—I've got a lot of other things to think about in the meantime."

## Chapter Seven

As Darcy predicted and he'd known full well himself—not that he'd wanted to admit it to her—Logan's painful shoulder kept him awake all night and felt worse the next day.

She picked him up the next morning since his truck was still at her place. After the drive to the clinic, his shoulder was even more uncomfortable. He grudgingly asked her to cover the 4-H horse exams after realizing with chagrin that the first one, a black Welsh pony owned by the Fowlers, was noticeably lame, and some of the steps of a lameness evaluation would be nearly impossible with his own injured shoulder.

He quietly watched from the sidelines in the fenced courtyard behind the clinic as Darcy went through each of the flexion tests meant to isolate sources of pain in the joints and soft tissue.

One by one, she lifted each back hoof and held the leg in a cramped, flexed position for sixty seconds, then watched as Kaycee led the gelding away at a trot. Then Darcy used a hoof tester on each foot.

After she completed the rest of the exam, she smiled

at the young girl and her father. "You have a lovely pony, Anna."

"Is Pepper okay?" The girl cast a worried look at the pony. "Can I take him to the workshop?"

"Right now he's too lame. I saw him last summer, and he was sore even then. We took X-rays of his feet, remember? We figured out that he easily grass-founders, so I talked about what you needed to do. Have you kept him off the pasture?"

Anna nodded vigorously. "I bring him in the barn every night."

"But—"

"That's right," her father interjected. "He's out there only nine or ten hours at the most."

A pained expression flickered in Darcy's eyes. "Was he sound over the fall and winter?"

Anna nodded again.

"That's because your pasture was winter brown. He didn't have rich green grass then—which is especially troublesome for a horse with this problem. His tendency for founder will always be the worst in the spring. Right now, both of his front feet are very warm and painful, and I can feel a strong pulse. I'm going to give him an injection to alleviate that pain for now and give you a tube of the pain medicine you used last year. And no more green grass for this boy. Promise?"

Kaycee ran into the clinic and returned with the syringe.

Anna looked away while Darcy administered the medication, and she dug her toe in the dirt. "Dad says he has to be in the pasture to eat, 'cause we don't need to buy hay for him in the summer. It's a waste of money."

Mr. Fowler cleared his throat, his face reddening.

"Why let all that pasture go to waste, right? Horses are supposed to eat grass. Surely a little can't hurt."

A muscle jumped along the side of Darcy's jaw line. "Most horses," she said patiently. "Not this one. If you want your daughter to be able to ride, he needs to be on a dry lot, with hay."

Muttering under his breath, the man grabbed the pony's lead rope and marched him to the back end of the horse trailer, where the pony obediently hopped inside.

"Marilyn is at the front desk and can give you a tube of bute for pain relief." Darcy watched him shut the gate. "If he isn't better within a week or two, give me a call."

"I never should have bought him in the first place. Big mistake."

"This little guy is a wonderful child's pony," Darcy said patiently. "He's a rare find with his personality and show experience. He's well worth any amount of extra care."

"Maybe you should buy him, then. I've just about had it with this whole business. I'd sell him to you cheap."

"Dad," Anna wailed, "Pepper is my best friend and—"

"Hurry inside and get that tube of bute," her father growled. "Then get in the car, Anna. We'll discuss this later."

Darcy exchanged weary glances with Kaycee after the truck and horse trailer pulled out onto the road and disappeared.

"Some people are so mean. I wouldn't want to be poor Anna," Kaycee muttered. "I think she's about to lose her buddy."

"Her dad isn't mean," Darcy said. "Not really. He just doesn't know anything about horses, and for all we know, maybe he can't really afford to be giving his daughter this opportunity."

"Yeah, well, I still wish the pony *and* Anna luck." Kaycee glanced at her watch. "Oops—I'd better see if your eleven-o'clock client is in the waiting room."

Logan followed Darcy through the back door of the clinic. "You did a good job with that exam and the client. I'm impressed."

She lifted a shoulder in a slight shrug. "Nothing too difficult."

Curious, he leaned his good shoulder against the door frame when she stopped at the sink in the lab to wash her hands. "I thought you'd done just small-animal work."

"No. I worked in a mixed practice before coming here." She pulled her lab coat on over her scrubs. "Plus I had horses when I was a kid and did quite a bit of showing until vet school, so at one time I even thought I'd go straight equine."

"Why didn't you?"

"Well, things don't always work out the way you expect." She hesitated. Looked away. "When I inherited my aunt's house, I was grateful to find a job in town, no matter what kind of practice it was—especially since Dr. Boyd was such a great guy."

"But it sounded like you've dealt with Pepper before."

"Yeah. Boyd was okay with me seeing horses if I wanted to. But when he got sick I had to take over the clinic, so I was too busy to pursue it. What little I've done has been more of a favor to the locals, really."

She cocked her head and lifted her gaze to his. "I'm sure you'll do very well here, but as you've now seen, there's also a strong demand for the small-animal side. So I just don't get it. You're throwing away a successful, established side of this practice if you don't let it continue."

He didn't answer. But she was right, of course. She

always had been. He'd known that before ever arriving in town.

But keeping on an extra vet had never been part of his goals. She didn't fit in his plans, and he only had to recall the situation in Montana to remind him why.

Try as he might to avoid it, Darcy was already slipping through his defenses. And where would he be then? Even though she didn't seem to be anything like Cathy, would he be second-guessing every move, every billing statement? Every country vet call that might be anything but?

"Okay, then," she continued coolly into the lengthening silence between them. "Fine. But just so you know, I've started looking into possible sites in town for my own clinic. I can't afford to delay if I'm going to be without a job, so sometime soon we need to sit down and talk before I sign a lease somewhere else."

Emma pushed aside her dinner plate and craned her neck to see Darcy's laptop screen. "That looks like an ice cream truck, Mommy."

Darcy laughed and gave her a quick hug, then scrolled through the next dozen photos in the online listing. "I guess you're right. But it's actually a mobile vet clinic."

Emma gave her a baffled look.

"See the door in back? People can walk inside with their pets to see the veterinarian."

"Dogs go in there?"

"Absolutely. People, too. I could drive it around the county and see clients in different towns. Or just park it here in Aspen Creek."

Emma eyes flashed with sudden fear. "I don't want you to go far away. Not like Daddy."

"Don't worry, sweetheart, I'm not going anywhere. I'd be home every single night."

A tear traced down Emma's cheek. "Daddy said he'd be back."

Yes, he had, but trust and honor hadn't meant much to him, and he'd ultimately paid the price for it, rest his soul. And the one still suffering for his selfishness was his little girl.

"Well, I've also been looking into some empty store-fronts on Main Street, and maybe that would work out better. You and I might start looking at some of them on Saturday. But right now, I need to get back to working on my bedroom floor."

"Can I help?"

"Um…no. But you can watch a DVD here in the kitchen if you want. You choose. When it's over it'll be time for your bath and storybooks."

Darcy had damp-mopped the bedroom when she first got home from work to give it time to dry fully. Now, after a painstaking hour of rubbing stain onto the hard-wood floor and wiping off the excess with a dry rag, she rocked back on her heels and studied the results as she peeled off her gloves.

"You're doing a great job."

At the sound of Logan's deep voice behind her, she spun around, startled. "I didn't hear you come in."

"I had to come back into town this evening and thought I'd stop in."

Darcy blinked in disbelief. She was never careless anymore. Not ever. One lesson had been more than enough. "Did I leave the front door unlocked?"

"No. Emma saw me through the front window and

opened the door. She said you were 'finger-painting' your bedroom and that I should take a look."

She laughed. "She must not think I'm very creative. It's all one color."

"Looks great, though."

"I read that medium tones would hide scuffs better than dark. I hope that's true." She studied the floor. "Next I need to apply sealer, buff it and add the polyurethane."

"I should be able to help by the weekend."

She snorted. "I don't expect that at all. Not for weeks. That shoulder still looks too painful."

"It's a lot better already."

"Right," she drawled. "Except that it's been only twenty-four hours. I see you flinch when you move it."

"That's just your imagination."

The twinkle in his eyes caught her unawares, and she glanced up at him in surprise. This wasn't the cold, distant stranger who'd shown up several weeks ago, and if she wasn't careful, she was going to start liking him a little too much.

Jerking her wayward thoughts back into line, she tapped the lid onto the empty can of stain and rose to her feet. "I figure I can put the furniture back in this room by Wednesday or Thursday, then start on Emma's room. The way it's going, I might get all of the floors done in a few weeks."

"I hope the kitchen flooring isn't a surprise. They can sure be a bear to take out. In the meantime, I brought you something to look at."

She belatedly realized that he was holding out some sort of catalog. She accepted it and studied the cover, suppressing the surprising sensation that raced up her arm at the inadvertent brush of their fingertips.

"These are…um…cabinets?"

"The resurfacing materials I told you about. Veneers for exposed cabinet sides, new doors, drawer fronts, hardware."

After days of mulling her options, she'd decided she was staying in Aspen Creek no matter what. But if she needed to establish her own clinic, she and Emma might end up in this little cottage for a long time to come. "These things aren't cheap or flimsy, right?"

"A friend of mine totally remodeled his home and used this company. The results were stunning. He chose the top of the line, though."

"So you just nail these pieces into place? I could probably do it myself, then, while that shoulder of yours is healing."

He shot her an amused look. "It might be just a little harder than that."

The laughter in his voice felt like dark velvet sliding over her skin and made her feel warm and shivery.

And for the first time since Dean left her, she found herself wondering what it might be like to be enfolded in another man's arms once again. Maybe even lose herself in a kiss…

But she had no business even thinking about that. Not with anyone. Emma, her career and a stable, secure home were all that mattered now.

## Chapter Eight

On Tuesday, ibuprofen throughout the day helped Logan see several horses that were brought into the clinic, though toward the end of the day, his shoulder was even more painful and he just wanted to get in his truck and go home

But Darcy was right. There was one thing he couldn't put off any longer. At five, he asked the staff to come into his office.

Marilyn edged in, her face pale. Kaycee fiddled with her necklace and didn't meet his eyes. But when Darcy trailed in after the others, she leaned against the wall, folded her arms and stared him down, clearly challenging him to do the right thing.

He just hoped what he'd decided *was* the right thing. "As you know, I bought this clinic planning to change the focus, update the building and search for staff experienced in an equine practice." He looked at each of them in turn. "I have reasons—good ones—for wanting to start fresh by interviewing and hiring new employees. It's a common approach in situations like this one."

If anything, Marilyn grew even more pale. Darcy reached over and rested a hand on one of hers.

Logan drew in a slow breath. "Some new owners let the previous staff interview, as well, and then make their decisions. That seems fair enough, but I don't think it's necessary here."

Kaycee scowled. "So here it comes."

"I've been here two and a half weeks now," Logan continued. "I've had time to see your efficiency and rapport with the clients, Marilyn. And Kaycee, you've done a great job with the horses and owners who've been in this week. I feel we'll all make a good team. How do you feel about working for me?"

Marilyn and Kaycee nodded, the relief in the room palpable.

Marilyn pressed a hand to her chest. "B-but what about Darcy?"

"She and I need to talk further." He looked down at a document on the desk. "One last thing. I need to have background checks done on anyone who works here— to safeguard our clients, staff and the reputation of the clinic. And that will include all of you."

After the last scheduled client was seen and Logan had left for the day, Kaycee stormed into the lab.

Darcy looked up from the X-rays she was reviewing of a dachshund with back pain. "What's up?"

"The more I think about it, the more I can't believe it," she fumed. "Background checks. Like we're criminals or something. I've been here for over two years and Marilyn for twenty. Not only that, but we've both lived here all our lives. What in the world does he think he'd going to find on us?"

"Nothing, I'm sure. And he probably knows it." Darcy turned off the light in the viewing box and tucked the films into a folder.

"It's just plain humiliating. Do I have the choice to say no?"

"If you did, you probably wouldn't have a job."

Kaycee's mouth pursed into a belligerent pout. "Maybe I don't even want it."

"Whoa, Kaycee, Think about what you're saying. Would you give up your good-paying job over this?"

"I just think it's wrong," she retorted.

"He's setting a wise policy. Can you imagine the flack if he inadvertently hired someone in the future who was on a sex offender registry? Or who had some other criminal record? Imagine the risk—and the liability he could face if something bad happened later on."

"I'll bet he isn't so perfect, either. I wonder what's in his background?"

At hearing the anger in Kaycee's voice, realization dawned. "Are you worried about…something in particular?"

Kaycee's eyes glistened with sudden tears.

"Honey, I don't know your whole story, and it's not my business. But I do know you're raising your brother and sister, so things must have been tough. You're an amazing young woman to have taken on such responsibility at…were you nineteen?"

"Almost." Kaycee gave a single short nod and looked away. "I…did a few things when I was a teenager. Bad things."

"I can help you find a lawyer if you want to be sure, but I doubt very much that any minor juvenile offenses were transferred when you became an adult. I imagine the documents were sealed."

"I don't have money for a lawyer," Kaycee retorted bitterly. "Especially not now."

"If you want, I can ask around for some advice— without mentioning your name, of course. Maybe you wouldn't even need to see a lawyer, unless there are problems with your records that need to be corrected. You could probably just start at the courthouse and ask someone in the juvenile office."

She shuddered. "Like that wouldn't be totally humiliating. It's a small town, and I know most of the people there."

"If you want, I could go with you. I can't imagine you capable of doing anything seriously wrong, though. And I don't think anyone could fault you for whatever happened in your past."

"But then there are m-my parents…" Kaycee bit her lower lip. "You know they're in prison, right? What does that say about me?"

"Their transgressions are part of their records, not yours." Darcy slid an arm around her shoulders and gave her a hug. "And I think you've become a far stronger person because of it. I would be very proud if my daughter grew up to be someone like you."

"Do you think I should just go ahead and tell Dr. Maxwell everything? I mean, would it be better if he heard it from me?"

"If you think he's going to hear things around town about your family, it might be more straightforward to get it all out in the open, so he hears the truth and not some exaggeration. But that's completely up to you."

\* \* \*

The answering service called at two a.m. to announce crisply that a client had an emergency and was requesting immediate help.

Logan flicked on the lamp, reached for a notebook on the bedside table and jotted down the address and phone number, ignoring the pain shooting down his right arm with every movement. He groaned and eased back into bed for a few seconds, considering his options.

There was no other equine vet within forty miles. He needed to take this call. But how was he going to manage a potentially complex case given his damaged shoulder?

At the multi-vet clinic in Montana, there had been plenty of staff. Vets were on a rotating schedule for after-hours emergency farm calls, as were the vet techs who were willing and able to leave home on short notice at night if a vet needed extra help.

Here, he could set up an alternating on-call schedule with Darcy, but she was a single parent with a young child, so how would that work? And the possibility of extra help on night calls didn't look promising, either.

Kaycee had younger siblings who lived with her, and Marilyn was office help, not trained as a vet tech. She would mostly be in the way, if she tried to help with a complicated case. Unless…

Glancing at the clock, he muttered "Forgive me" as he dialed Marilyn's cell. Then he called Darcy.

Twenty minutes later, Marilyn had arrived at Darcy's place to watch over Emma as she slept, and Darcy arrived at the clinic to ride with him to the farm.

"Double-time pay, huh?" Darcy said. "Marilyn could certainly use it."

"I just felt guilty about waking her up and grateful when she said yes."

He headed for the front driver's side door, but Darcy beat him to it. "No problem, but I'm driving so you can rest that shoulder."

The main highway was empty this time of night, the headlights cutting a narrow swath of light through the pitch-black countryside. Logan typed the address into the dashboard GPS screen. A crisp female voice directed them well out of town, then onto a maze of narrow gravel roads.

"I never would've found this place without a GPS," Darcy muttered.

The final turn took them down a narrow drive to a white ranch house and a metal barn. A woman emerged from the barn and waited anxiously as Darcy grabbed the plastic tote of supplies from the backseat of the truck.

"She's in here. Please hurry."

Bright banks of fluorescent lights illuminated box stalls flanking both sides of the wide aisle in the horse barn.

A big paint mare stood cross-tied in a large cemented area with rubber mats on the floor. A water hose snaked across the wet cement.

Blood had pooled on the floor by her front hooves. The gaping wound on the bulging muscle of her forearm was least ten centimeters wide and looked deep.

"I'm Dr. Maxwell," Logan said, offering his hand. "And this is Dr. Leighton."

"Margie Ford. We raise show paints here, and Buttons is one of our best mares. I heard a ruckus outside and found her fighting with a horse in the next corral. Two of the fence boards were splintered, so I think she ran into the sharp edges. It was bleeding pretty good at first, but I applied pressure for about twenty minutes. Now it's just seeping a little."

Logan leaned close and studied the damage, then listened to the mare's heart and lung sounds. "Has she been bred for next year?"

"We thought so, but she came back into heat yesterday."

"I need to sedate her to examine this. We need to determine just how extensive it is."

Margie nodded. "Absolutely."

Darcy drew a dose of xylazine into a syringe and handed it to him. He palpated the neck, found the jugular vein and, after temporarily occluding the flow of blood with his thumb, delivered the sedative.

The mare stood patiently through it all. As soon as her muzzle began to droop toward the floor, he donned surgical gloves and began gently probing the wound with his fingertips. "Did you remove any wood splinters?"

"I didn't see any, and didn't want to poke around in there to find out. I did start to rinse it off with the hose but figured it was better to leave that to you."

"Good. Sterile saline is better." He gritted his teeth as a wave of pain seared through his shoulder. "Darcy? If you could take over, that would be great."

"Got it." She donned surgical gloves, grabbed an IV bag of the saline from the tote and filled a syringe, then removed the needle. Using the syringe as a gentle water pistol, she began gently flushing dirt and debris from the wound.

After refilling the syringe a half-dozen times, she set it aside and began probing the wound, checking its depth and feeling for foreign objects.

Every movement was gentle and sure, and she was

exceptionally thorough. Logan relaxed as his confidence in her clinical skills grew.

Darcy looked up at Margie. "Fortunately, most of this is shallow. There's a central depth of around seven centimeters, though."

Margie moved closer and anxiously peered into the wound. "But she'll be all right? No major damage?"

"The bone wasn't compromised, so that's very good news. Now we just need to keep the wound clean and let it heal." Darcy reached for an autoclave bag, pulled out sterilized surgical scissors and trimmed away several dangling tags of shredded hide. "These small bits will die and just impede healing. It's best to clean up the edges of the wound."

"You're not going to stitch it all up?" Margie asked in disbelief. "Won't this leave a massive scar?"

"It looks bad to you now, but I don't think it will. I'd like to suture just the upper half of the wound and leave the lower five centimeters open for drainage." Darcy glanced up at Logan. "Dr. Maxwell?"

He nodded. "I agree."

"I'm going to give her a strong antibiotic today by injection and leave you with Bactrim tablets you can dissolve in water and give her twice a day starting tomorrow night." Darcy looked over at Margie. "Can you handle that?"

"Of course. No problem."

"It's a tricky place to bandage, given the tapering of the foreleg toward the knee," Darcy continued. "But I'd still like to wrap it for tonight and tomorrow to keep it clean, then come back tomorrow late afternoon to irrigate the wound and see how it's doing. After that we'll look at a progression of different types of dressings, depending on the stage of wound healing."

Darcy rifled through the tote at her feet and applied a dressing held by a thin layer of cotton wrap, followed by fluffy roll cotton and a cohesive elastic wrap over it all. "Done. But give us a call if the bandage slips, and one of us can come back to replace it."

"I'm so glad you two were able to come. It's great knowing that we've actually got equine vets in the area again." Margie blew out a relieved breath. "I'll be calling you from now on."

"Thanks, ma'am." Logan touched the brim of his hat as he and Darcy sauntered out into the darkness toward his truck.

Out here, so far from the lights of town, the sky was awash with glittering stars. It was chilly during the predawn hours, and he saw Darcy shiver.

He casually dropped his good arm around her shoulders as they walked. It was just a friendly gesture to share warmth, but he felt her tense, and he dropped his arm.

Interesting.

She'd felt so…right, nestled within that hug. He hadn't wanted to let her go. Somehow his thoughts had instantly conjured up images of long evenings over coffee. Candlelit dinners. She'd clearly felt anything but.

He had yet to hear anyone mention her boyfriend, spouse or partner, yet what was such a lovely, sweet and hardworking person like her doing all alone? There must have been someone, because she had a daughter… but where was he?

What if he'd been abusive?

A surge of protectiveness rushed through Logan at the thought, though a small voice whispered that her life was none of his business. He sat at an angle on the passenger side of the truck and casually watched her as she drove back to Aspen Creek.

Bluish smudges of exhaustion left dark circles under her eyes, but she was smiling to herself and humming a faint song completely out of tune.

Nope, it definitely was none of his business.

And yet he found himself clearing his throat. "You did a fine job out there."

She shot a quick glance at him. "Thanks, but it wasn't much, really."

"But it was. That suturing was done perfectly, and you didn't make a move that a top-notch vet wouldn't have made. So now I'm even more curious. You have real talent for the equine side of things. Why did you leave it behind?"

"It's a long story." Her jaw hardened and she gripped the steering wheel until her knuckles whitened. "And not all that interesting."

But he guessed it was.

In the dark intimacy of the truck cab, illuminated only by the dashboard lights, he felt emboldened enough to step over the bounds she'd clearly set…curious if the mystery surrounding her was somehow tied to her troublesome financial situation.

"Is it a secret?" he teased.

She rolled her eyes. "Not really. I can promise you my worst legal transgressions have been a few speeding tickets, and I didn't leave the previous practice under any sort of cloud. I enjoyed the work. I liked the clinic. But it was simply time to move on, so I did. Without regrets. Now Aspen Creek has become our home, with good friends, a great church and clientele at the clinic whom I enjoy very much."

It was an answer…and yet it wasn't.

He belatedly realized that he'd opened himself up to the same question, but she didn't ask the obvious. Instead, she settled into a comfortable silence. Dawn was brightening the eastern sky in ribbons of gold and mauve when she pulled up at the clinic next to her car.

Leaving the truck motor running, she glanced at the digital clock on the dashboard and climbed out of the cab.

"See you back here in a couple hours," she said with a wry smile. "Have a good night's sleep."

He watched her car pull out of the parking lot, its tail-lights glowing like rubies as it disappeared down the street.

He'd asked a simple, reasonable question about her past and she'd shut down like a door clanging shut on a bank vault…but not before he'd seen a flash of vulnerability in her eyes.

And now he had more questions than ever before.

## Chapter Nine

Wednesday passed in a blur, what with a busy clinic schedule and another trip out to Margie's place with Logan to check on the paint mare.

When Darcy finally picked up Emma at the sitter's and got home, she was too tired to make anything more than hamburgers and green beans for supper.

But afterward, once Emma was tucked into bed, she finished the final coat of polyurethane on the master bedroom floor, flopped onto the sofa—the only piece of furniture in the living room—and heaved a sigh of relief. One room done.

She'd been flippant while telling Logan she could do it all herself once it was clear that he'd be laid up for a while. Saving his time for more complex projects had seemed logical at the time.

True, she could follow directions and slowly get the floors done, but all of the steps took more time than she'd dreamed. And after prying at the vinyl on the kitchen floor for an hour, she knew it was going to be one of the most difficult things she'd ever done.

At a knock on the door she jumped, startled and a

little nervous as always about a stranger showing up on her porch after dark. Her heart had been broken after losing her elderly dog Elsie last fall, but as a single parent, Darcy also missed her fierce barking whenever someone approached the house.

No stranger would have guessed the noisy dog inside was a thirty-pound marshmallow.

"Yoo-hoo, are you home?" At the sound of Beth's cheerful voice, Darcy hurried to the front door and let her in.

"I have to follow up on everyone who won a handyman at the auction and make sure things are working out." Her arm curved around a clipboard, Beth surveyed the furniture piled in the kitchen and the bare floor of the living room. "Wow. You're sure making progress. Is Logan working out for you?"

"Very well. He repaired the picket fence and also started the flooring, but then injured his shoulder. He also has some great ideas for the kitchen cupboards, though there might not be enough hours to cover any of that."

"And how are you two getting along?" Beth waggled her eyebrows. "I was just at the salon getting my hair trimmed, and he seemed to be the hot topic of the day. Sooo handsome. So nice. So eligible. Just thought I'd mention it in case you've had any thoughts in that direction."

"No. Absolutely not. It can be open season on Dr. Maxwell for as long as it takes for someone to tie him down. Really."

Beth gave her a speculative look, her mouth twitching. "Sounds like an awful lot of protest."

"Well, I mean it. You know what happened back in

Minnesota with Dean. I *trusted* him. How can I dare fall for anyone else and be sure it won't happen again? I was completely clueless." Darcy snorted. "As in, too stupid to live."

"I predict you're going to find the right guy someday. A guy you can completely trust and love forever. And then you'll have to eat your words. For the record, I do think your new vet is pretty hot."

Well…yes. And he was turning out to be a much nicer guy than she'd first thought. But that didn't mean she would take a chance on him or anyone else. "It just isn't worth it. And what about Emma? I don't want to start dating and have her thinking she'll have a new daddy soon, then be heartbroken if the relationship doesn't work out. She is my priority."

"How is she doing, by the way? I heard she had an asthma episode after church last Sunday, when my husband and I were out of town."

"She was fine after using her rescue inhaler. This time of year is tough for her, with the grasses and weeds, but molds and perfumes spell trouble, too. Since there were a lot of visitors at church for a baptism, maybe it was perfume."

"Poor sweetheart."

"She's been fine since. We just never know. Sometime she even starts wheezing without any of her usual triggers nearby. The doctor said her sensitivities could change over time. I'm just hoping they go away."

"Me, too. It's always a worry having something like that. By the way—different topic—we've missed you at the book club lately. Monday mornings, eight o'clock at my bookstore?" Beth teased. "Thought I would mention it since we haven't seen you for so long."

"I used to keep that first hour on Monday morning open so I could join you, but things have been a lot busier lately. Once we get into summer and people are traveling, the schedule at the clinic will slow down."

Beth gave her a knowing look. "When you come, bring that vet you're definitely not interested in. We have some new members who might like to check him out."

*Check him out, indeed.* Beth's words kept slipping into Darcy's thoughts as she worked through a busy appointment schedule the next day. How did she feel about that, really?

She'd told Beth the truth. She wasn't looking for a relationship. Dean had pretty much cured her of that basic human longing for companionship and love. She'd had to immerse herself in prayer to finally let go of the hurt and anger following his betrayal.

But did she really want to see Logan madly in love with someone else? It was selfish not to wish him happiness. She didn't even know him that well.

But with every day that she worked with him, with every conversation, she'd started to see new sides to him that had begun to touch her heart.

With several emergency call-ins and no extra time in her schedule to cover them, he had taken the extra appointments this afternoon so those clients wouldn't face long waits.

Now, on her way to the lab, she passed the open door of an exam room where an elderly woman hovered anxiously over her obese Maltese while Logan checked its heart and lung sounds.

It was Mrs. Peabody, dressed as usual in her faded print Sunday dress, sturdy laced shoes and a sagging sweater that had seen better days. Bent over and always short of breath, she religiously brought her dog into the clinic for the slightest signs or symptoms but was only able to pay a few dollars each time against her ever-growing account.

Darcy hated to accept even that much from her and had begun charging her less and less, waving off the old woman's protests by saying, "Today we're having a sale," or "I really didn't do that much, anyway."

Darcy lingered just past the door, hoping Logan wouldn't look at Mrs. Peabody's balance at the top of the clinic visit sheet. Hoping he wouldn't say anything less than tactful. If she asked about today's cost and he told her the truth, she'd probably succumb to a massive heart attack at his feet.

"I-is my baby all right?" The old woman's voice quavered. "I was so afraid this morning when his breathing didn't sound right. H-he's all I have left, doctor."

It was true. Her husband had died years ago, and her only child—a retired teacher—had passed back in December. Without her little companion, by now the crushing loneliness and grief might have taken Mrs. Peabody, as well.

There was a long pause. Darcy held her breath.

"He's a beautiful dog, ma'am. And don't you worry. His heart and lungs sound fine. There's one thing he needs to do, though."

"I suppose you want him to lose weight," she said on a long sigh. "Dr. Leighton says that, too. But he gets exactly the right amount of dog food."

"The weight loss formula?"

She nodded. "What Dr. Leighton prescribed. I buy it here."

"Then it's the extra little treats that have to go. Being overweight is very hard on his heart, so he needs less food and more walking."

Darcy continued on to the lab, the voices following her down the hall.

"But he loves his treats and looks at me so sadly if he doesn't get just a tiny bit off my plate," she said sorrowfully. "How can I refuse? What is life without small pleasures?"

Darcy smiled to herself, waiting for his response. *Good luck, Dr. Logan.*

Footsteps came down the hall, and Logan appeared at the door of the lab. "Do we have any sample-size bags of light dog treats?"

"Top shelf, on your left. But—"

He grabbed a couple of bags and left before she could warn him about billing Mrs. Peabody.

His voice filtered down the hall as he explained the low-calorie treats and a proper diet.

Darcy once again held her breath when she heard him wrapping up his advice and saying farewell.

Then warmth washed over her like a gentle hug as she heard his next words.

"No—of course not." His voice dropped to a conspiratorial whisper that Darcy could barely hear. "No charge for today. We weren't that busy, and I didn't really do anything. Anyway, we all love to see you and your beautiful little dog."

After dialing the front desk and telling Marilyn there'd be no charge for the elderly lady toddling slowly down the hall with her dog, Logan left the exam room to head to back to his office.

As he passed the lab, Darcy stepped out the door and they nearly collided. He grasped both of her upper arms when she staggered, but quickly released her.

Her eyes widened. "Sorry."

He said it at the same moment she did, and they both laughed self-consciously as they stepped back. The air between them seemed to quiver with emotion and unspoken possibilities.

She readjusted the stethoscope draped around her neck. "How was Mrs. Peabody's dog?"

"Obese."

"She worries about him all the time, you know. He's the only friend she has. Her family is gone, and I hear all of her human friends have passed on, as well. Um… I couldn't help overhearing…" She angled an amused smile at him. "If you talk loud enough for her to hear, you might as well be using a loudspeaker. Sounds like you charged her as much as I do."

He felt himself flush a little. "This can't be run as a free clinic, but…"

"I know. You don't have to say it. She's just such a sweet old lady." Her eyes twinkled with silent laughter as her soft gaze locked on his and a faint blush stained her cheekbones. "I'm just relieved to find you have the same soft side for her that I do. And about those light treats? Tried already. The next time she came in, she told me he didn't like them—unless she slathered them with gravy. But I'm sure she didn't want to admit that to you."

"A losing battle?"

"Definitely a losing battle. She loves him up with food, and after seeing that dog for a year, I can tell you that it isn't going to change."

The equine practice back in Montana had been highly

professional. Successful. Busy. A well-run business—at least, until Cathy showed up. But from his first day in Aspen Creek, this town, these people and this practice had been proving to be so much more. Quirky. Warm. Populated with people who really seemed to care about each other.

"Does she truly understand how serious this is?" he asked. "Her little buddy isn't going to have a very long life if he doesn't lose weight."

"I figure it's like water dripping on a stone. If we talk to her every time she comes in, we may finally wear her down. I just hope it isn't too late." Darcy eyed him thoughtfully. "I'm guessing that this sort of thing wasn't an issue at your last practice."

He had to laugh at that. "Not often. But then, we weren't dealing with doting small-animal owners like Mrs. Peabody. Our clients included most of the large breeding farms in the county. A lot of training facilities and many of the smaller show stables. Anyone who wasn't concerned about optimal feeding and health care wouldn't stay in business very long."

"Do you miss it?"

"The practice?" He considered that for a moment. "I miss…what it was. The state-of-the-art, high-tech equipment that made it easier to provide the very best of care. Much of it is beyond the financial reach of a one-or two-vet practice. I miss the large staff."

"But things changed."

"Yeah. Some things changed." He lifted his uninjured shoulder dismissively. "So now I'm glad to be where I am. Where ideally I have more control if issues arise."

"Except with the Mrs. Peabodys of the world?" she teased.

"I have to believe that she'll eventually listen to reason. I'm not giving up on her."

"Good luck with that." Darcy patted his arm. "You keep trying, and I'll start praying. And sooner or later, it's gonna happen. He cares for the least of his creatures, you know."

He watched her head down the hall to an exam room, where another client was waiting.

*Praying.*

She'd said the word with such simple, straightforward faith. No hint of doubt, no hesitance about the power of prayer.

He knew the exact date when he'd last hoped prayer could alter the course of his life, and God hadn't been listening that time, either. Logan hadn't sent any more desperate pleas heavenward after that. But now he began to wonder. Was it ever possible to regain a childlike faith after so many things had gone wrong?

## Chapter Ten

Kaycee peered out of the kennel room in back and motioned to Darcy. "Could I talk to you for a minute?"

She closed the door after Darcy stepped inside. "I've been thinking about what you said."

"About…"

"About what might show up on a background check. Or surface because of some old…um…gossip."

"I see."

"Dr. Boyd knew everything and he was so nice about it. But now I wonder whether or not I should go ahead and tell Dr. Maxwell. Before he gets that background check done, I mean."

"And what did you decide?"

"I guess…well, maybe you're right. If I don't say anything and he finds out, maybe he'll think I was trying to hide all the bad stuff. Or that I can't be trusted. But I can't just go up to him out of the blue. That would be so weird, you know?"

"So…what do you want me to do?"

"I…um…wonder if you could come in with me. You know, like having someone in my corner?"

"Moral support."

Her mouth twisted. "It still makes me mad, having to do this. If you live in a glass house you shouldn't throw stones, right?"

"What?"

Kaycee shifted uncomfortably and looked away.

"Kaycee?"

"Just something I found out about him on Google. It doesn't matter. I'm just really afraid I'll mess this up. And if I do and he fires me, what am I gonna do?"

"Do you want to catch him right now before he leaves for home?"

"No." Kaycee's eyes rounded. "Well…maybe. Yes. If I think about this too much longer, I'm going to be sick."

Logan looked up from his computer screen in obvious surprise when Kaycee and Darcy walked in his office door. "Is something wrong?"

Kaycee plopped into one of the chairs in front of the desk and mutely looked down at her hands, suddenly looking far younger than her twenty-three years.

Darcy took the other chair and waited for the girl to speak. After a long, awkward moment of silence, she turned to Logan. "Kaycee needs her job very much. But she's concerned about some things in her past and wants to be up front with you."

Logan's gaze softened with understanding as he shifted his focus to Kaycee. "If this is about the background checks, I got that information today, and they were perfectly fine for all three of you. I fully expected they would be, by the way. I hope you weren't too upset about having it done, but…well, I've been in situations in which more care would've saved people a lot of grief."

Kaycee lifted her gaze to meet his, her eyes hard and narrowed. Then she looked away. "I can imagine."

Logan tilted his head and frowned as he studied her for a moment, then he leaned back, his elbows on the arms of his chair and his fingertips steepled. "Is there anything you wanted to discuss?"

Mystified by the uneasy currents of emotion in the room, Darcy glanced between them. "Kaycee?"

The girl closed her eyes as she drew in a deep breath. "Okay. Just in case you were to hear gossip around town, I wanted you to hear everything from me first. My parents abused and dealt drugs for years, so I pretty much raised my brother and sister ever since I was in middle school. I...um...got caught shoplifting at the grocery store a couple times. But I had to try, 'cause there wasn't any money and sometimes we had nothing to eat."

"I'm sorry you had to go through that," Logan said gently.

"It's better now." Kaycee's voice took on a belligerent edge. "The kids live with me, they're on Badger Care state insurance, and the state helps out now that Mom and Dad are in prison. We're doing just fine." She launched to her feet as if ready to flee. "I promise that I'm trustworthy and I'll work hard. I *need* this job more than you could know."

An easy smile on his face, Logan stood and offered his hand to her across the desk. "Then it sounds like we have a perfect deal, because I need you, too. I'm glad to have you on board."

"That took some courage," Darcy said quietly after Kaycee left. "She's one of the strongest kids I've ever met. What a relief to hear that her background check was clear."

"It wasn't, actually."

"What?" Darcy leaned back in her chair, aghast. "But you told her it was."

"I told her it was *fine*, and I meant it. When I asked the sheriff to run criminal background checks, he said he couldn't help me much because Kaycee's juvenile records were sealed. But Marilyn stopped me after work one day, and said she wanted me to know the truth in case someone gossiped about Kaycee later on."

"Oh."

"That poor kid has had a real struggle raising her siblings, but even as a teen she fought to keep them out of foster care and together. How many kids her age would've taken on that responsibility?"

"Not many could have handled it. That's for sure."

"From all accounts, she's done a fine job ever since. She keeps them clean and well fed, they never miss school or activities, and she helps with homework. There are many parents who don't do half as well. I'm impressed, and I need employees like her."

Warmth and relief settled around Darcy's heart. "That's just about the kindest thing I've heard in a very long time. A lot of people would take one look at her past, assume she could be a risk and just let her go."

"Then they would be wrong. Her parents aren't going to be out on the street for thirty years, and before being incarcerated, they were guilty of abuse and neglect. So how could I not give her every chance to succeed?"

Darcy wanted to reach across the desk and kiss him in heartfelt thanks for his quiet compassion. And then kiss him again for his kindness in helping Kaycee hang onto her pride during what had to have been a terrifying confession.

"That's exactly how I feel." Her gaze locked on his.

She felt her pulse escalate as she rose and took a careful step back lest she find herself impulsively giving in to that temptation. "I realize I've misjudged you, Logan. Thank you from the bottom of my heart."

Saturday morning dawned bright and sunny, with the promise of clear skies and seventy degrees throughout the day.

It was a perfect day for opening all the windows in the little house and tackling the floor in Emma's room. But it was also perfect for making good on her promise, and that promise had to be kept.

So after the clinic closed at noon, she picked up Emma at the babysitter's house, took her home for lunch, then got ready to leave again.

"Are you ready to go?" Darcy helped Emma into a pink sweater with kittens and puppies embroidered on the front. "Hannah is waiting for us."

Emma fidgeted while Darcy fastened her buttons. "I want to go *now*. Please? What if there aren't any puppies left?"

"There will be, I promise. Remember all the photos we looked at last night on the rescue website?"

"They were every color. Puppies and big dogs, too."

Darcy smiled and gave her a hug. "Have you decided which ones are your favorites?"

The little girl frowned. "I can't remember."

"Well, we'll take lots of time. If you can't decide, we can always go back again."

They walked out to the car and Darcy buckled her into the booster seat, then got behind the wheel and turned the key in the ignition. At the *click-click-click* sound she dropped her head against the headrest and groaned.

"What's wrong, Mommy?"

"It won't start."

"But what about the puppies?" Her voice rose to a wail. "You promised!"

"Well, we might—"

At the distinctive sound of Logan's diesel pickup pulling into the driveway, Darcy glanced in the rearview mirror. *Good timing, buddy.*

She climbed out of her car and met him halfway. He held out his hand, and she blinked in surprise at her cell phone. "Oh, my— I thought it was in my purse."

"Marilyn noticed it at the clinic, but she was heading for Minneapolis for the weekend, so I said I could drop it by."

"Many, many thanks. We don't have a landline, so I wouldn't have missed it until I tried calling AAA road service."

He looked over her shoulder. "What's wrong with the car?"

"Won't start. It's doing a clickety-click thing when I turn the key in the ignition, and Emma is pretty upset." She turned to help the child out of her booster seat. "I bought a new battery two months ago, so I'm guessing it's the starter."

"Mommy said we could get a puppy today, and now we can't," Emma said sadly. Her face brightened when her gaze veered past Logan to his truck. "Maybe you could come! Will your car go?"

"That's a pickup, honey. And no, we don't need to bother Dr. Maxwell. I'm sure he's very busy."

"Actually, I'd like a good excuse to not go home." He sauntered to her car and tried the ignition. "I'd guess the starter, as well. Do you have a good mechanic?"

"Red's seems to be good. So, why don't you want to go home?"

"This is the weekend I'm finally dealing with all of the unpacked moving boxes still stacked in the house. I can't stand looking at them any longer, and I might have company coming next weekend."

Company?

Maybe a girlfriend from Montana?

Of course he would still have relationships with people back there. Maybe really close ones. It shouldn't have been any surprise, but she still felt a little pang in her heart.

"Should you be doing that lifting?" she asked. "What about your arm?"

He cautiously rolled his shoulder, then grinned. "It's actually pretty good. Another week and it should be fine."

Emma tugged the sleeve of Darcy's sweater and looked up at her with a pleading expression. "He *wants* to go see the puppies. Maybe he'll want one, too. Please?"

"Even if you call the road service now, there'll be no mechanics to check your car until Monday—or later. I'll get her booster seat, and we can be on our way." Logan reached into the car to grab it and put it into the backseat of his truck.

"If you do this for us, then we have to return the favor. How about we come out tomorrow afternoon to help you after church? We can even bring a picnic basket with lunch."

"You don't need to." He thought for a moment and gave her a lopsided smile. "Then again, lunch sounds mighty nice. Deal."

Her eyes twinkled. "Oops. I just remembered that

I won't have a car. But I have a wonderful idea—you could come with us to church this time!"

"Uh…"

"Pastor Mark is wonderful, I promise. Every Sunday, I feel so…so renewed by his sermons. It's hard to explain, but I feel like a better person. More able to deal with everything in my life, because my faith has been uplifted. Growing up, my parents made me attend their church, and I didn't want to go. Now I really hate to miss."

She took a deep breath. "I'm sorry. I don't mean to be pushing something at you that you don't want. I should have my car fixed in a couple days, and then Emma and I can come help. We'll still owe you a return favor, after all."

He stared out into the backyard for a long moment as if sorting through his thoughts.

"I had the same upbringing you did, but…bad things happened. God and I reached an impasse when I learned that my faith really didn't help. But I'll pick you two up tomorrow and take you to church if that's what you want."

She could see he wasn't thrilled—he was simply determined to do the right thing. She barreled ahead anyway before he could change his mind. "Perfect. That's so nice of you! Emma and I will pack a lunch and come out to help you unpack, or clean, or whatever. It's the least we can do."

Emma scrambled into the truck, and he clicked the seatbelt into position. "This is sure a pretty booster," he teased, ruffling the top of her hair. "I've never seen a pink one. You must be a big girl now."

She nodded vigorously. "I'm *four*."

"Just the right age for a puppy, then."

Darcy directed him to the highway leading out of town, then up a narrow lane leading through the forest toward Hannah's house.

All the way, Logan kept up a steady patter of silly conversation with Emma that kept her laughing.

Darcy felt an ache settle in her chest at how hungry Emma seemed for male attention.

But of course she was. In time she probably wouldn't remember much about her father, but having a loving male influence in her life was something she would always miss.

Hannah's house stood at the very end of the lane. She was out in the yard and gave the truck a startled look when Logan pulled in and parked, but relaxed as they all climbed out.

"You made it," she exclaimed as she picked up Emma for a big hug. "I'm so glad. I have all sorts of little guys who are eager to meet you—and some older ones, too."

She sized up Logan with a sweeping glance and grinned. "I have just the thing for you, too."

She led the way to the backyard, probably Emma's favorite place in the whole world.

The perimeter was enclosed in high chain link fencing, with three separate large runs to the right. In back stood a new red metal barn with crisp white trim and a large enclosure with colorful chickens inside.

Emma stood on her tiptoes, looking at the far end of the yard. "Is the pony here?"

"She's probably way out in the pasture right now." Hannah reached over and gave Darcy's hand a quick squeeze. "I asked Ethan to take the kids to a matinee so there'd be a bit less commotion. But I want you to be the first to hear—he and I have set a date. The Fourth of July weekend!"

Darcy's heart filled with joy for her closest friend in Aspen Creek. "I'm so thrilled for you both. This is the best news I've had in a long, long time."

Hannah beamed. "And next week the contractor will be breaking ground on the new animal shelter in town. It's finally happening."

Darcy nodded. "Hannah and several other women in town have been managing a private, licensed animal shelter system on their own properties until enough money could be raised. They've done a wonderful job."

"And Darcy has been a great help to us, donating her free time after clinic hours and helping with the fundraising. Once we get the facility done, we'll be able to do so much more."

"Where are the puppies?" Emma spun around to look in every direction. "Are they gone?"

Hannah led them all to the barn and ushered them inside, where the space had been divided into six large pens with pet doors leading outside to individual runs, plus areas for horse feed, dog food and supplies.

Emma rushed to the pen at the far end, where puppies were squealing and standing on their hind legs at the chain link fence, vying for attention.

"I'm grateful every single day that insurance covered the fire," Hannah said as she led Darcy and Logan down the aisle to join Emma. "The old barn wasn't big enough anyway, and this one makes our work so much easier."

The other pens held an assortment of older dogs. Some cowered at the back corners and avoided eye contact. Others bounced to the front of their pens and frantically yelped for attention.

"Oh, my," Darcy whispered, halting in front of a pen. A thin, bedraggled dog stood at the back, its head hanging low and muzzle pressed into the corner, the picture of depression and hopelessness. Heavy mats of hair hung from its body, exposing taut flesh pulled painfully tight by the twisted mats.

Logan stopped next to her and stared. "I'll never understand why people are so cruel. What's the story on this one?"

"She just came yesterday," Hannah said. "Abuse. Neglect. The neighbors who finally reported her said she was kept in a small, filthy pen and never let out—not even for a walk. From her behavior, I suspect little or no friendly human contact for ages."

"I sure hope the owners were arrested."

Hannah shook her head. "I have no idea if she even has a name, so I've been calling her Cedar. I called your office yesterday for an appointment. She'll be in Tuesday."

Logan frowned. "Let's fit her in on Monday so we can check her over. With a good clipping and bath, we can see what's under that mess."

"I had hoped we wouldn't ever see one as bad as Belle, who was dropped off last winter. But I guess I shouldn't overestimate human nature." Hannah whistled, and a gleaming chestnut-colored dog—a springer-shepherd mix—loped into the barn, its tail wagging. "This is Belle, who came to us as a surprise one night. I'm not sure who looked worse—Belle or this poor gal—but now Belle has her forever home right here."

An old, deep red golden retriever with a white muzzle limped in, its banner of a tail waving.

"And this is Maisie, who will never leave, either,

right?" Darcy leaned over to give her some good rubs beneath her collar.

"Never." Hannah laughed wryly. "I really try not to adopt everything that come along, honest. But these two just stole my heart."

Down at the puppy pen, Emma held her hands flat against the chain link and shrieked with delight. "They're licking me. It tickles!"

A thin yellow lab mix in the next pen stood watching, her achingly hopeful gaze pinned on Emma, her tail wagging slowly as if she didn't quite dare to hope.

When Emma noticed, she moved in front of her pen and stared into her soulful eyes. "This one is lonely, Mommy. She's so sad."

The lab's tail moved a little faster as she pushed the black tip of her nose through the fence.

"I think she likes me. She doesn't want to be here."

"That's because she's waiting for someone to love who will love her right back for the rest of her life," Hannah said softly.

A single tear fell down Emma's cheek. "How come she doesn't have a family?"

"Some people think a puppy would be fun and cute, but have no idea how much work a puppy is…or they just lose interest. Dogs sometimes end up in a shelter if their owners get sick or pass away."

Darcy moved over to the pen and hunkered down next to Emma to take a better look. "What's the story on this one?"

"That's Bonnie. She's around three years old and had a good home, but her elderly owner died suddenly, and no one in the family was willing to take her. She was too depressed to eat for a week. She's doing better as long as I hand-feed her, so at least her ribs don't show quite as much. She came with vet records that show she's up to date on vaccinations and worming."

Emma looked up at Darcy. "This is the one, Mommy."

"I thought you wanted a playful little puppy, sweetie. You've been talking about that for a long time."

"Not anymore." Emma lifted her chin to a stubborn tilt.

"What Hannah said about dogs giving us their life-time love is true about the puppies, too," Darcy said.

Emma's lower lip trembled. "I want this one."

Hannah smiled down at her. "Well, I'm sure your mom would want to check her over very carefully, and then you would all need to get to know each other during several visits. My first rule here is that no one can make snap decisions, because if they regret it later, the dog suffers yet another confusing, upsetting change. That's not fair."

"Can she come out now?"

"Let's see how she does. Just don't move quickly or try to grab her, okay? We need to take it easy. She's a sweet dog, but this change to a new place has been scary for her."

Hannah reached for a leash snapped to the front of the pen and went inside. Murmuring to Bonnie, she stroked the animal's thin side and then gently scratched behind her ear.

Reassured, the dog came closer and licked Hannah's hand. "You see? She's very sweet. I understand she was a very well-mannered pet. It's just that the noise, strange dogs and unfamiliar people can be terribly intimidating."

Darcy watched as Emma edged slowly up to Hannah.

"Can I pet her?"

"Talk to her a bit first."

"You're going to be mine," Emma whispered. "And you'll be happy. You can sleep on my bed with my dollies and me."

Darcy bit back a smile as the dog extended her nose to sniff Emma's hand, and wagged her tail faster when Emma gently stroked her neck.

"She likes me, Mommy!"

"Yes, I think she does. She's probably hoping to find a new friend, just like you are." Darcy glanced over her shoulder and found Logan hunkered down in front of Cedar, the newest rescue. "What do you think—"

But he wasn't listening. He was murmuring gentle words to the ragged dog, promising all sorts of wonderful things. Toys and treats and soft beds, and the company of someone who would care for her forever. She was still at the back of her cage, but she was watching him intently. Her single, wary step in his direction was a victory.

This was yet another glimpse of a man she found more intriguing as the days and weeks passed. She'd never expected to discover a deep sense of kindness and caring in the cold, remote cowboy she'd met on that first morning he'd arrived.

And now, the evidence of his soft heart was confirmed, because it looked like Logan had just found himself a dog.

Logan slowly opened the door of the dog pen and let himself inside, then sat down in one of the front corners to appear as nonthreatening as possible.

The emaciated dog fled to the back of the pen when the door opened, as far from him as possible, and stood hunched and shaking, her tail tucked between her legs and lowered head pressed against the chain links to avoid looking at him.

His heart twisted painfully at her terrified reaction. She was expecting a beating. What kind of vicious animal of a human being could vent his rage and cruelty on a poor dog?

Even though he'd seen many similar cases of abuse over the years, just the thought of them always made him feel ill and angry and even a little helpless. How many others were never rescued? He helped whenever he could, but it broke his heart to think of any animal suffering.

And another thought always lurked in the back of his mind. If the perpetrator was this cruel and had a wife and kids, what was happening to them behind closed doors?

He began to hum softly, his gaze fixed on a distant point away from Cedar, his posture relaxed. And then he began to croon to her again, a quiet litany of praise and encouragement.

"Here—try this." Hannah opened the door of the pen a few inches and tossed him a small plastic bag filled with dog treats. "I keep these on hand for just this sort of thing. The dogs love them."

He caught the bag. "Thanks."

"I spent quite a bit of time with her yesterday, and she finally came close enough for me to pet her, but she seems to be more wary with men. I can't wait to get started on clipping her. She'll feel so much better."

Logan tossed a dog treat midway across the pen and continued talking to the dog. "I've got more of these," he said softly. "Things are going to be so much better for you now."

He'd pursued his lifelong dream of working with horses, but on the rare free hours away from classes and labs and studying during vet school, he'd volunteered at a shelter.

This was what he'd imagined when he'd first started dreaming of vet school as a child. He'd wanted to rescue damaged animals and make them whole, and then bring them all home. It just wasn't possible to adopt them all, of course. In those childish dreams, he hadn't considered the sheer magnitude and impossibility of such a plan.

But when the dog in front of him finally dared to look his way and gave a single, tentative wave of her tail, he knew that this one had just found her forever home.

With him.

## Chapter Eleven

It was yet another perfect spring day, with the sweet scent of lilacs in the air. A profusion of bright flowers along the foundation of the old church nodded in the light breeze.

Feeling as if he had his father's hand on his collar to shove him forward, Logan self-consciously followed Darcy and Emma up the steps of the white clapboard Aspen Creek Community Church.

The steeple soared toward the clouds above wide double doors that welcomed the crowd of parishioners arriving for worship.

A big crowd, he realized. Kids chasing each other on the grass, burning off energy, adults of all ages greeting each other warmly with hugs and handshakes. A number of them approached Darcy with cheerful smiles, and some even welcomed him with a masculine thump on the back, though he recognized only a few.

"Let's sit in the back," Darcy whispered as they entered the cool darkness of the church, redolent with the scents of flowers, candle wax and lemon furniture polish.

They slipped into a pew and Emma settled between

them with a small felt bag of books, crayons and coloring books she'd taken from a rack as they came in.

She looked up at Logan, her troubled eyes searching his face as if she were trying to remember something important. She leaned closer. "My daddy used to come with us. But he died."

Darcy heard her, too, and reached over to take Emma's hand for a gentle squeeze.

"We gotta be quiet now," Emma whispered.

*Died?* The word hit him like a sucker punch to the chest, robbing him of breath.

He'd certainly known there must have been someone in Darcy's life at some point—a boyfriend, a significant other, maybe a husband. But he hadn't brought it up. He hadn't felt it was his business to pry.

Now, after coming to know this little family, he imagined the wrenching loss of someone they had loved. How it must have devastated both of them.

He felt a stab of guilt, remembering all of the doubts he'd had over Darcy's apparent financial troubles, and his worry that it might make her a liability in the office—just like his ex-fiancée.

He'd imagined careless spending. An addiction to online shopping—which had brought his spendthrift sister to the brink of bankruptcy more than once. Or maybe lavish vacations. Gambling. Jewelry, maybe—though there'd certainly been no evidence of that.

But instead of enjoying luxuries, she'd had to deal with the financial burdens of burying a young husband and perhaps years of illness before that. Starting over in Aspen Creek. Making a home for her little girl. Juggling the heavy responsibilities. Motherhood. A career.

And then there was the new owner of the clinic, who had quickly implied that she soon wouldn't even have a job.

He closed his eyes, feeling like a complete jerk, as the congregation began to sing the lyrics of a contemporary praise hymn on a large screen behind the altar.

And then a small hand slipped into his. He looked down at the concern on Emma's sweet face and felt a renewed stab of guilt.

"If you're sad about my daddy, it's okay," she whispered. "Mommy says he's dancing in heaven with the angels and my grandma. And someday we'll be there, too. We just gotta pray, and believe in God with all our hearts."

Her childlike trust nipped at his thoughts as he stared blindly at the words on the screen. Had he ever accepted his own faith with such absolute conviction? He'd been rebellious as a kid. Then he'd grown closer to his faith as an adult. Until…

The singing had stopped. The congregation was standing for prayer. He belatedly rose to his feet as the prayer ended and the pastor began to speak.

"Our first lesson for today is from Ephesians chapter 4. 'All bitterness, anger and wrath, insult and slander must be removed from you, along with all wickedness. And be kind and compassionate to one another, forgiving one another, just as God also forgave you in Christ.'

"Our second lesson is from Philippians chapter 4. 'Don't worry about anything; instead, pray about everything. Tell God what you need, and thank him for all He has done. If you do this, you will experience God's peace, which is far more wonderful than the human mind can understand. His peace will guard your hearts and minds as you live in Jesus Christ.' Please be seated."

Pastor Mark's rich baritone voice felt like a soothing balm as he moved on into his sermon, weaving those Bible verses into life's choices, mistakes and forgiveness. If he'd had a window into Logan's heart, he couldn't have chosen a message that hit home so perfectly.

Ah, forgiveness. It was easy to say, but so hard to do.

How did you forgive a surgeon who'd failed at a simple procedure to save his mom? The doctors who misdiagnosed his dad until it was too late? Cathy, with her calculated lies?

Or the God who had never listened to his prayers?

Each had caused immeasurable pain, a loss that could never be returned. Surely none of them had even given their responsibility for pain or suffering a second thought.

He felt his heart harden all over again. But this time, he took a slow, steadying breath and tried to let his anger go.

After church, Darcy asked Logan to stop by her house so she and Emma could change clothes and pick up her picnic basket.

On the drive out to his place, Emma chattered nonstop in the backseat of the pickup about puppies and horses, but Logan seemed unusually distant, and Darcy wondered if roping him into going to church had been a mistake. Had he felt out of place, still too new to the community to feel at ease in the company of so many close-knit strangers? Or had she said something wrong?

Now, after several hours of unpacking moving boxes and putting things away, they all sat around his kitchen table, finishing off ham-and-cheese sandwiches, chips and quartered Honeycrisp apples,

When Emma wandered into the screened porch off

the kitchen to play with her dolls, she set aside the last part of her sandwich. "You seem awfully quiet. Is something wrong?"

He took a last swallow of lemonade and didn't answer.

"I guess I was pretty thoughtless. I railroaded you into taking us to church, and didn't stop to think that maybe you're of a different faith and wouldn't want to attend ours. Is that it?"

"It's been a while since I've gone to church. You were right—he's a fine pastor, and he made me think. I'm glad I went."

But his solemn expression didn't change.

"Then what is it? Something's wrong."

"I didn't realize you'd lost your husband." He regarded her with troubled eyes. "Emma told me. I'm sorry, Darcy. I know it must have been really hard for you both."

She'd always accepted sympathies without offering any explanation, knowing the truth was so awkward, so revealing about her past life, that it tended to open an uncomfortable chasm in conversations that niceties couldn't bridge. And really, what could anyone say?

Dean had been unfaithful and she had been a fool.

But at the depth of compassion in Logan's voice, she knew she couldn't let any misconceptions lay between them.

She leaned back in her chair to look into the screened porch, where Emma was still occupied with her dolls but beyond hearing range. "It was…complicated," she said slowly, lowering her voice.

"You don't need to say anything. I know it's not my business."

"But it is, I guess. Whether we work in the same clinic or just in the same town, we might both have long careers here, and I don't want to hide the truth." She took a deep breath. "Dean and I were classmates in vet school. Love at first sight, married quickly. We had big plans. When we graduated, we went into a lot of debt developing a mixed equine and small-animal practice in a leased facility north of Minneapolis."

She ran a fingertip down the condensation on her glass of lemonade. "Dean had always wanted the best, and he made sure we bought it. But his taste for class didn't end with top-of-the-line ultrasound equipment and digital X-rays."

"I think I can guess what's coming."

She shrugged deflecting his sympathy. "Emma was just two when I discovered he was having an affair. He oversaw the office manager and the accounting while I spent my time away from the clinic, being a mom. So I never noticed the billing discrepancies—money he'd diverted for entertaining his girlfriend, I guess. And I didn't realize that many of his late-night vet calls didn't actually involve horses."

"Ouch."

"Needless to say, when I found out, I felt like an absolute fool for trusting him. I guess it's not an uncommon story—faithless husband, faithful wife—but it gets worse."

She glanced out at Emma once again to make sure she was still in the screened porch and too far away to hear.

"A few months after he moved out, he was in the Caribbean with his gorgeous twentysomething girlfriend, living the high life on money he'd siphoned from our joint accounts before moving out. He had a scuba accident in deep water."

Logan's jaw dropped. "I'm so sorry. How in the world did you…"

"Of course, his latest girlfriend took off. At least she

called to tell me about what happened, but she wanted no part of the funeral arrangements. I had friends who said I should just leave him down there—have his ashes scattered and be done with it. But what about Emma? It just didn't seem right. Would she need the closure of a service to remember and a grave to visit?" She sighed wearily. "After he left our practice, he had no life insurance. So a ton of paperwork and over fifteen grand later, he's now buried in Duluth, his hometown. And I'm still paying off those expenses, plus the loan I'd cosigned for his fancy new truck while we were still together."

"How did Emma take all of this?"

"She misses her dad terribly, though I hope she never hears the truth about him. But do I miss him? Not so much after all he did to destroy us and hurt his daughter. The verse from Ephesians at church today is actually what got me through it all, though I had to post it above the kitchen sink and recite it hundreds of times before the message finally got through. My anger was hurting only me. It had no effect on the one who caused it."

His eyes were deep with understanding, and she wondered what he might have been through in his own life.

"So," she added with a half smile, "you might be running into clients who think we'd be quite a pair, because they sure have said that to me. But I promise you I'm not ever going down that road again, so you don't need to worry. I've been there, done that, and it was a disaster—except that it gave me Emma. So never again."

"I bet there'll come a time…"

"Nope. *Never.*"

He laughed. "Then I guess that does make us quite a pair."

Curious now, she waited for him to elaborate, but he

sat back in his chair and fell silent for a few moments before clearing his throat.

"I've been thinking about my original plans for the clinic. I agree with what you said earlier—that my original plans were narrow-minded. I was ignoring the obvious—that shutting down the small-animal clinic would be a big mistake."

"This is about misguided sympathy for me, isn't it?" she asked flatly. "But I can build a solo practice of my own. You should do what's best for you, not me."

"And that would be to keep the small-animal side going for the clients who already depend on it, with an associate vet who's excellent at what she does."

"You should think on this for a while. When you moved here, you—"

"I realize I was wrong."

She considered his words, then looked up and squarely met his gaze. "If we're truly talking business here, I want the chance to buy into the practice, just as I would've with Dr. Boyd—twenty percent per year, until I'm a full partner."

"Sounds fair enough."

"But if you decide otherwise, I'm going out on my own. Let's take the next week to think this over, and then we can decide which way we want to go."

She'd kept an eye on Emma while they were talking, but now she wasn't in sight, and Darcy heard a faint telltale cough.

"Excuse me." She rose, grabbed her purse from the bench in the front entryway and hurried for the back porch.

Emma had curled into a ball on a wicker love seat, her dolls strewn across the floor. She coughed again when

Darcy sat down next to her. "Hey sweetie, how are you doing? Want to sit in Mommy's lap?"

Darcy pulled her onto her lap to sit upright and stroked her back, then rested her fingertips lightly along Emma's ribs.

"Is she all right?" Logan pulled up a matching wicker chair and settled into it, watching them with an expression of concern.

"I think so. I don't hear her wheezing, and she's not laboring to breathe. But at the first cough I always start watching her closely, just in case." She kissed the top of Emma's head, then reached into her purse and withdrew a zippered vinyl bag. "We just want to be careful. Right, honey?"

Emma nodded somberly. "I get scared sometimes."

"I know you do, sweetheart, but we take really good care of you, right?" Darcy pulled a plastic peak-flow meter from the plastic bag, swiftly set it up and gave it to Emma. "Okay now…big breath out. Big breath in—and blow."

Emma dutifully blew into the plastic mouthpiece.

"Good job!" Darcy looked at the measurement showing along the length of the device, then had her do it once more. "Looks good, honey."

Logan asked, "So, it's okay?"

"Super. This gives us a measurement of lung function, and she's in her normal range. But I think she and I are just going to sit here for a while and have a nice rest. Then I'll get back to helping you out."

By late afternoon, the haphazardly placed furniture in Logan's great room and bedrooms had been arranged, and most of the paintings hung.

Now all of the moving boxes had been emptied and flattened as well, the kitchenware and linens stored.

Exhausted, Darcy took a final look around the main floor. "You have such a beautiful home. I love the wood-work and that massive stone fireplace."

"I barely glanced at the house when I flew in to look at the practice," Logan said with a rueful smile. "I'm just thankful it turned out to be a nice place and not a money pit."

"It's hardly that. And it's such a beautiful place for entertaining. Dr. Boyd used to host parties here for his staff and clients at Christmas and on the Fourth of July. No one ever wanted to miss his summer hog roast, or the gorgeous decorations at Christmas. He always had a dazzling twenty-foot tree in the great room, and the pine trees lining the driveway were covered in lights. Traditions to continue, right?" she teased.

"He must have had a team of elves to do all that," Logan said wryly as he adjusted a lampshade. "It must have taken weeks."

"He did it all himself for years, I understand. But by the time I came on board, he'd started hiring a decorating service for Christmas and a catering service for all of the parties." She glanced at her watch. "Well, I suppose we ought to go. Can you give us a lift?"

"Of course…unless you think Emma might like a ride. I saddled Drifter a few minutes ago, and she's ready to go."

Emma had been coloring at the kitchen table, but she whirled around at his words. "Really? I can ride a horse?"

"It's about time—you were a big helper today. You even colored some pictures for my fridge." He grinned down at her. "And I'm pretty sure I have just about every size of helmet in the tackroom, so we can find one your size."

They all walked in the shade of towering pines on the way out to the barn, the fallen needles under their feet releasing the crisp scent of pine.

Emma impulsively grabbed Logan's hand and skipped along beside him. "Someday I'm going to have a pony and ride all day long. At night, too."

Logan cast a glance over his shoulder at Darcy. "Hear that, Mom? You're going to need a larger yard *and* a barn. And you'll need a pony with headlights."

"That might be a while." Darcy leaned down to pick up a pine needle and crushed it between her fingers to release the Christmassy aroma. "But I look forward to it. I want her to have the same childhood I did."

He turned around and walked backward in front of her. "What kind of horses did you have?"

"A grade Welsh mare when I was six, which was a lot like giving me car keys. Then a gradual progression of horses after that, each one a little better. I lived on those horses. Mom said the only time she saw me in the house was when I was sick. I started showing horses when I turned eight, but when I started vet school, I no longer had time."

"Sounds like an idyllic childhood."

"It was, with incredible freedom. My friends and I rode bareback for miles in every direction on the roads and trails. I wouldn't let Emma do that now, though. The world is a scarier place. So, what about you?"

A corner of his mouth lifted in a faint grin. "You rode for fun. I was working cattle and helping start our two-year-olds under saddle. I think Dad thought my sister and I would break less easily if we got dumped, so he turned that job over to us when we got into middle school."

Later, as she stood along the fence and watched Logan

patiently leading the palomino and her elated daughter up and down the long driveway for at least the twelfth time, her thoughts kept slipping back to the conversation after lunch.

She'd said what she'd truly believed, until now.

After Dean's cruel betrayal, she'd intended never to risk falling for anyone else. For whatever unknown reasons, Logan had said the same thing.

But those words had now carved an empty, aching place in her heart. Was that really what she wanted? To become lonely and bitter like her mom, and continue their long family legacy of failed relationships?

It didn't take any thought to imagine which would be the most positive example for Emma. But did Darcy have the courage to risk taking a chance?

Probably not.

She watched Logan sauntering toward her, his sleeves rolled back, the first two buttons of his pale blue oxford shirt open to reveal his tanned throat. With those broad shoulders and his face shaded by his black cowboy hat and dark Oakley sunglasses, and he looked like a cowboy in a Levi's commercial.

The palomino's long white tail swept the ground as Logan turned her around and headed toward the highway once again. "Last trip," he called out over his shoulder. "Been a long day, and this cowboy's done for. But Emma thinks you should take a spin."

Delightful memories from her own youth deluged her as Darcy watched them return from their final trip up the lane and back.

The trail rides.

The horse shows.

And oh, the Minnesota State Fair—the most exciting of all. The cavernous cement arena had been called the Hippodrome back then, and every time she'd ridden through the wide entryway to compete in a quarter horse class, her adrenaline had soared and she hadn't been able to stop grinning.

After helping Emma dismount, she stepped lightly up into the saddle and adjusted her reins, the joy of being back on a horse again sending sparkles of delight down every nerve.

Logan looked up at her, his eyes twinkling. "I don't suppose we need to talk about the brakes."

"Probably not. But it's been a while."

He tipped his head in acknowledgment. "She was my reining horse, just so you know, and she did pretty well in working cow horse classes."

Power steering deluxe, then. Delight washed through Darcy as she almost imperceptibly tensed the muscles of her calves and Drifter eased into a super slow jog on the soft grass-covered side of the lane, her head nice and low.

Darcy twisted in the saddle to look at Logan. "I may never bring her back. Is that okay?"

He laughed, but before he could answer, she cued the mare with a faint touch of a leg, and Drifter rocked into a slow lope, smooth as butter.

With other delicate cues, the mare did flying lead changes on the straightaway. Rollbacks and 360s, and when the highway came into view, Darcy sent her into a faster loop and cued her for a sliding stop.

Drifter sat down into the slide, as perfect as if she'd been headed for biggest shows in the country.

Awed, Darcy leaned forward to hug the horse's neck,

then pivoted her toward the barn and let her saunter slowly on a loose rein during the half-mile trip home.

Back at the barn, Emma watched Darcy with amazement, and Logan leaned against the fence, one boot heel hooked on a fence board. The knowing look on his face made her grin in return.

"I haven't had a horse for years, and you just made my day. My week. Maybe my year," she breathed. "She's spectacular. I'd love to work cattle on her."

"Back in Montana, my sister and I showed quite a bit. The mare is definitely quick."

"I've never owned a reining or cutting horse, but I've ridden a few. It's so exhilarating—I can't even explain it. They make me feel like I'm dancing."

He looked up at her with a strange, indecipherable expression. "I know exactly what you mean."

She swung out of the saddle, tossed the stirrup over the seat, and rested a hand on the mare's neck. Drifter hadn't even broken a sweat. Her breathing was slow and steady.

Darcy paused with her hand on the girth. "Are you riding now, or do want me to unsaddle her?"

"Unsaddle. She's cool and doesn't need to be walked, but I can put her into one of the dry lots while I take you and Emma home."

"I don't suppose you'd like to sell her."

He chuckled. "Charlie and Drifter will never be sold."

"How about if I throw in my house? My car? Oh, wait. It doesn't run. Just the house, then. I don't have much else of value."

"Sorry. Not even your house." Laughing, he brushed an errant strand of hair away from her face. "But you and Emma are welcome to come out anytime."

"Tomorrow! Can we come tomorrow?" Emma begged. "Please?"

"Probably not, sweetie," Darcy said. "I'll be working all day, and you'll be at Mrs. Spencer's, playing with your friends. In the evening I need to work on your room. But maybe another time."

Emma didn't speak a word on the way home, and when they arrived she yawned and silently climbed down from Logan's truck.

"Looks like we're going to have a quiet evening," Darcy said as she followed Emma to the house with Logan at her side. "But I think she's just overtired. Thanks so much for the wonderful day."

At the steps of the porch Darcy impulsively gave Logan a quick hug and stepped back, suddenly feeling a little flustered and awkward at unexpectedly crossing that invisible line between friends and something more.

Yet how could she regret something that felt so right?

## Chapter Twelve

"Looks like the wrecker beat us here," Logan murmured when he took Darcy home on Monday after work. "Did they know where to take your car?"

"Red's. I talked to Red this morning, and he said he could at least check it over by tomorrow afternoon. He's going to drop off a loaner car after he gets done for the day. Just in case it doesn't come in time, Mrs. Spencer said she would drop Emma off after six."

"You've got one whole hour of freedom." He grinned at her. "So, what would you like to do?"

"I'll be prying up more pieces of that old linoleum in the kitchen. I figure at an hour every day, I'll be done in 2025. Easy."

"Perfect. Let's go in so I can help."

"Oh, no," she protested. "All of that prying and tugging can't be good for your shoulder. Anyway, I'm saving you for when the floors are all done so you can help me do the cabinets and countertops."

He followed her into the house anyhow, on the pretext of taking another look at the kitchen layout, but soon joined her on his hands and knees, shoving a scraper under the stubborn, brittle old flooring.

A wonderful aroma was emanating from a Crock-Pot on the counter, and he thought he detected the sweet scent of apple pie. If Darcy invited him to stay for supper, he definitely wouldn't be saying no.

"The bedrooms are both done, and the old wood flooring is beautiful," she said, blowing a lock of hair out of her eyes. "I thought of doing the living room next but decided to get the worst part over with. Isn't this fun?"

"Well worth the effort, though." He shoved his scraper under another piece of flooring that abruptly released and sent a small missile zinging across the room.

"It sure feels like it when you hit a spot where someone didn't go crazy with the glue." She sat back on her heels, grabbed a rubber band from the counter, and pulled her thick, wavy hair into a haphazard ponytail. "You can't imagine my elation when an entire two-foot-square section came off like a breeze. Best thing ever."

With what Darcy had already done on her own, they reached the middle of the room by the time Emma came home.

"That's it—I'm done," she announced. "Who wants supper?"

Just as he'd hoped, there was a beef roast in the Crock-Pot with tender whole potatoes, carrots and onions. The rich gravy surrounding it all was redolent with garlic and seasonings he couldn't name.

And after that came the pie. Wonderful pie.

The flaky, buttery crust sparkling with sugar crystals was perfection, the cinnamon-laced apples inside tender with just the right amount of juiciness.

"Thank you," he said when Darcy handed him a cup

of coffee. He turned to Emma. "If I've ever had a better meal, I can't remember it. Your mom is an amazing cook."

Emma nodded. "I like macaroni better."

He hid a smile, remembering the neon-orange boxed macaroni of his childhood. "I'll bet that's good, too."

"We put lots of cheese in it, and crunchy stuff on the top."

"Those are buttery bread crumbs, Emma," Darcy said with a laugh. "Do you remember what else we use? You always help."

Emma's face scrunched into a frown. "Um…brown noodles."

"Whole wheat pasta."

"And…?"

"White stuff."

"A white sauce, with extra seasoning. Good job remembering, sweetie. Maybe you can help make it for Dr. Maxwell someday."

Not boxed macaroni and cheese. Homemade. He found himself wishing he could join them every day, instead of facing meat on the grill and a salad at his place, alone, week after week. "I would love that, Emma."

"Mommy would like that, too. And she *really* likes your horses." Emma nodded solemnly as she glanced between her mom and him, then brightened. "Maybe you could even be my daddy."

"Emma!" Darcy shot a mortified, warning look at her daughter, high color rising to her cheekbones.

The little matchmaker looked back at her, clearly mystified at why her mother was upset. "But you said—"

"I'm not sure what you think I said, but I have never

alluded to anything of the sort, and you just can't start asking guests something like that."

"What's *looded*?"

"*Alluded*. I didn't say…" Darcy made a small noise of frustration, but now her mouth was twitching as she tried to suppress a smile. "It's just that these things are between adults."

"Sienna has a daddy. And she gots a playhouse, too." Emma sat back in her chair, her lower lip thrust out in a pout, clearly thinking that Sienna had gotten a much better deal.

Ah, yes. The playhouse. Logan and his tomboy sister had grown up making forts up in the hayloft and ramshackle tree houses out in the cattle pastures with their cousins. But in a little girl's world in the Midwest, apparently playhouses were the ultimate prize.

Emma pushed her plate away. "Can I go now?"

"Yes, you may be excused." Darcy leaned out of her chair and caught her as she headed for the living room and gave her a hug. "Hannah says we can go back again tonight to see the puppies. Would you like that?"

"Yes!" All of her woes instantly forgotten, Emma threw her arms around her mother's neck and gave her a kiss on the cheek. "Now? Can we go now?"

"Dishes in the dishwasher first, and then we can go as soon as we get the loaner car."

Logan cleared the table while Darcy rinsed the dishes and put them in the dishwasher. "We should go together. I can drive, and I'd like to go out there anyway to check on Cedar."

"That poor, sweet dog. She probably has some ulcers under all of that matted fur."

He nodded. "Hannah was going to bring her in this afternoon, but she had some sort of emergency at the hospital."

Emma pulled her shoes on at the speed of light and waited at the door. "I'm ready!"

All the way to Hannah's house she chattered nonstop, which precluded any other conversation.

"Sorry about that," Darcy said as they all got out of the truck.

"It's actually a revelation, discovering how much a four-year-old can talk."

The final wisps of sweet-smelling pine smoke drifted upward from the ashes in a metal fire ring in the backyard, scenting the air as they walked back to the barn behind Hannah's house.

Darcy shot an amused glance at him as they stepped inside the barn. "I remember rocking Emma as a baby, longing for the day when she could talk and tell me what she was thinking. Then she hit two, and hasn't stopped talking since."

Emma coughed as she made a beeline for Bonnie's cage. Darcy knelt beside her, quietly talking to her about caring for a dog.

Emma coughed again.

Logan went on to Cedar's pen and felt his heart grow heavy when he found the cage empty. The pile of soft blankets in the corner was missing, and even the feed and water bowls were gone.

Apparently Cedar hadn't made it.

"I should've taken her to the clinic when we were here last," he muttered, feeling a sense of loss. It had been three years since he'd lost his dog, and he'd never been able to bring himself to buy another.

He'd seen Cedar for only a short time, yet when her

soulful eyes had made that long connection with his, he'd simply known that he had to take her home.

Darcy looked up as he moved on to look at the other dogs, then the puppies. "Did you say something?"

"No…"

"It's been just a few days since we were here, but Bonnie already looks a little better, don't you think?"

The yellow lab was pressed against the front of her pen, wagging her tail, her attention focused on Emma. "Definitely a brighter affect."

"Hey, guys," Hannah called from the doorway. "Sorry I'm late. We roasted marshmallows after supper, and then I had to help with homework. I've got someone for Logan to see, but I can't bring her down here. Brace yourself. She looks far worse now."

He followed Hannah to the garage, where she kept an isolation pen.

His heart lifted when he saw Cedar curled up in a ball on fresh blankets. The heavy, tangled mats of hair had been clipped away, revealing ulcerations where the mats had pulled relentlessly at her skin. She had bald patches, as well.

"Besides everything else, the poor thing had the start of mange, as you can see," Hannah said unnecessarily. "I've seen it before, so when I started to clip her and discovered it, I took her up here to the isolation pen right away and disinfected everything she might have touched with bleach water. She had her first dip with a scabicide this evening, but from now on I'll do it weekly for a month."

"It's good you caught it." Logan looked down at the miserable dog, who had yet to lift her head at the sound of the voices nearby. "I'd like to bring her back to the clinic tonight to check this out under a microscope, if it's all right with you."

"Absolutely fine. Do whatever you need to do while she's there. I've got a kennel that you can borrow to put in the back of your truck."

"And… I'd rather not bring her back."

Hannah's eyes widened. "What?"

He smiled, remembering the depth of trust and intelligence in Cedar's golden-brown eyes when she'd finally responded to him the last time he'd been here. "Whatever the adoption fee is, I'll pay you right now. She's found her forever home with me."

Darcy scooped Emma into her arms and searched her pale face, then hurried through Hannah's yard. Once again she caught the scent of smoke, and again she felt a surge of trepidation when Emma broke into another spasm of coughing.

She stepped through the open back door of the garage and found Hannah and Logan deep in conversation on canine vaccinations.

She sank onto a folding chair with Emma in her lap. Now her coughing was tight. Wheezy. "I need my purse, now. Is the truck locked?"

"No." Logan glanced at them both. Then his eyes widened in alarm. He bolted out of the garage and returned in a moment with her purse. "Is everything in here?"

Hannah was a physician's assistant and had been down this road before. "Here, I'll find it."

She dug through the purse and found the clear plastic bag with Emma's asthma supplies, attached a clear plastic spacer to the quick-relief inhaler and placed it into Darcy's waiting palm.

Darcy shook it a couple times and depressed the top button. "Okay…big breath out…now a deeeep breath in—that's right. Hold it… Good. And another… Good girl."

Emma sagged against her, still pale, but in a few minutes the wheezing was lessening. Darcy rubbed her back in slow, comforting motions. "You'll be fine. Everything is fine."

Logan pulled up a folding chair next to her. "Hey, punkin, are you feeling better?"

Emma nodded almost imperceptibly, though Darcy knew how much even a light episode scared her. Who wouldn't panic if it was so hard to breathe?

"I'm so sorry—I wasn't even thinking when I let the kids have their little fire for marshmallows," Hannah said, her voice laced with regret. "I'll bet it was the wood smoke."

"Possibly." Darcy looked up at her. "But don't worry about it—she'll be fine."

Hannah rested a hand on Emma's shoulder. "Are her asthma episodes growing more frequent or worse?"

"No, though colds really exacerbate things, of course. The smoke sensitivity is fairly new."

"How often does she need the quick-relief inhaler?" Hannah asked.

"A few times a week at the most. Some weeks she's fine." Darcy dropped a kiss on Emma's head. "We haven't needed a trip to the ER in a long time. She's due to go into the clinic next month to see Dr. McClaren."

"You can get in sooner if need be," Hannah said. "Just give us a call."

It took only a few minutes for Logan to load Cedar into the plastic kennel and fasten it snugly in the back of the pickup, up against the cab so there'd be less of a breeze as he drove.

"What about Bonnie, Mommy? Can't we take her, too?" Emma twisted in her booster seat to look out the back window of the truck. "She could sit with me. *Please?*"

Darcy looked over her shoulder at Emma. "I told Hannah that we'll definitely take her, so don't worry. We're going to pick her up Sunday afternoon."

"Why not now?"

"Because I work the next four and a half days, and you'll be with Mrs. Spencer. We need to be home and spend time with her when she first comes to our house."

"You won't forget?"

"Of course not, sweetie."

"Promise?"

"Yes, of course. I promise."

"What about a pony?"

Logan laughed aloud and gave Darcy a sidelong glance that did something funny to her insides. "Yes, Mom. Why not a pony, too, as long as you're getting a dog?"

Darcy shot a dark look at him. "You are not helping."

The laugh lines at the corner of his eyes and the dimple in his right cheek deepened, but he kept his eyes on the road. After a few miles he glanced at the rearview mirror again. "Looks like your little cowgirl just fell asleep."

Darcy slumped in her seat. "That's not good. She'll wake up when we get home. A nap will set her bedtime back for a good hour—and that's if I'm lucky. She's quite a live wire at night."

"Maybe she can help you with the floor."

"You wait. Someday you'll have kids, and then you won't take these things lightly. Sleep means everything to a mom—or dad—who has to work every day."

"I suppose you're right," he said quietly, giving the rearview mirror another glance. "But I doubt I'll ever know firsthand."

When he pulled into her driveway, he parked behind an older model sedan with dents in the bumper and a Red's Auto frame around the license plate. He opened the back door of the truck. Emma was still asleep.

"I can get her," Darcy said, opening the opposite door.

"Nah, I've got her—you grab the booster seat." He lifted her into his arms and carried her to the front porch and waited while Darcy unlocked the door. Then he walked to Emma's bedroom and laid her on her twin bed.

"Looks like you just got a break," he whispered as he stepped back and watch Darcy carefully remove Emma's shoes and jeans and cover her with a light blanket. "Does she need her pajamas on?"

"That would be pushing my luck. She might even stay asleep for the night if I don't disturb her."

They both tiptoed out of the room, and Logan headed for the front door, where he hesitated, then turned back with a look of regret.

"I suppose I should get Cedar settled at the clinic."

She nodded, regretting the fact that he needed to leave. "I suppose."

"Thanks. For the wonderful meal. And for…the company."

"And thank you for helping with the floor, and taking us to Hannah's. And—" she considered her words "—thank you for being so sweet to Emma. I know it means a lot to her."

His gaze locked on hers. He took a single step closer, close enough that she could pick up his familiar scents of pine and fresh air, and a faint aftershave she couldn't name. And for just a moment she felt enchanted, as if she might be taking the most important step in her life.

But then he shook his head as if he'd felt that same connection and was just as afraid as she was. He walked out the door.

And the moment was lost.

## Chapter Thirteen

With news spreading throughout the county about the new equine vet in Aspen Creek, Logan found his schedule filling up with farm calls. He spent most of his time on the road in his vet truck and very little at the clinic.

Foaling problems and other reproductive issues were always intense throughout the spring, often involving late-night calls, and there were a number of large horse breeding farms within a thirty-mile radius delighted to finally have a good equine vet in the area.

The hectic pace had helped him gain some perspective—along with a lot of time in his truck to think.

But now it was already Saturday afternoon, he'd spent the last hour in his office catching up on email and bills and reviewing Marilyn's accounting, and he needed to get to the airport in the Twin Cities on time or he'd hear about it for months.

"I'm off," he said to no one in particular. "See you folks Monday."

"You've got your cell phone, right?" Marilyn called out from the front office. "And you're on call this weekend?"

"Darcy is on for the rest of today. I've got Sunday."

"And you did talk to her, right? I left a couple messages on your desk."

He'd managed mostly to avoid Darcy since Monday night, when he'd been on the verge of sweeping her into his arms and kissing her senseless right there in her living room. What had come over him?

He'd thought a lot on the way home Monday night and during the four days since then. To his chagrin, he finally realized that she seemed to be avoiding him, as well, except for some brief businesslike exchanges.

"She knows she's on call tonight. I texted her."

"No, this is something else. It's about Emma, and an award, and a very important event. Something about the poor child facing a broken heart, if I understood correctly."

He glanced at his watch. "Darcy's already left for the day, and I've got to run. I'll call her later."

Marilyn's voice followed him down the hall as he waved to Kaycee and went out the back door. "Today. It has to be today."

Distracted by the news of a Middle East bombing on the public radio station, he was well into heavy traffic on southbound 494 before he remembered to call. Soon he was into even more traffic leading into the airport.

He had Susan in his truck and was headed out of the Twin Cities when his phone rang.

He grabbed his phone and pressed the screen to route the call from the hands-free speaker mode in the truck and into his cell. "Hello. This is Dr. Maxwell."

"So sorry to bother you," Darcy said, her voice tinged with embarrassment. "But I figured you hadn't gotten my message, and I promised Emma that I would try again. She's quite upset, thinking you won't be able to come."

He gripped the phone a little tighter. "What's this for?"

"Sunday school tomorrow, right after church. It's the last day of the classes until after Labor Day, and there'll be desserts and coffee, and prizes for the kids. She's getting an award for good attendance and is sure all of the kids will have both parents there, so she'll feel left out. She wonders if you could come as just her friend."

He glanced over at Susan. From her upraised eyebrow and knowing little smirk, he could tell she'd heard every word.

She shrugged. "Go for it. I don't mind. I'll probably sleep in anyway."

He returned to the call. "What time?"

There was a long pause. "I'm so sorry—I forgot you were having company. I didn't mean to interrupt."

She hung up before he could say another word.

"Sounds like she's not too happy." Susan rolled her eyes. "Tell me she's not another girlfriend like that last doozy. Puh-leeze."

"The woman on the phone is the other vet at the clinic."

"All the better, bro. Mutual interests and all that?"

He ignored her little jibe and focused on the slow-down of the traffic ahead. "So, how are the kids? I haven't seen them since Christmas."

"They're with their dad for the weekend, probably driving him crazy. I figure it serves him right." She looked away. "I just needed some time to get away and think things through, you know? Big decision."

Logan spared her a quick glance. "How did the counseling go?"

She snorted. "Would've helped if Rick had decided to go. But he never would've admitted to any responsibility for our problems, anyhow."

"Did it help you to talk to someone?"

"I went a few times, then gave up. One side of the story couldn't ever get to the real problems, right?" She bit her lower lip. For all her bravado, Logan saw a single tear trail down her cheek.

"I'm so sorry, sis."

"Me, too." She laced her fingers on her lap. "You know, if he had just made a little effort—tried to help around the place, or offered to help with the kids' homework once in a while—I would have been okay with that. But he was gone most of the time and impatient when he got home. The house was never clean enough. He didn't like what I made for dinner. Where was his underwear, and why didn't I have the lawn mowed before he got home? Enough is enough."

*Enough is enough* was probably Rick's assessment, as well. As for her part in this mess, Logan knew that Susan had perpetually run up heavy debts by shopping at high-end stores and never seemed satisfied with what she had. But he'd wisely learned to hold his tongue on that score.

One wrong word and she would rail that he was always on her husband's side and neither of them had ever loved her, and then there would be no chance at all to get through to her.

"If it's all that bad, then I'd say you deserve better. Want me to go back to Montana and give him what-for?"

She gave him a watery smile. "He would back down

if he saw you coming, but I doubt it would make any difference in the long run."

"So, how long are you staying here?"

"Just 'til Monday afternoon. Much as I'd like to stay away longer, Rick has an important company meeting in Houston, so I have to get back to take care of the kids."

He reached across the cab to give her hand a quick squeeze. "I'm glad you came."

"It's funny, the things you imagine when you're young…" Her voice turned wistful. "A knight in shining armor sweeping you away. Buckets of money. A loving family. Growing old together, and still in love after fifty years. Then reality comes along to remind you that life just doesn't end up that way, except in the movies. Of course you know all that—you were going to marry that despicable woman in Montana, and then she tried to drag you down with her. What did she get? Was it twenty years?

"Something like that." He sighed heavily. "She had everyone at the clinic fooled. Most of all me."

"Which just proves my point." Susan wearily leaned against the headrest and rolled her head to face him. "Mom and Dad divorced, then Uncle Jake, and two of my best friends did, too. I've come to realize that it's a mistake to think you're going to be happy, because eventually everything just turns to dust. You're the only one in our family who's smart enough to stay single."

After they made it to Aspen Creek, he looked in on Cedar at the clinic, then drove home and got Susan settled in an upstairs guest room.

Down in the great room, he turned off the lights and settled in his favorite leather chair to stare at the moonlit landscape outside. With the windows open, he could hear the wind sighing through the trees and inhale the sweet scent of pine that was so reminiscent of his life back in Montana.

One of the horses whinnied, and in the distance coyotes were yip-yipping to the moon. All he needed was the sound of a few beef cattle bawling now and then to feel right at home, but in a year or so he would have a herd established here. With a return to cattle ranching and his vet practice, his life would be complete.

But though Montana had been his home, he had no yearning to go back. It held only bitter memories now.

*The only one smart enough to stay single.*

His sister's words rolled through his thoughts again and again, a litany that might have been meant as praise but only reminded him of how empty his life had become.

Darcy was struggling financially under the burden of her profligate husband's thoughtlessness. She didn't have a fancy house or a fine car. She was the sole support of her little family with all of the heavy responsibilities that went with it.

But she had what really mattered, and it reminded him of what he had lost.

A cozy and welcoming home. A sweet child or two. A life of someone to talk with over dinner and bedtime stories to read at night.

These were the things he'd longed to have, when he thought he was going to marry Cathy. The opportunities he'd lost when she betrayed him.

But his life was going to get better. He might be totally gun-shy when it came to risking his heart ever again. But in a few days he could bring Cedar home from the clinic, and at least he'd have a dog.

In the morning, he'd heard no footsteps moving around upstairs and Susan hadn't started a pot of coffee in the kitchen, so Logan assumed she was still sleeping. He drove to church with just minutes to spare.

The congregation was seated and already singing a beautiful old hymn when he slid into the back pew. He looked around, seeing things he hadn't noticed the last time when he felt awkward and out of place.

Beautiful old stained-glass windows—six on each side. The sunlight beaming in from the east that splashed the parishioners with jewel-like colors.

He knew the building was very old—a plaque on the outside proclaimed it was on the Register of Historic Places. But the soft ivory paint looked freshly done, the woodwork gleamed with loving care and the windows sparkled.

Throughout the service, the Bible verses Pastor Mark used and the sermon he gave flowed over him. The heartfelt praise songs seemed to lift him up. During the final prayer, he looked up at the brass cross hanging over the altar and realized that this place filled him with an utter sense of peace. Forgiveness. And even an unexpected ray of hope that seemed to fill in some of the ragged and empty places in his heart.

And he found that for the first time in his sorry life, he wished a church service wasn't already over.

Afterward he couldn't see Darcy and Emma anywhere in the crowd drifting down the central aisle to shake the pastor's hand, so he stayed at the back until the line thinned out, then joined the stragglers.

Someone slid a hand around his elbow. "Howdy, stranger," she chirped. "So good to see you here."

It was Hannah.

"Glad to be here."

"That tall guy over there—talking to the lawyer—is my fiancé, Ethan. I'll make sure he comes over and says hello if Walter ever stops talking."

"Actually, I'm looking for Emma and Darcy. They're at some sort of Sunday school ceremony."

"Downstairs. The kids and parents were mostly sitting in the back during the service and slipped away during the last song so they could get ready." She pointed to the right. "The stairway is over there."

He nodded his thanks and descended to the lower level, where apparently everyone in Aspen Creek had gathered. Chairs and tables with tablecloths had been placed around the large meeting hall, but there were so many people standing that he had no idea where to look for Emma.

Beth appeared at his side. "You did come! Emma will be so happy." She pointed to the opposite side of the room. "You should find her over there with her mom. The little ceremony will be starting soon, but don't worry—it shouldn't take more than an hour."

Logan made his way sideways through the crowd, apologizing as he went. When he finally spied Emma, he smiled at her. "Hi, little lady. I hear you've having a big day."

She squealed with delight and rushed to him, her

flouncy pink skirt bouncing and her arms raised, so he scooped her up into his arms.

She wasn't his, yet he felt such a surge of protectiveness just holding her that it nearly took his breath away.

"I knew you'd come! Mommy didn't think so, but I *knew* you would."

Darcy materialized in front of him with a small cup of pink punch. "You don't want to spill your punch on Dr. Maxwell, so you'd better hop down, honey."

Emma wrapped her arms wrapped her arms around his neck. "No."

"Let me set your drink aside, then." She looked up at Logan with a grateful smile. "I just figured that you had company and wouldn't want to come. Thank you so much. As you can see, it means a lot to Emma."

"I'm glad you let me know. Susan is still asleep back home or I would've brought her."

Darcy's welcoming expression shuttered. "That would have been very…nice. I hope you two have a great time."

"It won't be, but I'm glad she came. She's pondering the end of her marriage and just wanted to get away."

"Oh." Darcy blinked. "Oh, dear. I'm sorry."

"It's not the first time, unfortunately. But she's my only sister, and I always do whatever I can to help."

Ever since she'd heard Logan mention he was having company this weekend, Darcy had envisioned him with a beautiful girlfriend from back in Montana. Probably a mad, passionate affair with marriage on the horizon.

She'd found herself feeling a deep sense of loss over what could never be.

Which made no sense at all.

After her experience with Dean, she'd been so sure that she'd never fall for anyone again, for nothing could be worth risking such crushing heartache.

Yet despite her convictions, and her doubts about him when they first met, Logan had proved to be the kind of guy she'd once dreamed of meeting, and she'd found herself falling for him a little more with every passing week. And more than that, he was wonderful with Emma, who idolized him. He'd once said he would never have kids, but how could that be?

Discovering that Logan's weekend guest was his sister had literally taken Darcy's breath away. But still…

A loudspeaker squawked.

At the far end of the meeting hall, the head of the Sunday school program gripped a microphone and began reading off the names of the children who had won prizes for memorization. Then she began reading the perfect attendance list from youngest on up.

Darcy looked up at Emma, who still refused to leave Logan's arms. "You need to get down, sweetie. She's about to call your name."

Logan swung Emma down to the floor and watched as she fell into line with the other four-year-olds. As the little ones marched across the stage, Emma waved at Darcy and Logan, her face beaming with pride.

Someone touched Darcy's arm, and she turned to see one of the older women in the church whose name she couldn't recall.

"You have such a lovely family," the woman said in a loud whisper. "You must be so proud. Such a handsome young husband and pretty little daughter. Not many families stay together these days."

Her voice was one that carried.

Embarrassed, Darcy smiled at her and edged away. She caught a glimpse of Beth giving her a sympathetic smile through the crowd.

She didn't even want to imagine what Logan thought of the elderly woman's assumption after he'd been so kind to show up. He'd made it clear that he had no intention of ever settling down.

"Let's go," she whispered to him, as soon as Emma came back to her side. "This program will take a while."

It took time to make it through the crowded room, but once they made it outside, she took a deep breath of fresh air.

Emma lifted her certificate up high. "I got good 'tendance. And I learned a *lot*."

"I'll bet you did, Emma," Logan said. "Great job."

"Did you get good 'tendance, too?"

"Yes, ma'am. My mom and dad made sure of it. And I'm still learning."

Emma spied some dandelions scattered like little disks of sunshine in the grass and bent to pick them.

Darcy waited until she was completely engrossed, then touched Logan's sleeve. "Thank you again for coming. It meant all the world to her."

"Glad to do it. It got me back to church again, and I'm beginning to realize just how much I've missed it."

"You were there? You could have joined us—" She bit her lip, realizing that he might have intentionally found a different pew.

"I didn't see you or I would have. I got there a little late."

"I-I'm really sorry if you were embarrassed about

what the woman said downstairs. I didn't know what to say without making a scene."

"Any man in that room would be honored to claim you and Emma as his family." He went very still, his expression unfathomable as he searched her face. "You said you were never taking a chance again, but no one with a decent heart would ever treat you like your husband did. I can promise you that."

She watched him head for his pickup, feeling a little breathless and more than a little confused. Had he just encouraged her to look elsewhere, or had he meant those words for himself?

## *Chapter Fourteen*

After getting home from church and making lunch, Darcy called Hannah to arrange a time for picking up Emma's new dog, but as Hannah and Ethan were leaving to check out wedding venues, they promised to drop Bonnie off on their way.

Emma was overcome with awe when Hannah appeared at the front door with Bonnie at her side.

"She's here! She's really here!" Too excited to contain herself, she ran in circles and jumped up and down, her arms flailing, then threw her arms around Darcy's legs.

Clearly terrified, Bonnie yelped and scrambled backward.

"This probably isn't the best introduction," Hannah said dryly as she reached down to comfort the dog. "Got any suggestions?"

"Emma and I need to have a little talk." Darcy said with an apologetic smile. "Can we meet you in the backyard in a couple minutes?"

Darcy closed the front door, then knelt down and rested her hands on Emma's shoulders. "Have you ever been really scared about something? So scared you just wanted to run and hide?"

Emma nodded.

"Well, poor Bonnie is really scared, too. She had a good home, then ended up at Hannah's rescue center where there were strange people and noisy dogs that frightened her, because she only knew her quiet home with an elderly man. And now she's here, facing another change."

Emma's eyes filled with worry. "She doesn't want to come here?"

"She'll be fun and playful later, but right now we want to make it easy for her to get to know us. So you need to be slow and quiet and very gentle. Can you do that?"

Emma nodded and took Darcy's hand.

"Let's go, then. Just don't forget. Today is a quiet day."

Hannah was in the backyard with Bonnie still on the leash when they came outside.

The golden lab tentatively wagged its tail when Darcy and Emma approached.

"Let's sit down on the picnic bench, sweetie, and let her come up to you. But don't grab her around the neck—at least for now. Dogs can see that as a form of aggression."

Emma sat quietly as the dog nervously surveyed her surroundings, then slowly approached and sniffed her knee. "I hope you like us, Bonnie. You're going to be my friend."

The lab sat down and rested her head on Emma's lap.

"Looks good to me," Hannah said. "Now I'd better get going, because Ethan has the car running. Let me know if you have any problems."

After Hannah shut the gate behind her, Darcy stood

and unsnapped the leash. "Let's let her explore her new home, all right?"

Emma giggled as the dog crisscrossed the yard at a jog, nose to the ground. She explored every nook and cranny. Sized up the fence. When a squirrel chattered from its perch on an overhead branch, Bonnie launched into a volley of barks. Then she stared at the screened porch and tentatively rested a paw on the lowest step. Every few minutes, she came back to Emma and nudged her knee with her nose as if asking her to join her.

"I'd say this went just fine," Darcy said with a smile. "Let's let her check out the house."

Inside, the dog continued checking every corner, until at last she settled down and followed Emma into her room. She curled up on the rug by the bed, watching Emma play with her dolls.

"If everything's all right, I'm going to go back to the kitchen and figure out what we're having for supper. Call if you need me, okay?"

Darcy hunted through the freezer and pulled out a package of chicken thighs that she defrosted in the microwave, then threw into the Crock-Pot on high with seasonings, sliced onions and barbecue sauce.

Eyeing the floor, she dropped to her knees and chipped at another section of the vinyl. She sat back on her heels with awe when a large section came up. *Thank You, Lord.*

The next piece came up just as easily, and soon she had the final section pulled free and the hardwood floor exposed. Overjoyed, she called out to Emma to come see what she'd accomplished.

Emma didn't answer.

Frowning, Darcy jumped to her feet and hurried back to the bedrooms. "Emma?"

*Success.*

She was lying on her bed, a book in her hands, with her head on Bonnie's side. And both were fast asleep.

When her cell phone rang twenty minutes later, Darcy had finished hauling out the last of the vinyl and was busy scraping at the pools of petrified flooring glue that remained.

Surprised at the Montana number on the screen, she set aside her scraper and answered the call.

"Hey, this is Susan—Logan's sister. I made him give me your number."

Baffled, Darcy tried to image any reason why she would call. "Is he all right?"

Susan laughed. "More than. I insisted that I wanted you and your daughter to join us for supper, but he thought you'd be busy—something about a floor. I told him that was a lame excuse to not ask. We'll eat at six, if that works for you?"

This wasn't just an invitation, it was an expectation. "I—I guess so."

"Don't worry—this isn't the Inquisition or anything. I'm just curious about what he's gotten himself into by moving so far away, and figured it would be nice to meet you. He says you're going to be his business partner."

Talking to her was like an encounter with a steamroller, and Darcy felt a little breathless. "He did? We've discussed it, but nothing is final yet."

"Whatever. Six, then?"

"That's good. What can I bring?"

Susan bellowed at her brother, her voice muffled.

Then she came back to the call. "He says some sort of easy dessert would be good. Maybe brownies? But you really don't have to bother. He's got ice cream here."

Darcy turned the Crock-Pot to low so the chicken would be done around bedtime and could be refrigerated for dinner tomorrow. Then she considered her ravaged kitchen before reaching for one of the three-ring binders where she kept her favorite recipes protected in plastic sleeves.

Something easy, yes. But she had no doubt about Susan's intent. Tonight she would be assessed and probably found wanting as part of Logan's new practice. Darcy had a feeling that people did not pass muster with his sister, no matter who they were.

But she wasn't going to fail at dessert.

At six, Darcy pulled up at Logan's place and helped Emma out of the car, then reached for the handle of her covered pie carrier.

"I think Bonnie will be lonely at home," Emma said with a worried frown. "Should we go get her?"

"She's better off at home—especially on her first day with us. She'll be fine in the house."

As they walked up to Logan's front door, Darcy started imagining what they would find. From Susan's strong voice and no-nonsense attitude, she expected a woman topping six feet with broad shoulders, just like her brother. Someone who was a serious contender in women's boxing.

When the door opened, Darcy felt her jaw drop.

Susan offered a delicate hand. "You must be Darcy. I'm so glad to meet you—and this young lady must be Emma."

Susan was all of five feet tall, probably a hundred

pounds, with bright blue eyes and a tumble of blond curls down her back. If she wasn't doing some sort of petite modeling or television work, she was seriously missing a golden opportunity.

Darcy blinked. "So nice to meet you."

"Logan just put the steaks on, and we've got romaine salad, garlic French bread and baked potatoes. That seems to be his only skill set, so I hope it's all right. Won't you come in?"

She led the way out to the screened porch in back, where the table was set and a bright profusion of wild-flowers had been arranged in a quart-size canning jar.

Logan was at the grill on the stone patio beyond. Setting aside his long barbecue fork, he came inside. "So you've met, I suppose? Susan, Emma just won a big award at Sunday school today."

"You were in church?" Susan eyed him closely, her eyes sharp and assessing. Then she smiled and offered her hand to Emma. "Congratulations. Your mom must be very proud."

Emma nodded, her gaze veering toward a low set of shelves where Logan kept a stack of paper and a box of crayons. "Can I color now?"

"Of course." Susan watched her collect the supplies and spread them on a glass-topped wicker coffee table in front of a matching wicker love seat. "I can see that you know where things are around here. Help yourself."

Susan and Darcy brought out the foil-wrapped pota-toes, salads and dressing. By then, Logan was bringing the foil-wrapped French bread redolent with garlic and butter and a platter of juicy rib eyes.

If steaks were Logan's one achievement in the culi-nary arts, at least he was a star.

When everyone was seated, Susan gave Logan a pointed look. "Grace?"

He nodded.

They all reached for a neighboring hand and said a simple table prayer. Then Logan passed the steaks. "The most rare are on the right."

Darcy cut part of her steak and put tiny pieces on Emma's plate, along with a buttered half of her baked potato and some diced lettuce.

She then cut a bite of steak for herself. "Oh, my. This steak is perfection."

"It's the maître d'hôtel butter." Susan looked up at her. "He adds it on top at the very last minute, then it melts over the grilled meat. Butter, a little fresh parsley, lemon, garlic, salt and pepper. Our mom always used it, too. And growing up on a cattle ranch, we learned to use only prime beef when it comes to steak."

Darcy looked over at Logan and smiled. "I am in awe. Everything is just wonderful."

While they were finishing the meal, Susan and Logan intelligently debated politics and world news, then segued into the Colorado Rockies game stats and whether they had a good chance this year.

Whatever his opinion, Susan automatically took the opposite view. The competitive conversation was like watching a tennis match that had been choreographed to a fine point over the years.

Content just to listen, Darcy smiled, intrigued by this side of him.

Susan broke off the debate with her brother and looked at Emma. "I hear you love horses. I'll bet Logan would saddle up a horse if you'd like to ride. Then we could enjoy dessert afterward."

Emma nodded vigorously, but Darcy shook her head. "Really, we can't take more of your time. I'm sure you'd much rather visit with each other. And honestly, we really can't stay that long. We got a new dog today, and she's in the house."

"Kenneled, right?"

"Um…yes, but…"

Susan shrugged. "It won't take Logan long to bring a horse up from the barn. It looks like Emma is more than a little excited."

Of course she was. After that enticing invitation, she was bouncing in her chair.

From the look Logan gave his sister as he stood, he suspected that she'd just skillfully engineered a setup.

"Behave," he said quietly to her as he headed for the screen door.

"Can I come with you now? Please?" Emma quivered with anticipation. "I won't be in the way."

He extended a hand. She scrambled out of her chair and held on to it as they headed through the backyard toward the barn.

Darcy rose and began gathering plates, while Susan picked up the serving dishes. "Thanks again. This was all lovely, but I do hope we didn't intrude on your time together. You leave tomorrow, right?"

"Back to the soap opera that is my life." Susan raised an eyebrow. "I assume Logan told you about why I'm here."

"Um…"

"No worries. I assumed he did." She gave a rueful laugh as she began loading the dishwasher. "I seem to be an expert at finding good men. I'm just not so good at keeping them. So, how about you? Were you married long?"

"What?"

"You have to admit that any good sister would worry about her little brother, especially after what he's been through. I worry about him making another mistake."

"Unless you're talking about a business relationship, I think there's been a misunderstanding. He and I aren't… an item."

Susan stopped, a dirty plate in hand, and turned to give her a flat look of disbelief. "Really."

"I work at the clinic. I may well buy into the practice and become a partner. And I think we're becoming friends. Nothing more." She shrugged. "Anyway, just in passing conversation, he has mentioned that he has no plans to settle down with anyone. Not ever. So take it up with him, but it doesn't sound like you have any reason for concern."

"And yet he's gone to church with you. Twice."

Darcy gave a helpless little shrug. "As coworkers. Friends. It's not uncommon."

"For him it is. Logan has not stepped into a church since our mom and dad died. He's been angry about what happened to them for so long that I thought it would never happen. And yet he apparently put those feelings aside. For you. And after that deal with Cathy—" She broke off and studied Darcy's face closely. "So you *don't* know?"

"Know what?"

Susan seemed to reconsider her words. "I thought he would never take a chance on someone new, yet here he is. Why?"

"I—I have no idea." But from somewhere deep in her memory, Kaycee's narrowed look at Logan and her words *glass houses* and *throwing stones* surfaced.

Maybe it was time to do some sleuthing on her own, because neither Kaycee nor Susan was very forthcoming.

"Understand that I have nothing against you. You seem like a great person." Susan dropped the plate in the dishwasher and shut the door. Her voice gentled, but it also held a thread of steel. "But I didn't come here to think over my marriage—I already know which way that's going. I came here because of you."

Shocked, Darcy stared at her. "Me?"

"Logan and I talk on the phone almost every week, and I could tell something was different. After a lot of badgering, I finally got just a little information out of him. How he's spending time with you outside work. How much he likes your daughter."

"But really, there's nothing going on here. He helps out with some things at my house because of an auction."

"I think there's more—at least, on his part."

Darcy felt a warm little ember come to life in her heart, even though she knew what Susan said wasn't true.

"Apparently there's a lot you don't know about his past, but you won't find anyone on this planet better than my brother. But I promise you—I won't let you break his heart. Because if you do, you'll be answering to me."

## Chapter Fifteen

On Monday, Logan took Susan back to the airport—a strangely silent trip. Then he returned to Aspen Creek and discovered two emergency calls added to his already full schedule.

The rest of the week sped by—equally hectic, despite the fact that few mares were still foaling in late May, and the breeding season for next year was essentially over.

He'd barely seen Darcy since dinner last Sunday afternoon beyond some passing, casual greetings at the clinic. But today he was done and back at the clinic by five, determined to catch her before she went home. He'd spent the week feeling edgy and out of sorts, like he'd lost something but didn't know how to get it back.

And he suspected Susan had something to do with it.

He waited until Kaycee and Marilyn left for home at five thirty, then found Darcy in the lab running a CBC in the hematology analyzer. "Is this for someone in an exam room?"

She shook her head. "A dog we're keeping overnight. What's up?"

"I couldn't get a thing out of my sister before she

left, but I get the feeling that she might have been—" he searched for the right word, but when it came to Susan, that could be a challenge "—intrusive."

Darcy's shoulders sagged as she turned to face him. "I honestly had no idea what she was talking about, but she seemed to think an awful lot of hanky-panky was going on around here. Apparently—don't laugh—between you and me."

"I figured as much."

"She also hinted at all sorts of big secrets in your past. And—" Darcy gave a helpless laugh. "—I actually think she threatened me, sort of. Not that I took her seriously. I mean, she's got to be under five feet tall."

"That's where a lot of people underestimate her," he said with a wry smile. "She wrestled me to the ground and broke my arm when she was only ten."

"Maybe so. But as an adult, she seems like a wonderful sister who just wants to watch out for her brother, and I respect that."

He sighed, remembering some of the times when she'd tried to interfere a bit too much. "I'd like to discuss this a little more, but not here. Could you meet me for dinner tonight—just you and me?"

Her gaze flickered. Then she turned back to the analyzer. "I've got Emma, remember?"

"Could you find a sitter for an hour or two? There's a little restaurant out by the lake. Excellent food, and it's quiet."

"I just don't have anyone I can call on such short notice."

"At least let me stop at your house so we can measure the cabinets. Then you can get them ordered whenever you're ready."

"The sooner the better." She glanced up at the clock.

"I'll have just forty-five minutes before I need to pick her up, so we'll have to make this quick."

After closing up the clinic and setting the alarm, Logan followed Darcy to her house and parked in front. From inside came the sound of loud barking until Darcy unlocked the door and called out Bonnie's name.

"I'm glad to have an alarm system again," she said with a smile as she let the dog out into the backyard. "She sounds so fierce, no one would ever guess she's such a softy."

"So it's worked out well?"

"More than. She's housebroken, she doesn't chew on things and she's totally devoted to Emma—follows her around like a shadow and sleeps on the foot of her bed." Darcy filled a stainless-steel dog bowl with kibble and set it back down on the floor. "I always recommend that clients check the local shelters for an older dog before bringing home a puppy, and this is why. How's Cedar?"

"A little better," he admitted. "I brought her home a week ago. She's had three dips in scabicide, so the mange is clearing up and her bald spots have peach fuzz coming in. I keep telling her she's quite the fashion plate, but I don't think she believes me."

Darcy laughed. "Just don't let her look in any mirrors."

"The housebreaking is going fairly well. I don't think she'd ever been inside before, so that scared her. And she hadn't ever learned all of the good citizenship rules. But it's coming along. Once her coat has grown back, I'll start taking her to the clinic and on calls with me so she's not alone all day."

"A perfect life, then, if she can be with you 24/7." She looked at her wristwatch. "So, what did you want to discuss? I'll need to go after Emma before long."

He blew out a long sigh. "As I started to say at the clinic, I want to apologize for my sister. When she got Emma excited about riding Drifter last Sunday and sent the two of us off to the barn, I figured she had a reason. I thought she might pry a little, but not that she'd go so far."

"She's worried about you."

"But it wasn't appropriate for her to interfere, or to try to warn you away."

"It was lovely to see someone who cares so much for family that they'll try to intercede. But as much as I do like her, it wasn't really necessary." Darcy gave a dismissive wave of her hand. "You'd already made it clear that you aren't looking for any relationships here in town. It sounded to me like you were saying 'been there, done that, not going through it again.' And as you might imagine, I can totally empathize. So, case closed."

"I need to talk to you about something else that I should have told you already, but it's a little complicated, and we don't have enough time." His gaze fell on a stapled, typed list several pages long that she'd left on the counter. "Veterinary equipment?"

A blush rose to her cheekbones. "With costs, for either a storefront office or a mobile vet clinic. It makes me a little dizzy to look at those numbers, but I want to be prepared either way."

"You talked about buying into the practice. Staying on board," he said slowly. "Is that off the table now?"

"Of course not. But we haven't really sat down to talk it over yet, either. Without any concrete numbers, I don't know which direction is the best way for me to go. So I just want to keep my options open."

He nodded. "I need to talk to the bank and also my

lawyer. When I get something drawn up for you to consider, I'll let you know."

"Perfect. So, what do you think of the kitchen floor?"

He surveyed the bare hardwood, impressed. It still needed all the steps of finishing, but the vinyl was gone, and a thorough sanding made it look a hundred times better. "You did all this?"

"Worked on it every night. The bedroom floors are completely done. Last night I ran the barrel sander and edger over the kitchen floor, so next I can apply the sealer." She reached for a tape measure on the kitchen counter. "Once we take the measurements, I can do some ordering."

"What have you decided?"

"At first I wanted to just reface the cabinets. But after studying the poor condition of these, I'd rather replace them all. White upper and lower, with granite counters—ideally white with gray veining."

"Sounds good."

"I've chosen the style of cupboards in a catalog at the lumberyard. The lower ones have soft-close drawers, and some have special dividers. There are even toe kick drawers at the very bottom, floor level, to add more storage."

He looked at her in awe. "You amaze me."

"The floors have taken hours of unskilled labor and a lot of YouTube videos while trying to get it right. The cabinets I just need to choose."

"I mean everything. Your skill as a vet and dedication as a mom. Doing all of this work on the house yourself would overwhelm a lot of people. And then there's your cooking. That dessert you brought Sunday night was amazing. Cloud—"

"No, *kladdkaka*." She grinned, her hazel eyes sparkling. "Pays to know a Scandinavian, I guess. We have the best desserts. And that one took just ten minutes in the oven."

"I've never had anything like it. It tasted like chocolate silk."

"Well, now. You might need to stop by now and then for supper, just to see what we're having."

They got down to work taking measurements, then checked them a second time.

By then it was time to go. They both headed out the front door onto the porch, and she locked the door behind them. "I really appreciate your help with this. I'll order the cabinets tomorrow and let you know when they're ready."

He gave her a quick one-arm hug, then caught her hand in his and gave it a little squeeze. "I just hope you'll like it all when you're done."

The shadows under the covered porch and the lowering sun made the space seem more intimate somehow, more private. When he drew her a little closer, she didn't resist.

And then, without a plan or even conscious thought, he bent down and kissed her.

## *Chapter Sixteen*

Startled, Darcy stiffened, then found herself melting into Logan's kiss. A sparkling sensation washed through her, filling her with warmth and wonder.

Despite every resolution she'd made since Dean walked out on her, she curved her arms around Logan's neck, pulling him even closer.

It was Logan who finally broke away.

He smiled down at her with that little half smile that deepened just one of his dimples, sending a shiver of awareness down her spine. His eyes darkened as their eyes locked.

Then he dropped another swift, gentle kiss on her mouth that sent Fourth of July sparklers coursing through her veins all over again. And in that brief, sweet moment, he left her longing for more.

When had she ever felt that way? Dazed, she tried to collect her thoughts as he jogged out to his truck.

The answer was *never*.

Not with Dean. Certainly not with anyone else she'd ever dated.

She stood on the porch well after Logan's taillights disappeared down the street.

True, it had been so long since she'd been in Dean's arms that she could barely remember any emotion he might have stirred, and now even those fading memories were clouded by his deceptions.

Had he ever really cared for her? Loved her? Had there ever been a time when their relationship had been honest and real?

She'd thought so…but maybe she'd only been a convenience. Easy prey. Just a bright student at the top of their class who would thus be a good money earner. A logical choice. Another set of hands at the clinic.

Maybe he'd been having affairs all along and she'd been too blind to notice, caught up as she was with caring for their daughter, and working day and night to make their new clinic succeed.

But that was the past and this was now. And this felt different.

Even now she imagined she could still detect Logan's crisp aftershave and the fresh scent of soap on his skin.

Shaking off her thoughts, she hurried to Mrs. Spencer's to pick up Emma with just minutes to spare.

"You look funny, Mommy," Emma announced when Darcy walked in. "You're pink."

"Hmm…must've been the nice spring sun today."

Mrs. Spencer, a hefty woman shaped like a barrel, was no-nonsense and plainspoken with adults, but she enthralled kids from infancy to teens with her sense of humor and a laugh that shook her belly.

Now she gave Darcy a head-to-toe perusal and pursed her lips. "I'd say it might be that handsome young vet of yours. He could make a statue blush."

"Mrs. Spencer." Darcy glanced around the living room, hoping there were no other adults around. "Please."

The older woman's ample middle shook as she chuckled. "From the chatter down at the cafe, I'd say everyone in town knows there's something going on between you two. Don't think it's any secret."

"Well, tell everyone in town that it isn't true. We've not gone on so much as a single date. I just work for him. And… I won him at that church auction, so that's why he's been doing some work at my house."

"Right. But I've seen sparks between you two when I've been at the clinic with my Rufus." Mrs. Spencer waggled a forefinger, her eyes twinkling. "Great move on your part, I'd say, bidding at that auction. Anyway, I'm glad to have two vets in town in case Rufus gets sick again."

Darcy cast a wary glance around the toy-cluttered living room.

Rufus, with claws sharp as scalpels and teeth to match, was a disagreeable cat whether sick or well, and he had a memory like a five-gigabyte hard drive when it came to remembering the clinic staff who had dealt with him.

He also had a penchant for eating bizarre things like rubber bands and stretchy little hair ties left by the girls at the day care, which meant repeated trips to the clinic.

Mrs. Spencer followed her gaze. "Don't worry, dearie. I've started closing him upstairs when the kiddies are around so they can't play too rough with him."

Darcy suspected the rough behavior might be the other way around. "I know you must be really tired at the end of each day, but would you know of anyone who might be willing to babysit for an occasional Saturday night?"

"So I was right." She chortled. Her eyes gleamed in triumph. "It's always nice to help young sweethearts along."

Darcy couldn't help but roll her eyes. "You do know I could be talking about needing you for a church meeting at night. Or...or..."

"Well, whatever you're up to, I can always use a little pin money, so just give me a call. If I can't do it, you can always ask my niece. She might even come to your house."

On the way out to her car, Darcy tried to keep a firm grip on Emma's hand as the child skipped and hopped and then tried going backward. "What has gotten into you, sweetie? Are you this glad to go home?"

"Mrs. Spencer said you like Dr. Maxwell, so if you have a date then he can live with us. And then he could be my daddy 'cause I like him *lots*."

Darcy stifled a laugh as she tried to keep up with Emma's childish logic, though the potential for further embarrassment was obvious.

"Sounds like an interesting plan, sweetie—except things are never that easy. Keep it to yourself, okay? It would happen only if it was meant to be, and I doubt very much that it will."

After Emma had her bath, stories and bedtime snack, and finally fell asleep, Darcy worked into the night staining the kitchen floor to match what she'd done in the bedrooms.

As painstaking as the process was, it gave her way too much time to think.

She'd never thought a kiss could be so sweet. So compelling. Logan's kiss had reverberated through her long afterward, and though once she might have dismissed her reaction as silly schoolgirl nonsense, even now she could feel the touch of his mouth on hers and the dizzying way he'd made her feel.

All with just a kiss.

Obviously she was way too susceptible and needed to get a grip. She had to make sure it didn't happen again.

After Dean, she'd been absolutely sure she never wanted to risk a relationship again. Nothing could possibly be worth the stress, the uncertainty. And from what Logan had once said, he felt exactly the same.

But what could have possibly gone badly enough in his life to make him that adamant?

He was intelligent, compassionate, dedicated, with good career. Handsome...and he was obviously great with kids, because Emma loved him. Just thinking about how sweet he'd been with old Mrs. Peabody and her dog still made Darcy feel warm inside. The list went on and on.

Then again, she'd blithely ignored the warning signs about Dean, and she'd learned that painful lesson all too well.

She'd be a fool to ignore Kaycee's muttered comment about something dark in Logan's past, and his sister's veiled reference about someone named Cathy. And what had Susan meant about a consuming anger that he'd never forgotten?

Out-of-control anger was something she never wanted to face again with any man. Ever.

The last swipe of the rag wet with stain took her to the kitchen door. Evening out that last swath of stain with the dry rag in her other hand, she surveyed the beautiful old hardwood that was now coming to life, then closed the can of stain and peeled off her gloves.

After a shower, she curled up on the couch with her laptop and pulled up Google. Thought long and hard about what she was about to do.

And then she typed in Logan's name.

Logan picked up his cell phone. Stared at it, then looked down at Cedar, who was sitting by his chair at the kitchen table. "So what do you think, old girl? Should I do this?"

The moth-eaten dog, now mostly covered in peach fuzz hair, laid her head on his thigh and looked up at him.

"Is that a yes? I could use some help here. Extend the invitation—yes or no?"

Cedar blinked.

He'd been on farm calls all morning and Darcy had worked at the clinic until noon, so he hadn't seen her since he'd kissed her last night. Even now he was second-guessing that move.

He'd never been so uncertain about a relationship in the past, through the few that had come and gone. He should have been far more uncertain about the last one and then avoided it all together.

But now, knowing about Darcy's past and her justified fear about involvement, he felt like he was traveling through unknown waters, as unsure as any teenage boy facing the terror of asking for his very first date.

What did he want here, really?

He wasn't even sure, except that being with Darcy and her little girl gave him a deep feeling of completion that had never been a part of his life. Whether he and Darcy were trading light banter or discussing vet cases, just talking to her made him smile. Made him want to be better, somehow. Made him long to be a part of a family. *Her* family.

And Emma...what a little pistol she was. Bright and talkative and curious, she made him laugh and made him want to protect her from anything that might ever dare try to harm her. He only had to look down at her to feel a sense of warmth settle in his heart.

Though after he'd impulsively kissed her mom last night, he might have thrown that all away.

He punched in Darcy's number, sat back in his chair and thanked God for church picnics and second chances.

"I didn't expect to be here today," Darcy said as she surveyed the shady city park. "What a perfect way to enjoy a Saturday afternoon."

Dozens of kids from the Sunday school classes were swinging, climbing on an old-fashioned jungle gym and lining up for the slides. Emma had already taken off at a run for her preschool friends, who were playing in a massive sandbox.

Darcy angled a look at Logan over the top rim of her sunglasses, then adjusted them into place. "How did you happen to find out about it?"

He shrugged. "There was a note about the Sunday school picnic in the church bulletin last weekend."

"It was nice of you to invite us. I'd forgotten about it, but this was good timing. I put down the first poly-urethane coat on the kitchen floor this morning, and we needed to get out of the house. The fumes are really pungent." She frowned, looking at the long, food-laden tables in the picnic shelter. "I'll bet we were supposed to bring food. This is a potluck, right?

"Got it covered." He reached into a cooler in the back

of his truck. "I bought a gallon of potato salad and a couple dozen M&M's cookies at the grocery store on my way to pick you up."

He handed her a blanket, and he carried the food as they strolled together through the sun-dappled shade of the massive oaks, nodding to the church families who had already spread out blankets or commandeered picnic tables. "Do you see a spot you'd like?"

"Up there on the knoll overlooking the playground."

She shook out the blanket in the deep shade beneath the massive branches of an oak while he took the food down to the buffet set up.

He brought back cups of icy lemonade. "They'll be having horseshoes, volleyball and also a softball game for the teenagers after lunch. Pastor Mark will say the prayer in a few minutes and then lunch will start. Are you glad you came?"

"It's a perfect day for this, and I'm so happy Emma's having a chance to play." She smiled softly, her gaze fixed on Emma and her little friends industriously digging in the sandbox. "Next year she'll start kindergarten, and I hear that once she starts school, she'll grow up in the blink of an eye. I feel like I have to savor every moment and memory before these years are gone."

She took a sip of lemonade. "I have to admit, I was a little surprised when you called about this."

"To tell you the truth, it's been a long time since I've had any part of being in a church family. If you'd told me six months ago that I'd ever be at a Sunday school picnic, I would've said you were crazy. But I'm honestly glad to be here. Especially with you and Emma."

"She adores you, you know." Darcy took another sip of her lemonade and flicked away an ant crawling across the blanket. "Probably too much. So I need to know something. Maybe this isn't the right time and place, but it really can't wait. I won't let her little heart be broken again by someone who disappoints her."

She fell silent for a moment, then looked across the picnic blanket and met his gaze. "I did a search of your name on Google last night. I suppose you already know why."

He knew what she was going to say. Back home, too many people already had. He stilled, quietly waiting for her to rail at him, then turn her back on him for good.

"I never would've thought to check, but your sister alluded to some trouble before you moved here. There were a lot of links to your name, but I couldn't bring myself to click any of them. It seemed wrong somehow. I'd rather that you told me yourself."

"And you'll believe me? I doubt it."

She fixed her piercing eyes on his. "I haven't known you long, but I've seen the kind of man you are. Tell me."

He didn't ever talk about his past—not with friends or family. Not with the counselor Susan had hired. Any words he managed to find did disservice to the depth of his grief and loss. None came close to truly honoring his late wife.

But he sensed that any chance to move on, any chance for a future, depended on getting this right. He took a slow breath and sent up a silent, rusty prayer.

"I was married in vet school," he said slowly. "Gina was a year behind me. The sweetest, prettiest girl I'd ever met, and she totally stole my heart. We loved the same things—skiing, camping, high adventure stuff. I couldn't believe I'd found someone who loved all the things I did. We both wanted a big family and a horse farm in Montana, but we'd been married just two years when she died of stage IV breast cancer that showed up out of the blue. I was devastated beyond words."

"I am so, so sorry," Darcy said softly.

"Afterward, I joined a large vet practice and totally immersed myself in work. I was alone for five years. After losing Gina, I couldn't even look at another woman. Then one day, the group hired a new bookkeeper."

He looked away, and had to pause before he could continue. "I'd been wallowing in my grief since Gina died, but this gal was so sympathetic, so understanding and kind, that I fell into spending more and more time with her. She seemed like a lifeline to me, but she must have thought I was a sitting duck. Looking back, I'm not even sure when it happened or if it did. But suddenly she was happily announcing that we were engaged."

Darcy scanned the sandbox at the bottom of the hill, where Emma was building a sand castle. Then she looked back. "I'm almost afraid to hear the rest of this."

"Every expression of sympathy, every seemingly heartfelt emotion Cathy expressed was a ruse to mask her real intent. I was only a cover who unwittingly helped allay suspicions about her because, after all, she was with me, and I was a full partner. She embezzled around forty grand before being discovered, and then she disappeared. When they caught her, the money was gone—gambled away at casinos."

"So they got nothing back at all?"

He snorted. "In court she tried pinning it all on me. She said it was my idea, that I'd forced her into it. She said I'd kept the money myself and they needed to go after me instead. But the casino records and security videos showed otherwise. I don't gamble, and her attorney couldn't prove that I was ever in a casino with her."

"At least you were vindicated, then."

"Not entirely." He heaved a sigh. "The investigators found no proof against me, so I was never charged. Cathy went to prison a couple years ago. But the situation cast a veil of distrust over me as far as the other vets and clients were concerned. There are people who are still sure I helped her, pocketed the money or at least turned a blind eye. Even out on vet calls, I still got endless questions and innuendoes, and some clients questioned my character and professional skills. I finally gave up because it just wasn't worth it anymore. That's when I started looking for a practice somewhere in Minnesota or Wisconsin."

"What an awful situation to go through. I just can't imagine." She reached over to rest a hand on his forearm. "I wish I could have done something."

She already had, and she didn't know it. He'd arrived in Aspen Creek feeling betrayed and bitter, determined to keep his distance from anyone who tried to get too close. But she and her little girl had slipped beneath his defenses and reminded him of what good and decent people were like.

And now, he felt like he once again had a chance at a normal life. And if he could spend it with her, he would be well and truly blessed.

He rose to his feet and offered her a hand up. "Looks like we ought to get down to the picnic shelter—most everyone has already gone through the line."

He started to step away from the blanket, but she caught his hand and tugged him back.

She looked up into his eyes. "I'm proud of you, Logan. For how you dealt with all of that, and for the man you are. Those people out West were so wrong about you. How could they not see it?"

This time, it was Darcy who started the kiss.

Lightly resting her hands on his chest, she raised up on her tiptoes to brush a kiss against his cheek. The wooded park, the sounds of adults talking and children playing and everything else in the world seemed to fade away, until it was only Darcy and him in this moment.

And when he gently pulled her into his arms for another kiss and she looked up at him again with those beautiful, luminous eyes, he felt like he was coming home.

## Chapter Seventeen

The last week of May started unseasonably warm and muggy with rain most every day, but nothing could dampen Darcy's mood.

Tomorrow was the start of the three-day Memorial Day weekend. The clinic would be closed throughout, except for emergencies, and since she'd chosen Shaker-style kitchen cabinets that were available in the warehouse, they were already being delivered this afternoon.

Marilyn looked up from her computer screen. "I thought you were leaving at noon," she said with a smile. "Sounds like you have an exciting day."

"I'm on my way out now. And yes—you have no idea how thrilled I am to be almost done with the house. Just the cupboards, countertops and then some bathroom re-modeling are left, and then everything will be done. For now, anyway."

Marilyn looked back at her screen. "It looks like Dr. Maxwell will be out on calls until four. Is he helping you tonight?"

"We're starting after supper, if all goes well."

"I guess you got a good deal at that auction in more

ways than one." Marilyn winked. "How is everything going with you two?"

Darcy shrugged, trying to contain her smile. "Pretty well, I think. We've been meeting at one house or the other for supper since the Sunday school picnic on Saturday. Emma is delighted because she gets to see the horses more often. And of course, she thinks Logan is her hero."

And, Darcy admitted only to herself, with each passing day she and Logan were becoming closer. Just the sound of his voice made her blood thrum in her veins, and every hour spent with him made her realize that she'd been truly blessed to find someone so wonderful.

It was way too soon to be thinking about a future together. But maybe, someday, if all went well...

"Just so you know, Kaycee and I will both be out of town this weekend. She's going to take her brother and sister to see relatives in Madison, and I'll be going to the Twin Cities with my husband."

"See you Tuesday, then. Travel safe." Darcy headed out the rear entryway and started to climb behind the wheel of her car.

"Wait!" Marilyn stood at the back door, waving frantically. "You need to see this."

Darcy followed her into the clinic. "What's up?"

Marilyn scurried down the hall ahead of her.

"It's on my computer screen. I...um, don't usually look at Facebook while I'm here." She gave an embarrassed little shrug. "But I was just starting to eat lunch at my desk. I happened to take a peek at my profile, and this came up in my feed. I don't know who this is—he calls himself the Aspen Creek Sentinel. His posts pop up now and then, usually about something around town, and he's often a little snide. A lot of locals comment on his posts. But *this*…"

Darcy leaned over to read the post. It had been shared from a newspaper website in Montana and included a photo of a beautiful young woman. The snippet of headline read Convicted of Fraud and Embezzlement, Woman Goes Free.

Darcy stared, her mouth suddenly dry. "Can you click on the link?"

"I already read it, and I printed it off. It's not good news. Did you know about this?"

Darcy felt her stomach twist into a cold knot. "I know she stole something like $40,000 from a vet clinic where Logan worked and tried to blame him. Why have they released her?"

"I don't understand all the mumbo-jumbo legal stuff, but it sounds like she's getting a retrial and has been released on bail." Marilyn reached over to grab some sheets of paper from the printer, stapled them and handed them to Darcy. "But the kicker is that she says she gave her lawyer new evidence that Logan was responsible in the first place—so he should have been tried, not her."

Darcy's stomach twisted even tighter. She closed her eyes in disbelief. "If that's true, he could be arrested and extradited back to Montana."

"*If* it's true?" Logan's voice came from behind her, the measured, emotionless tone cutting through her like a scalpel. "You apparently think it's a possibility?"

She whirled around to face his stony expression. "No—of course not. I meant if she or her lawyer come up with something, the court would have to check it out, and…" She faltered to a stop. "But surely she has falsified something, or flat-out lied. You said she was like that."

"All I know is that I had nothing to do with it. And whoever discovered this news must be standing on quite a soapbox around here." He cast a pointed glance at the papers in Darcy's hand. "Because three of my clients today had already heard about it, and one said he was taking his business elsewhere."

"That's so unfair. What are you going to do?"

"I've called my lawyer in Montana, and I'm going back. If Cathy has cooked up something plausible enough, there could be a long road ahead. And with the type of friends she probably made in prison, I don't even want to imagine it."

"What can I do? Just tell me," she pleaded.

"Nothing." He shrugged dismissively and turned away. "Nothing at all."

He'd known it was too good to be true—finding this idyllic little town, the kind of practice he'd dreamed of. Finding a woman and her little girl who had both touched his heart from the first time they'd met.

Well, maybe not the *first* time, he amended, remembering that first stony encounter at the clinic. But after that first meeting, things had warmed quickly, and he'd discovered such hope, such possibility, that maybe he would finally be on track toward the life he'd always wanted.

Then he'd heard that flicker of doubt in Darcy's voice and he'd pounced on it—seizing the chance to distance himself. No matter how much he cared for her, or how much he hoped she and little Emma could become his family someday, God willing, he knew what was coming, and she didn't deserve to be any part of it.

He'd already seen it happen.

The friendly greetings turned wary, the whispers of doubt among clients and people he barely knew. After all, some folks figured that shady lawyers could set free the most evil of men, so whether he was vindicated or not, there would be many who still thought another criminal had been freed.

And then the rumors would go on and on, expanding exponentially. Tainting the well that had once held only goodwill. And Darcy would suffer for it all only if she had any connection to him.

His first day here in town had been a case in point.

A client with an appointment in the clinic had overheard a misspoken statement. Offered it up to the local gossip mill.

So when Logan arrived at the café for an early lunch an hour later, the café clientele had turned on him as one, angry at his supposed mistreatment of one of their own.

Small in comparison to the catastrophe back in Montana, but awkward all the same.

He resolutely pushed open the door of the café, wondering if this visit would bring another charred hamburger and spilled beverage to his table. Prepared to ignore any comments and rebuffs, he found his usual front window booth and sat down without looking at the menu.

Marge, the morning waitress, came by with her pad and pencil. "The usual, Doc?"

He nodded, and she scurried off to the kitchen.

One by one, heads turned. Most of them silver or gray and all of them familiar—mostly retired folk who could while away long hours over a shared slice of pie and coffee refills without regard for a time clock back at the job.

At the nearby round table, where a trio of older women usually reigned, all three heads turned. All of them frowned, and he braced himself.

"We wish you all the best, Doc," Mabel announced. "We read the news online and think it's abominable. It's clear enough that they ought to throw that tootsie back in jail."

The woman with the shortest silver hair nodded. "Just trying to get off the hook herself, I'd say. Some people would lie to their mothers if they thought it would do them any good."

The oldest woman—Mrs. Peabody—nodded. "We're all writing letters, you know. If that judge doesn't realize what a fine man you are, then he's going to find out. If you need character witnesses, we'll go to Montana."

That she would offer such a thing touched his heart. She barely had enough to live on as it was. "That's really kind of you all," he said, smiling at each lady in turn. "I appreciate it."

Wally, the old duffer with purple tennis shoes, came up to Logan's booth and pounded a fist on the table. "We've seen how good you are to Doc Leighton and her little girl, and we've seen you around town. You're good folks. If things go south, we'll take up a collection. Mark my words."

Logan hated to think what even a few dollars meant to some of these people. "Thank you, Wally. But I don't think things will come to that."

"If they do, we'll send you news from home. You can have mail in prison, right?"

Mrs. Peabody gasped. "Wally, no one is going anywhere. He'll get things straightened out, because he's innocent."

Beth had told him about the community spirit here when he'd first arrived. How folks banded together to help their own, and stood by their friends.

So how ironic it was, to learn that he'd become a part of that kinship when he might soon have to leave?

Darcy eyed the mountain of cardboard boxes stacked in her kitchen and sighed.

She'd been excited about this delivery and the chance to help Logan install the new cabinets today. With Emma safely out of the way at Mrs. Spencer's, they could've gotten so much done.

And she'd been so happy about the long weekend ahead, because she and Logan had planned be together every day.

She'd lined up Mrs. Spencer's niece to babysit several times over the long weekend, so if the stormy weather forecast cleared, she and Logan had planned to rent kayaks to explore the St. Croix, and later on take his horses on a long trail ride.

They were also going to take Emma along for cookouts at the park and take her wading at the beach. Simple things. The kind of family times that she always recorded with lots of iPhone photos so she could create photo books, and Emma could see glimpses of her happy childhood after she'd grown.

But now Darcy had seen Logan angrily blow her comment about his legal situation all out of proportion, and he wasn't answering his phone or responding to texts. How could he have become so volatile over a single misconstrued comment when everything had been going so well? How could he not be willing to discuss it and work things out?

It didn't make sense.

And it made her worry.

Had this relationship been heading toward the boundaries that she'd sworn she'd never cross? A deeper commitment that could lead to heartbreak?

Dean had changed over the years. He'd become defensive and petulant, and his anger had grown way out of control the year before he finally walked out on her.

Darcy had done her best to shield Emma from their verbal battles, but on that last night her little girl had awakened and come out into the living room at just the wrong time. Seeing her pale and frightened face had been the final, defining moment.

Whatever Darcy's beliefs about marriage and forgiveness and trying to make things work, raising Emma in a safe, loving home, with a good example of how men should treat their families, mattered most of all. She would have left with Emma the next morning if Dean hadn't already gone.

Now she could look back and see that his unconscionable outbursts likely correlated to times when he was totally enamored with some other woman. He'd probably been consumed with frustration and anger over the complexities of being a cheat—while still inconveniently involved in a business with his wife.

Maybe he'd even felt a little guilt, if Darcy wanted to give him that much benefit of the doubt.

But no good and decent father put his selfish desires above the welfare of his daughter and the bounds of marriage. And no man—no matter how appealing—would ever have a place in Darcy's heart if he had Dean's dark and angry side.

*Ever.*

And that brought her back to Logan.

She wandered through the house, adjusting the tilt of Aunt Tina's artwork on the walls. Running her hand over the furnishings she'd arranged in the living room and bedrooms now that the beautiful old floors glowed with burnished charm.

Despite what Logan thought he'd heard her say, she did trust him to be honorable in all things, because she seen him with clients, Emma and the staff.

Even when he hadn't realized that others could inadvertently overhear him, his kindness had never wavered. He'd erased more than one bill for an elderly client on welfare and examined a child's puppy when there was no way the family could pay. And that was just when she'd been around to notice.

There was no way Logan Maxwell would have embezzled that money in Montana. No way at all.

But unprovoked anger...that was another issue entirely. One she would never tolerate. Should she call him on it? Make herself perfectly clear on that score?

Apparently it was a moot point, if they were no longer speaking.

With a sigh, she grabbed her keys and purse to go after Emma, who would be far better company than an irritable Montana cowboy who apparently didn't know what he was throwing away.

But if she managed to track Logan Maxwell down, she would definitely be letting him know.

## Chapter Eighteen

Storms rolled through late Friday night, and Saturday morning was unseasonably hot and muggy. By afternoon the humidity was ninety percent and felt like wearing a blanket in a sauna.

With the clinic closed for the long weekend and both Marilyn and Kaycee out of town, there was no one to ask about any calls from Logan, and there were no calls on the office answering machine when Darcy stopped in to check on the two canine patients that had needed to stay over the holiday.

The kennel girl always came early to clean cages and feed any animals before going to her next job, so Darcy had rarely seen her, but everything was clean and in perfect order back in the kennels.

Coming back down the hall, she paused at the door of Logan's office. There was no sign that he'd been here today—the desk was tidied, with no half-empty coffee cups or the scattered papers of a task in progress. The computer was off.

She started to call his cell, then dropped the phone back into her purse.

If he glanced at his incoming calls, he'd see that she'd tried several times already. Many more tries and she would seem like an obsessive, scorned woman bent on confrontation.

If he had any desire to talk, he knew her number.

The stormy sky was darkening as she drove home with Emma after stops at the grocery store and the old-fashioned ice cream store for a hamburger and a sundae.

But it was the sudden sickly green tint overhead and the deadly calm air that had her worried.

"Can we go to the park?" Emma craned her neck to look around and pointed. "We could go that way."

Darcy glanced at the rearview mirror. "I'd like to, sweetie. But we have groceries that need to be in the fridge, and it looks like rain. Maybe we can go after supper."

"Please?"

"Later." Darcy pulled to a stop at the next corner and turned right.

The flowers at the base of the stop sign were as still as a watercolor painting, ominous for all their beauty. The leaves on the trees were motionless.

The birds were silent.

Darcy flipped through the radio channels as she drove the last few blocks to their house, catching only snatches of music and talk shows.

No one on the radio seemed concerned. It was probably nothing. Maybe just a front blowing through.

But as she drove slowly up Cranberry Lane, past the stately brick homes that overshadowed her own little cottage, she began to see curtains pulled back to reveal worried faces and a few of the neighbors standing outside with hands on their hips, staring up at the sky.

At home, she drove into the garage, grabbed the groceries and Emma and hurried into the house, clicking the garage door closed with the remote on her key ring. Even here, the towering oaks were motionless.

Lightning cracked in the distance, followed by a long roll of thunder.

Bonnie scrabbled at the back door as Darcy unlocked it. She raced outside, then threw herself at the door to come back in.

As soon as the door reopened, she came in with her tail tucked and pressed herself against Darcy's leg.

Emma wrapped her arms round the dog. "I'm scared, Mommy. Bonnie is, too."

"It's okay—I promise. We've got a nice, safe basement, so we can go down there if the weather gets worse, and there haven't been any sirens going off, so—"

A low, piercing siren split the air, rising to an earsplitting high note, then slowly undulating. Another siren began in some other part of town, and the discordant wails sent a shiver down Darcy's spine.

"That's our cue, sweetheart. Let's go." On her way to the stairs, Darcy shoved her cell phone in her pocket, then grabbed her purse, a flashlight and the old-fashioned portable radio Aunt Tina had always kept on top of the fridge. She took Emma's hand and descended the steep, narrow wooden stairs with Bonnie close at her heels.

At the bottom, she pulled the cord dangling in front of her to turn on a single bank of fluorescent lights over the washer and dryer.

Emma trembled. "I don't like it down here, Mommy. It's scary."

It wasn't a place Darcy enjoyed much, either. The house had been built in the 1900s and no doubt remodeled many times, but the four basement walls were original—constructed of massive, uneven stones held together with cement, and the floor was perpetually damp.

As a child she'd thought it reminiscent of a dungeon in some spooky, medieval castle, but during the intervening years, Aunt Tina had painted the walls a stark white. It was less gloomy now, though the lights still threw dark shadows in the corners where anything in a little girl's imagination might hide.

Darcy squeezed Emma's hand and smiled. "Do you know what? Even with a dehumidifier, it's too damp down here ever to finish off as a family room, but I think I'll put another coat of white on the walls and have a lot more lights installed. At least it will be nicer if we have to come down here again during a storm."

Emma wrapped her arms around Bonnie's neck. "Can we go back upstairs yet?"

Rain and hail battered at the narrow basement windows. Lightning flashed and thunder roared and a loud *crack!* shook the house, sending dust swirling down from the floor joists above their heads.

At the far side, cement steps led up to the sloped cellar doors leading to the backyard. They'd been padlocked for as long as Darcy remembered, and she'd never tried to open them, but now they rattled and bucked against the high winds, the hinges squealing.

*Logan.*

His name slammed into her thoughts. A warning, a plea. Where was he? What if he hadn't answered his phone because he was lying somewhere hurt, unable to call?

Or maybe he'd already been arrested and extradited back to Montana—though she had no idea if such things could happen that fast.

Thinking about his sharp comment and remembering Dean's temper, she'd assumed the worst about his behavior. She hadn't tried calling again.

She felt her heart wrench.

If something bad had happened, she hadn't had a chance to say goodbye. Then again, maybe it was just this weather giving her such dark thoughts.

Now the screaming of the warning sirens competed with the strident wailing of emergency vehicles, and Darcy's heart pounded.

Ten minutes later, silence fell.

Emma hugged her dog tighter and looked up, her eyes round and frightened. "Is our house okay, Mommy?"

"I think so. Just take my hand while we go up."

Darcy slowly made her way up the stairs and opened the door into the kitchen.

The sky was starting to lighten, but the wind still sent buffets of rain against the windows. She walked through the house, checking the windows for damage and surveying the yard, with Emma and Bonnie close at her heels.

"The house seems fine, but I'll need to stand outside to see if we lost any shingles. Look here—out the front window."

A massive oak lay uprooted in the neighbor's yard, blocking his drive and most of the street. One branch had broken away the front porch.

Power lines lay in tangles on the street beneath its upper branches and were sparking and snapping between the neighbor's house and the next one down.

"They won't be going anywhere soon." Darcy flicked a light switch. Sure enough, the power was out. "But our drive is clear, and none of the power lines are compromised at the other end of the block, so I believe we can get out safely. I'm going to try."

Emma's eyes filled with worry. "Where are we going?"

"I need to check on Logan, so you get to play with Mrs. Spencer for an hour or so. I just don't want…" Darcy hesitated. "I just want you to have some fun for a while. It'll be really boring if you come with me."

The rain slowed, then stopped. She glanced at her cell phone again. No calls, no texts. But of course not—she would have heard the alert.

She called 911 for police assistance to check on the neighbors, and the power company to report the downed wires.

Biting her lower lip, she tried calling Logan again. No answer. Then she dialed Mrs. Spencer.

If Logan no longer cared about her, so be it.

But she had to make sure he wasn't lying injured somewhere at his place and in need of help. And if he was, she couldn't waste another minute. *Please, Lord, let him be all right.*

## Chapter Nineteen

The streets were clear to Mrs. Spencer's house, though after Darcy dropped off Emma and headed out of town, she encountered numerous uprooted trees and heavy branches blocking the streets.

After zigzagging through town to avoid the blockages and power company utility vehicles, she finally made it onto the county road leading out to Logan's. The damage was even greater out here, cutting a swath heading to the northeast through the heavy timber.

At the lane leading up to his place, she repeatedly had to get out of her car to drag heavy branches to one side. Up around the house and barn, the damage was worse.

Several large pines had toppled over in his yard, and one had broken through the fence. Another one had landed on roof of his house at a crazy angle, and it looked as if some of the branches had crashed through the shingles and into the attic.

"Logan?" She ran toward the barn, calling his name, then surveyed the corrals. Not even the horses were in sight, though when a whinny echoed from the barn, she found just the bay gelding in a box stall. At the house, she jerked open the front door and ran through the rooms, searching for him to no avail.

His truck was still in the garage. But it didn't appear that he'd left for Montana on his own volition or otherwise.

His billfold and truck keys lay on the kitchen counter. A plate on the counter held a raw steak, ready to grill. Where in the world was he? And where was his dog?

Every doubt she'd had about him, every nonchalant thought about easily walking away from him after that last tumultuous encounter, all dissolved, leaving her feeling bruised and empty.

She didn't need explanations or apologies or even promises…she just needed to find him and make sure he was all right. Nothing else mattered.

Because Logan Maxwell had truly stolen her heart.

Exhausted, Logan rubbed his free hand over Drifter's muddy neck and continued the litany of reassurances that he no longer believed.

State forest backed up to his secluded place on three sides, his driveway was long, and traffic was rare on the county road passing his property.

If not for the rusty mailbox, a stranger driving past wouldn't even know his place existed, much less think to traverse his twenty acres of timber and meadow unless hunting illegally. And without any phone reception out here in this hilly terrain, there was no way to call for help.

So he was here alone, except for his injured horse and a dog that kept running off. He would hear Cedar barking her head off somewhere, and then she'd come back, even during the worst of the storm today. If she was hunting, she hadn't brought back any evidence of prey, but she'd looked more weary with every trip into the forest.

If he even moved a few feet, his beloved Drifter would bleed out. So he'd stood beside her to compress her wound and keep her still, and tried to keep the sharp branch impaled in her chest from moving. The miracle was that it hadn't severed a major artery...yet.

There was nothing else he could do unless someone happened by—as improbable as seeing a penguin toddle past—except for mulling over the stupid things he'd done in his lifetime and wishing he had another chance to do them right.

And he could pray.

Since last night he'd had plenty of time for that.

He'd started out angry at God last night for taunting him with the inevitable loss of his beloved mare, right after he'd walked out on the best thing in his life. *Darcy.*

Though he still counted himself a believer, for years his rebellious heart had refused the thought of prayer in a time of need. Why bother? His prayers had sure never been answered before when it mattered most.

He'd prayed relentlessly, tearfully, as a teenager when Dad had his heart attack and died. Had prayed desperately when Mom died months afterward. And during the long months of Gina's illness, he'd begged God to save her.

None of his prayers had saved the people he loved.

But today he'd stood out in the forest through a fierce storm, with lightning crashing all around him, refusing to give up on Drifter's life. And in his exhaustion and desperation during those interminable hours, the words of his family's pastor nudged at him, prodded at the wall of ice around his heart. *God created this world and the*

*laws of nature that exist. He doesn't want terrible things
to happen...he doesn't cause them, Logan. But when they
strike, he wants to surround us with his loving arms and
give us strength, and hope, and peace. And the people
around you are an answer to your prayers.*

As the hours passed, he finally began to understand
how wrong he'd been about those prayers. God had answered in other ways. The wonderful, supportive hospice
staff. The friends and family who had hovered like angels to offer loving comfort. Who had stepped up to help
with the harvest, the cattle, the horses, and helped Susan
and him deal with the deluge of decisions that followed.

From far away came the sound of Cedar barking.
Barking. Barking. Slowly coming closer. But it was a
different sound this time—more agitated.

If she was after a badger or other fierce wild prey,
there wouldn't be a thing he could do to help her. *Please,
Lord, bring someone to help me...and please keep that
foolish dog safe.*

She fell silent. Then he heard her crashing through
the brush close by.

And this time, there were footsteps behind her.

If she hadn't heard Cedar's frantic barking, Darcy
never would've known which way to go. She pulled to
a halt the moment she saw Logan and his mare.

Drifter was caught in a tangle of downed pine trees,
with an undoubtedly sharp broken branch protruding
from her chest.

Pale, clearly exhausted and weaving on his feet,
Logan was holding that branch steady and stemming
the flow of blood from a wound on her neck that might
well have sliced an artery, given its position.

She instantly assessed the situation. "One of us needs to stay. The other needs to bring back the right equipment—stat. Tell me what you want me to do."

"I need to stay and keep her stable."

Darcy had never run so fast in her life, through the brush. Picking up random deer trails. Praying. She made it to the clinic and back in under an hour, laden with everything she could carry that they might need.

After delivering an intravenous sedative, she spread a sterile surgical drape on the ground and laid out her instruments, surgical gloves and a bag of sterile saline for flushing the wounds. "You or me?"

"It had better be you. I'm not sure I could even hang on to a scalpel right now."

Within an hour she'd meticulously cleaned the wounds. Repaired the neck injury.

Sutured the inner layers of the gaping chest wound, and sutured what she could of the outer layer. After delivering an intramuscular dose of long-acting antibiotic, she gathered up her equipment and rolled it up into the surgical drape.

"It's the best I can do out here without better light," she said, giving Logan a closer look. He was muddy and streaked with blood. Given the gash on one cheekbone, some of that blood was his own. His shirt was torn, and from what she could tell, he was barely staying on his feet. "You look awful. Why don't you start home? When Drifter is more alert, I can lead her back to the barn."

"I'll wait."

"No, you should go. There's no way I can carry you home if you collapse, and I doubt the EMTs could get here anytime soon. They probably have their hands full with all that happened in town."

"How bad was it?"

"I saw a lot of trees down, some damaged roofs. But I just saw a part of town on my way out here, so I don't know about the other areas. There were a lot of sirens."

"Your house okay?"

"Good. But yours didn't fare quite as well. There's a tree down on your roof, and another one broke your fence line."

He nodded. "That corral fence went down in the storm last night. Charlie was easy to catch, so I put him in the barn, but Drifter was still racing around in the yard. I opened the pasture gate in case she headed that way. Figured I could get her into the barn that way, but lightning struck close by and she just kept running until she crashed into this."

"Why didn't you call me? I would've come right away."

"I figured helping me would be the last thing on your mind. A little later on I came to my senses and figured at least you might send someone else, but then I realized that there's no reception out here. If I left her, she might've bled to death."

Darcy wanted to shake him. "You angrily miscon-strued what I said to Marilyn at the clinic. You gave me no chance to explain, and then you walked away. But I certainly would have helped you anyway. That's what friends do. But just so you know, Dean acted like that all the time, and I'll never, ever go through that again. Not with anyone. So—"

She faltered to a stop and took another hard look at him. His gaze veered away.

"Wait. You did that on purpose?"

He didn't answer.

"Why?" She thought back over the last few weeks. Despite her resolution not to become romantically involved with anyone after her disastrous marriage, she'd thought she and Logan were becoming closer. She'd even kissed him. Twice. But clearly he hadn't shared her feelings. He'd been trying to get rid of her, for goodness' sake. Embarrassment burned through her. "Never mind. I can guess."

"Look, you've built a good life for yourself. You don't deserve to be mixed up in my problems," he said wearily. "You have no idea what it's like. The rumors. The doubts. Even after you're proven innocent, people figure you're guilty and just got off easy. It's why I finally left my last practice. And now, apparently it has caught up with me here."

So this wasn't about a brush-off, then. He'd been trying to *protect* her? In a completely awkward and somehow endearing way, but still.

"Look. I'm sorry that your ex-girlfriend is trying to stir up trouble. I'm sorry that you might need to go back to Montana to prove her wrong and get this straightened out. But I know from the bottom of my heart that you're totally innocent. I know what kind of man you are, and none of that stuff in Montana matters. I just hope it can be straightened out for good, so you'll never have to deal with it again."

A faint smile crooked one side of his mouth. "I have it on good authority that the morning crowd at the cafe all want to be my character witnesses. One old duffer even offered to take up a collection for my defense."

"That would be Wally. Purple shoes?"

"Yep—and he also promised to send me prison mail if things don't work out."

She laughed. "After a slow start with the locals, it sounds like you've won them over, after all. Just think. You've got an excellent staff at your clinic. A devoted following in the over-eighty crowd, and a dog smart enough to go for help. She came and got me, you know. I was headed the wrong away and she kept barking and trying to lead me here."

Drifter's ears flickered. She raised her head a few inches as she started to coming out of the sedation. Logan stroked her neck. "About the future…"

She felt her heart still.

"I've talked to my banker and my lawyer about drawing up an offer for a contract, with annual payments leading to full partnership. Just what Dr. Boyd planned, if you're still interested."

It was what she'd hoped for. The perfect resolution. Starting a practice of her own would have involved a huge investment and a great deal of risk.

Yet…it took some effort to smile.

Was that all there was between them—just a business contract? Had she been wrong all along about where this might be going?

One day she'd be locked into a full partnership— granted, in a career she loved—and when he found a beautiful bride and had two beautiful children, she'd get to stand by for the rest of her career and see them all have a beautiful life.

The thought was depressing.

He'd moved a little closer while she was thinking those cheery thoughts, and now he rested a hand on her shoulder and gently lifted her chin with his other forefinger. "I thought you'd be happy. Isn't this what you wanted all along?"

"Yes—yes, of course."

"If you'd rather just be an associate, that's fine, too. But I thought you'd rather have a legal stake in the business, come what may. It would give you more financial security."

"Absolutely. Thanks." She looked away, not quite able to meet his eyes, knowing he would see only disappointment, not satisfaction. *Legal* stake? This was only *business*?

Then she lifted her gaze to his.

The warmth in his eyes sent a shiver straight to her toes.

"I know it's early days, but—" his voice roughened "—I love you, Darcy. If we can only be partners, so be it. But if you say there's even a chance for us, you'll make me the happiest guy in Aspen Creek."

She reached up on tiptoes and pulled him down for a kiss that answered his question and more. And when he drew her into an embrace, she melted against him, wrapped her arms around his neck and kissed him again.

And looked forward to what the future might bring.

# Epilogue

Logan slipped an arm around Darcy's waist and leaned over to kiss her cheek, then picked up Emma as the bridal party gathered under the trees. "You two look beautiful tonight, ladies."

Darcy grinned up at him. "Mighty good-looking yourself, cowboy. You clean up exceptionally well."

The old phrase was certainly appropriate—not two hours ago, they'd been performing an operation on a severe colic case, and they'd made it out here to the county park with minutes to spare. Now, Logan was wearing a dark sports jacket and gray slacks, while Emma wore a flouncy, fluffy dress with matching pink socks and shoes.

Darcy had resisted buying a dress for herself, then found a silver sheath dress with matching shoes at the last minute.

They slipped into the back row of chairs, where Emma wouldn't be a distraction if she got restless. "Can I stay up for fireworks, Mommy?"

Darcy doubted she'd last that long, but smiled. "You can sure give it a try."

The small crowd was settling into the white chairs

facing a simple altar set up along the shore of Aspen Creek. Off to one side, the harpist finished playing the beautifully haunting strains of "Somewhere in Time." Then the violinist seated next to her joined in a duet of "Ave Maria." The sweet, achingly emotional violin sent shivers through Darcy, and she closed her eyes to savor every note.

"This couldn't be a more perfect evening or a more beautiful wedding," she whispered. "I'm just so happy for Hannah and Ethan."

The harpist began a solo of Canon in D by Pachelbel. Everyone rose and turned as the wedding party came down the aisle—Molly and Cole, the niece and nephew whom Hannah had adopted, and their two dogs, each sporting a big white bow.

"I hear Ethan's paperwork is completed, so he will be adopting the kids, as well," Darcy whispered. "Hannah says he's thrilled about making it official."

Hannah and Ethan walked down the grassy aisle next, arm in arm, to join the children. Hannah's radiant expression and Ethan's adoration of her touched Darcy's heart.

Throughout the open-air chapel, she saw other friends and neighbors and people from church, and her heart warmed. Coming to this town after closing a painful chapter in her life had been one of the best decisions she'd ever made and had led her to the most wonderful man she could have imagined.

She smiled to herself, remembering that first day when she found an unexpected stranger in the clinic and thought he spelled disaster for her future in Aspen Creek. And later, when she'd gone to auction and ended up losing Edgar but gaining the best prize of all. Surely

God's hand had been guiding her, because otherwise she might never have ended up so blessed.

After the wedding buffet, some of the guests left, but the rest settled on a hill in the park to watch the fireworks display. Emma curled up in Logan's lap, her eyes already closing as the dazzling explosions of diamonds filled the sky.

Logan looked down at her with chagrin. "I hope you'll both remember this as a really special day, so I got each of you something. But I'm afraid she won't be awake to see hers until tomorrow."

"What is it? Can you tell me?"

He took another look at Emma's sleeping face, then lowered his voice to a whisper. "I hope she'll be happy to find that her preschool pal isn't the only little girl with a playhouse."

"She will love it! Thank you so much!"

He grinned. "That's not all. Remember Pepper?"

"Anna's pony. Oh, no—did her dad make her give him up?"

"He stopped by this morning." He looked down at Emma to see if she was still asleep, then continued in a lower voice. "Anna's riding instructor found them a pony a little better suited for her. He said he wanted a good home for Pepper and has given him to Emma as a gift."

"That's wonderful," Darcy breathed. "Emma will be so thrilled."

Logan slipped something from his pocket and handed it to her, then draped an arm around her shoulders and drew her close. "And here is something for you. Not quite as big as a pony, unfortunately."

Her heart stilled as she stared at the small box in his hand.

"You can open it later if you want, but this just seemed like the perfect place to give it to you."

She turned the small box over, savoring the moment. Wondering if she was holding the key to her entire future in the palm of her hand. Slowly, very slowly, she lifted the lid, barely able to breathe.

Inside lay a platinum engagement band strewn with diamonds, with a glittering solitaire at its center. "Oh, it's…it's stunning!"

He gave he shoulders a little squeeze. "Try it on and see if it fits."

She slid it on her ring finger, feeling utterly dazzled. So happy she could barely contain her emotions.

His eyes twinkled. "So what do you say, Darcy Leighton? Same date next year?"

Mindful of her sleeping daughter, she turned to cradle his beloved face with her hands and leaned closer to draw him into a kiss.

The biggest and brightest of the fireworks were now filling the sky, but they didn't begin to match what she felt, with Logan in her arms.

\* \* \* \* \*

# HER SINGLE DAD HERO

Arlene James

I know some truly intelligent, talented, loving, beautiful professional women, and quite a few of them live in Oklahoma, but only one is my niece. Hillary, your many accomplishments speak volumes, but your faith is especially eloquent. I'm so proud of you!

Do not conform to the pattern of this world, but be transformed by the renewing of your mind. Then you will be able to test and approve what God's will is— His good, pleasing and perfect will.

*—Romans 12:2*

## Chapter One

The sprawling old house creaked and groaned in the afternoon heat. Its cedar siding expanded with reluctant moans, while the steep, gleaming metal roof snapped impatiently beneath the relentless July sun. Such was summer in south central Oklahoma.

Having grown up here on Straight Arrow Ranch, Ann Jollett Billings found the heat of mid-July no surprise. She was used to worse, frankly, and better, having spent the past six years in Dallas, Texas, being a manager in the finest hotel that city had to offer. Despite the opulence of her usual surroundings, however, what Ann now found difficult to bear was not the utilitarian inconveniences of her childhood home but the silence.

She couldn't recall the last time that she'd had more than a few quiet hours to herself, let alone two whole days. Managing a hotel meant being on call virtually around the clock; managing a ranch, not so much, even apparently during the "busy season." At least her brother had claimed this to be the busy season before he had taken off to Tulsa with his new wife and adorable baby girl to settle personal business and put his condo on the market, leaving Ann in charge of the family ranch during his absence. She'd taken the time to fully computerize their bookkeeping, which would allow Rex to track everything online. Their sister, Meredith, a nurse, had left the afternoon after Rex, on Sunday, to take their father, Wes, to Oklahoma City for his second chemotherapy treatment. The house had been as silent as a tomb ever since.

So who was pushing a chair across the kitchen floor? That noise, Ann suddenly realized, could not be anything else.

"Oh, Lord," she prayed softly, "please don't let this be happening. Not here. Not now."

Rising from the battered old desk in her father's study, Ann crept to the door that led into the foyer and listened. The screeching stopped, but other sounds ensued. She was definitely not alone in the house. Her imagination, fueled by her years in Dallas, conjured numerous scenarios, none of them innocent. Reason told her that theft was a rare thing around the small town of War Bonnet, Oklahoma, which lay five miles or so away. Rarer still in the outlying rural surrounds, but perhaps one of the employees of the custom cutter hired to install the new feed bins and harvest the oat and sorghum crops had assumed that, with Wes and Rex gone, the house would be empty and, therefore, easy pickings.

Well, she was no helpless female. Never had been; never would be. At five feet eight inches in height and a hundred thirty-five pounds, she had enough heft to do some damage, if necessary, though more than once she'd wished otherwise.

"All right. If this is how it has to be," she whispered,

"then give me strength, give me wisdom, give me courage, and send that thief running."

Moving quietly in her expensive Gucci flats, black jeans and lace-trimmed, jade-green silk T-shirt, she eased open the door of the coat closet at the foot of the front stairs and reached inside for the baseball bat that had been stored there since her brother had left home for college twenty years earlier. She could have taken the shotgun or the rifle from the high shelf, but it had been too long since she'd used a gun. Besides, she knew how to swing a bat for maximum effect, having played four years of fast-pitch softball in high school and three in college.

Holding the bat at her side, she slunk in long, silent steps across the foyer, through the living room and dining room to the door of the kitchen, glancing out the windows as she went. She saw no new vehicles parked alongside the dusty, red-clay road that ran between the ranch house and the outbuildings that sheltered machinery, fodder and livestock, primarily the horses used to work the two-square-mile Straight Arrow Ranch. The regular hands—Woody, Cam and Duffy—lived off-site and would have simply come to the front door if they'd needed to speak to her.

She lifted the heavy wood club into position and darted through the door into the kitchen. A dog—a mottled, black-masked blue heeler with brown markings, one of the better herding dogs—wagged its tail expectantly beside a kitchen chair pushed up to the counter, atop which kneeled an impish redheaded boy with his arm buried up to the elbow in the owl-shaped cookie jar.

"Hello!" sang out the boy, his bright blue eyes hitting a chord of familiarity within her. Completely unrepentant to have been caught stealing cookies, he turned onto his bottom, pitched a cookie to his dog and crammed another into his mouth. "Mmm-mmm."

Stunned, Ann let the bat slide through her hands until she could park the butt on the floor and lean against the top. "Thank You, Lord!" she breathed. Then, in as reasonable a tone as she could muster, she demanded, "What do you think you're doing?"

He blinked at her, his freckles standing out in sharp contrast to his pale skin.

"Eatin' cookies," he answered carefully as if any dummy could see that.

His eyes were the brightest blue she'd ever seen, far brighter than her own pale, lackluster shade. He had eyes like sapphires. Hers more closely resembled the sun-bleached sky of a hot, cloudless summer noon. Suddenly she remembered where she'd seen eyes like them before, and to whom they belonged. Dean Paul Pryor. The very reason she was stuck in this dusty backcountry.

She had first met Pryor at her brother's wedding reception, when Rex had identified him as the custom cutter who would be harvesting their oat and remaining barley crops and installing the new feed storage and mixing station while Rex, his new bride, Callie, and her baby daughter were in Tulsa on a combined honeymoon and business trip. Pryor had presented himself again that morning when he'd reported for work.

Dean Paul Pryor was everything Ann disliked in a man: tall, gorgeous, confident, masculine. She suspected he stood taller than her brother, who was at least six foot two. Dean might even be as tall as her dad, at six foot four. Solidly built, he outweighed her by at least fifty pounds. Add the short, thick, wheat-blond hair, gem-like blue eyes and the square-jawed perfection of his face, and he had everything he needed to make most women melt at his feet. But not her.

He'd mentioned that morning that he had his son with him. She hadn't expected the boy to be so young, however. This child couldn't be older than six or seven.

"Where is your father?" she asked icily, taking a choke hold on the bat again.

"Workin'," came the laconic answer.

Obviously the father, as well as the son, needed to be taught some manners. Well, this wouldn't be the first spoiled brat who she'd had to deal with or the first lazy, uninvolved parent she'd had to set straight. *This* was why she didn't have children, why she never intended to have children. One of the reasons.

"Come."

Shrugging, the shameless imp helped himself to several more cookies. What he couldn't stuff into his mouth, he crammed into the pockets of his baggy jeans before hopping down onto the chair and then the floor. As she had no intention of eating the cookies or anything he'd touched, she allowed it. He began to push the chair back toward the table, its feet screeching across the wood planks.

"Leave it!" Ann ordered, her eyes crossing at the high-pitched noise.

The dog barked sharply as if in agreement, and the boy again shrugged. Ann again pointed to the door, and he happily set off, the dog falling in at his side.

"Mmm, Mizz Callie mawkz ze bezz cookeez," he said around the mass in his mouth as Ann escorted him through the house.

"Didn't anyone ever tell you not to talk with your

mouth full?" she scolded, stopping to put the bat back in the closet.

Nodding, he looked up at her with those big blue eyes, gulped and said, "You sure are pretty. And you got red hair like me." He grinned suddenly, displaying an empty space in the front of his mouth where a tooth should be. "Come and meet my dad, why doncha?" With that, he turned, opened the front door and ran outside, the dog scampering after him.

Her mouth agape, Ann snatched a faded ball cap from its wall peg, a shield against the relentless summer sun and the possibility of freckles, crammed it onto her head and went after the miniature thief.

From the corner of his eye, Dean Paul Pryor caught sight of his son in the field just south of the big red barn. As previously instructed, Donovan stopped at a safe distance to watch as Dean used the small, rented crane to drag a cone-shaped steel bin on stilts from a flatbed trailer and carefully, painstakingly stand it upright. Dean let out a sigh of relief as four workers in white hard hats guided the stilt legs of the bin to the concrete base. Donovan, meanwhile, munched his cookies and watched, rapt, as the workers settled the five-ton bin, one of several, and began bolting it down.

Smiling, Dean shook his head. He should've known that nothing, not even chocolate chip cookies, could keep the boy away from the construction zone. What red-blooded boy could resist the lure of heavy machinery and risky maneuvers? At least Donovan had sense enough to keep his distance.

Just then one of the workers dropped a fist-size nut

meant for an enormous bolt. The nut bumped across the uneven ground.

The boy darted forward, yelling, "I'll get it!"

Dean's heart leaped into his throat. Abruptly letting out the clutch, he killed the engine on the old crane and bailed out of the cab, waving his arms and shouting over the sound of screeching metal as the full weight of the bin suddenly came to rest.

"Donovan! No! Get back! Get back!"

The boy froze in his tracks then began creeping backward. The worker who had dropped the nut quickly retrieved it and began threading it onto the bolt sticking up from the concrete base. Pocketing his mirrored sunglasses, Pryor strode toward the boy. To Dean's surprise, Ann Jollett Billings got to Donovan before he did, pulling the boy backward several steps. Dean temporarily ignored her.

"Son, I meant it when I told you that you couldn't help with the feed bins," he said firmly. "It's too dangerous. That's why I sent you to the house."

"You *sent* him to the house?" Ann demanded.

Dean swept off his hard hat. He never could ignore her for long, and as always she was a sight for sore eyes, especially with that familiar old baseball cap on her head.

"Hello, Jolly," he said around a grin.

She gasped. "Jolly!"

The nickname, a reference to her middle name, Jollett, had once been used by those closest to her, but Dean had momentarily forgotten that particular circle had never included *him*. The look she gave him said so in no uncertain terms, the message coming across loud and clear. He sucked in a quiet breath.

"You really don't remember me at all, do you?" he

asked on a wry chuckle, scratching his nose to hide a hurt that he had no real right to feel.

She tossed her long, wavy hair off her shoulder with a flick of her hand. "Should I?"

"We went to school together."

"We did not."

"Oh, we did," Dean insisted lightly. "I was ball boy for the softball team all four years you played."

Ann stiffened. "That was you?" Obviously she didn't like being reminded of those she had once considered beneath her. "Ah. Well, you're younger than me, then."

"Not that much younger. Three years."

"A lifetime in high school," Ann retorted dismissively.

"High school," Dean said drily, "doesn't last forever. Three years makes a difference at thirteen and sixteen. Not so much at twenty-five and twenty-eight."

She lifted her pert little nose. "Matter of opinion."

Stung, as he had so often been in the past by her, he switched his attention to the boy. "Get your cookies?"

"You sent him to the house to steal cookies?" Ann yelped.

"How is it stealing," Dean asked, frowning as he plunked his hard hat onto his head again and pulled his son to stand against his legs, "when Callie left the cookies for him and told us where to find them?"

He saw the shock of that roll over her, deflating her anger, but then she lifted that stubborn chin again.

"He should at least knock."

Dean looked down at the boy. "Donovan, did you knock?"

"Yessir."

"I was sitting at the desk in the study, right next to the front door," Ann argued.

"I sent him to the *back* door," Dean Paul pointed out, "because his shoes were dusty." He looked down at Donovan again. "What did Miss Callie say you were to do if no one answered?"

"Go in and he'p myself."

Dean looked to Ann, who colored brightly even as she sniffed, "Well, no one told me."

He lifted his eyebrows to tell her that wasn't his problem. Then he looked down at his son and said, "Why don't you and Digger go explore the corrals while I take care of the big feed bin." He speared Ann with a direct, challenging look then. "If that's all right with you."

"Yes, of course," she muttered.

"Just don't go into the stables," Dean warned his son.

"Mr. Wes said it was okay."

"Yes, he did, but you're not to go in there alone. I'll take you inside to look at the horses later. Understood?"

"Yessir." The boy reached into his pocket and produced a cookie for his father. Despite the boy's grimy hands and the melting chocolate, Dean took it and bit off a huge chunk.

"Yum."

"Don't tell Grandma," Donovan said in a husky whisper, "but Mizz Callie makes the best cookies."

Dean held a finger to his lips, but the boy was already running toward the big red barn and the maze of corrals beyond it. Smiling, Dean polished off the remainder of the cookie in a single large bite.

"He may be right," Dean mused after swallowing. "All I know is that they're really good. Don't you agree?"

Ann jerked slightly. Then she nodded, shook her head, nodded again. "I'm sure they are."

He swept his gaze over her. "You haven't even tried them."

Was she that vain now, this polished, sophisticated version of the fun, competitive girl he used to know—and admire? Did that svelte figure and the fit of those pricey clothes matter more to her now than a little sugar, a moment's enjoyment? Oddly, it hurt him to think it, but it was none of his business. Nothing about her had ever been any of his business, much as he might have wished it otherwise.

"He's awfully young to be out here with you, isn't he?" she asked pointedly.

"Donovan's been coming into the field with me since he was toilet trained," Dean informed her. "I figure he's safer with me than anywhere else. I always know where he is and what he's doing. Besides, I want him with me. The day's fast coming when he can't be."

"I see. Well, it's your business."

"It is that."

"And I don't care for sweets," Ann called defensively as he turned away and began to trudge toward the newly installed feed bin, plucking his sunglasses from his shirt pocket.

"It shows," he drawled, and not just in her trim figure. Her attitude could use some sweetening, in his opinion, but he couldn't fault her shape.

Telling himself to put her out of mind as he had so often done before, he strode to the feed bin, climbed the attached metal ladder and began releasing the chains with which he had hoisted the heavy, white-painted steel bin into place. Tomorrow he would begin harvesting the oats that would be stored in this particular bin.

The second bin—this one painted green—was even

larger and would contain the sorghum crop. This, too, Dean would harvest, but only after the oats were in, as much more heat would strip the oats of their protein content. After that, a blending plant would be built.

Rex and Wes Billings had decided to take the ranch onto an organic pathway. Wes had started the process months ago when he'd allowed Dean to plant and oversee the two forage crops without any pesticides. To Dean's surprise, Rex had even given up his law practice in Tulsa to permanently move home to the Straight Arrow Ranch and oversee the transition, while his dad received treatment for his cancer. Wes imagined that Rex's wife, Callie, had something to do with that decision.

If Rex was happy living on the Straight Arrow and practicing law in War Bonnet, the tiny Oklahoma town where he, Ann and their younger sister, Meredith, had all gone to school, then Dean wished him well, but he couldn't imagine that Ann would follow suit. She had long ago let her disdain be known for this community and everyone in it, himself included, not that she'd ever seemed to know he was alive until now.

So why, Dean wondered, did he feel particularly slighted? Why had Ann Billings always had the power to wound him?

Ann marched across the pasture to the road. Red-orange dust settled on the toes of her buttery, pale leather flats as she crossed the hard-packed dirt road that ran between the big sagging red barn and the house. She told herself that Dean Pryor's disdain meant nothing to her. Why should it? He was just another local yokel. She'd barely noticed him in high school—and yet now that she thought about it, he'd always been there on the periphery during what she thought of as her jock phase.

Memories of that time in her life made Ann mentally cringe. She hadn't stopped to think back then that being able to compete with her brother, out-swinging half the guys on the baseball team and generally acting like a tomboyish hoyden would mark her as less than feminine. Her middle name, which she shared with her mother and grandmother, had been a source of pride for her, even when the coach who'd given her extra batting practice with the boys' baseball team had shortened Jollett to "Jolly" and the nickname had stuck. It hadn't occurred to her that being seen as "one of the guys" would literally mean being seen as one of the guys. Even now, though, all these years later, she couldn't seem to outlive either the nickname or the impression.

Around War Bonnet and the Straight Arrow, she was Jolly Billings, the mannish, unfeminine daughter of Wes Billings, and nothing she could do would change that. No matter that she rose every morning at daylight and ran for miles to keep her figure. Never mind that she spent hours every day on her makeup and hair or wore the finest Manolo Blahnik shoes and Escada suits, not that the clodhoppers around here even knew the difference.

No, she didn't belong here, could never again belong here. Suddenly she longed for the anonymous, frenetic energy of Dallas and the quiet, reserved presence of her fiancé, Jordan Teel. At 41, Jordan was thirteen years her senior, but then Ann had always been mature for her age. That, she told herself, was why she had forgotten Dean Pryor, the younger batboy for the softball team.

She heard the phone ringing before she got back to the house and hurried inside to find her brother calling.

Pushing aside thoughts of Dean Pryor, she took notes as Rex advised her of the contractors who would soon be journeying from Ardmore and Duncan to bid on building a garage behind the house and remodeling the master bedroom for him and Callie. Ann promised to take the bids, scan them and email them to him.

As they talked, she heard Donovan's high-pitched voice outside, speaking to his dog, Digger. Before long, Ann mused, her little niece, Bodie Jane, would be running around the place much like Donovan did now. That was what she and Rex had done. They'd run wild, practically living on horseback and knocking out every step their dad had taken around the place until school had intruded.

Being the youngest, Meredith had spent more time with their mom, Gloria, but Ann had desperately wanted to do everything that Rex and Wes had done. That, no doubt, had been her downfall.

Unbidden, other words ran through Ann's mind.

*You sure are pretty. And you got red hair like me.*

At least Donovan thought she was pretty, and it seemed to matter that she had red hair like him.

Not that she cared one way or another what the Pryors thought.

She yanked off the ball cap and touched a hand to her long, stiffly waving locks, wondering when its shade had ever before been a plus for her. She wished Callie had told her that she'd given the kid free run of the house before she'd taken off to Tulsa with Rex and Bodie. Maybe then she wouldn't have come off so…tough. Maybe she'd have had a chance to appear soft and womanly.

On the other hand, Dean Pryor had known her a lot longer than she'd realized. She'd probably never be able to overcome the image of her hard-slugging, hard-driving, super-competitive past with him.

Not that it mattered. Actually, it didn't matter one whit what he or anyone else around War Bonnet thought of her.

*Jolly.*

She shook her head. It had been a long time since anyone had called her that.

Not long enough.

## Chapter Two

"Watch it, Dean!"

"Sorry."

So much for *not* thinking of Ann Billings. Dean Paul pulled his attention back to the job at hand, getting the lift chains on the feed bin released without braining any of his help or injuring himself. A man could easily lose a finger if he didn't focus. Besides, what did it matter? He'd never been anything but an underclassman to her, and he was still obviously underclass in her estimation.

He could live with her low opinion of him, but it burned him up that she'd thought his son had been stealing cookies. Dean had learned to swallow his anger and focus on his joy a long time ago. Nevertheless, he couldn't help wanting to give her a piece of his mind where his boy was concerned. He listened as he worked and caught the sound of his son talking to his dog in the distance. The exact words escaped him, but the tone of Donovan's voice assured Dean that all was well. His five-year-old son, born Christmas Day, was the gift of a lifetime, in Dean's opinion.

Smiling, he released the last heavy link and let the

chain fall, calling, "Heads up!" He tossed the heavy, locking S hook to the ground and descended the ladder.

When Rex had told him that Ann would be here to oversee and help with the build-out and harvest, Dean had felt a secret thrill of anticipation, but apparently nothing had changed in the last decade. She still obviously thought she was too good for the likes of him. And maybe she was. God knew that he'd made more than his fair share of mistakes in this life already.

Being a father to his son was not one of them, however. Being Donovan's dad had shown Dean that he could do anything that he had to do. It had also given him more joy than he had known the world could contain. That was all he needed, more than he'd ever expected, enough to keep him thanking God every day.

No matter how hard things got, Dean would thank God for Donovan Jessup Pryor. Those sparkling blue eyes and that happy smile gave Dean's life purpose. That little red head warmed Dean's heart as nothing else could. He just wished he had better answers for the inevitable questions that Donovan had begun to ask.

*How come I don't have a mom?*

*Why don't she want us?*

Dean had asked those same questions his whole life and still had no satisfactory answers for them. Grandmothers and aunts were wonderful, but they weren't mothers. At least Donovan had a father who loved and wanted him. At least he'd been able to give his son that much.

It was more than Dean had had.

Hopefully it would be enough, for Dean didn't see himself marrying anytime soon. He could barely afford to feed himself and Donovan, let alone a wife and any other children. In a perfect world, he'd like a half dozen more kids.

But Dean Paul Pryor's world had never approached anything near perfect. The closest he'd ever come was the day a nurse had placed a tiny, redheaded bundle in his arms and exclaimed, "Merry Christmas!"

He had wept for joy that day, and the memory still made him smile.

What was another snub, even one from Ann Jollett Billings, in the light of that?

He shook his head and got back to work. The men helped Dean chain up the first of ten-ton storage bins and connect it to the crane. Then Dean climbed into the cab of the crane and started the engine. Donovan and Digger showed up again, the boy's curiosity alive on his freckled face. He grinned and waved, showing the empty space where he'd knocked out his baby tooth jumping from the tire swing in their front yard. Dean sighed, torn between satisfying that little boy's love of all things mechanical and keeping his kid at a safe distance.

His first instinct was always to keep Donovan as close as possible, and soon that would no longer be close enough. Donovan would start kindergarten in a month, and their days of constant companionship would come to an end. Sighing, Dean killed the engine on the old crane once again and climbed down out of the cab. He walked to his pickup truck and extracted a hard hat and a 40-pound sandbag then waved to the ever-hopeful boy.

Donovan darted across the field, stumbling slightly on the uneven ground, the cuffs of his oversize jeans dragging in the dirt. He'd torn the pocket on his striped polo shirt. Grandma would have to mend it before putting it into the wash. His socks would never be white again but a pale, muddy, pinkish orange. He needed boots for playing out here in these red dirt fields, but he grew so fast that Dean dared not spend the money for them. The dog loped along behind him, its pink tongue lolling from its mouth.

Dean patted the side of the truck bed, commanding, "Digger, up!" Obediently, the dog launched himself into the bed of the truck. "Stay."

Panting, the heeler hung its front paws over the side of the truck, watching as Dean adjusted the liner of the hard hat and plunked it onto Donovan's head.

"I could use a little help with these big bins."

Donovan's smile could not have grown wider. "Yessir."

Dean lifted the sandbag onto his shoulder and walked with his son to the crane. Reaching inside, Dean pushed down the jump seat in the rear corner of the cab. Then he tossed the sandbag into the opposite corner before lifting Donovan onto the jump seat and belting him down.

"Sit on your hands," he instructed, "and keep your feet still."

Donovan tucked his hands under his thighs and crossed his ankles. Nodding approval, Dean climbed up into the operator's seat again.

"Keep still now," he cautioned again as he started the engine once more.

So far as he could tell, the boy didn't move a muscle as Dean guided the crane to lift the feed bin from the tractor trailer, swing it across the open ground, position it and carefully lower it, guided by the hands of his temporary crew, into place. Thankfully the job took only one try. When the chains at last went slack, Donovan hooted with glee. Dean glanced over his shoulder, smiling.

A wide smile split his son's freckled face, but he sat

still as a statue. Dean's heart swelled with pride, both because the boy was truly well behaved and because he had derived such pleasure from watching the process. Dean killed the engine and swiveled the seat to pat the boy's knee.

"Good job."

"That was so cool!" Donovan swung his arm, demonstrating how the steel bin had swung through the air, complete with sound effects.

Chuckling, Dean slid down to the ground. "Stay put. We've got two more to do."

After all three bins were in place and secured, Dean released his son's belt and lifted him down from the crane cab.

"You're the best oparader!" Donovan declared.

"I'm an adequate crane operator," Dean said. "Couldn't have done it without you." He leaned inside to grab the sandbag with which he'd balanced his son's weight, hefting the bag onto his shoulder once more.

Still wearing his hard hat, Donovan proudly walked back to the pickup truck with his father. "I helped, Digger," Donovan told his dog.

Caramel-brown ears flicking against his mottled dark gray head, the animal waited for a discernible command. Dean dumped the sandbag into the bed of the truck and ruffled the dog's fur before snapping his fingers next to his thigh to let the dog know he could hop down. The dog vaulted lightly to the ground.

"Why don't you guys go play in the shade while I load the crane onto the trailer?" Dean said, pointing to the trees in front of the house across the road.

"Can't I help?" Donovan whined.

"Not this time," Dean told him, taking the boy's hard

hat. "I think I remember a swing on the porch. I'm sure it's okay if you and Digger want to swing for a bit. Then, after I talk to Miss Ann, we'll go look at the horses."

Donovan dug the toe of his shoe into the dirt. "O-kay."

"Sure is hot out here," Dean said, lifting off his own hat to mop his brow with the red cloth plucked from his hip pocket. "You need to be in the shade. Maybe we can stop for a snow cone on the way home."

Donovan's eyes lit up. He loved the sweet, icy treats, especially the coconut-flavored ones that turned his mouth blue.

"Yay! Come on, Digger." They ran across the dusty road and into the trees.

Dean sighed. Cookies and snow cones. They'd be dealing with a sugar high this evening for sure. Well, five-year-old boys hardly ever stopped moving. He'd burn it off before bedtime. Besides, Donovan was a good eater. The only vegetables he wouldn't touch were Brussels sprouts and cooked greens. Big for his age, he was pretty much a bottomless pit already.

Dean shuddered to think what it was going to take to feed his son at fifteen. He worried that they might have to move away from War Bonnet for him to make a decent living, but most of his work came during harvest time, and even with Oklahoma's elongated season, he hadn't yet been able to make those earnings comfortably stretch through the whole year.

Putting aside those thoughts, he went back to work, thankful that Rex Billings had tapped him for this extra job. Soon he had the rented crane loaded. While the crew chained it down so that it was ready for pick-up, he traded his hard hat for the clean, pale straw cowboy hat that his grandma had bought him for his birthday just two weeks earlier. Then he walked to the house, weary to the bone, to get payment from Ann. After showing Donovan the horses, he'd drive straight to the bank with her check, deposit it and pay his help.

When he stepped onto the porch, he found Donovan and Digger on the cushioned swing, Donovan singing softly as he pushed them both. The boy started to get up, but Dean waved him back as he stepped up to the door.

"I'll only be a few minutes. You stay right there."

"Okay, Dad."

Dean opened the screen door and rapped his knuckles against the heavily carved inner door. After only moments Ann stood frowning up at him. He didn't know what she had to be unhappy about or why she seemed intent on taking it out on him. Her grumpiness did not, unfortunately, detract from her looks.

She had an unusual face, a longish rectangle with a squarish jaw and chin, prominent cheekbones and a high forehead. It was the sort of face that could have been outfitted with features from either gender, but hers were unmistakably feminine, from her perfect lips to her dainty, straight nose and the gentle curves of her slender brows over her big, exotic eyes. Those eyes were like orbs plucked from a clear blue sky, ringed in storm gray around shiny black pupils. They suited her as nothing else could have. He'd always thought her one of the most beautiful girls, even when she'd had freckles splattered across her nose and cheeks. He kind of missed those freckles.

Aware that he was staring, he cleared his throat. "All done for now."

She inclined her head, her red hair sliding across her face. Of a more muted shade than Donovan's, more golden, less orange, it glistened like copper pennies. Dean frowned. Hadn't her hair been brighter at one time? He fought the insane urge to rub locks of it between his fingers to see if the color rubbed off and exposed the brighter hue he seemed to recall.

Turning, she led the way into the study where he had conducted his business with her father and brother. Dean lifted off his hat, stepped inside, pushed the door closed behind him and followed. Leaning over the desk, she signed a check, tore it from a large, hard-backed checkbook and handed it over.

"I really didn't know about the cookies," she said defensively. "Callie didn't tell me."

He glanced at the check, folded it and stashed it in his shirt pocket. "I suppose she had a lot on her mind, what with the wedding and all."

The young widowed mother had come to keep house for the Billings men and help take care of Wes, who was fighting cancer. It had quickly become obvious to everyone who saw them together that she and Ann's brother, Rex, were made for each other. They had married within weeks.

Ann dropped down into the chair behind the desk, muttering, "I suppose. I don't really see what the rush was, though."

Surprised, Dean lifted his brows at that. "Don't you?"

"No," she stated flatly, laying both of her hands on the desk blotter. "I don't."

He saw the big diamond on her left hand then, and understanding dawned. Along with unwelcome disappointment. "Ah. And how long have you been engaged?"

"Not long," she said, smiling and leaning back in the

desk chair, "but I don't intend to rush things. A proper wedding takes time to plan."

His throat burned with a sudden welling of acid. "Does it? I thought Rex and Callie's wedding was everything *proper*."

"You know what I mean."

"No. Sorry, I don't."

Ann rolled her pale eyes. "Well, for starters, I won't be getting married *here*."

He nodded, an ugly bitterness surging inside him. "Got it. War Bonnet's not good enough for you."

Blinking, she rose to her feet. "No, that's not it at all. It's just that the majority of my friends and most of my business contacts live in Dallas now."

"Uh-huh."

She folded her arms. "What's that supposed to mean?"

"Nothing. Just…" He really needed to shut his mouth and get out of there. Instead, he said, "You haven't changed much, have you? Except you're coloring your hair now." He knew it suddenly, and she confirmed it by lifting a hand to her hair, something like guilt flashing across her face.

"What do you mean, I haven't changed? I've changed a lot."

"No, you haven't," he said, knowing he was being rude but unable to help himself for some reason. "You're still a snob."

She jerked as if he'd hit her. "I am *not* a snob."

"Really? Couldn't prove it by me." He might as well still be the ball boy to her athletic highness.

"What do *you* have to do with it?" she demanded.

"Not a thing," he told her, thumping his hat onto his head and turning away.

"And what's wrong with my hair?" she demanded.

He looked back at her. "I like the real you better, that's all."

"You don't know the real me," she snapped.

He let his gaze sweep over her, liking what he saw, missing what he didn't see, wishing otherwise on both counts.

"Don't I?" he asked. "You still look and act like the queen of War Bonnet High to me."

With that, he finally got out of there, calling himself ten kinds of fool. The queen, after all, couldn't be expected to do more than barely acknowledge her servants.

Calling herself the very worst kind of fool, Ann guided her father's pickup truck off the dusty road and over the rough cattle guard between the pipes supporting the fencing. She didn't know why she'd come. Rex had told her simply to make sure that Dean could get his equipment in and out of the field without problem. As the weather had remained hot and dry, Dean could have had no issues whatsoever, so she really had no reason to trek out here and inspect the job site. His rudeness the day before should have been reason enough to forgo this particular chore, and yet she'd found herself dressing with ridiculous detail for an encounter she had no desire to make. Why should she care what he thought of her, after all? Yet, here she was in all her feminine glory, including denim leggings, a matching tank top and a formfitting, crocheted cardigan that perfectly matched her white high-heeled sandals.

Dean had obviously taken down a section of the barbed wire in order to get his combine into the field. He was even now using a come-along to draw the post back into position, the wires still attached, so he could temporarily restore the fence. Ann beeped the truck's horn to stop him then killed the engine and got out.

Watching her pick her way across the ground on her high heels, he let the wire stretcher drop, stripped off his leather gloves and took off his sunglasses, dropping them into his shirt pocket. The hard hat had been replaced by a faded red baseball cap, which he tugged lower over his eyes. Dirt gritted between her toes as she made her way toward him, but she refused to show any discomfort. At least the early-morning temperature wouldn't melt her carefully applied makeup or frizz her hair, which she'd painstakingly set on heated curlers after her shower and predawn run. Resisting the urge to tug on the hem of her tank top, she plastered on a smile and tucked her muted red hair behind one ear so he could see the dainty pearl earrings she was wearing.

"I meant to tell you yesterday," she announced. "Rex had the hands move all the cattle to the east range, so you don't have to worry about replacing the fence until you're done here."

He glanced around, his gaze landing on her feet. "Okay. Good to know. Thanks."

She heard barking a second before Digger shot out of the thigh-high golden oats, a yellow bandanna clenched in his doggy teeth. Giggling wildly, Donovan careened behind him. The dog skidded to a halt, facing Donovan, who snatched at the bandanna. Turning, the dog took off again, making straight for Ann and Dean. Before either could react, the animal bolted between them and came to a taunting halt just beyond. Shrieking with laughter, Donovan gave chase. Right across Ann's toes.

"Ow!" Yelping in pain, she reeled backward.

Dean lurched forward, grabbing her by the arms and

pulling her into his embrace even as he scolded the boy. "Donovan Jessup! Watch what you're doing."

The child immediately sobered, turning to face the adults. "I'm sorry."

Ann staggered against Dean, her elbow digging into his side, his very solid side. His large, heavy hands cupped her other elbow and clamped her waist, steadying her. Those were the hands of a real man, strong, capable, sure. She felt dainty, safe and cherished in that moment.

"You okay?"

Aware that her heartbeat raced, she ignored her throbbing toes to smile and nod. "Yes. Thank you."

"Good," he said, dropping his arms and stepping back. "Next time you come out here, maybe you'll wear boots."

Ann gasped, her silly illusions abruptly shattered. "And maybe you'll control that wild thing you call a child," she snapped, regretting the words the moment they escaped her mouth.

Dean's expression instantly hardened. "Let me walk you to your truck," he stated firmly.

Setting her jaw, Ann intended to refuse—until she caught sight of Donovan's face. The dismay on that small, freckled face smacked her right in the chest. She bit back the caustic reply on the tip of her tongue and allowed Dean to clamp his large, hard hand around her arm just above her elbow. They moved across the ground in silence. She teetered and danced across the uneven terrain while he strode purposefully along beside her.

When they reached the truck, he opened the driver's door and all but tossed her up behind the wheel before stepping close, looking her straight in the eye and commanding flatly, "Don't ever speak that way in front of my son again."

"I won't," she capitulated softly. "I'm sorry."

Dean relaxed a bit and sucked in a calming breath. "He's five. He makes mistakes, but he's a good boy. He'd have apologized again if you'd given him a chance."

She nodded. "I was just…hurt. And I didn't realize that he's so young."

Dean shifted until he was halfway inside the cab, draping his left arm over the top of the steering wheel. "He's big for his age, I admit." He rubbed a hand over his face before asking, "Your toes okay?"

For some reason she couldn't seem to breathe as easily as she ought to, but she managed to squeak, "I think so."

"Next time," he said quietly, pointedly, "wear boots."

"Don't you like my shoes?" she asked, truly curious about that.

A crease appeared between his brows. "What's that got to do with anything?" Angling his head, he looked down at the floorboard. "Your shoes are fine. That's not the point." He looked her in the eye, adding, "If you're going to come out here, you need the proper footwear."

"Unfortunately, I only have dress shoes and running shoes."

"Well, you better go shopping, then."

"In War Bonnet?"

He chuckled. "Most of us drive to Ardmore or Duncan or even Lawton or Oklahoma City."

"That's more than an hour away!"

"I'm told that it can take more than an hour to drive across Dallas."

He had her there. "True. But I know where to shop in Dallas, and I wouldn't have to drive across town to do it."

Shrugging, he backed out of the cab and straightened. "Risk your toes, then. Just don't say I didn't warn you."

Great, she thought. So much for showing her feminine side.

She just could not win with this guy. No matter what she did, it turned out wrong. She didn't know why it mattered.

Somehow, though, it did matter. A lot.

Still, she had a job to do here, and she was all about doing the job. That, at least, she could manage. If she needed boots to do the job, she'd figure out how to get her hands on a pair of boots. Couldn't be that difficult. Right?

## Chapter Three

Ann had once owned numerous pairs of boots, but she'd thrown them all away, convinced that such masculine attire should no longer be tolerated. She wondered if her sister had done the same, however. Long ago she and Meri had worn the same size shoes. In fact, they'd worn the same size everything, then Ann had experienced a sudden growth spurt during her freshman year in high school and shot up several inches. Everyone had expected Meredith to follow suit, but she never had. Still, looking in Meri's closet was worth a shot.

Though Meredith's surviving cat had traveled to Oklahoma City with Meri and their father, Ann opened the door to her sister's bedroom with some trepidation. Meredith had an apartment in the city and, while on temporary leave at the moment, worked as a nurse in the very hospital where Wes was even now receiving his chemotherapy. Generous to a fault and sweet, Meri was, nevertheless, manic about her cats, one of which had been accidentally killed on the day of Rex's wedding.

Her room showed her obsession. Every kind of cat contraption imaginable filled the space. Connecting tubes, scratching posts, toys, feeding stations and an elaborate litter pan/carrier thingy. Meri even had framed photos of her cats, including the dead one. Meredith still blamed the local veterinarian for not saving the poor thing. Ann certainly would not have done away with the cat, but one cat per house seemed quite adequate to her. Meredith claimed that Ann just didn't understand, and Ann supposed that was true. She was more of a dog person, really.

The intelligent face of Donovan Pryor's dog came to mind with its perky, twitching ears and alert black eyes. That dog certainly seemed smart and playful, a great companion for a little boy.

This space was too small for the amount of cat junk crammed into it, Ann noted. There was hardly room enough for the bed.

After searching her sister's closet, Ann found three pairs of Western boots. All proved too small, so she reluctantly accepted defeat before carefully closing the bedroom door behind her.

Her next step took her into War Bonnet, but Mrs. Burton's Soft Goods had long since closed, and the local grocery sent her to the Feed and Grain, which offered nothing more than work gloves and tool belts. She stopped at the gas station to refuel her BMW coupe for the drive out of town, and that was where she ran into the one person she had most hoped to avoid.

Jack Lyons had been a fixture at War Bonnet High for at least two decades. So far as Ann knew, he had never married. All indications were that he ate, drank and slept sports. Yet it was common knowledge that he had turned down positions with much larger school districts, and for that he was greatly revered by the local populace. Coach Lyons had spotted Ann's athleticism early on, but he hadn't offered her extra batting practice until she'd buckled down and gotten serious about improving her stats and landing a softball scholarship. The extra practice had meant working out with several of the guys on the baseball team.

Those practice sessions had involved lots of teasing and laughter, but Ann hadn't cared. Like every other kid who played for Lyons, his respect meant everything to her. She hadn't always managed to hold her own against the guys, but she'd done so often enough to be good-natured about it when she failed. This had prompted Lyons to tag her with the Jolly nickname, a play on her middle name, Jollett. Ann had done her best to live up to the label.

Under his tutelage, the softball team had won their district championship four years in a row, with Ann as the team's number-one slugger. Coach Lyons had written her glowing recommendations, and she'd managed to win a minor scholarship to Southeastern State in Durant, where she'd studied business management and marketing. For the next three years she'd driven home as often as she could, and she'd never failed to stop by the school and say hello to Coach Lyons. He'd always seemed happy to see her. Then, near the end of her junior year, she'd stopped by the field house just in time to overhear a conversation between Lyons and another teacher.

"Saw Ann Billings pull into the parking lot a minute ago." It had sounded, strangely, as if the other teacher, Caroline Carmody, was warning Coach.

He had sighed and said, "Guess that means she'll be here soon."

Ann had paused beside his office door to listen, puzzled.

"What's the deal with her?" Caroline had asked. "She's been out of school for years. Why is she still coming around?"

"The awkward ones are like that sometimes," the coach had opined.

"You think she's awkward?" Caroline had asked.

Jack Lyons had snorted. "She's taller than half the male population. She could outhit most of the teenage boys I've worked with, and if you cut off her hair, I'm not sure you could tell the difference."

Horrified, Ann had slapped a hand over her own mouth to keep from crying out in pain.

"It's true she's not the most feminine girl I've ever known," Caroline had said with a chortle. "If she comes back to War Bonnet after college, she'll probably wind up an old maid out on that ranch with her mom and dad."

Lyons said something else, but Ann hadn't stayed around to listen. She'd run as quickly and quietly from the field house as possible.

Some serious thinking had followed, and her conclusions had been painful.

Her parents had not encouraged her to date during high school, and the pickings around War Bonnet had seemed slim at best, especially once she'd started outdoing many of the guys at sports. For most of her college career, she'd focused on academics, sports and working enough to help her parents afford tuition and expenses. Her disinterest in partying had ruled out a great many prospective dating partners, but she hadn't worried about it. Now, suddenly, she wondered if something might be fundamentally wrong with her, if she was seriously lacking in the feminine qualities necessary to attract male interest.

Horrified by the future painted for her by Coach Lyons and the teacher, Caroline Carmody, she had taken steps to ensure that she would never be War Bonnet's pathetic spinster. Telling her family that she wanted to focus on hotel management, she had transferred to the University of North Texas for her senior year. The move had required her to give up her scholarship, take several extra classes and delay graduation until the age of twenty-two, but she'd made up for all that with hard work and early success in her field.

She'd told only one other soul about the fears she'd nursed for so long.

Her fiancé Jordan's only response at the time had been to say that War Bonnet's loss was Luxury HotelInc's gain. Later, when he'd proposed, Jordan had reminded her that no one in War Bonnet could possibly value her as much as he and LHI did.

Ann had successfully avoided conversation with Jack Lyons until that very morning at the gas station. Jack climbed up out of his vintage Mustang and reached for the gas nozzle. He'd put on a bit of weight, but he still looked almost exactly like he had the day he'd impacted her life. His gaze slid over Ann on the opposite side of the pump with a friendly, disinterested nod then came back for a second look.

"Jolly!" he exclaimed, making Ann cringe.

"Coach," she returned quietly, willing the slow old pump to fill the coupe tank faster.

Lyons walked around the pump to take a long look at the coupe.

"Very nice. Series 4?"

She nodded.

"I always knew you'd make good," he said, smiling. "You still in Dallas?"

"Yes. I manage a hotel there."

His gaze raked over the car again. "Big, fancy hotel, I imagine."

"You could say that. I, uh, I understand you're head coach now."

"Athletic director," he corrected proudly.

She put on a smile. "Ah. Congratulations."

"Thanks. How's your dad? Heard he's been ill."

She nodded. "Undergoing chemotherapy."

"Oh, I'm sorry to hear it."

"I'll tell him you asked about him."

Lifting her arms, she swept her hair back with both hands, trying not to fidget beneath his stare.

"Is that an engagement ring I see, or have you taken to wearing a house on your finger?" he quipped.

Feeling rather smug about it, Ann straightened the cushion-cut diamond. "I am engaged, as a matter of fact."

"Congratulations. Dallas boy?"

"Not a boy," Ann said pointedly, "and not from Dallas, at least not originally. He's actually from New Hampshire, though he's moved around a lot. Right now he's filling in for me while I'm here helping out."

"So you're coworkers, then."

"Not exactly. He used to be my boss. Now he's upper management in another area of the company."

"So when you're married you'll be living where?"

"I'm not exactly sure," she admitted. "Jordan is working that out with the company now."

"Won't be in War Bonnet, though, will it?"

"No. It won't be in War Bonnet."

Jack nodded. "Well, don't be a stranger."

The fuel pump clicked off. Ann turned away with a sense of satisfaction mingled with relief, saying, "I'll try not to. I really need to get going now."

He pushed away from the truck. "Important doings, huh?"

"Boot shopping."

"Ah. Where you headed?"

"Duncan, I suppose." Ann replaced the cap on the neck of the gas tank.

"Try the Western wear store on 81," he advised.

"Okay."

"Good seeing you," he said, wandering back toward his vehicle.

Smiling, Ann climbed into the car, started up the engine and drove away, thinking how odd it was that the man who had so impacted her life would never know how he had changed things for her. Had she not overheard that conversation that day, she might well have finished school, come back to War Bonnet and…what? She'd had some vague notion of taking over the ranch at some point, but other than that…

For some reason, Dean Pryor's face sprang up before her mind's eye, so real in that instant that she gasped.

Heart pounding, she shook her head. Dean Paul Pryor was nothing to her. He could never be anything to her. Why, he didn't even compare to Jordan.

She told herself that was because Jordan existed on an entirely different plane than the men in War Bonnet. He was suave, polished, always expertly groomed. She'd never seen him in anything other than a classically tailored suit. Jordan's idea of casual wear was a suit without a tie, but even then he tended to favor silk T-shirts in place of his usual handmade dress shirts. She wondered if he even owned a pair of jeans. He must. They'd been friends for years, and she'd seen photos of him swimming and skiing. Surely he didn't wade up out of the ocean or come down off the slopes only to relax in a nice three-piece, Italian wool suit. It was just that most of their interactions had taken place in more formal surroundings.

Truthfully, Ann didn't have much of a life outside the hotel. Being on call twenty-four hours a day, seven days a week put a damper on a girl's social life. That was why she and Jordan had become friends in the first place; she just didn't have a lot of other options.

When Jordan had returned to Dallas to temporarily take over for her during her leave of absence so she could help her father through this health challenge, Jordan had immediately confessed that he'd formed feelings for her when he'd been her boss that had gone beyond friendship. He'd declared that he meant to sweep her off her feet, and then he'd done just that. In the three weeks they'd had to bring him up to speed on the current operations of the hotel before she'd left for Oklahoma, they'd become engaged.

Strangely, however, Jordan, Dallas and the hotel no longer seemed quite real. Instead, Dean Pryor, War Bonnet and the Straight Arrow were her current reality. Surely it was natural, then, to compare Jordan to Dean.

And yet, she could not bring herself to do it. She simply refused to compare her fiancé to Dean Pryor in any way. She didn't even want to know why.

"Yep, those are boots, all right," Dean pronounced, staring down at Ann's feet on Friday morning. He was very glad that he'd kept his sunglasses on after she'd driven up and gotten out of the truck, for he feared that she'd have read in his eyes exactly what he thought of those pink-and-pearl-white, pointed-toe monstrosities.

Apparently he didn't cover his opinion up well enough, because she brought her hands to her shapely hips and demanded, "What's wrong with them?"

"Nothing!" he exclaimed, shaking his head. "They'll protect your toes out here just fine."

She frowned at the rounded toes of his scuffed, brown leather boots then tilted her head, obviously comparing her own footwear with his. Her boots were designed for riding, with toes so sharp that they almost curled upward at the tips. She had clearly chosen them based on color and style rather than function, but he wouldn't embarrass her by saying so. Unfortunately, Cam wasn't that circumspect.

One of the longtime hands at Straight Arrow Ranch, Cam had evidently known Ann from childhood. How else could he have gotten away with calling her pet names?

"You always did like fancy duds, Freckles," Cam declared, strolling up to the harvester where Dean and Ann stood talking. "Oo-ee! You bought them boots right outta the window of the Western wear store up there in Duncan, didn't you? Why, them things been there nigh on thirty years, I reckon." He grinned at Dean, shaking his head. "Just goes to show that something'll come back in style if you wait long enough, don't it?"

Dean kept his jaw clamped and rubbed his nose, while Ann turned red. She lifted her chin and seemed about to turn on her heel when Donovan ran up behind her. He just naturally threw his arms around her thighs and hugged her, startling a high, shocked yip out of her. To

Donovan, anyone he saw more than twice was a close, personal friend.

"Hello!" he sang, swinging around her body as if she were a maypole, a long-legged maypole wearing hideous boots.

She recovered quickly, smiled and smoothed a hand across Donovan's back. "Hello. Where's your dog?"

For an answer, Donovan put his head back and yelled, "Digger!" The dog bolted from somewhere to the boy's side. "Here he is."

"That's one fine dog," Cam declared enviously. "Show her what he can do."

Thinking that it might take her mind off the boots and Donovan's unorthodox greeting, Dean complied. He put Digger through a series of tricks then nodded to Donovan.

"Ready?" Donovan fell to his knees. "Digger, protect!" Dean commanded.

Instantly the dog knocked the boy to the ground and stood over him with all four legs, growling, teeth bared, while Donovan lay still beneath the animal.

"Digger, safe!" Dean said.

The dog moved to sit beside the boy, its tongue lolling happily from its mouth. Donovan hugged and petted the dog, crooning softly to it.

"That's amazing," Ann said.

"Wish I had me a dog like that," Cam said, not for the first time. "You ought to think about training dogs for a living, Dean."

Dean chuckled. "Not much call for that around here, I imagine."

"I'm not so sure about that," Ann said. "Lots of local

farmers and ranchers use herding dogs. They might be interested in the kind of protective training Digger has."

Dean shrugged. "You can't train just the dog. You have to train the owner, too."

Donovan got up, and Dean went to dust him off, but Ann reached him before Dean did.

"How does your mama manage your laundry?" she asked, ruffling his hair.

"Don't got a mama," Donovan announced baldly. "Grandma does my laundry."

"And a chore it is, too," Dean said quickly, whacking dirt from Donovan's bottom. "Run and get the water jug now. We've got work to do."

Donovan nodded, but he stood looking up at Ann for a second longer. "I like your boots," he said before taking off with Digger on his heels.

"Thank you," she called after him, turning a wry smile on Dean. He had to clear his throat and swallow to keep from laughing as he turned toward the cab of the harvester.

Cam said, "That reminds me. I need to check the water in the east range." He ambled off toward the four-wheeler that Rex had recently purchased.

Dean traded his cowboy hat for the ball cap then turned toward the combine. To his surprise, he felt Ann's hand on his shoulder. He turned his head to find her biting her lip.

"Um, obviously I could use some…guidance."

Guidance. Somehow he thought this could be a momentous admission for Ann Jollett Billings. Letting go of the rails, he turned to face her.

"About?"

She looked down at her toes then up at him. "I've

been away from the ranch for a long time. Obviously I don't have a clue about what boots to buy."

The grin he'd been trying to hold back since she'd first climbed out of her dad's old truck broke free at last. "They sure saw you coming, didn't they?"

She smacked him in the shoulder, which made him laugh. Then she laughed, too.

"They were in the window. I thought they were the latest style. I didn't even look at anything else."

"I hope they were cheap, at least."

"I don't know." She told him what she'd paid, and he nodded.

"Cheap enough." He considered a moment and made a decision. "I've got to take Donovan shopping for school supplies tomorrow. If you want to come along, we'll see about getting you into a proper pair of boots."

"Oh, I don't want to intrude."

"Donovan would love it if you came," Dean pointed out, "especially as Digger will have to stay home." He shook his head. "The truth is, I'm not sure how he's going to manage school without Digger. Donovan was eighteen months old when we got that dog. I'm having to find ways to wean them apart."

"I see. Well, if you're sure."

"I'll work till noon," he told her. "Then we'd planned to grab lunch in town and go shopping after that. Sound okay to you?"

To his surprise, she nodded. "Sounds fine. Thanks. I'll be ready."

"Saturday it is," he told her, turning away again. He climbed up into the cab and tried not to be too obvious about watching her walk back to her truck.

Something about the way a woman walked in a pair

of jeans and boots, even ugly boots, made a man sit up and take notice. Like he hadn't noticed before this. To his disgust, he'd noticed when she'd worn a softball uniform and cleats. Not that it mattered. The woman was engaged to be married, after all, and on her way back to Dallas and her hotshot career as soon as her dad could do without her.

Sighing, Dean straightened his sunglasses as his son ran toward him, hauling the heavy water jug by its handle. He reached down a hand for the water jug as Donovan shoved it toward him. He stashed the jug in a corner then helped Donovan scramble up into the cab of the harvester before following him and settling into the operator's seat.

Donovan leaned against his back and said straight into his ear, "She sure is pretty, ain't she, Dad?"

He meant Ann, of course. Donovan had been playing pint-size matchmaker since Ann had literally caught him with his hand in the cookie jar. For the past year or more, since he'd come to understand what going to school really meant, Donovan had gone on the lookout for a mom. Dean figured it was as much concern about him being on his own during the time Donovan would be in school as it was the boy's natural desire for a mother. The boy didn't realize that most husbands and wives spent relatively little time together and that almost no fathers were blessed with the almost constant companionship of their children.

Dean mentally sorted through a number of possible replies, everything from correcting Donovan's grammar to playing dumb. In the end he chose casual honesty.

"She's pretty."

"And you like red hair, don'cha?"

"I do. But you realize that she doesn't actually live here, right?"

"Huh?"

"She's just visiting, son. Before long she'll go on back to where she came from and stay there."

"Huh. Is it a long ways off?"

"Yep. Afraid so."

Only a few hours away by car. Worlds away by every other measure.

But then that had always been the way with him and Ann Billings.

Donovan couldn't know that, of course.

Dean hoped that he never would.

## Chapter Four

Jordan laughed when Ann told him about her boot-shopping experience, but not for the same reason that Dean had laughed.

"Why bother?" he asked during their phone conversation that evening. "You're only going to be there a few weeks. It's a foolish waste of money and time."

"You wouldn't say that if you could see the fields here. I can't wear my good shoes in this red dirt. They'll be ruined!"

"I suppose you have a point," Jordan grudgingly conceded. "I don't understand why the hired help can't handle things there, though. You have an important job here, and your family ought to realize that."

"Nothing is more important than my father's health, Jordan," she pointed out, "and the ranch hands work the livestock. They know little about the crops, especially now that Dad and Rex are moving into organic production."

"And what do you know about it?" he demanded.

"Only what I've been told," she admitted, "but someone has to give the orders, Jordan. I'm needed here. At least until Rex returns or Dad gets better. I thought you understood that."

He made a gusting sound. Then he said, "I guess I just miss you. We didn't have much time together before your brother's wedding pushed everything forward."

"The wedding didn't push things forward that much," she replied lightly before changing the subject. "Speaking of weddings, I've been thinking about a date for ours."

"Oh, I have, too," Jordan said briskly. "A date opened up here at the hotel for the last Saturday of July, and I think we should take it."

Ann bolted upright on the leather sofa in the living room of the ranch house. "The end of July! But that's…" She quickly did the mental math, torn between elation and panic. "That's eleven days away!"

"Eleven days and a year," he corrected, chortling. "Surely you didn't think I meant *this* year? You said you wanted a traditional wedding, after all. That takes time."

Ann blinked, feeling suddenly deflated. "Right. Of course. How silly of me." She slumped back onto the sofa, frowning.

Her brother, Rex, and Callie had waited only a matter of days to marry. She'd thought their wedding a paltry thing compared to Rex's first one, but she couldn't deny that she'd never before seen the kind of joy on her brother's face that she saw when he looked at Callie. She knew that he regretted the failure of his first marriage, and she thanked God that he'd been given a second chance with Callie.

"There's always the possibility that the Copley-Mains wedding will be rescheduled and we'll have to pick another date," Jordan said. "I'm told that Samantha Copley changes her mind every other day."

"Oh," Ann mumbled. "Yes. I expect she'll change her mind in the middle of the ceremony."

"Well, we'll take the date anyway, and if she changes her mind again we'll adjust," he said lightly before changing the subject to business.

They spent the next hour talking about hotel issues before someone called Jordan away to handle something unexpected. Something unexpected was always coming up. That was why the manager lived on-site. Ann had tried to maintain a separate residence at first but had quickly realized the futility of it.

She went to bed that night feeling uneasy, though she couldn't say why. She and Jordan were a good match. She loved him, and Jordan was eager to marry her. Wasn't he?

Of course he was! He'd made that abundantly clear. She smiled, telling herself that she was going to dream about her wedding.

Instead, she dreamed about a dog performing tricks and protecting a freckle-faced little redhead on command. And the tall, blond, blue-eyed trainer who so obviously devoted himself to that little redhead. She woke in the morning both dreading and looking forward to the shopping trip to come.

No doubt, Callie would have offered to make lunch for Dean and Donovan, but Ann hadn't had much experience in the kitchen. She could open a can, build a passable sandwich and operate the microwave, but she'd followed a recipe only a few times in her life, with mixed results. Meri was more domestic, having spent more time with their mother while Ann had hero-worshipped their older brother and done her best to compete with him.

Nine years her senior, Rex had always been patient with her—to a point, and Ann had always pushed to keep up with or even surpass her big brother. Only later did she realize how unattractive men found women who could and did compete with them. No matter how often she prayed that God would help her suppress her masculine traits, no matter how hard she tried to be more feminine, she just couldn't seem to overcome these undesirable tendencies. Still, she felt compelled to try.

Thankfully, Jordan seemed not to see that side of her. He knew her deepest, darkest secrets, and they didn't seem to matter to him. He valued her as a competent manager and organizer, and he obviously found no fault with her looks. They had much in common when it came to their careers and lifestyles. He'd seemed unconcerned when she'd told him that she wanted to wait till they were married to be together as man and wife, and had said that he wasn't currently a man of faith, but was open to Christianity, and promised that they could discuss it later when they had more time. She'd told herself that was a good sign.

Dean knew her from before, though. She already had a deficit to overcome with him. She couldn't risk spoiling lunch. So, after a longer than usual run and a light breakfast, she took her time dressing. She styled her hair with hot rollers and carefully applied makeup. She chose a pale floral lace tank top with skinny jeans and vanilla, leather spike heels. Once convinced that she appeared as feminine as possible for the task at hand, she went to the office and waited, going over the books and internet articles that Rex had left for her.

She heard footsteps on the porch at a few minutes past noon and was at the front door when the first knock sounded. Opening it the next instant, she greeted Dean with a smile. He wore a clean chambray shirt with the cuffs of his sleeves rolled back and the neck open. The blue heightened the gem-like color of his eyes, and the pale straw of his hat looked very much like the color of his blond hair. He was an amazingly attractive man, even in faded, dusty denim.

Next to him, Donovan wore a blue-and-green striped shirt, baggy jeans and a big smile. He looked up at her and proclaimed, "You look real pretty!"

Ann found that little-boy smile more and more difficult to resist. "Thank you, Donovan."

Dean looked her over and said, "Especially like the shoes."

She narrowed her eyes at him, pretending that she was not very much pleased. "They just aren't too good for tramping across fields."

"Exactly. I am extremely impressed that you can walk in them, though." He shot her a cheeky grin, flashing those dimples at her. "Ready to go?"

Rolling her eyes, she reached over and took her small handbag from the half-moon foyer table. "I am now."

"Did you remember to bring socks?"

Socks. Of course. "Uh, one moment."

Turning, she hurried up to her room, where she snatched a pair of clean socks from the dresser. She had long ago gotten rid of sports and school memorabilia, leaving only the purple, tailored bed coverings and drapes. Before she left here this time, though, she was going to repaint this dresser and the shelving unit across the room. What had possessed her to paint all the drawer fronts and shelves different colors, anyway?

She rushed back downstairs, socks in hand. Dean and Donovan had stepped inside . "Thanks for reminding me," she said to Dean.

"Voice of experience," he told her, opening the front door.

She went out first, checking to be sure that she had the key before hitting the lock and pulling the door closed behind Dean, who followed Donovan. Her dad rarely locked the house, but her years in Dallas simply wouldn't allow her to walk away from an unlocked house. Dean's slight smile told her that he found the precaution unnecessary, but she would never forgive herself if she returned to find her dad's TVs and computer missing, not to mention her own electronic devices.

Of course, the horses and cattle could be taken by anyone bold enough to pull a trailer onto the place, though Wes had installed some motion detection devices at vulnerable spots along the fence line. He had an alarm panel set up in the office, and occasionally a coyote or bobcat set off one of the motion detectors. He'd warned her not to get upset if the alarm woke her, just to check the security screen, and if she saw nothing suspicious take a look at the recording in the morning. Rex, who was apparently some sort of expert on such things, had set up the recording component and arranged for cloud storage, but that security arrangement did not include the house, which seemed shortsighted to Ann.

She followed the Pryors to Dean's somewhat battered, white, double-cab, dually pickup truck. At least she supposed it was white under that thick layer of orange-red grime.

As if reading her thoughts, Dean said, "Hope you don't mind if we wash the truck before we head home." He opened the front passenger door with one hand and the backseat door with the other.

"We had to unload ever'thing so we could," Donovan informed her as he scrambled up into his car seat. "Gotta get out all the tools and stuff afore you can wash it."

Dean chuckled as he buckled Donovan into his seat. "Quite a job, isn't it, bud?" He glanced at Ann, who had yet to slip into her seat. "Donovan earned some extra money to buy school gear by helping me unload the truck bed this morning."

"I'm gonna get some cool stuff!" the boy exclaimed excitedly.

Ann smiled and stepped up into the surprisingly comfortable bucket seat. She was buckled before Dean slid in behind the steering wheel.

"War Bonnet Diner okay for lunch?"

"Is there any place else?"

"Not if you're hungry."

"I'm starved!" Donovan declared from his car seat in back.

"That makes two of us," Dean said, glancing into the rearview mirror as he pushed his sunglasses into place on his nose.

For a starving man, he didn't seem in much of a hurry. He drove in a leisurely fashion that had Ann setting her back teeth. In Dallas, where everyone was in a hurry all the time, he'd have been run off the road. The trip into War Bonnet covered fewer than six miles, but it seemed to take forever. They pulled into town, stopped at the blinking red light just past the Feed and Grain on the edge of town, far longer than required to determine that no other vehicle could possibly impede their pathway, and rolled on.

Dean waved as they passed the gas station then tooted his horn at a madly grinning middle-aged woman in the grocery store parking lot.

"My aunt Deana," he explained.

Every other driver they passed waved or called out a greeting. War Bonnet boasted only a single city block of business buildings, including the town hall, bank, post office, a junk shop that billed itself as a collectibles store, a pair of empty spaces and the café. The school and athletic fields lay on the southwest side of town, beyond the four or five blocks of houses that comprised the remainder of War Bonnet, along with the small church on the southeast side. Her family had attended that church for most of her life, but her parents had switched to Countryside Church after she'd left home.

With tornadoes an ever-present danger in Oklahoma, the joke around War Bonnet was that a good-size dust devil could wipe it off the map. The little whirlwinds routinely whipped up red clouds of dust that danced down the streets, lashed the blooms off flowers, spattered windows with grit and stung eyes. One had even disconnected the electricity to the tornado siren near the school. After that the cable had been buried.

Dean found a parking space in front of one of the empty storefronts, and they walked up the sidewalk to the little café, which bustled with activity. The undisputed social center of the community, the café featured a long counter with eight stools, two booths in front of the plate-glass window and five tables, for a total capacity of thirty-six diners. Donovan begged to sit at the counter, but there were only two stools open, so Dean steered him toward a table in the back corner near a jukebox that hadn't worked in over a decade.

After escorting the boy to the bathroom to wash his hands, Dean ordered a hamburger and onion rings. Donovan asked for fish sticks and fries. Ann decided to try the fruit plate and chef's salad. It was better than she'd expected, but Dean's thick, fragrant hamburger made her mouth water. She'd forgotten how good a simple hamburger could smell. When Donovan offered to trade her fries for grapes, she gave him the grapes and declined the fries then accepted onion rings from Dean.

The moment she bit into the crisp ring, memories swept over her, fun times spent in this place with school friends and family. After she'd gotten her driver's license, she and her friends had hit this place after school, loading up on milk shakes, fries and onion rings before heading off to whatever commitments claimed them. She'd found such freedom in that. No more school buses to catch, no adults around to police their behavior—not that they'd misbehaved really. None of her group had drunk alcohol, used drugs or even dated much. They'd been too busy with school, sports, church, chores and getting their livestock ready for the county fair. True, they'd teased and gossiped and gotten loud, even broken out with the occasional short-lived food fight, but essentially they'd been harmless.

"Ann Billings," said a female voice, jolting her out of her reverie. Opening her eyes, Ann stared at the small, rounded, older woman. Something about her seemed familiar, but the short, curly, iron-gray hair and thick, owlish glasses brought no one to mind. Then the woman cupped her hands together and clucked her tongue, saying, "First your brother, now you. Will all the prodigals return to Straight Arrow Ranch?"

"Mrs. Lightner!"

The old dear smiled and held out her arms as Ann rose to her feet and bent forward for her hug. When she straightened again, she said to Dean and Donovan, "Mrs. Lightner was my Sunday School and piano teacher."

"Dean, Donovan," greeted the older woman, nodding at each. "I'm surprised to see you all together."

"We're going shopping!" Donovan announced happily.

At the same time, Ann said, "Dean is doing some work for the ranch."

"I'm harvesting out at the Straight Arrow just now," Dean explained calmly. "And Donovan's ready to buy school supplies. Ann's going along to find a pair of boots."

"School supplies," Mrs. Lightner echoed. "First grade, is it?"

"Kindergarten," Dean corrected. "He turned five on Christmas Day."

"He's such a big boy that I thought he must be six at least," Mrs. Lightner said. She turned her full attention on Donovan, saying, "You'll do very well, I'm sure."

Donovan nodded eagerly. "Yes, ma'am." He frowned then. "But how come they won't let me take my dog?"

"I'll need Digger with me," Dean told him.

"Oh, that's true," Mrs. Lightner confirmed, nodding sagely. "Even though it's just half a day, your dad will miss you. He'll need the dog to keep him company.

You'll have lots of new friends and teachers, but Dad will be missing his right-hand man."

Donovan sighed. Then he abruptly brightened, split a look between Ann and his father and shook a finger in Dean's face, proclaiming, "You need to get a wife."

"Whoa!" Dean cried, shoving back his chair.

"Out of the mouths of babes," Mrs. Lightner chortled.

"Your grandma can shake a finger at me, buddy, but you cannot," Dean scolded lightly, crumpling his napkin and dropping it beside his plate. "Now, let's get this show on the road. I have things to do today."

Donovan crammed the last bit of fish into his mouth, rubbed a paper napkin over his face and slid down off his chair. Ann stood as Dean pulled his wallet from his pocket and tossed several bills onto the table.

"You're driving, so let me pay for lunch," she said quickly, hoping that would squelch any suppositions that Mrs. Lightner might have about the two of them dating.

He looked at her, his face blank, shrugged and slid his wallet back into his pocket, leaving the gratuity on the table. "Suits me."

Relieved, Ann reached for her purse. At the same time, she felt an unexpected and puzzling sense of disappointment. She didn't have time to think about it, though, as Mrs. Lightner surprised her by sliding her arm through Ann's.

"How is your father?" the older woman asked.

"He's in the city with Meredith for chemotherapy," Ann told her. "Meri calls every day. It sounds pretty tough, but we're trusting that he'll come through okay."

"Everyone here at the town church is praying for him," Mrs. Lightner said.

"Thank you," Ann replied. "We appreciate that."

"So how long are you going to stay?" Mrs. Lightner asked, walking with her to the cash register.

"As long as I'm needed. At least until Rex and Callie get matters settled in Tulsa and come home. My fiancé is filling in for me with my job," Ann said pointedly.

"You're engaged?"

"That's right. If you were at the wedding, you probably saw him."

"I did attend the wedding but not the reception," Mrs. Lightner mused, obviously thinking. She looked up suddenly. "Distinguished, older man, graying temples, expensive suit?"

*Older man? Graying temples?* Ann would have said silver, not gray, but the expensive suit nailed it. She put on a smile. "That's right."

Mrs. Lightner looked to Dean, who waited by the door with Donovan. "Well," she said, "to each her own." Then she hugged Ann again, said her farewells and left.

Stung for reasons that she couldn't quite explain, Ann waved over the waitress, paid the bill and followed the Pryors out onto the sidewalk. She watched them strolling along in front of her, Dean's large, capable hand resting against his son's narrow back while Donovan talked excitedly about some subject that escaped her. Then again, Donovan never seemed to speak in any other fashion. He was an excited, happy, obviously well-loved little boy. And apparently something of a matchmaker.

She wondered where his mother was, then she realized that she'd been trying very hard *not* to wonder. Donovan had told her, of course, that he didn't have a mom, that his grandmother did his laundry, but Ann purposefully hadn't pursued the subject because she really hadn't wanted to know. Knowing the situation would somehow open her to...speculations, unwelcome, unnecessary, troublesome speculations of the sort that no engaged woman should entertain. Especially a woman as unsuited to being a mother as Ann thought herself to be.

Standing aside, she waited while Dean belted Donovan into his safety seat. Then, to her surprise, Dean walked straight past her on his way around the truck. She knew instantly that she'd somehow insulted him, probably by insisting on paying for lunch.

"Dean."

He halted at the front of the truck and reached out a hand to thump a thumb against the hood, but he didn't turn or speak.

"I didn't mean to upset you."

He turned his head then, that cold, blank look on his face. "What makes you think I'm upset?"

"I don't know. I—I just thought it was fair that I pay for lunch."

Nodding, he looked away. "Uh-huh. I really didn't expect anything else from you, Jolly." With that, he walked around the truck and opened the driver's door. He stood there, waiting, until she opened the passenger door and got into the truck.

She didn't know what to say or think, and she really couldn't get into it with Donovan sitting there in the backseat. As it was, the boy sensed the tension.

"Everything okay?" he asked, leaning forward.

Dean turned a warm smile over his shoulder even as he reached for the ignition switch. "Sure, bud. What could be wrong?"

Apparently satisfied, Donovan sat back and began enumerating the items he intended to buy. Ann smiled and nodded.

Like Dean said, what could be wrong?

Or was she avoiding the more important questions? Like, why couldn't she escape the feeling that something very important was wrong?

Why did it suddenly feel as if her whole life was wrong?

## Chapter Five

"Look at this, Dad!"

Donovan held up a red plastic container in the shape of a car with real wheels. Decals depicted the windows and other details, but it could be rolled.

"It's a pencil case," Dean explained, opening the thing to expose the sharpener and storage compartments.

"Cool! Can I get it?"

Dean pulled out his phone and activated the calculator function. "Well, it's not on the list, but let's see if it's in your budget." He helped the boy find the price, figure the tax and deduct the amount from his available funds. Next they checked to make sure the pencil case would fit in Donovan's chosen backpack. "Looks like you'd still have enough to finish your list, so if this is the bonus item you'd like to choose, you can get it."

Crowing, the boy spun around on the heel of his shoe. The pencil box functioned in several ways, one of them being a toy, all for under five dollars. Donovan couldn't have been happier. Ann couldn't have been more impressed. Whatever else he might be, Dean Paul Pryor was a great father. Dean had clearly taught his son the value of a dollar, how to shop and prioritize and to be happy with the most functional things. Later, when they moved on to clothing, she found herself seeking his guidance for her own purchases.

"What do you think of these boots?"

"Real good-looking," he answered, turning one over in his hands. "I'd buy them myself if I could afford them. For Sunday best."

"Not for every day?"

He shook his head, set down the ostrich leather boot and reached for another, one with a rounder toe, lower heel, wider vamp and crepe sole. He tossed it in his hand, saying, "This boot here is lighter by several ounces, easier to get on and off, far better padded where it counts most and it's got a steel toe." She looked down to see a much more scuffed boot in a different leather finish on his own foot.

"Mine's roughout," he said. "You can get this same style in a true suede or a slick leather, even exotics, though I don't recommend that."

She reached for a slick leather in a medium reddish-brown.

"You'll have to polish that one to keep it looking good," he pointed out, "but it's a better-looking boot, for sure."

"I don't mind a little polishing," she said, turning the boot over in her hand.

He smiled. "Try it on."

She quickly discovered what he meant about padding where it counted most—and that her skinny jeans looked a little odd tucked into the tops of these boots, which were not as tall as the showy pair she'd bought in Duncan. She decided to let Dean advise her on the proper cut of jeans to go with her new boots.

The new jeans felt strangely familiar when she slipped them on, and she couldn't help smiling when she recalled wearing Rex's old hand-me-downs. How simple and carefree life had seemed back then. Secure in the love and acceptance of her family, all she'd cared about was the day's activities. She'd never even stopped to wonder what anyone else thought of her. Frowning, she suddenly worried that she might be slipping back into harmful old habits.

When she stepped out of the dressing room, however, Dean's eyes lit up with unmistakable approval. Still, she couldn't help feeling concern.

Twisting at the waist, she asked, "You don't think they're too masculine?"

He barked laughter. "On you? You're the girl who rocked a pair of cleats and a batting helmet. Now you're worried about looking masculine?"

Was he saying that she'd looked good in cleats and a helmet or that it was too late to worry about her femininity? At least Donovan's opinion seemed unambiguous.

"She looks pretty, don't she, Dad?"

Dean ruffled the boy's shaggy hair, saying, "Of course."

Still doubtful, Ann turned her back to the mirror and looked over her shoulder in time to catch Dean's expression in the mirror.

Rolling his eyes, he said, "Look, who's going to see you, anyway? It's not like you'll wear these things anywhere but the field. Right?"

That was true. No one but the ranch hands and these two would likely see her dressed like this. It was far too late to try to impress Dean, and the ranch hands still thought of her as that little girl who ran around the place in her brother's outgrown clothes, so what did she have to lose?

"I'll take them," she decided, and just for old times' sake she'd take a couple of lightweight, long-sleeved shirts, too. If nothing else, they'd help keep the freckles on her arms at bay. She'd leave them here when she returned to Dallas, and Jordan would never be the wiser. Meanwhile, she'd at least be more comfortable while on the job at Straight Arrow Ranch. And maybe—just maybe—she'd feel some of that old, carefree joy, too.

The snoring from the backseat made Dean chuckle. He had no doubt that they'd worn out the boy. Donovan had been dragging his steps long before they'd gotten back to the truck. He'd been snoring almost before his belt had been buckled on his safety seat. Dean knew his son well, though, and he wasn't buying it.

After nearly an hour of silence, as soon as Dean turned the dually onto Straight Arrow Road, Ann asked, "Dean, what did you mean earlier when you said that you didn't expect anything else from me?"

He'd suspected that she'd been stewing about that, but he still hadn't decided exactly how to answer her. He wouldn't be giving her an explanation in front of his son, though. Lifting a finger to his lips, he brought the truck to a safe stop beside the house and shifted around in his seat.

"Hey, pard," he said quietly, "I'm going to walk Miss Ann to her door now. Okay?"

Donovan's eyes popped open. He sat up straight and grinned. "Sure."

Dean looked at Ann, who bowed her head to hide her smile. "You wait right here. I won't be long."

"I'm real tired," the boy said, sounding anything but. "I'll just take another nap."

"You do that," Dean replied, glancing pointedly at Ann again before opening his door and stepping out of the truck, leaving his hat behind.

She let herself out before he could gather up her packages from the backseat and get around to do it, but he supposed that was to be expected considering how he'd acted earlier. He felt a certain amount of shame about that now. He'd had no right to feel slighted by her before; she just seemed to have that effect on him sometimes; too often, actually. Catching up to her, he walked alongside her, his arms laden with bags and boxes, until they were well beneath the trees on the pathway to the porch.

"Let's face it," he finally said, "Donovan was matchmaking back there at the diner, and it made you uncomfortable. I expected you to show Mrs. Lightner that he's barking up the wrong tree, and you did just that."

"So he's done this before," Ann mused.

"Uh, not really," Dean had to say. "It's not like single women are thick on the ground around here. My grandma's always urging me to get out and date, and it's obvious that he *wants* a mother. I—I think it's a matter of you showing up at the right time, and that hair."

"Just as he's about to start school, you mean."

"Exactly."

She reached up and touched her head. "The hair, though…"

They stepped onto the porch.

"*He* has red hair. *You* have red hair," Dean explained. "To him that means you look like his mother. Makes you a prime candidate."

"Ah."

"Of course, I know you're not interested in us." Even though he'd had a terrible crush on her as a boy. She hadn't known it, still didn't know it, and he had no intention of informing her, no more than he had of explaining that her eagerness to rid Mrs. Lightner of any hint that they might be dating, or were even friends, had unexpectedly hurt him.

"Look, Dean," Ann began, but just then the front door opened, and her sister, Meredith, stepped out. "Meri!" Ann exclaimed. "I wasn't expecting you until tomorrow."

"Dad couldn't wait another day to get home. He's terribly ill, though, Annie. I had to pull the car right up to the back door to get him into the house." That probably explained why Dean hadn't spotted the vehicle when he'd driven in, that and Ann's question.

"Oh, honey, I'm sorry I wasn't here when you arrived," Ann was saying. "I wish you'd let me know you were coming."

"I meant to, but frankly I had my hands full just getting him here." Meredith glanced at Dean then, adding, "Looks like you've got your hands full, too." He stepped forward as she reached out and began shifting his burdens to her and Ann, while she explained they'd been shopping.

"Thanks so much for your help with this, Dean."

"My pleasure," he told Ann. "Please let Wes know that Grandma and I are praying for him."

"That means a lot," Meredith said.

"Don't hesitate to call on us if we can do anything else."

Nodding, Ann said, "Say goodbye to Donovan for me."

"Absolutely."

He walked away heavy of heart. Wes Billings was a good man, and Dean hoped fervently that he would beat this awful disease, for Wes's sake but also for the sakes of his children and everyone who knew them. He sensed instinctively that if Wes didn't make it, Ann would likely never step foot in War Bonnet again. Something about that struck Dean as deeply, desperately, sadly wrong.

To Dean's surprise, Ann showed up at Countryside Church the next morning. He'd assumed that her father's illness would keep her away. She'd grown up in this area, so folks greeted her warmly, not that they wouldn't have done the same for a stranger, but she was Wes Billings's girl, and that meant something around here. It didn't hurt that she looked like a peacock among hens in a shiny, cornflower-blue suit that ignited her eyes and made her skin glow. The slim skirt and high heels accentuated her height and long legs. How she walked in them he would never know, but he liked that she didn't try to hide her height. So many tall women did, and it just made them look uncertain and awkward. Ann Billings looked ready to take on the world and left the impression that she could do it without breaking a fingernail.

Still, she looked a little sad and lonely sitting all alone. If Donovan had been there instead of children's church, he'd have rushed up and thrown his arms around her. Dean didn't have his son's confidence that his greeting would be returned with equal warmth, so he contented himself with a nod and a mumble.

"Nice to see you."

His grandmother scolded him, in her fashion, after the service.

"You need to speak to her, Dean. You've had more to do with her than anyone here, I figure, and the Billingses have been good to us."

Betty Gladys Pryor was a stout, tall woman who wore her long, gray hair curled into a droopy bun on the back of her head and gave up her jeans and T-shirts for a dress only on Sundays, but Dean had never known her to own a pair of nylon stockings or a tube of lipstick. She'd worked alongside her husband in the field when they'd farmed wheat and raised two daughters, one of whom—Dean's mother, Wynona—had been a terrible disappointment. Betty still managed a good acre of a vegetable garden every year, as well as her grandson and great-grandson. She spoke her mind but never with rancor and faced each day with calm, patient acceptance and the expectation of joy. Dean had learned, with some difficulty, to value her advice and opinions, but if she had a failing it was thinking more highly of him than she had any reason to.

"Don't you go getting any ideas," he grumbled, even as he began to forge a path through the disbanding crowd to Ann's side. Betty snagged a forefinger in his belt loop and tagged along in his wake.

"How's your dad doing?" Dean asked as soon as he reached Ann, who had yet to leave her pew because of the people gathered around her. She turned a smile on him and spoke in a voice loud enough for all to hear.

"It's pretty rough right now. He isn't allowed many visitors for fear of infection while his immune system is at a low ebb, but Meredith is taking good care of him. He wanted me here today specifically to let y'all know that he appreciates your prayers and support."

"Anything we can do?" someone asked.

"Mostly keep up those prayers," Ann answered.

"You sure got those," someone else said.

"A card now and again would brighten his day," she suggested.

"We can make that happen," one of the women said, and she stepped away with two or three others to discuss a mail campaign.

The crowd began to break up. His grandmother edged forward then, and Dean introduced her.

"Ann, I'm not sure you've ever met my grandmother. Grandma, this is Ann Billings. Ann, my grandmother, Betty Pryor."

"So nice to meet you, Mrs. Pryor."

"Oh, call me Betty or Grandma. Everyone does. Forgive me if I'm stepping on your toes, sugar, but with Callie away, your sister nursing your dad and you running things up at the Straight Arrow, I'm wondering if you couldn't use some good old-fashioned home cooking about now. I'm no Gloria Billings, but I can put together a meat loaf right quick. What do you say?"

Ann looked to Dean, and he could see the relief in her eyes but also the polite protest she was forming. He spoke before she could.

"You put it together, Grandma. I'll deliver it."

Ann gave in without a fight. "Thank you so much. Callie put up what she could for us, but I'm not even any good at reheating it. I always get the oven too hot or the burner too high. And Meri has her hands full right now. If Dad could just get one decent meal…"

"Tell you what," Grandma said, taking Ann's hand. "I've got some chicken soup canned for when Donovan gets his usual winter croup. I'll send that over, too, and a few other things that are still sitting around from last year's garden. Maybe some creamed corn or bean soup would ease Wes's stomach. You can warm that in the microwave."

"Mrs. Pry—Betty, you are a Godsend," Ann declared.

Just then, Donovan came barreling through a side door. "Dad!"

His teacher waved at Dean to let him know that she hadn't just turned the boy loose. "Sorry!" Dean called. "Got a little held up."

"Donovan, please don't run or shout in the sanctuary," Dean instructed as the boy crashed into his side, waving his class papers.

"Yessir. Boy, we had a good story. Did you know about Lazarus?"

"I did."

"He died, and it was so long he was probably all stinky and everything, but Jesus brought him back." Before Dean could even remark on that, Donovan turned to his great-grandmother. Then he spied Ann and threw himself at her, nearly knocking her backward in his exuberance.

She laughed, staggering behind his hug. "Hello to you, too."

Donovan promptly backed up a step, tilted back his head and declared, "Wow, you sure are pretty."

Ann glanced around uncertainly, but then she smiled and said, "Why, thank you, Donovan."

He grabbed his father's hand and said to Betty. "She sure is pretty, ain't she, Grandma?"

"*Isn't* she," Dean corrected, trying not to look at Ann as he said it.

Grandma hid her smile behind her hand and nodded before answering. "She sure is. That color suits her very well."

Ann shook her head, blushing.

"Come on, you," Dean said, rescuing her by grasping Donovan's shoulders and turning him up the aisle. "We have to get going. Grandma has some cooking to do."

"Woo-hoo!" Donovan crowed.

"What did I say about shouting in the sanctuary?" Dean reminded him.

Ducking his head, Donovan lowered his voice to a near-whisper. "Woo-hoo." Dean started him toward the doors at the back of the long room. "I'm hungry enough to eat a horse," Donovan claimed to no one in particular, "A dead, stinky horse."

Behind them, Grandma and Ann laughed. Dean liked the sound of their mingled voices, and—not for the first time—he wished that he could be as free with his compliments as his son was with his. That ring on Ann's finger tied Dean's tongue, though, not that she wanted to hear compliments from him in any event, a fact he would do well to remember in the future.

By the time Ann heard tires on the red dirt road outside the ranch house later that afternoon, she was half out of her mind.

"That has to be Dean."

"Whoever it is, get them in here," Meredith barked, holding their father's head as he slumped into the corner by the bathroom door. "You should've called me," she scolded for perhaps the tenth time as Ann ran for the front door.

"Man's...got his...pride," Wes gasped.

Ann was still shaking her head about that when she opened the front door to find Dean ambling along the path toward the porch, a big cardboard box in his arms.

"Hurry!" she exclaimed. "We need your help."

He broke into long, loping strides. She stepped back, holding open both the screen and the front doors.

"What's wrong?" he asked as he slipped past her, the box clutched to his chest.

"Dad fell on his way back from the bathroom, and we can't get him up."

"Where is he?"

She hurried around him and quickly led the way through the foyer and along the hallway past the living room and back staircase into the spacious kitchen, where he left the box and his hat on the table. They rushed across the room and into the back hallway to the first door on the left.

Rex had brought in a hospital bed and opened a doorway into an updated bath behind the mudroom so their dad could make a convenient downstairs bed suite in the space their mom had once claimed for her crafts and sewing. The room was large enough to allow for a dresser and a couple comfortable chairs, a flat-screen television and bedside tables, and the wheelchair that Wes so hated to use. Ann and her sister had done their best to dress up the space with fresh paint, their late mother's needlework and filmy curtains on the large windows overlooking the side yard. The hardwood floors were clean, bare and even.

Meredith popped up from the far side of the bed by the bathroom door.

"Oh, thank God you're here, Dean. We can't lift him."

Dean shot across the room and rounded the bed, going down on his haunches next to Wes, who lay crumpled into the corner.

"You okay there, Wes? Did you hit your head?"

"I think he knocked his elbow against the wall, but he doesn't seem to have broken anything," Meredith answered.

"Pushed it…a little…too far," Wes panted, lifting an arm toward Dean.

Gingerly looping Wes's arm around his neck, Dean scooped his own arms around Wes's shoulders and hips, asking, "Do you think you can get your feet under you?"

"Think so," Wes muttered, wrapping his other arm around Dean.

"Okay. Let's get you up."

Standing, Dean literally lifted Wes with him. He scrabbled for a moment, but then Wes got his feet planted and stiffened his legs. Ann noted that as soon as Wes was standing, Dean shifted, keeping a supportive arm about her dad. Obviously Dean was doing his best to afford her father every dignity. Ann felt tears fill her eyes and quickly busied herself straightening the covers on her dad's bed. Wes sidled closer and eased himself down onto the edge of the bed, Dean supporting him all the way.

As soon as Dean backed away, Meredith stepped in and removed the slippers from their father's feet, lifting his legs up and onto the bed and making him comfortable.

"How's your stomach?"

Wes laid a large, bony hand across his flat middle. Despite the thirty pounds or more he'd dropped in the past weeks, he was still a big man, but the chemo had taken his once lush, cinnamon-and-sugar hair, giving him a cadaverish look that broke Ann's heart every time she saw him.

"Pretty rumbly."

Meredith plunked a basin down on the bed beside him, saying sternly, "No arguments. I don't want you getting out of this bed without help again. I've seen lots of men throwing up, you know."

"Not your father," Wes grumbled.

"Dad, that's what I'm here for," Meredith pointed out. "And I *am* a nurse, you know."

Sighing, he nodded. "I know."

Briskly, she set about filling a syringe from a tray on the bedside table. "I'm going to give you an injection now to settle your stomach. Then I want you to eat something before the medication knocks you out. All right?"

"Grandma sent over some jars of chicken soup," Dean said helpfully.

"I'll heat some up," Meredith volunteered, lifting the sleeve of Wes's T-shirt and wiping his skin with an alcohol swab before injecting him with the medication.

"Maybe Dean…will stay…and help me to the table," Wes said.

"Be happy to," Dean replied at once.

"You can eat on a tray here," Meredith argued, but Wes gave her a hard look.

"Table," he insisted.

Meredith rolled her eyes and pointed at the wheelchair. "As long as you use that."

Wes sighed. "Fine."

Meredith quickly finished up and left the room. Ann didn't feel that she should leave their guest, especially after he'd helped them.

"Betty sent some other things, as well, Dad," Ann said, nodding at a chair for Dean. He walked around the bed and sat down.

She perched on the side of her father's bed and smiled at Dean as Wes said, "Good of her."

"She's glad to do it," Dean told him. "Anything we can do to help." Wes put out his hand and Dean took it, saying, "Maybe you'd like to pray before your meal gets here."

"Please," Wes replied, closing his eyes.

Dean braced his elbows on his knees, Wes's hand clasped in both of his, and began to pray, quietly, calmly, competently.

Ann noticed that Dean's hands very much resembled her father's. Both were square-palmed and long-fingered, large and capable. These were the hands of working men, men who used their backs as well as their brains, strong, masculine, sure of their purposes and their abilities.

Suddenly she thought of Jordan's soft, well-manicured hands, and a shiver ran through her, something that felt terribly like revulsion. But that couldn't be right.

She loved Jordan.

Didn't she?

## Chapter Six

By the time Meredith had their father's lunch ready, Wes's stomach seemed settled and his strength somewhat restored. He didn't complain when Dean helped him into the wheelchair, and he managed to eat a fair-sized bowl of Betty's rich chicken soup with some hot bread that Meredith came up with from somewhere. His eyelids drooping, he began to nod off even before Ann had served up plates of meat loaf and green beans for herself, Meri and Dean, even though Dean protested that he'd already eaten a sandwich before coming over.

Wes insisted on staying at the table until Dean had finished his own meal. Ann had never seen a man make food disappear so fast—or been so grateful for it. He was wheeling her dad back into his room within minutes. Ann went with them and watched gratefully the careful, respectful manner in which Dean shifted Wes back into the bed, allowing him to do as much for himself as possible. She didn't have Meri's gift for caring, but Ann did her best to make her dad comfortable, kissed his cheek and left him drifting into slumber after hearing Dean promise to come again.

They returned to the kitchen to find that Meredith had dished up some ice cream for Dean. Chuckling, Dean sat down to the table again.

"You Billings women act like Grandma doesn't feed me," he joked, lifting his spoon.

"We just want to thank you for your help today," Meredith said, smiling at Ann.

She and Meredith finished their lunch while he polished off his ice cream. Then Ann walked him to the front door, Meredith calling out her thanks to his grandmother for the food.

"She'll be pleased to have been of service," Dean told her.

"I don't know what we'd have done without you," Ann began when they reached the front door, suddenly choking up. She could usually put her dad's illness out of mind and carry on, but today it had hit her especially hard, and she felt tears fill her eyes again.

"Mind a bit of advice?" Dean asked.

She shook her head, knuckling moisture from her eyes. "Seems like I'm always coming to you for advice."

"Don't let him see you cry. When my grandfather was ill, what worried him, what hurt him most, was seeing my grandmother's grief and fear. I realized that the best thing I could do for him was to hide my tears and allow him as much dignity as possible. Wasting away is hard on a proud, strong man."

Before she knew it, tears streamed down her face, and she couldn't stop them. She realized that she'd instinctively been holding them back, and now she knew why.

"Here now," Dean said softly, pulling her into his arms. "I shouldn't have said anything. Wes isn't wasting away. He's fighting. This isn't the same at all."

"It is," she whispered against his shoulder.

"No, no. Grandpa had lots more against him than cancer. He had a bad heart, and he couldn't put down the cigarettes. His lung cancer was too far gone when they found it, and that was ten years ago. They've improved treatment since then."

"You're right, though," she said through her tears. "We've been trying to baby him, and no father wants to appear weak in front of his daughters. On some level I knew, but...he's my dad." Her voice thinned and broke on the last word.

Dean's big hand cupped the back of her head and his strong arms just held her as she struggled to pull herself together.

"It's okay," he crooned. "Wes is going to be okay."

"I know," she managed after a long, tearful moment. "I believe that. I really do. It's just hard to see him this way."

"I understand."

She nodded, sniffed back the last of her tears and began to pull away. "I'm sure you do."

After a moment's hesitation, Dean loosened his embrace and shifted back. "Better now?"

Smiling, she wiped her face with her fingertips. "Yes. Thank you."

"No problem."

She finally met his gaze. "No, seriously. Thank you for everything."

He lifted his hand and gently cradled her cheek. "Anytime, Jolly. Anytime at all." Dropping his hand, he briskly added, "See you tomorrow."

Briefly touching the wet spot on his shoulder, she nodded. "Yes. Tomorrow." Chuckling, he turned and opened the door. "Say hello to Donovan for me."

"Promise." He went off with a wave, fitting his hat to his head.

Ann reluctantly closed the door and leaned her shoulder against it, wondering what was happening here. Just a few days ago, she'd felt nothing but disdain for Dean Paul Pryor. Now...now she felt a warm gratitude, a great respect and a good deal of liking.

She looked at the ring on her finger and frowned. More liking than seemed wise. She didn't even mind when he called her Jolly anymore.

Troubled by her thoughts and feelings, Ann found a few minutes, later that afternoon, to call Jordan. He answered the phone after only a few rings, which told her that he wasn't especially busy. At times he had to let calls go to voice mail and get back to her when he wasn't dealing with hotel issues. She felt a good deal of relief at the sound of his voice.

"Well, hello there, Oklahoma. I was just thinking of you."

"That's nice to know," she told him, "especially after the day I've had."

"Rough going?"

"Dad's very sick. I guess it's to be expected, but it's really hard to watch."

"How long do you think he has?"

Stunned by the casual manner in which Jordan had tossed the question out there, Ann gasped. Then she got angry.

"Jordan! How dare you say such a thing? He's not dying."

"You said—"

"He's going to beat this, Jordan. He's fighting, and he's going to beat this."

"Of course he is," Jordan said soothingly. "I didn't mean that the way it sounded. It's just that I miss you and can't help but wonder how long we're going to be apart. That's all I meant."

But was it? And why didn't Jordan's reassurance comfort her as much as Dean's had?

She told herself that it was all about proximity. Dean was here; Jordan was a hundred and fifty miles away. Dean could see what was happening with her father. Jordan's reality was the hotel and its myriad problems and details. He had only secondhand information about what went on at the ranch, so how could she expect him to understand her fear and pain?

The vision of Dean sitting at her father's bedside quietly praying came to her, and she knew that Jordan would not even begin to do such a thing. He'd likely be horrified if asked to. Not so long ago, that idea wouldn't have bothered her a great deal.

Now, somehow, it did. Very much.

Once he started praying, Dean couldn't seem to stop. He'd only been fifteen when his grandfather had died, but he remembered those dark days all too well. The shock of learning of his grandfather's illness still reverberated through him whenever he thought of it. Within a very few months—weeks, really—a seemingly strong, almost invincible, man had weakened, shriveled, faded and quickly passed from this life to the next. The family hadn't even had time to adjust to the idea of his illness before he was gone.

Dean didn't want to see that happen to Ann and her family. He hated the very thought of Wes's suffering, and Ann's tears made him want to storm Heaven's gates on their behalf. After leaving the Straight Arrow, he tried to turn his mind from their situation, but the feel of Ann in his arms, the dampness of his shirt, the cracking of her voice all weighed on his mind. Yet, what could he do other than pray?

He did so silently and often throughout the rest of the afternoon and evening, and Grandma somehow knew it. She came to him as soon as Donovan was tucked up in his bed for the night.

Dean sat on the stoop in the corner of the porch that wrapped around the front of the two-story, white-clapboard, T-shaped house. Grandma dropped down beside him, pulled her knees up and hugged them. She didn't beat around the bush.

"How bad is Wes?"

Dean shrugged. "I don't know. He looks bad. No hair, pale, thin. But I can't say whether he's going to make it or not. The chemo is obviously pretty rough, but I doubt even the doctors know what the real status of the disease is yet."

"Well, treatment has improved a lot."

"That's what I told Ann."

Several telling heartbeats later, Grandma asked oh-so-casually, "How is she?"

Dean tried to sound just as casual. "Worried. Broken up. She tries to keep it together in front of him, but she and Meredith both need to back off a bit and let him do what he can for himself."

"I don't suppose you told her that." Dean shrugged, and Betty patted him on the knee. "You did tell her that. Well, don't take it so hard. She'll think about it and realize you were trying to help."

"No, it's not like that," he said. "It's just that I upset her, made her cry. I brought up Grandpa and scared her."

"Hmm." Grandma touched the faint stain on his shirt. "Cried on your shoulder, did she?"

"Now, don't make more of it than there is," Dean warned. "Her dad's ill. She was upset."

"Uh-huh."

"*And* she's engaged."

"Engaged isn't married," Grandma said, getting up to go inside. "Just saying."

"And I'm just saying that you're being silly," Dean told her as she walked across the porch.

"Well, if I'm silly, we can both laugh about it later," she drawled. "Good night, hon."

"Night," Dean muttered as she went inside.

She *was* being silly, Dean told himself, very silly. And so was he.

Once he'd had Ann in his arms today, he hadn't wanted to let her go. He'd wanted to sweep her up, carry her off and promise to make everything okay. He'd wanted to kiss away her tears and return that saucy, bring-on-the-world smile to her face. He'd wanted…all sorts of things to which he had no right and for which he had no hope.

And so he prayed. For Ann. For her dad. And for himself.

In the end, he decided that the best thing he could do was keep his distance from Ann Billings. It wouldn't be easy, given the situation, but it would be wise. So that, ultimately, became his prayer.

*Lord, make me wise.*

By the time Ann arrived in the field on Monday morning, Dean was already hard at work. She waved, and he waved back but didn't stop the combine or try to speak to her. Donovan ran up, his dog on his heels, to give her one of his body-blow hugs and a smile as wide as his face. Seeing that he was essentially alone in the field while his father worked, she offered to take the boy back to the house with her, but he claimed that his dad "needed" him to watch the water cooler that sat on the open tailgate of the truck until he was "needed" in the cab of the combine.

Ann had to admire Dean's parenting skills. He kept the boy close and taught him responsibility by giving him small jobs that he could perform while playing. One day Donovan would realize those jobs were imaginary, but hopefully by then he'd also realize how deeply and skillfully his father cared for him.

She let the happy boy show her how Digger drank from the stream of water that fell from the spigot of the cooler when he turned it on, then she left him to scamper around with his dog until Dean took him up into the cab of the harvester. No doubt Donovan would grow bored shut up inside the cab of the harvester all day. This way, Dean broke up the monotony for him while keeping him within sight and allowing him a certain freedom.

Only as she drove back to the house did she wonder if Dean might be avoiding her, but she had no real reason to think that. Telling herself that she couldn't trust her feelings just now, she pushed aside the suspicion and focused on what needed to be done. Fearing that she was becoming too fond of Dean, she didn't go out to the field the next day. After all, if she couldn't trust him to do what needed to be done by now, she'd know it already. On Wednesday morning Dean called to say that he'd finish the oat harvest and would be delivering the fodder to the appropriate new storage bins later that afternoon.

Wes felt well enough to watch from the living room window as Ann went out to oversee the delivery. She hadn't expected Dean to have extra hands with him, but the oats arrived in a pair of two-and-a-half-ton trucks. Dean, Donovan and the dog rode in the first; two other men came in the second. Well past trying to impress Dean, Ann had dressed simply in a lightweight, long-sleeved top, tied at her waist, work jeans and her new, plain boots. With her hair caught in a ponytail low on the back of her head, she'd crammed her old baseball cap onto her head before going out to wait for them.

Dean got the first truck into position, and the men were hauling out a huge vacuum hose to siphon the oats from the truck bed into the storage tank when Donovan and the dog came to greet her. As usual, Donovan nearly knocked her over with his hug. Laughing, she bent and scooped him up against her before setting him down again, Digger barking and scampering around them happily. The kid was surprisingly heavy, a solid hunk of boy. Dean left the truck and walked over to them, smiling.

"Well, look at you," he said, stripping off his sunglasses. "You've turned into the best-looking ranch hand I've ever seen."

As soon as he said it, he ducked his head, as if embarrassed, but Ann had never felt so flattered. Glancing around, she muttered thanks and caught the other men sneaking looks at her. Suddenly feeling a bit self-conscious, she turned and moved a little distance off. After a moment Dean followed, sliding his glasses back onto his face.

"Everything go all right?" she asked casually.

"It's a good harvest. Oats are in excellent shape. Wes should be pleased."

Ann nodded. "I'll tell him."

"We'll get started on the mixing station in the morning. Once the sorghum is in, you'll be able to mix your feeds right here."

"I'll make sure Dad and Rex know where we are with the schedule. I assume you'll be wanting a check now."

"It can wait until tomorrow. I won't pay these men until then."

"All right."

He stepped off, waving for her to follow and slapping his billed cap onto his head. "If you want to come over here, I'll show you where the mixer will stand."

"Sure."

Rex had given her a good idea about it all, but Dean explained in detail. The whole thing made perfect sense now that she fully understood. Suddenly the dowdy, dusty old ranch where she had grown up was starting to feel like a thriving, modern business, not that it had ever been failing. Her dad had kept the ranch in decent shape financially, but she knew that he had worries now that the medical bills were stacking up. Even with insurance, the bills came in with dismaying regularity. With Rex pumping new investment and energy into the place, though, she didn't doubt that the Straight Arrow Ranch would quickly be more prosperous than ever. Ann sensed that her dad was eager to get out here and be part of it all again; she prayed that would soon be the case.

Dean apparently felt the same undercurrents. He glanced around, smiling, and lifted his shoulders. "It's kind of exciting, what's going on around here."

"I think so."

He seemed surprised by that. "Really?"

"Well, sure. Dad and Rex have big plans for this place."

Turning a slow circle to take a good look around, Dean said, "I wish them every success." Coming to a stop, he looked down at her, a wry smile curving his lips. "And frankly I wish I had their vision and business acumen."

"What makes you think you don't?"

"Oh, the fact that I work sunup to sundown and just barely manage to get by," he said lightly.

"You're raising a son on your own," she pointed out, "and you've got a lot of skills."

"Maybe so, but I haven't figured out how to best make them work for me yet," he said with a wry smile. "But I will. Eventually." One of the men called to him, and he lifted his chin in acknowledgement. "Gotta switch the trucks."

"I'll leave you to it." She began backing away, lifting a hand in farewell.

He paused before striding resolutely toward the now-empty truck. Something about that seemed reluctant to Ann, as if he didn't want to part company with her. Or was she projecting her own feelings onto him?

Shaking her head at her own foolishness, she hurried around the second truck. As she did so, she heard Dean's workers talking.

"Purely ridiculous," one of them was saying, "tottering around out here on those spiky little heels, all that heavy makeup. She's really come along, though."

"I'll say. I thought she might be kinda cute under all that gilding."

"Dean thinks she's downright hot."

Ann caught her breath and quickly adjusted her route before they saw her.

Was it true? Did Dean think she was hot now?

She didn't know if she was more shaken by the idea that he might truly find her attractive or the unmistakable opinion of his men that she looked better today in her utilitarian ranch clothing than in the expensive designer wardrobe that she usually wore. Suddenly she remembered Dean's comment the day she'd bought these clothes.

*You're the girl who rocked a pair of cleats and a batting helmet.*

Could he really have found her appealing even then?

*I like the real you better.*

He'd said that when he'd come to pick up his first check. He'd also called her a snob.

And he hadn't been wrong.

She'd known it, to her shame, at the time, though she hadn't wanted to admit it, especially not to herself. Secretly, she'd felt justified in her attitude, even while knowing better. What had made her think that she could raise herself by looking down on those she'd left behind? That was what it had amounted to.

War Bonnet was small and simple, its folk goodhearted and unpretentious. In many ways life here seemed slower and less complicated than that to which she had become accustomed. Strangely, it also felt less lonely, despite the dozens and dozens of employees, coworkers, guests and friends who surrounded her every day in Dallas.

As she stepped up onto the porch, she caught sight of her father's drawn face in the living room window. He smiled and nodded, obviously eager to hear what Dean had said to her. Strangely, Ann found herself eager to discuss it with him.

How could she have forgotten the ease with which she and her father had conversed and worked together? When had she lost that precious connection with him? Ashamed that it had taken a life-threatening illness to reestablish their relationship, she silently prayed for forgiveness for her neglect of her father and her baseless feelings of superiority. As she removed her shabby baseball cap and hung it on the wall peg, she begged God to spare her dad's life. She had ten years of foolishness to make up for.

Even as she turned to her dad and began to report on Dean's progress, she knew that she needed to speak with her fiancé about their future. Things had changed, and Jordan needed to know.

She made the call immediately after dinner, while Meredith settled Wes into his bed. The call went to voice mail, but before she could make her way back downstairs, her phone rang. Seeing Jordan's photo on her screen, she walked out onto the porch and sat cross-legged on the swing to answer.

"Hi. How are you?"

"Busy," came the terse reply. "You?"

"Things have calmed down a bit. Dad's feeling better every day. The oat harvest is in. We start building the feed mixing station tomorrow. Then we can start the sorghum—"

"That's all very interesting," Jordan cut in, sounding anything but interested. "Unfortunately I've got a situation on my hands here, and I need to resolve it. We booked three gold level suites this weekend and only have two available."

"That's an easy fix," Ann said. "Move into my apartment and give your suite to the third guest."

Silence. Then a chuckle. "Of course. That's why we need you back here. You always see every problem with such clear-eyed perspective and come up with the easiest, most common-sense solutions."

Ann smiled, but then she sighed. "I only wish that were true. Jordan, we have to talk about where we're going to live. I know I said it didn't matter to me, but I don't want to move any farther away from my dad than Dallas."

"You know LHI wants you here in Dallas," he said easily. "So I don't see a problem."

Dropping her feet to the floor, Ann sat up straight. "That's great for me, Jordan, but what about you?"

"Hmm, well, Marshal said something recently about Arizona."

Shocked, Ann yelped, "Arizona!"

Marshal Benton, the CEO of Luxury Hotels, Inc., and Jordan were great friends. Jordan had a gift for befriending people, and he could keep a confidence better than anyone. When she had worked for Jordan, Ann had felt that they were great friends. He was one of the very few people to whom she had poured out her heart, so it shouldn't have been surprising that this was the first she'd heard of Arizona. Except…

"Don't you think that's something your fiancée should be consulted about?"

"It wouldn't be permanent," Jordan said in a soothing tone. "He has in mind a sort of research and development position. I'd be scouting out spots for new hotels, including possible purchases of existing properties, and reporting directly to him. After Arizona, they're looking at Idaho and Seattle."

"So you'd be traveling."

"That's right."

"But Jordan, I thought once we married—"

"Ann," he interrupted, "did you miss the part about me reporting *directly* to Marshal? This is a vice presidency. I don't have to tell you how huge that is. Besides, it's not like we're in a rush to set up housekeeping in a little bungalow with a white picket fence somewhere and fill it with kids. That's not us. Right?"

Donovan's grubby little face flashed before Ann's mind's eye. She thought of the way he threw himself into every hug, of that snaggle-toothed smile beaming up at her and the supreme confidence with which he barreled through each day. If ever a little boy knew he was loved, Donovan did. In that moment she could almost feel the coarseness of his flaming red hair, packed with sand, beneath her fingertips.

*You sure are pretty.*

Her heart turned over in her chest.

She realized belatedly that Jordan was still talking about his proposed vice presidency, but suddenly she couldn't bear to hear any more.

"I'm sorry," she interrupted, pushing up to a standing position. "I need to check on Dad."

"Ah. All right. Well, I'll move into your rooms tonight. Give housekeeping a chance to really go over my suite."

"That's fine," she said, just wanting to end the call.

"We'll, um, reconvene when you head back this way."

"Yes. Sounds reasonable."

"Don't make it too long, Ann. Please," he said smoothly. "You're needed and missed here."

She wondered why that felt so sadly impersonal, but she merely said, "Thanks," and hung up. What, she asked herself, had happened to the ambitious career woman who would have rejoiced at this news? More to the point, what had happened to the simple, happy girl who had once lived here? And did some part of her still exist?

## Chapter Seven

What was it, Dean wondered, about mornings that made sound carry so clearly? Or had he unknowingly been listening for the rasp and thud of the door on the ranch house across the road? Either way, he didn't have to be told who headed this way, along the meandering path beneath the trees to the shallow ditch beside the road and then across it to the field just south of the barn.

Mentally congratulating himself for keeping his focus on the job at hand, he scraped up a metal washer with gloved fingers and awkwardly maneuvered it onto the second of two bolts sticking up out of the yard-square concrete pad and held out his hand for the metal "foot" that Donovan was even then passing to him. Dean worked the holes in the L-shaped foot over the bolts protruding from the concrete pad and picked up a pair of metal nuts to spin onto the threads of the bolts. Using a wrench, Dean tightened the nuts.

With two such feet now in place, he need only to secure two more. Then he could attach legs to the feet, which together would support the mixing pan with its interior paddle wheel, dump chute and openings for input channels from each of the feed storage bins. By simply manipulating levers on the channels, Rex, Wes or the ranch hands could accurately measure the amount of oats and sorghum that they wished to mix. Dumping the feed from the mixing pan into a truck or trailer bed would be a simple matter of pulling a lever.

Well aware that Ann had arrived on the scene, Dean rose and nodded in greeting, prepared to move to the next corner of the concrete mixing station foundation. Instead, both his jaw and the wrench dropped.

Gone was the snooty hotelier who wouldn't be seen without her perfect makeup and designer clothing. In her place stood a softer, calmer woman, her vibrant hair lying in a braid across her shoulder. Wearing nothing more than mascara and lightly tinted lip gloss, her pale, pearly skin showed the faint stippling of freckles. She might have been seventeen again in her jeans and plaid shirt tied at the waist over a bright blue tank top. For a moment Dean couldn't think, couldn't move, couldn't breathe.

Then he reached up and resettled his cap, hearing himself say, "There's the girl I've missed all this time."

She laughed, almost as if relieved, and closed the distance between them in swift, long strides. For once, Donovan did not throw himself at her, his head swiveling back and forth between them, curiosity sparking in his brilliant eyes. Hearing her laughter, Dean could not restrain himself. He shook off his gloves and reached out his hands to her, which she took without the slightest hesitation. Only his son's presence kept Dean from pulling her into his arms. Still, as her shoulder bumped into his and she smiled up at him, he bent his head toward hers. Only when his thumb brushed over her engagement ring was he able to check himself. Even then he couldn't let the moment pass without comment.

"Welcome home, Jolly," he said softly, smoothing her cheek with one hand as his thumb swept over her engagement ring with the other. "It's good to finally see you."

Her sky-blue eyes plumbed his for a moment. Then Donovan stepped forward, her faded old cap in hand.

"Miss Ann, you dropped something."

"So I did," Ann said, smiling. "Thank you, Donovan." She took the cap, slapped it onto her head and reached out to drag the boy in for a hug.

Dean found himself swallowing down a sudden lump in his throat and immediately got back to work. He expected her to ask an obligatory question or two and take her leave, but to his surprise, she didn't just stick around, she pitched in. When next he reached for a washer, Ann beat him to it, saving him the trouble of having to scrape it up with the seam of his glove.

After he'd gotten all four metal feet secured, he went to the dually to lift the metal legs from the truck bed. Four feet long and made of heavy, V-shaped channeling, the legs connected to the feet via flattened flanges at the bottoms. They were too heavy for Donovan, even one at a time, so Dean gave him the job of dispensing the bolts, washers and nuts, filling his pockets with each.

"Where's your extra help today?" Ann asked, helping him lay out the legs at each corner of the foundation.

"Tending their own business. They're all small ranchers and farmers around here just picking up an extra buck when they can. I don't need them for this. Doesn't make sense to pay someone to basically hand me what won't fit in my tool belt."

He picked up the first leg, crouched, rested the upper portion against his shoulder and lined up the holes in the flanges on the leg and foot before holding out his gloved hand for the first bolt. Donovan dropped it into his palm, and Dean began working it through the two holes, leaning this way and that to keep the leg lined up. Seeing his problem, Ann walked around behind him and grasped the top of the leg, holding it steady in position.

"Looks to me like you could use an extra pair of hands, though."

Dean shoved the bolt home. "You looking for a job?"

"So what if I am? You hiring?"

He placed the washer and spun on a nut before tilting his head back and smiling up at her. "Depends. How cheap do you work?"

Her eyes narrowed, lips skewing to one side. "Hmm. Job like this… Can't settle for anything less than smiles and hugs."

Dean chuckled and winked at Donovan. "We've got those to spare. Don't we, son?"

Donovan put his head back and beamed a snaggle-toothed smile at Ann, who laughed. It was as if the years literally fell away, but this time, Dean mused, he was part of her crowd, not just hanging around the periphery.

Working together, they quickly got the legs bolted into place. Dean brought out the ladder and set the square metal brace that spaced the top of the legs and held the mixing pan. This part had to be riveted then welded into place, which required significant strength. The first time that the ladder rocked, Ann caught hold of it and made sure that it stood solidly in place while he fixed the rivets.

His welding kit was small, perhaps too small. He

hadn't wanted to rent the larger welder, however, when he had a perfectly usable small welder. Unfortunately the small welder couldn't sit on the ground, but was too large for the top of the ladder. Dean started thinking aloud about building a platform.

"Can the brace hold the mixing pan as it is?" Ann asked.

"Sure, but it won't hold several hundred pounds of fodder like this."

"But it will hold that welder, won't it?"

He realized suddenly what she was saying and grinned. "You use that head for more than just a place to park that pretty face, don't you?"

She blushed, actually blushed, and he realized that he was flirting.

"I've never been told that I was stupid," she countered drily.

"No, ma'am, you are not," he agreed, going for the mixing pan.

The pan itself was fairly lightweight, especially without the mixer, chutes and door attached. It was, however, cumbersome. Ann hurried over and helped him carry it by the chute openings to the station. She then shoved as he hauled the pan up the ladder. Getting it wrestled into place proved a feat. He could've done it, but it went much more quickly because Ann climbed the ladder to help him. They performed a strange dance there four feet above the ground, arms over, under and around, bodies shifting and sliding.

When they were done, and the pan was at last appropriately seated, Ann had somehow worked her way to the inside and moved up a rung, turning her back to the ladder, so that they stood pressed together on that narrow structure, staring into each other's eyes. He had pocketed his sunglasses, and she had knocked off her cap again. With one movement he could have gathered her fully against him and kept her there. The impulse was so strong that he slid his hands across her shoulder blades. Her lips parted, and she seemed to be drawing in breath in preparation for his kiss.

Then Donovan called, "You dropped your hat again," and Dean realized that he'd almost kissed Ann Billings on a ladder in the middle of a field in broad daylight with his son running around below them. The engaged-to-be-married Ann Billings.

Dean jumped backward off the ladder, landing with a huff in the red dirt. As he gathered his welding gear, he was exquisitely aware of Ann carefully turning on the ladder and descending step by step. He wasted no time climbing that ladder again, this time to deposit his welding gear in the newly placed pan. Ann passed him the helmet and long gloves necessary for the job.

"You two back away," he ordered, "and do not look directly at the welding arc. Hear me, Donovan? You can damage your eyes looking at that bright light."

"Yessir."

"Let's get a drink," Ann said to the boy, sliding an arm over his shoulders. She walked him to the back of the truck and let down the tailgate to get at the water cooler while Dean struck a spark and ignited the torch.

He took his time with the welding, moving his ladder as necessary. Ann and Donovan sat on the tailgate of his truck with Digger, swinging their legs and talking. He couldn't hear what they were saying, but he saw the way Donovan leaned against her from time to time and heard their occasional laughter. The thought came to him that she would make a wonderful wife and mother.

But not for him and Donovan.

That rock on her finger told him well enough that he had nothing to offer her. He could never afford a ring like that, never give her the kind of life she was accustomed to, the kind of life she deserved. He was still that silly freshman boy dreaming about a girl who remained worlds above him.

After he finished the welding, Ann and Donovan returned to help him finish installing the mixing pan. They formed an efficient team. Donovan had worked with his father long enough to know each tool by name and which one was used for which job. He passed the correct tool to Ann, who handed it up the ladder to Dean, saving Dean many steps and much time. As a result, the job was finished sooner than expected. Donovan was jubilant.

"We get to go fishin' after, right, Dad?"

"That was the deal," Dean confirmed, stowing the last of his gear in the toolbox in his truck bed. "If we finished early enough, we'd go fishing."

"Ann helped so she can go, too, can't she?" Donovan suggested happily.

Hope and excitement leaped inside Dean, but he kept his face impassive. "Sure. If she wants to."

Ann grinned and ruffled Donovan's bright hair, saying, "I'd like that, but I need to be here for my dad so my sister can take care of some errands."

Dean told himself that it was just as well and his disappointment was entirely out of proportion to the situation, which highlighted his personal foolishness where Ann was concerned. He wasn't fourteen anymore, after all. As a boy, he'd learned that wishing didn't make a thing so. It was past time that he gave up this juvenile fantasy of him and Ann Billings.

"If you'll come to the house, I'll write your check," she was saying. "The amounts were all spelled out in your agreement with Rex."

Nodding, he lifted a hand to indicate that she should lead the way. Donovan and the dog fell into step beside him. Ann walked backward much of the time, chatting with Donovan about what sort of fish he hoped to catch and whether he baited his own hooks.

"'Course I do!" Donovan declared, glancing up at Dean.

"He tries," Dean clarified. "He's certainly not squeamish about it. The only question is whether or not there's enough of the worm left to stay on the hook."

Ann wrinkled her nose. "Gotcha."

"They squish real easy," Donovan muttered, and Dean bit his lip to keep from laughing while Ann delicately shuddered.

They reached the porch, and Dean pointed to the cushioned porch swing, speaking to his son. "Why don't you and Digger enjoy the swing while I go inside with Miss Ann?"

"Aw, Da-a-d," Donovan whined.

Ann ruffled his hair again. "I'm sorry," she apologized, "but my father is very ill, and he can't be around too many people right now. Or dogs."

Donovan's eyes widened solemnly. "What's wrong with him?"

"It's called cancer."

Frowning up at her, Donovan asked, "You're not going to get it, are you?"

"No, no." Ann smiled. "No one can get cancer from someone else, but cancer patients can get all sorts of illnesses from other people while they're getting treatment.

He'll be better before long, then you can visit him. In fact, I'm sure he'd like that."

Mollified, Donovan crawled up onto the swing. Digger hopped up next to him, and Donovan began to swing them both as Ann and Dean went into the house.

"I won't be long," Dean promised.

They headed straight into the office, Ann hanging her cap on a peg in the entry hall on the way. Dean swept off his own cap and stuffed the soft part into his hip pocket. She went to the desk, checked something on the computer and got out the checkbook.

"You know," she said, scribbling away, "I wouldn't mind seeing your business plan."

Shocked, Dean chuckled. "Business plan? What business plan?"

"Surely you have one," Ann commented, signing the check. "Everyone does these days." She began carefully tearing the check out of the book. "I don't mean to be nosy. It's just that I find what you do fascinating, and I'd like to see how it all works. I mean your agreement with Rex is very finely drawn."

Dean hung his thumbs in his belt loops. "Jolly, Rex is a lawyer. He drew the agreement. Seemed fair to me, so I signed it. The closest thing I have to a business plan is a budget."

She leaned back in the old desk chair, staring up at Dean. "Seriously?"

He shrugged. "Unless you consider prayer a business plan."

"Dean!" she exclaimed, rocking up onto her feet. "You're smarter than that."

"Apparently, I'm not," he admitted testily, yanking his thumbs free. "There wasn't time for things like business plans and market studies when I started. I didn't expect to be a father at twenty, but that didn't change the fact that when Donovan was born, I had to make money as quickly as possible. I had land but no equipment because Grandpa had bought all the machinery on timeshare and it all went back to the manufacturer when he got sick. I had no credit of my own, so I sold most of the land, bought some equipment and went to work farming for others. It's just that simple."

"I understand," she told him, handing over his check. As he folded the check and slipped it into his shirt pocket, she said, "But it's not too late, you know. A good business plan could grow your business significantly."

He shook his head. "Look, I'm not like you. I didn't finish college, so I work with my hands. Grandma and I stretch every dollar as far as it will possibly go. And too often it doesn't go far enough. But we manage, and at least I don't have any debt."

"I think you could do better than manage," Ann suggested gently. "Who carries your line of credit?"

Exasperated, he snorted. "Haven't you been listening? I don't have a line of credit, and I don't care to. I may not be making lots of money, but at least I'm not in debt."

"A line of credit isn't about debt," she pointed out patiently. "It's about leveling out your monthly income and normalizing your budget so you don't get caught short. You have more than enough of a track record now to apply for a line of credit, so if you want, I could take a look at your books, help you draw up a business plan and secure that line of credit so you don't have to worry about months with no income."

Thunderstruck by both the implications and the offer, Dean's first instinct was to refuse. He'd been operating on his own for five years now, and he was who he was, a simple, hardworking man. If that wasn't good enough for her, well, when had it ever been?

On the other hand, how stupid would he be to turn down expert help just because his pride had been pricked? And if there was a way to even out his monthly income so he didn't find himself completely broke at the worst time of the year, he owed it to his son to at least investigate the possibilities. Besides, as foolish as it seemed, when he came right down to it, he wasn't sure he could refuse the opportunity to spend more time with her.

He swallowed his refusal and his pride with it. Nodding, he said, "I'll, uh, be on another job for a few days. Then I've got to get that sorghum cut for the Straight Arrow. Will you be available after that?"

She nodded decisively. "I will."

He felt a rush of relief. "Great. Thank you."

She put out her hand and he took it, shaking to seal the pact. She smiled suddenly, and it was all he could do not to pull her into his arms for a hug. Instead, he dropped her hand like a hot potato and turned toward the door.

"Okay if I look in on Wes before I leave? I won't get too close."

"Sure. Go on back," she said. "He might be asleep, though."

"I'll be quiet," Dean promised, "just in case."

He strode away, passing Meredith as she came down the stairs, the strap of her handbag on her shoulder.

"All done for the day?" she asked.

"Yep. Just going to say hi to your dad before we head out."

Mindful of Donovan waiting on the porch, Dean

didn't pause. He journeyed on down the hall, tiptoeing up to the open doorway of Wes's room. He found the older man in his bed watching television. The grayness of Wes's skin troubled Dean, but he put on a cheery smile and hailed Wes from the doorway.

"How you doing, Mr. Billings?"

The other man cleared his throat. "It's Wes. And I'm doing fine."

He didn't look fine, but Dean said only, "Good to hear it. The mixing station is all done. I think you're going to be real happy with it."

"I'm sure we will be. We're always happy with your work."

"I appreciate you saying so. I'll get started on that sorghum by midweek."

Wes gave him a tired smile. "We'll look forward to seeing you then."

"If you need me before that, you just call. Ann knows how to reach me."

Wes nodded wearily. "Good of you."

"I'll let you rest," Dean said, turning away.

"See you soon," Wes rasped.

When Dean looked back, the older man's eyes were closed as if he'd fallen asleep. Dean stood there a moment longer, until he was sure that Wes's chest rose and fell in regular breaths, before he slipped back down the hall to report to Ann.

"He's sleeping now."

"Did you get to speak to him?" Ann asked.

"A bit. You'll call me if I'm needed, won't you?"

She nodded, smiling slightly. "I wish Rex would get back. If Dad falls or collapses…"

"You just call me," Dean stated flatly. "Anytime.

Wherever I am, whatever I'm doing, I'll come. You have my word on it."

"Thank you."

"Save it for when—if—I actually do something."

"I feel better just knowing I can call on you if I need to," she told him.

"Anytime."

He meant it. Anytime Ann called, he'd come, no matter why or when. Even if he was fishing.

That said something sad and rather pathetic about him, but so be it. He could fight his attraction to Ann and his disappointment that she would never feel the same way about him that he felt about her. He could tell himself that he was being foolish and unrealistic. He could pray for wisdom and strength. But he couldn't change who and what he was; in truth, he wouldn't want to try.

One thing being Donovan's father had taught Dean was to be himself. Only by being his authentic self could he help his son grow into his true self. Knowing one's true self was a necessity. Sharing one's true self with another was a gift, an act of love and trust.

It saddened Dean to think that Ann would never know the deepest, truest parts of him, but she was meant for another.

He stepped out onto the porch and pulled the door of the ranch house closed behind him. "Let's go catch some fish."

His son's bright smile lightened his heart.

It was enough. It had to be enough.

## Chapter Eight

Ann had known difficult days but nothing like those immediately following the construction of the mixing station. That very evening after Dean left, Wes ate something that didn't agree with him, and within the hour an unrelenting nausea set in. Several times Ann picked up the phone to call Dean, but in truth he could do nothing that Meredith wasn't already doing. Just because having Dean there would make *her* feel better was no reason for Ann to call him over to the house, especially as she had no right to the comfort and support he offered.

In fact, having Dean around was dangerous. She'd come to realize that he was dangerous to her heart, as well as her peace of mind. That didn't keep her from hoping that he'd stop by to check on Wes.

In a very real way, she missed Dean. She'd sort of gotten used to seeing him on a daily basis. Yet, her father was so ill that Ann didn't feel comfortable leaving Meredith alone with him and going to church on Sunday.

By Sunday evening both sisters were worn to frazzles, and Wes seemed no better. Meredith had already consulted Dr. Alice Shorter by telephone, and she called the doctor again, as instructed, very early on Monday morning. Dr. Shorter drove out to the ranch straightaway, bringing intravenous medications with her.

On the plump side and fiftyish, with long, straight, thick blond hair, Dr. Shorter had a dry, ready wit, remarking to Wes, "If you wanted to see me, Billings, you didn't have to go to such extremes. You could've just invited me to dinner."

Wes chuckled then clutched his loudly rumbling belly with one hand. "Don't even…mention…food."

"Sorry. Let's get you comfortable."

While Meredith set up the IV, Dr. Shorter conducted a routine examination before announcing, "Well, you're dehydrated. No surprise there. We'll get some fluids and medication in you and calm this down." She nodded at Meredith, adding, "At least your nurse knows her stuff."

"She's good," Wes managed with a smile. Meredith didn't even look up from securing the IV in her father's arm.

Watching from the foot of the bed, Ann said, "We're lucky to have her."

"Blessed," Wes corrected. "I'm blessed…with both… my daughters."

Ann smiled at that, glad she could at least be here to help run the ranch while Rex was gone. She couldn't care for their dad the way Meri did, but at least she could contribute in some ways. And to think that in the beginning she had secretly resented having to put her life on hold to come here and do this. The selfishness of that shamed her, and she was deeply, deeply grateful for this time with her father and sister.

"What set you off?" the doctor asked.

Wes made his face, flattening his lips in a stubborn expression that she knew all too well, so Ann answered for him.

"Catfish. He had an intense craving for it. We thought it would be mild enough for him, so we brought it in from the diner."

"The fish, maybe," the doctor said. "The grease it's fried in, probably not."

"I should have thought of that," Meredith said guiltily. "Callie would have."

"Callie had training, if I'm not mistaken," Dr. Shorter pointed out. She poked Wes in the chest with a gloved forefinger then, adding, "And so did you."

He rolled his eyes. "Sounded...*so* good."

The doctor turned to her kit and found a syringe. "Doesn't feel so good now, does it?"

"Nope."

His poor stomach rumbled so loudly that the doctor handed him the basin sitting on the bedside table. "Need to puke?"

Wes gritted his teeth, swallowed and closed his eyes. "No."

Alice Shorter shook her head and injected medication into his IV tube, muttering, "Men and their pride."

"Not pride," Wes ground out. "Self-respect."

She patted his shoulder. "I forgot. Christians are forbidden pride. Have it your way."

"You know... I will," Wes said, one corner of his mouth hitching up in a smile.

Ann could tell that he was already beginning to relax. To her surprise, the doctor reached down and squeezed his hand. Even more surprising, he grasped her hand and held it for several long seconds. The three women—Ann, her sister and Dr. Alice Shorter—stood quietly around his bed until he began to breathe easily and slipped into peaceful sleep. Meredith's hands trembled as she smoothed her light golden brown hair back from her face and twisted it into a long rope.

"It's different when it's family, isn't it?" Dr. Shorter said softly, and Ann recognized the sound of experience in her voice. Meredith nodded.

Abruptly, the doctor began packing up her bag. A few seconds later she stripped off her gloves and dropped them in the trash can. Then she was heading for the door.

"He'll sleep for a while. Call me if you need me."

"Thank you, Dr. Shorter," Meredith murmured, following the older woman from the room, Ann on her heels.

They picked up the pace in the hallway, but the doctor was out the door before they could catch up to her. Wandering back into the kitchen, where her sister went to the refrigerator for the tea pitcher, Ann brought her hands to her hips and thought over all that had just happened.

"Do you know," she said after a moment, "I think Dr. Shorter might have a crush on Dad."

Meredith looked around, taking an ice tray from the freezer, and she raised her eyebrows. "Don't be silly. I've heard that she's an atheist, and you know Dad's a very outspoken Christian."

"He's also a very attractive man, even ill."

Meredith shook her head, cracking the ice tray over the sink. "Doesn't mean anything. He would never be interested in her."

"No? Meri, Mom's been gone since 2012. What would be wrong with Dad finding someone else?"

"Nothing." Meredith dropped ice cubes into glasses. "I hope he does. Once he's well again."

And what if he's never well? Ann wondered. Doesn't he deserve every moment of happiness he can find, well or not?

The house phone rang, and Meredith reached out to answer it.

After greeting whoever was on the other end and a moment of chatter, she said, "Ann's right here. Want her to take this in the office?" She held the telephone receiver away from her ear and said to Ann, "It's Rex. I'll bring your tea to you."

"Thanks, sis."

Ann hurried to the office and picked up the cordless receiver there. She listened while Meredith filled in Rex on their dad's most recent health issues. Then Meri hung up on her end, and Ann and Rex got down to business. Rex had been going over the books online and had some questions. Ann had paid a couple of bills he hadn't expected to come in for several weeks yet, and he wanted to see the statements. Meredith brought her iced tea while Ann was scanning up and emailing the billing statements. As soon as her sister left the room, Ann took the opportunity to ask Rex about Dean, shading her question in tones of concern.

"Just how much do you know about Dean Paul Pryor? I have a few concerns."

"Problems with his work?" Rex queried, sounding surprised.

"His work is fine, but he doesn't really seem very fiscally sound. I can't help wondering just how much you really know about him."

"I know everything I need to know," Rex insisted. "Dean's as honest as the day is long and the hardest working young man you'll find anywhere."

"I know he works hard," Ann ventured carefully. "He just seems...well, he's awfully young to be a single father."

"That's true, but he didn't have to take responsibility for the boy at all," Rex pointed out. "The mother was a college student, same as Dean. When Dean proved to be the biological father, he took custody of the child, and that was that.

"He might have been a little wild at one point," Rex conceded, "but everyone agrees he's been an excellent father, especially since he became a Christian not long after his boy was born."

"I certainly can't argue that point," Ann said, trying not to let her smile sneak through into her tone.

"Dean may not be the best businessman, but he's young, and he'll learn," Rex insisted.

"I'm sure you're right," Ann agreed. In fact, she meant to make certain of it by helping Dean learn what he needed to know to solidify and grow his business, starting with a business plan. Business, after all, was what she did best, and a hardworking, loving, responsible father deserved all the expertise and help he could get.

Now she just had to figure out how to protect her silly heart while she helped this handsome single dad make the most of what he did best.

When Dean arrived at the sorghum field at dawn on Wednesday morning, Ann already stood beside her dad's old truck, dressed in running shorts and a tank top, her hair in a ponytail. Waving, she jogged around to the passenger side of the truck and hauled out a square pan covered in a dish towel. Parking the thing on the front fender of the truck, she smiled cheerfully and pointed to it. Dean brought the dually and the combine that it was hauling to a slow, shuddering halt in the center of the narrow, rutted, red dirt road.

She looked better than she had as an eighteen-year-old, all long, slender muscles and womanly curves.

A sleepy Donovan craned his neck to see what had caught his father's attention. His gaze went to the pan on the fender of the Straight Arrow pickup truck, and he happily exclaimed, "She brought food!"

Digger, in the front passenger seat, perked up at that. Dean had to laugh, not just because of his son's and his dog's interest in the food but because he hadn't given that cloth-covered pan a second thought.

"Looks like it."

Leaving the rig where it sat, he killed the engine and got out. By the time he unbuckled Donovan and crossed the ditch to Ann's truck, she had folded back the cloth and the sheet of waxed paper beneath it and helped herself to the biggest sticky bun he'd ever seen.

"Meredith put these up last night," she said around a big bite. She chewed and swallowed before adding, "Since I wasn't about to miss these bad boys, I figured I'd better bring enough for everyone."

Dean figured that he was grinning as broadly as Donovan, who practically soared with glee.

"Can I, Dad?"

"Sure. It'd be rude not to eat these after Miss Meredith baked them and Miss Ann brought them all the way out here."

"There's no clean way to do it," Ann warned, "so I brought packets of wipes. Dig in."

Dean used his hands to peel off a bun for Donovan then took one for himself. Tasting of butter, brown sugar, cinnamon and pecans, the things practically melted in the mouth—and all over the face and hands. Ann had brought coffee and milk, too. Dean was not a big coffee drinker, but it had never tasted so good as it did that morning.

They ate leaning against the truck, watching the sun play peekaboo over the horizon.

"I meant what I said about the business plan," Ann told him between bites. "If you'd let me look over your books, I think I could help you formulate a good plan and set up a line of credit."

"I told you I'd do it," he reminded her lightly.

"I know. I just thought we could get started sooner rather than later. Like tonight maybe?"

He wondered if she was rushing to get out of town, but then he thought of her dad and discarded the notion. She wouldn't leave until Wes was better and Rex returned, which could be sooner than anyone realized.

"I'll bring the books over tonight," he decided.

She smiled and bit into her sticky bun. He ate three big buns and drank two tall cups of coffee before Donovan, Digger and Ann could finish off their own. To say that Donovan needed a wipe after he was done was akin to calling the Red River a stream.

Ann seemed a little horrified by what she had wrought with her sticky buns. She broke out the wipes and went to work. By the time she was satisfied that the entire Straight Arrow Ranch wouldn't stick to Donovan, her wipes had been all used up. Dean poured the last of the coffee on a ragged bandanna and cleaned himself well enough to proceed with his day. He was going to be dusty and sweaty in an hour's time, anyway. Ann, however, was another story, and her attempts to take care of herself with the used wipes only made matters worse.

She was a good sport about it, and cute as a button

in the bargain. Dean could've stood there and watched her wipe and rewipe all day, but they both had work to do. He allowed himself just so much fun before he took her by the arm and walked her to his truck.

"Come with me. I keep a container of baby wipes under the backseat."

"Okay, so I grossly underestimated the number of wipes needed," she admitted, skipping along beside him to the truck.

"Baby wipes are one of mankind's greatest inventions," Dean told her, opening the back door of the dually and reaching inside. He felt around under the seat until he found the cylindrical container and hauled it out. "One of the first things you learn when you have a kid is that you can never have too many baby wipes."

"Got it."

Popping the top, he pulled out two and handed them to her so she could clean her hands. When she had that job whipped, he gave her another wipe for her face, though he really hated to see the sticky, brownish circle around her lips go. He wished he'd taken a picture with his phone. She seemed so far removed from the polished, big-city hotelier who had greeted him that first day, more like his Jolly—if such a person actually existed. She was certainly making a hash of cleaning her face.

"Hold on. Hold on," he said, chuckling. "First of all, fold that thing so the clean side is up."

She looked down at the wipe and folded it. "Okay."

"Now, start here." He touched his own face.

She wiped the wrong cheek.

"No, no. The other cheek."

She moved her hand. "Like this?"

"Almost. To your right. Got it. Now move in. And turn your wipe over."

Exactly as instructed, she turned the wipe over. Then her gaze came back to his, and he pointed to a spot on his own cheek. She lifted her hand to her face once more. He realized only as she slowly swept the wipe over her lips that they were still looking into each other's eyes, and abruptly his breath seized.

Suddenly, as the sun shot golden rays across the fields, igniting tiny fires in the red-orange dirt of the road, they somehow stood apart from the rest of the world, wrapped in an intimate, electric awareness. As if in a trance, Dean lifted his hand and brushed the backs of his fingers against her cheek. Then he turned his hand and lightly cupped the curve of her jaw. She tilted her head ever so slightly, leaning into his palm, her eyelids growing slumberous, lips parting. Emboldened, he slid his hand to the back of her neck and felt her lean toward him.

Then Donovan slammed into his side.

"Dad, Dad! Can I go under the wire with Digger? He's got some armerdiller or ground squirrel over yonder."

The dog's barking finally penetrated Dean's consciousness. "Uh…" Blinking, he stared down at his son and found a reasonable answer. "No. Might be a skunk he's found. Better hang with me until we get the combine into the field."

Donovan dug a toe into the dirt. "Aw."

Ann was already halfway across the road when Dean looked up again. "Rex tied a red flag on the section of fence that can come down," she called. "He's had pipe laid over the ditch so you can drive right over." Of course, Dean could see the movable cattle guards temporarily bridging the ditch.

"Great!" Dean shouted after her, fully aware that she was running away from what had almost happened between them. He didn't blame her. She was engaged to be married, after all. To an older, established, successful man. But Dean couldn't escape the certainty that, given just a moment longer, she would have allowed the kiss that hadn't happened.

In light of that, Dean had to wonder if working on a business plan with her was such a good idea, but even as he wondered, he knew he was going to do it. Somehow, with her, he couldn't seem to help himself. So, that evening after supper, he left Donovan with his grandmother and drove back to the Straight Arrow with his account books.

Meredith answered the door. "Come on in. Annie's on the phone, but Dad would love to see you."

"I'll be happy to visit with him for a few minutes. I promise I won't tire him."

"He's feeling better," Meredith told him. "It'll be fine."

"Thanks for the sticky buns this morning, by the way. They were great, really good."

Meredith shot him a smile over her shoulder as he hung his hat on the wall peg and followed her into the living room. "Callie put them in the freezer before she left. All I had to do was thaw them overnight and shove them in the oven this morning."

"Well, you did a good job of it," Dean insisted politely.

"What you really mean is that sister-in-law of mine can sure cook."

"That, too," Dean admitted with a chuckle.

"Meredith has her own talents," Wes said from his recliner. "She's a top-notch nurse, my Meri."

"Oh, Dad." Meredith patted the top of his bald head affectionately on her way to the kitchen, saying, "Call if you need anything."

Dean couldn't say that Wes looked much improved, but his color wasn't so gray, and something about his smile seemed brighter, healthier. Easing into the room, Dean nodded at his host, who waved him toward the comfortably worn leather sofa. Wes immediately clicked off the television with a remote controller.

Dean sat and stacked his ledgers atop his knees. Wes glanced at them but remarked only, "Ann says the sorghum looks good."

"It does. Rex's timing has been perfect with the harvest."

"Boy's a natural," Wes proclaimed proudly. "Always suspected it, but it took him a while to figure it out. Well, everyone has to take their own path."

"I hear he's a really good lawyer, too."

"Oh, yeah, he is," Wes stated without hesitation.

Dean had to grin. He knew just how Wes felt about his son, and he was glad that the feeling didn't necessarily fade with time.

"Ann's done a good job for us, too," Wes added, and Dean quickly agreed.

"She has."

"Between you and me, I'm seeing some changes I like in her lately. Not sure that big-city fiancé of hers would approve, but she seems more her true self to me now than she has in a long time."

Dean said nothing, but privately he thought Ann's fiancé a hopeless fool if he didn't completely and wholeheartedly approve of Ann and all she was.

Maybe she wasn't perfect, but no simple human being could be. She was, however, and had been for as long as Dean had known her, all things lovely and fine.

What man in his right mind would not approve of—and appreciate—that?

Conversation had moved to that morning's breakfast of sticky buns, with Wes joking that he'd needed a sponge bath after finishing his, by the time Ann swept into the room. She smiled distractedly at her father and twisted the heavy diamond on her finger in a way Dean had never seen before this. He knew at once that something troubled her.

"You okay?"

She flashed a smile and waved a hand in a gesture that didn't quite appear as careless as it might have. "It's…" She shook her head. "A work thing."

He didn't like to even think about the job waiting for her back in Texas, but he could see that something weighed heavily on her mind just now.

Lifting the slender books in his hands, he suggested, "Maybe I should just leave these with you for now. You can look them over at your convenience and get back to me later."

To his disappointment, she pressed trembling fingertips to her temple and nodded. "Maybe that would be best."

His spirits plummeting, he got to his feet. "I'll let y'all enjoy your evening. It was good to see you, Mr. Wes. Take care now."

Uncertain what to do with the books, he placed them on the coffee table and moved toward the door, sliding sideways past Ann. He'd nearly reached the foyer when she suddenly announced, "I'll walk you out."

Surprised, he stopped then almost wrapped an arm around her waist as she came up next to him; Wes called out a farewell just in time to remind Dean that would not be a good idea. Stuffing his hands into the pockets of his jeans, he tucked his elbows in tight as he stepped into the entry hall with Ann right at his side.

They skirted the stairs in silence. When they reached the foyer, he took his hat from the peg but kept it in one hand, opening the front door with the other, holding it wide until Ann pushed through the screen. She crossed the porch and stepped down onto the well-beaten pathway, but then she paused and waited for him to pull the door closed, sidestep the screen and catch up to her.

Half a dozen innocuous topics of conversation slipped through his mind, but something sat so heavily on hers that he couldn't bring himself to start a conversation. Finally, just as they approached the edge of the trees, she spoke.

"Can I ask you something and get an honest answer?"

Even though little, if any, traffic could be expected along this private road at this time of evening, Dean had pulled his truck to the side of the road nearest the house, parking practically in the shallow bar ditch. He stepped across that narrow ditch, reached in through the open window and laid his hat on the seat of the truck. Turning, he put his back to the passenger's door and leaned against it, folding his arms.

"Sure."

She shook her head with obvious agitation, her eyes gleaming in the dusky light. Darkness often didn't fall until nine o'clock at this time of year, and they had no moon this early in August, only the light of the stars and the ambient illumination from the vapor lights near the barn and the rear of the house. He wondered if the sheen of her eyes could be from tears.

"An *honest* answer," she repeated sternly. "Don't spare my feelings."

He stilled, everything in him focused on this woman before him, this woman he had wanted for so long. His heart pounded as he imagined the questions he *hoped* she would ask.

"I've always been honest with you, Jolly. I always will be. You have my word on that."

He'd never meant any words more than those.

## Chapter Nine

Watching her face, Dean knew for certain that Ann was on the verge of tears, but he made himself stay as he was, and finally she came out with it.

"Do you think I'm feminine?"

That couldn't have been what he'd heard. He'd been hoping for something along the lines of, *Do you like me?* or *Do you think of me when we're not together?* or maybe even *Do you think there's a chance for you and me?* But…no, he couldn't have heard her right.

"I beg your pardon?"

Her hands balling into fists, she practically shouted it at him. "Do you think I'm feminine?"

The question was so stupid that for a moment he still couldn't wrap his mind around it. As a result, his tone may have been a bit sharper than he'd intended. "Of course. How could you be anything else?"

She shifted, mirroring his stance with her arms folded. "But what, specifically, is womanly about me?"

"What is—" He nearly swallowed his tongue. When she looked in the mirror, did she not see what he saw when he looked at her? Dropping his arms, Dean slapped his hands against his thighs. "What isn't? Jolly, you're the most—"

Throwing up her hands, she interrupted hotly, declaring, "I have *no* feminine accomplishments. I can't cook. I don't know the first thing about kids. Half the time I can't even figure out how to dress!"

"What's that got to do with anything?" he wanted to know, shoving away from the truck.

"I have no close female friends," she went on. "I can't sew. I can't…grow flowers or make jewelry or…" She whirled her hands in angry circles. "I can't do anything that most women do!"

Dean just stood there, still not believing what he was hearing.

"I'm not like other women," she declared, and he could tell that she was working herself up to a real meltdown about this. Every time he opened his mouth, she spouted something nonsensical about being too masculine or broad-shouldered or tall.

Then she complained about her hair and her freckles.

"What's wrong with red hair and freckles?" He liked red hair and freckles. That was how he'd wound up with a redheaded, freckle-faced son.

"Your face is beautiful, freckles and all," Dean interrupted bluntly, but she couldn't even hear him at this point, having moved on to the color of her eyes, which were apparently "washed out and faded, like old jeans."

Frustrated, Dean did the only thing he could think to do, the thing he most *wanted* to do.

He took one long step, breaching the chasm between them, reached out with both arms and pulled her flush against him, capturing her lips with his.

For an instant, everything froze. But then he tightened

his arms and poured everything he had into that kiss, everything he'd felt for so long, everything he wanted with this woman. In seconds she melted, and her arms slid up around his neck.

Kissing Jolly was everything he'd ever dreamed it could be.

Not feminine? He wanted to shake her for being so stupid. Then he felt her smile, and he was lost to the wonder of having her, at last, exactly where he wanted her. Where she surely belonged.

Didn't she?

If that were so, though, why was she suddenly pushing away from him? And laughing.

Frowning, Dean watched her back up a step and raise one hand as if to hold him off. Her laughter faded to a huge grin, but he still didn't like the look of it.

Was she laughing at him?

She clapped her hand to her chest then and said, "That was my fault. I know that men speak with actions more than words, and I didn't exactly give you a chance to really say anything, so you made your point the most efficient way you could. And, well, I just want to thank you."

A chill ran through him, followed by an unexpected surge of white-hot anger that stunned him with its intensity.

"Thank you," he echoed with deadly calm. "That's what you've got to say to me after that kiss? Thank you?"

Her smile faded, and she dropped her hand, moving from gratitude to apology. "I'm sorry. I was having a big old pity party, and I dragged you into it. That wasn't fair."

"You think that was about pity?" he demanded, aware that he was shouting but not quite able to control his tone. She just stared at him, clearly clueless. "You may not have 'feminine accomplishments,' as you call them," he managed, leveraging volume into sarcasm and curling his fingers to indicate quotation marks for emphasis, "and you may be better at some things than most men, but the only *masculine* thing about you is your stubborn, blind, ridiculous inability to see what's right in front of you!"

Her eyebrows jumped into pointed little arches, and she looked down as if expecting to find something sprouting from the ground.

"Uh, I don't—"

"I'm talking about me!" he snapped.

"You?" Her gaze jerked up to meet his.

Parking his hands at his hips, he bluntly admitted, "I've wanted to do that for years."

"You've wanted to kiss me for years?" she squeaked.

"But never more so than recently," he told her, "and I'm tired of you never seeing or acknowledging my—" he almost said *feelings for you,* but he was too much the stubborn, blind, ridiculous male himself to give away that much, especially now, so he settled for "—attraction to you."

She looked stunned as if he'd punched her in the gut, and he suddenly felt completely drained, emotionally and physically.

"Dean," she began, "I didn't… I never…"

The words just died away, and that was it, all he could handle.

"I have to go," he muttered abruptly.

Striding around her, he hopped across the ditch in one long stride and kept right on going until he'd circled the truck and reached the driver's door. She stood as if rooted to the ground while he opened the door, shoved aside his hat and wedged himself inside the slanting truck. After he started the engine, wrenched the steering wheel as far right as it would go and swung the truck in a wide U-turn, he hit the brake. She had followed the motion of the truck but still stood with her arms dangling at her sides, her jaw agape. Shaking his head, Dean pushed the gas pedal and drove away, leaving her there, staring after him.

"Lord, help me," he whispered.

Would he *never* learn? He couldn't just answer her idiotic questions and listen to her rant. He couldn't let it go at the kiss. He'd had to tell her that he'd carried this torch for her for years.

Oh, what had he done? What *had* he done?

What had she done?

Ann watched the red taillights of Dean's truck grow smaller and smaller in the darkening distance, torn between elation and shame.

On one hand, she was thrilled beyond words that the most masculine man she knew found her attractive. That kiss left no doubt about that. None. She lifted trembling fingers to her lips and found them curved in a smile.

On the other hand, she was an engaged woman, pledged to marry another, and he was the one who should be giving her such thrilling assurances. She should never have dragged Dean into it.

The problem was that when she'd asked Jordan if he thought she was too masculine, he'd replied that what mattered was her *brain*. He'd then gone on to say that she had one of the finest managerial minds he'd ever encountered and how essential she was to the success of the Dallas hotel, which had run a slight deficit before she'd taken over, even with him at the helm. He'd talked about how much she was missed there and asked again how soon she could return. All of his words had been flattering, but the conversation had left her shaken. It had been as if she was talking to her *boss* rather than her fiancé, and doubts had suddenly overwhelmed her. She'd asked herself if Jordan truly loved her or if she was just a wise career choice for him.

Feeling vulnerable and frightened that her perfect future might not be so perfect after all, she'd told herself to steer clear of Dean, but for some reason she hadn't been able to stick to the plan. When Dean had actually gotten up to leave the ranch house, she'd panicked. In some strange way, he had become her anchor in a world that had turned upside down.

Her father's illness, her return to War Bonnet, her growing concerns about her engagement, Rex's continued absence, her confused feelings about Dean and Donovan…it all whirled around her, a tornado of emotion. Even the good things seemed too much all of a sudden. Her success here at Straight Arrow—Rex seemed pleased with the way she'd kept things running—relaxing into a simpler lifestyle, feeling finally as if she'd really come home, reconnecting with her dad and sister, the comfort of church and Christian fellowship somehow piled one atop another until she felt buried by everything that had happened these past few weeks. She'd wanted to grab hold of Dean and never let go again.

But that kiss…

Never in her wildest dreams had she imagined anything like that kiss. Minutes later she still tingled all the way to her toes. Guiltily, she realized that not one of Jordan's few kisses had ever made her feel even remotely like this. She had presumed that she was the problem. After all, hadn't she known for years now that she was not like other women? Or was she?

All through the night she tossed and turned, torn between the delight of Dean's kiss and all that it seemed to reveal, and guilt that she had enjoyed Dean's kiss so much more than her fiancé's. By morning she had decided that the only thing to do was to call Jordan and have a frank talk with him.

She did it early, very early, so she wouldn't interrupt Jordan's working day and in order to give them the time necessary to say all that needed to be said. She did it before she even got dressed. Because of the hour, she wasn't surprised that he didn't answer on the first or second ring. When at last he picked up, she immediately apologized.

"I'm sorry to call so early, but we really need to talk."

"Ann," Jordan groaned. "We spoke just last night."

"I know, but something's happened."

"Your father?"

"No, no. Me." Drawing her legs up beneath the bedcovers, she held the cell phone to her ear. "I, um, kissed someone. Rather," she hurried on, "someone kissed me. But… I—I did…*participate*."

She heard dead silence on the other end of the line.

"Jordan, I'm sorry, but I felt you had a right to know."

"Do you want to break our engagement?" Jordan asked carefully.

"Do you?"

"Ann," he said softly, warmly, "these things happen when couples are separated. Given the stress you've been under and the fact that you're a woman working in an almost exclusively male field now…" He sighed. "Well,

I can't say I'm happy, but I'm not surprised, either. Just don't let your head be turned by one of the local yokels back there in Oklahoma. Your life is here in Dallas. We can really build something together, Ann. Don't lose sight of us and the future we have. Please. I—I don't think I can do this without you."

Melting, Ann said, "Jordan, that's so sweet."

"It's a onetime thing, right? Just a onetime thing."

She started to tell him that it wouldn't happen again, but she barely got the first two words out before another call rang through. "It won't— Oh, Jordan, I'm sorry. This is my brother. It must be important for him to call so early."

"That's okay, darling," Jordan said. "We can talk again later."

"Thank you. Yes. Just give me a little while to take care of this." She quickly tried to put an end to the call and get to Rex, who sounded harried.

"Oh, good. I caught you before you left the house," he said as soon as he heard her voice. "I have a delivery of building supplies coming in two weeks earlier than expected. Some sort of scheduling mix-up. The transporter just called to say that his trucker has driven through the night to get to us first thing this morning so he can make another delivery somewhere in north Texas before nightfall."

Rex went on to detail where the supplies needed to be off-loaded and stored, just in case Duffy, whom he'd awakened from a sound sleep, didn't understand or remember his instructions. Then Rex told Ann that she would have to coordinate with Stark Burns, the local veterinarian, who had partnered with Rex on the order so they could take advantage of a bulk discount. Only after Stark deemed the order complete would Rex transfer payment to the supplier.

"I'll call him after we hang up," Ann promised. Because she hadn't seen their father yet this morning, they had nothing to talk about there, so she ended the call.

Only then did she realize that she'd accidentally put Jordan on hold. Remembering her parting words to him, that she just needed a little while to take care of Rex's call, she feared that Jordan was still on the line.

Swiping the correct button, she spoke. "Jordan, I'm so sorry. I didn't mean for you to hold."

The line was open, and she did hear him speak but distantly. "Don't know," he was saying, "and I don't care. Some dusty, drawling redneck, I imagine."

Ann heard another voice, a feminine one, but she didn't recognize it or understand the words until the speaker came closer. "Doesn't seem her type," the woman said, and Ann suddenly knew to whom that voice belonged. Gena Johns, one of the customer service clerks who worked the main reception desk. But what was Gena doing in Jordan's—Ann's—suite at this time of the morning?

"Who *is* her type?" Jordan was asking, his tone dry.

"You, obviously," Gena answered, sounding petulant.

"Guess that's why Marshal gave me this assignment," Jordan said, his voice growing louder then fading as if he bent toward the phone and backed off again.

*Assignment?* Ann thought, freshly stunned as Jordan asked Gena to hand him his shirt. *What assignment?*

As the ramifications of what she was hearing began to sink in, Ann dropped the phone into her lap. This couldn't mean what it seemed to mean. Could it? Tears filling her eyes, she shook her head. It was a mistake.

She'd misunderstood. Gingerly, she picked up the phone again and held it to her ear.

"…believe she's still buying it," Jordan was saying, "but I may need to move up the wedding date."

"You said you'd jilt her before it got too far," Gena whined.

Ann closed her eyes, horrified.

"That *was* the plan," Jordan said. "If it could be done before the wedding arrangements were too far underway. But things change."

"You're really going to marry her?" Gena demanded.

"If that's what it takes to get her back here and keep her with LHI," Jordan answered bluntly.

Ann slapped a hand over her mouth as a sound of horror escaped her.

"Look," Jordan said calmly, "if her father hadn't gotten sick, she wouldn't be playing cowgirl in Dirtville now and none of this would be necessary. But it's like Marshal says, we can't take the chance that her family will guilt her into staying on to run the family business. I promised him I'd get her back here ASAP, and trust me when I tell you this is the way to do it."

He would know, of course. Ann had told him exactly how to guarantee her cooperation.

"I've got a huge promotion riding on this," Jordan went on. "So if I have to drive down to that waste of space again to sell it and march her up the wedding aisle to get her back here, that's what I'll do. Not that it matters much because I'll be living in another state, anyway."

Ann couldn't bear to hear any more. Crushed, tears coursing down her face, she broke the connection and fell back on the bed.

An assignment. A project. A promotion deal.

That's all she was to Jordan, all she'd ever been.

Some small, sane part of her supposed that she ought to be flattered because Marshal Benton and Luxury Hotels, Inc., thought enough of her to go to such lengths to keep her on the job. Such filthy, underhanded, sneaky, hateful lengths. And she'd given them the nefarious plan herself.

It all made terrible sense now. Jordan had shown up in Dallas not long after her dad's cancer had been confirmed. Ostensibly, he had come to relieve her so she could take off time to help out here at the Straight Arrow, but he'd needed to be brought up to speed before she could leave the hotel *that he had managed before she had taken over.* Of course, he'd used that time to sweep her off her feet and get an engagement ring on her finger, ensuring that she'd return to Dallas as quickly as possible—long after she'd confessed her personal history and fears to him. And she'd fallen for the whole charade, hook, line and sinker.

Foolish didn't begin to cover her idiocy.

Ann turned facedown into her pillow and sobbed, her entire world shattering around her.

She had believed that Jordan loved her.

She had thought that he wanted her for herself.

She had trusted in the future that he had promised her. Maybe it wouldn't have been quite traditional. Maybe she wouldn't have been a mother or a homemaker, but she'd have been a wife, a partner, half of a couple.

Or so she'd thought.

In truth, she was nothing more to Jordan Teel than a means to an end, an assignment that he meant to leave behind at the first opportunity.

Only one man, it seemed, had ever seen her as a

woman, and now she had to wonder if even that could be real. Maybe all Dean wanted was a mother for his son. At best he might want Jolly, the silly, thoughtless girl Ann used to be. He didn't really know the person she was now. How could he when she wasn't sure that she knew herself anymore?

She couldn't trust anyone or anything right now.

For the first time, her soul felt as dry as kindling.

*Oh, Father God, help me!* she cried silently, but her prayers seemed to bounce off the ceiling and fall back to her shoulders, driving her deeper into despair.

Eventually she heard the long blast of a horn and realized that the hauler with the building supplies about which Rex had warned her had arrived. Pulling herself together enough to crawl out of the bed, she pulled on jeans, boots and a nondescript T-shirt then found her phone and dragged herself out of the room without so much as glancing at a mirror.

She was creeping down the upstairs hall and looking up the veterinarian's phone number when that horn blasted again. Meredith stepped out of her room, belting her robe over her pajamas.

"What's going on?"

"Mix-up with a delivery schedule," Ann explained dully, moving toward the stairs. Meredith caught her by the arm, turning her back.

"You okay? You don't look well, Annie."

"Couldn't sleep last night," Ann muttered. "Then Rex called early. Gotta go."

She tapped the number displayed on the screen of her telephone and let it dial Stark Burns's number. Meredith's hand fell away as Ann turned once more for the stairs, lifting the phone to her ear.

Burns sounded wide-awake when he answered the call. Ann told him what was needed, and he replied that he was on his way. She flipped on porch lights to let the trucker outside know that she would be with him momentarily then trudged across the porch and along the path to the road. To her surprise, what awaited her was a full-blown tractor-trailer rig with a skid loader on the back.

By the time Ann and the driver figured out how best to position the trailer to off-load the materials meant for the Straight Arrow, Duffy had arrived. Burns quickly followed in a one-ton flatbed truck. After Burns agreed that the order was complete, the trucker agreed to load certain bundles onto Burns's truck if Rex verbally signed off on the arrangement and put through payment.

Ann contacted Rex, who took care of his end of things, and the trucker proved he knew his business by quickly off-loading his shipment then backing the rig straight down that red-dirt road well over half a mile before he could turn it around and head it south to Texas. Burns, in his usual taciturn manner, wrote a check for his part of the order and took himself off again.

Ann dragged back into the house to face Meredith's frown. "What was that man doing here?"

"Which one?"

"That so-called animal doctor."

Meredith could not forgive Burns for failing to save her injured cat. Ann sighed and explained about the building supplies, then for the first time in memory, she decided to forgo her Thursday morning run. Instead, she took a long shower then got dressed again and went downstairs to face her family with wet hair and red-rimmed eyes.

Fortunately Meredith had already related her tale of a sleepless night, bungled scheduling and early-morning calls, so their dad commiserated rather than questioned.

No one seemed to notice her missing engagement ring, which sat atop her dresser, boxed, addressed, and waiting to be brought to the War Bonnet post office.

## Chapter Ten

Missing. Dean expected Ann to show up in the field every day, but the woman had gone missing.

She had always been the gutsy type, but obviously that kiss had driven her away, maybe all the way back to Texas. He had a perfect excuse, the business plan, to stop by the house, but he couldn't quite work up the courage. If she didn't want to see him, he was not about to force his company on her.

Yet he felt a burning need, which only grew as time passed, to at least clap eyes on her. Part of him needed to know that she was well; part of him needed to know that she didn't hate him or, even worse, scorn him. Mostly he just wanted to see her. Sometimes he wondered how he had gone for so many years without just *seeing* her. They didn't even have to talk; he just needed to look at her and know that she still existed in the world.

The wounded part of him felt some residual anger over her reaction to that kiss, but then he closed his eyes to sleep at night and the memory of it washed over him afresh. He remembered the feel of her in his arms, and he couldn't help smiling.

If only she hadn't thanked him, hadn't suggested it was all about pity.

If only he hadn't carried the image in his head all these years of this vibrant, laughing, confident, beautiful girl who could melt him with a careless smile and knock a ball out of the park with the same ease. No other girl he'd ever met had measured up to her.

And she'd wanted to know if she was feminine!

He still wished he'd shaken her. Right after he'd kissed her. Maybe before.

And maybe he should just keep his distance. Besides, she would surely be in church on Sunday.

Except, she wasn't in church on Sunday. Meredith was there, and when Dean asked about Ann, Meredith said, "She insisted on staying home with Dad this week."

*Yes, of course she did*, Dean thought, *because she knew I'd be here.* Smiling, he said, "I hope that means Wes is improved."

"Much," Meredith confirmed. "He's still weak, of course, and his immune system is increasingly compromised, but at least his nausea is gone. That will only last until his next chemotherapy session, but for now he feels better."

"Glad to hear it," Dean said, and he meant it. He lifted a hand to the back of his head and asked, "Would you happen to know if Ann's had a chance to look over my books? She was going to help me with a business plan."

Meredith shrugged. "Sorry. I couldn't say. She's spent a lot of time in the office lately, though. Maybe that's what's keeping her so busy. Should I tell her you asked?"

Shaking his head, Dean backed away. "Naw. I'll give her a couple more days. Thanks, though. Do give my best to Wes." He left Meredith nodding.

Certain that Ann was avoiding him, Dean stayed away from the ranch house on Monday, but by Tuesday evening, though tired to the bone, he couldn't bear it anymore. Telling himself that the longer this went on, the more awkward their next meeting would be, he cleaned up, left Donovan with his grandmother and drove back to the Straight Arrow.

Meredith answered the door, smiling warmly. Dean pulled his hat and nodded in greeting but didn't beat around the bush.

"Ann here?"

Her smile seemed to fade slightly. "Sure. I'll go up and get her. Meanwhile, will you see Dad? He's feeling like a caged tiger these days."

"Be glad to."

Meredith waved him inside, took his hat, hung it on a peg on the wall and pointed toward the living room as she started up the stairs, calling out, "Dean is here, Dad."

Wes brought his recliner into its upright position and stood, turning to face Dean. He appeared much improved, maybe even a little heavier, as if his skin wasn't quite as loose over his bones. "Hey, there, Dean Paul. How's it going?"

"Harvest is coming along fine," Dean answered carefully, walking into the room.

"I'd shake your hand, but I'm not supposed to," Wes said cheerfully. "They're afraid some common old bug will get me before the cancer can."

"Lots of folks are praying healing and protection on you," Dean told him, "against old bugs, new bugs, cancer and everything else."

"And I appreciate it," Wes said with a broad smile. "Appreciate it and count on it. Now, take a seat." As

Dean moved toward the sofa, Wes added, "I want to know what's going on with Ann."

Dean paused, halfway between the sofa and standing. Before he could formulate any sort of reply, Ann spoke from the shadows at the foot of the stairs.

"I keep telling you, Dad, nothing's going on. Rex just has me buried with work, and I'm worried about you. Am I not allowed to worry about you?"

"Yes, sugar, you're allowed to worry about me," Wes conceded. "You're not allowed to worry yourself sick."

"*I'm* not sick," Ann snapped, already turning toward the office door across the foyer. "In here, if you please, Dean. Let's get to it."

Glancing at Wes, who sighed deeply, Dean straightened and followed Ann into the office. What he saw there shocked him. She had dark rings around her eyes, wore no makeup at all and appeared haggard, as if she hadn't slept in days. Her hair had been swept up into a messy ponytail, and her faded, rumpled T-shirt looked like something left over from her high school days. Dean had never seen her so unkempt. Worse, she appeared dull, lifeless, as if she cared for nothing and no one.

"Your annual income is more than adequate," she stated flatly, standing behind the desk and flipping through some stapled papers. "You pay too much for insurance and way too much in taxes. Fire whoever is doing your taxes for you."

"That would be me," Dean noted flippantly, trying to inject a little humor into the moment.

She glanced up at that, shrugged and said, "You don't know what you're doing. Pay someone who does. You'll save money." With that, she tossed the papers at him.

"That's it?" he asked, both surprised and dismayed.

"No. There are phone apps to keep track of your mileage, fuel costs and so forth." She pulled a sheet from another pile and slung it across the desk. "I made a list for you."

He ignored the list and reached for her hand. "Ann, what's wrong?"

Jerking free of him, she turned her back and pulled a folder from a shelf. "Here's my recommendation, a step-by-step plan for realigning your budget, capitalizing and growing your business." She plopped the folder onto the desk, saying, "Study it. Hire a CPA. Get with Rex after he comes home. He'll steer you to the right bank and—"

"Jolly," Dean interrupted softly. "Talk to me. Please."

"I *am*," she snapped, frowning.

"Forget the business stuff," he began.

"Business is my thing!" Ann insisted hotly. Leaning her palms flat against the desktop. "Business is what I'm best at, management especially. Some people would go to great lengths, *very* great lengths, to secure my advice and expertise." Straightening, she folded her arms and glared at him.

He didn't know how or why, but he was suddenly standing on very shaky ground here. Drawing in a steadying breath through his nostrils, he spoke calmly.

"I'm sure that's true, and I appreciate everything you've said and done. Truly I do."

Despite her outburst, she shrugged as if it made no difference to her one way or another. Dean folded the paper and stashed it inside the folder, which he tucked under his arm, thinking furiously. Something was very wrong here, but he didn't have a clue what it might be. He turned reluctantly toward the door. Then inspiration struck, and he turned back again.

"You missed church on Sunday. Maybe you'd like to go to prayer meeting with me tomorrow night." Ann blinked at him before shaking her head. "Why not?"

*Don't say that kiss. Don't say that kiss. Please, God, don't let her say it's because of that kiss.*

She lifted her chin, but her eyes remained downcast. "I don't have anything to wear."

He raked his gaze over her. "That's an absurd reason."

She opened her mouth as if she would argue, but he didn't give her the chance.

"Don't you feel moved to pray for your father's health? When was the last time you joined with a group of others in focused prayer?" She stared at him for several seconds, robbing herself of any opportunity to refuse. "I'll pick you up at six thirty," he said, turning to open the door. He walked out before she could speak again, pulling the door closed firmly behind him.

He spent the rest of the night and almost the entirety of the next day praying that she wouldn't close the door in his face when he came for her.

To his immense relief, Ann stepped through the front door of the ranch house the next evening before he even got to the porch. Dressed in a flared skirt and familiar lace T-shirt, with no makeup other than some subtly colored lip gloss, her long, vibrant hair hanging straight past her shoulders, she looked like a sixteen-year-old in her mom's high heels.

He fell for her all over again, just like the chubby, awkward thirteen-year-old he'd been the first time he'd laid eyes on her in the dugout at the War Bonnet High School baseball field. She hadn't even known he was alive back then. To her, he was just some kid who delivered a fresh ball to the ump after she smashed one over the fence or who darted out and snatched up her bat after she tossed it aside to run the bases. To him, she'd been as near perfect as a girl could get.

One of them had changed. But not enough. She was still the girl who could knock the ball out of the park, while he had moved on from ball boy to...barely-getting-by dad.

He wouldn't trade Donovan for a college degree or a career, but he couldn't help wanting to be more for her, for a chance with her. Not that he'd ever have such a chance. If he could help her somehow, though, that would be enough. Whatever had gone wrong for her, if he could find a way to help that would be enough. It had to be.

Smiling, he said, "Love your hair like that."

Lifting a hand to her side part self-consciously, she actually seemed shocked, but all she said was, "Shouldn't we go?"

Dean had lots of practice at hiding disappointment. Keeping his smile in place took hardly any effort at all. "Right. Let's move."

He lifted an arm, and she stepped down off the porch onto the path, striding quickly toward the truck parked at the side of the road, so quickly that she stayed a half step ahead of him. He had to rush past her and leap across the ditch to get the passenger door for her. She slid up into the seat without even glancing at him. Sighing, he jogged around and got in behind the steering wheel, started up the truck, made the U-turn and headed toward the church.

Just as he turned the dually into the parking lot of

Countryside Church, he glanced down and saw her left hand dangling off the armrest. Her very naked left hand.

Before he could think, he blurted, "Where's your ring?"

She turned dull eyes on him then looked away again, moving her hand to her lap. "Probably in Dallas by now."

He quickly pulled the truck into a parking space, his mind abuzz with questions. Had she broken her engagement? Was that what lay behind her downcast mood of late? Was she heartbroken? Confused? Uncertain what or who she wanted? Or all of the above?

Before he could ask any of those questions, she'd bailed out of the truck and started across the graveled lot. His heart thudding, Dean threw the transmission into park, killed the engine and went after her, catching up within steps. Impulsively, he slipped an arm across her shoulders. She didn't even break stride, giving him no reaction at all. Uncertain what to do next—she could be having the ring cleaned, after all—he decided, perhaps cravenly, to go with small talk.

"School starts in exactly one week. Can you believe it? We haven't even hit the middle of August yet, and school is about to start." She nodded but said nothing. "I don't mind admitting that I'm not looking forward to it," he went on. "My little boy's growing up, and it's tough to take."

As if that had penetrated her blankness, she stopped and turned a surprisingly endearing look on him. "You're a good father, Dean." A hint of a smile curved one corner of her mouth. "A lousy businessman but a good father."

Relieved to see something like real emotion in her, and anxious to further lighten her mood, he chuckled. "Well, I've got you to help me with the business part, and things like tonight help with the father part. You know, I never really prayed until Donovan came into my life," he admitted. "Then suddenly I had this helpless, amazing, *tiny* person to take care of. Scared the fool out of me. I knew I'd die to protect him but that I *couldn't* always. So I started praying, and now sometimes I feel like that's all I do."

Nodding pensively, Ann threaded her fingers through his. "I can see how that might be. But Donovan's going to be fine. You're giving him everything he needs to get through life."

"Like your parents did for you," Dean pointed out subtly.

She blinked up at him.

Just then, one of the deacons, a middle-aged man, hurried past them and pushed open the glass double door, holding it wide. "Coming in?"

Dean hadn't exactly been a regular at midweek prayer meeting in a while, especially since the children's choir director had resigned to have a baby. With the children's program on hold, Dean usually stayed home with Donovan so Grandma Betty could come to the meeting, but tonight they had switched so he could bring Ann with him.

"Yes, thank you," he called to the deacon, stepping out again, Ann's hand firmly clasped in his.

Together they walked into the building. The place felt oddly quiet, serene, even, though Dean knew from the number of cars in the parking lot that dozens of people had to be inside. He was glad that each and every one had come, but tonight the person he cared about most was the woman at his side, holding his hand.

He was beginning to think that he would always want her at his side, always need her to hold his hand.

\* \* \*

Simply holding hands with someone should not have been so comforting, but Ann had never been so shaken, and unlike most women, she was truly lousy at sharing her feelings. She'd known Jordan for years before she'd told him how an overheard conversation had driven her into hotel management. And he had used that knowledge to try to break her bond with her family and keep her on the job—when, now that she thought about it, the job was really all she had to hold on to.

She told herself that latching on to Dean would be foolish in the extreme because eventually she must go back to her job in Dallas. At first she'd thought otherwise, that when her engagement ended, her job would also, but then she'd checked online for comparable job openings, and everything she'd found would take her even farther away from her dad and the rest of the family than Dallas.

Strangely, it wasn't so much that she wanted to go back to the Dallas job. Her life in Dallas seemed sterile and lonely now. Over these last few weeks, she'd gotten used to sharing a home with her father and sister again. Having company, sitting down to meals together, enjoying real conversations, even trading those small, casual expressions of affection—a touch, a kiss on the cheek, a quick hug—those things all made life so much more... worthwhile. She just didn't know what she'd do with herself on a productive, day-to-day basis if she *didn't* go back to her job at Luxury Hotels, Inc.

Nevertheless, Rex, Callie and baby Bodie would be home soon, and Rex would once again pick up the reins of the Straight Arrow operation, not that he'd ever completely relinquished them. Ann feared that she would feel displaced and in the way once he stepped back into his managerial role.

On the other hand, in only a few more days her dad would return to the hospital in Oklahoma City for more chemotherapy; it wouldn't be the last, and she hated the idea of not being here for him as he fought this disease. Seeing him so ill after the chemo infusions broke her heart, but how could she walk away while he battled for his very life?

Beneath the shock of Jordan's lies, she felt lost and uncertain. She'd been able to keep panic at bay with work and a stoic refusal to face the future. Now that Dean had noticed she wasn't wearing her ring, suddenly Jordan was behind her, and the future stared her in the face. The time had come to begin making plans.

During the meeting, she asked for her father's healing and comfort, but her private, unspoken prayer sought clear, obvious direction for her life. Try as she might, though, she couldn't see her way forward. Where should she go? What should she do? For what job should she apply? She had only questions, no answers.

Throughout it all, Dean held her hand in his. He became her anchor in the rocky sea of uncertainty that had become her life.

As the meeting progressed, however, and those around her lifted their voices in prayer, often for her father, Ann's strength began to return. She didn't know what she was going to do, but she began to feel that she could figure it out in time. In too many ways, she still felt at sea, but the storm began to calm, and she started to believe that she would make it to land, though just where she might wash up she couldn't quite imagine yet.

By the end of the evening, she was very glad that she

had come, though she almost hadn't. In fact, she couldn't really say why she *had* come. At 6:00 p.m. she'd been determined to tell Dean to get lost, and then suddenly she'd wondered what she had to lose by going with him. After running upstairs to trade her jeans for a skirt and her boots for shoes, she'd told Meredith that she was going out for a while and had been sitting on the porch when he'd arrived at thirty minutes past the hour. She hadn't analyzed why she'd changed her mind; she'd just done it.

Maybe it was because Dean somehow made her feel safe and appreciated, the *real* her, the one so few people actually knew.

As they walked back to the dually after the prayer meeting, Dean slid his arm about her shoulders again. His support felt so good that she couldn't help leaning into him just a bit. He opened the passenger door for her and held her hand as she stepped up into the truck. Settling behind the steering wheel a few seconds later, he smiled at her.

The silence felt easy and calm as they drove back to the ranch. When they got there, rather than pull to the very edge of the road as he usually did, he stopped the wide-bed truck right in the middle. Then he got out and came around to open the door for her. She waited, appreciating the gentlemanly gesture.

"Thank you," she said simply.

"You're welcome," he responded, but when she turned toward the house, he caught her by the left hand, bringing her to a halt. "Why did you send back the ring?" he asked softly, enunciating each word carefully.

She didn't have the energy or the will to tell him the whole story, so she finally came out with, "It's not going to work out between me and Jordan."

Dean pressed his thumb over the vacant space on her ring finger. "You're breaking up with him?" She nodded, and then Dean was pulling her to him. "Good."

He wrapped his arms around her, dipped his head and kissed her.

Her head swimming, she pulled back enough to ask, "Is that all you have to say?"

Step by step, he backed her against the truck, asking, "What do you want me to say? That it's the best news I've heard in ages? Because it is."

Then he was kissing her again, and it was so difficult to think when he was kissing her. She tried to be sensible, though. Even as her arms slid up around his neck, she broke away again, trying to clear her brain.

"Dean," she said desperately, "I'm not sure I'm cut out for what you may have in mind."

"Hush," he told her, pressing a fingertip to her lips. "This is all I have in mind at the moment. I've waited years for this, longer than you know." He bowed his head to hers, whispering, "I've prayed for this."

He drew her like metal to magnet, so that he was no longer kissing her. She was kissing him.

By the time he stopped and said that he had to get home to Donovan, she could barely kiss him for grinning. Pushing away from her, he took several deep breaths, carefully stood her a safe distance away from the fender, then reluctantly trudged around to the driver's door and opened it then paused to shake his head at her.

*"Am I feminine?"* he parroted in a wry, silly voice. "That has to be one of the stupidest questions ever asked." He shook his head again before getting into the truck and slamming the door. Starting the engine, he gave her a hard look. Then he grinned and began back-

ing toward the drive at the rear of the house, where he could turn the truck around.

Ann laughed, practically dancing on air as she strolled through the trees to the front door.

## *Chapter Eleven*

Dancing on air.

That was how Dean felt for all of twenty-four hours. He couldn't stop smiling, and he couldn't seem to just walk anywhere. When he went down for breakfast on Thursday morning, he expected Grandma to ask why he was so happy. He didn't know what he was going to tell her.

Nothing was settled between him and Ann. She'd ended her engagement with that Jordan Teel character, and she'd kissed him, Dean, but that was all that had happened. So far.

That didn't keep Dean from dreaming and planning. He told himself that with her business know-how and his hard work, they could really build something together. He hadn't looked at her business plan yet, but when he realigned his budget, surely he could work in a reasonable payment on an engagement ring. Maybe he'd never be able to afford a diamond the size of that thing she'd taken off, but then size couldn't matter as much as the man who offered it. Could it?

All Dean really knew about Jordan Teel was what he'd

seen at Rex's wedding: an older man who spent a lot of money on clothes. Apparently Teel hadn't recognized Ann's uncertainty about her feminine appeal. Dean neither knew nor cared why she had confided in him about that, but he thanked God that she had. He would happily reassure her on that score at any time, not that he particularly wanted to tell his grandmother that.

Thankfully, as she placed his eggs before him, Betty asked only, "How was prayer meeting last night?"

"Good," he answered, taking up his fork and glancing at her. "I think it did Ann a lot of good."

Betty patted him on the shoulder as she headed back to the stove. "Prayer always does."

And that was it. Donovan was too busy smearing jelly on his toast to pay attention to anything the adults had to say. Dean smiled and ate his eggs.

Half an hour later the dually bumped over the pipes that Rex had laid out to bridge the ditch into the sorghum field, where Ann sat on the fender of her dad's truck, wearing running clothes and smiling broadly. The combine sat far in the distance, across already harvested acres, but Dean brought the dually to a halt. Only Donovan's presence kept Dean from jumping out, sweeping Ann into his arms and kissing them both stupid.

"I won't be long," Dean said to his son and his dog, opening his door and getting out.

He couldn't keep the smile off his face as he strolled over the uneven ground to greet her. "Good morning."

She nodded, her ponytail bouncing, and said, "Thought I'd come out to see how far you've gotten." Squinting across the field, she added, "Dad's heading back to the city for another treatment, and he's wondering when you'll be done. I wanted to reassure him before he goes."

"We're just about done here," Dean told her. "I'll be delivering the last of this to storage before next week."

"That soon?"

"Mmm-hmm." He pointed to the trailers already loaded with the rich fodder. "Tell him not to worry. We're making good headway."

"That will make him feel better, I'm sure."

"When will he get back home?" Dean asked.

"Not sure," she answered, shaking her head. "Meri says that a lot depends on how he handles things at this stage." Ann sighed, adding, "I can't shake the feeling that I should go with them. She had a hard time getting him home by herself last time. Would it be a hardship for you if I wasn't here to sign checks for a few days?"

Dean shook his head. "I don't have any help to pay right now. I can manage until you get back. Go if you need to."

She looked off to the east then, saying, "I'd forgotten how pretty the sunrise is out here."

"Not as pretty as you," he said, smoothing an imaginary tendril of hair away from her cheek.

Glancing down, she tilted her head just enough to maintain brief contact with his hand. "You don't have to say that."

"I've always thought you were the most beautiful girl in War Bonnet."

Pegging him with those sky eyes of hers, she smiled slightly. "You really mean that, don't you?"

"With all my heart."

Her smile grew, and she looked down at her hands,

asking, "Have you had a chance to look at the business plan I drew up for you?"

"Not yet, but I will. Tonight, hopefully."

Nodding, she hopped off the fender and moved toward the driver's door. "Okay." She opened the door and got inside the truck. He reached out and caught the edge of it before she could pull it closed.

"Ann."

"Yeah?"

"I don't know why you broke up with that Dallas guy, but if he doesn't fight for you, he's an idiot."

Sadness tinged her smile, and she shook her head. "I'm the idiot," she told him, "but at least I found out in time."

Dean crouched behind the open door, bringing his gaze level with hers. "Then he doesn't deserve you."

She laughed and rolled her eyes. "Right. I'm Jolly Billings, the best slugger ever to come out of War Bonnet High."

"And don't you forget it," he told her with a grin, coming to his feet and at the same time bending at the waist so he could kiss her forehead.

Still laughing, she started the engine. He backed away and closed the truck door.

"Go or stay, just take care," he told her through the open window.

"Say a prayer for us."

"Several," he promised.

She blew him a kiss before starting the truck forward.

Dancing on air, even as he trudged back to his own vehicle, he watched her drive out of the field and go on her way.

Then that evening he sat down to study her business

plan. The crash back to earth came as a very painful jolt indeed.

He tore the thing apart, came at it from every angle he could find, but no matter how he looked at it, her plan could not possibly work without a serious injection of capital to fund a real expansion of his business. Where he was supposed to get that kind of money, he didn't know, couldn't even imagine. Even if he took a mortgage out on the house and remaining acreage, the resulting funds would not do what Ann suggested needed to be done. As things stood, he *might* be able to establish a modest line of credit, but that was about it.

Certainly if he could find a way to get his hands on the capital that Ann believed he required, her number projections looked great, but he could see no way to come up with that much cash. Or *any* cash, really, not if he intended to feed, clothe, house and transport his son, never mind himself.

He felt sick. Reality had just crashed his dreams. He thought of the plans he'd been forming in the back of his mind, some of which had hovered there for a decade or more, never seeing the light of day until just recently. Only lately had he even dared to actually *think* these things, let alone pray about them.

Now it was as if God had just told him in no uncertain terms that Ann was not for him.

Dean had traded a college degree and a career for fatherhood, the rewards of which were too numerous to count. He should be happy with that. He would have to be happy with that. It was all he could afford, all he'd ever be able to afford, no matter how hard he worked.

Maybe, after Grandma died—he prayed that wouldn't be soon, not before Donovan was grown and on his own—Dean could sell the house and remaining land, buy more equipment and a little trailer to live in. He could live on the move, following the work, and lay up a tidy sum that way then retire secure. That was no way of life for a family man, though. That was a single man's solution.

So obviously Dean was meant to be a single man.

He stopped sneaking peeks at engagement rings on the internet and concentrated on just getting through, hour by hour. Having learned that the key to overcoming self-pity was gratitude, Dean made a concerted effort to thank God for His every blessing, starting with the redheaded, freckle-faced boy who called him Dad.

Sadly, he couldn't help wondering how long it would be before he stopped seeing Ann every time he looked at his son now. Deflated and depressed, he finished the sorghum harvest and delivered it, truckload after truckload, glad that Ann did not put in another appearance. He assumed that she'd gone to Oklahoma City with her father and sister, but he carried his statement to the house that Friday evening as usual, intending to wedge it between the casing and the edge of the front door. He didn't even make it across the porch before the door opened, however, and Callie, Rex's wife, smiled at him, her little daughter on her hip.

"Dean Paul! Hello."

"You're back," he said stupidly, his stomach dropping all the way to his toes.

She nodded her shaggy blond head, and Bodie, her baby girl, copied her. "We just got in. Rex was going to come out to see you, but you beat him to it. He's in the office looking for the checkbook. Go on in."

Dean muttered his thanks as he followed her into the

foyer, but all he could think was that Ann would surely be heading back to Dallas now. It shouldn't matter, but somehow it did.

"Where's Donovan?" Callie asked. "I have some cookies for him."

"Oh, he's already belted into his safety seat in the truck," Dean told her.

"Well, you can take them to him," Callie said. "They're already bagged up, left over from our trip. I'll just go get them while you talk to Rex."

"That's very kind," Dean managed, kneading his work cap and painfully aware that he hadn't yet made his feet budge in the direction of the office.

She hurried away, and he faced that office door, which stood open, just waiting for him to enter. Dean liked Rex; he really did, but having him home felt like the death knell to every hope and dream Dean had ever nurtured.

"In some ways, I feel like my dreams have been dashed," Ann admitted, "and in others I feel as if I'm just now waking up to reality."

Her father reached out, his hand still surprisingly heavy and strong, despite the web of hoses trailing it, and patted her knee. "I'm glad you sent back the ring," he told her, "and I think you were wise to do it without explanation. I hope you'll tender your resignation the same way, but that's for you to decide."

Sighing, Ann shrugged. She didn't know why she'd waited until now to tell her father about her broken engagement. Something about hospital rooms seemed to invite confidences. Of course, she hadn't told him all of it, just that she'd mistakenly left the line open after a telephone call very early one morning and overheard Jordan telling another woman that marrying Ann was nothing more than a career move on his part.

"He's called, but I haven't answered. The thing is, I don't know what I'll do if I don't go back to LHI," she confessed gloomily.

"What do you want to do?" her dad asked, but she dared not answer that question. She wasn't quite ready to lay herself *that* bare.

It was too soon. A woman didn't just dump her fiancé and jump to another man. Not that doing so was even an option. Dean hadn't said anything about a relationship with her. All they'd done was kiss. Maybe if she could stick around long enough, things would develop into something serious between them.

Wes cleared his throat. "Maybe I should ask *who* you want."

Ann stared at him, wide-eyed. "Am I that obvious?"

Wes chuckled. "You're both that obvious."

Groaning, Ann squeezed her eyes shut. "Now, don't get the wrong idea. Dean had nothing to do with me breaking my engagement. Nothing happened between us until I ended things with Jordan."

Her father's pale blue gaze brightened. "So something did happen between you and Dean, then."

"Nothing of any significance," she stated flatly. Unless you called having your world rocked significant.

Grinning, Wes said, "Yes, I can see that. You know, sugar, there's nothing wrong with a woman going after what she wants. Dean is a good man. I'd venture to say there are few to none better."

As if she had to be told that. Not that Dean was perfect by any means.

"He has less education than me."

"So? Most likely he could finish his degree online these days. If he wanted to. I'm not sure it makes any difference. Dean's not the sort to work for anyone but himself."

That was true, and she certainly couldn't fault him for it. But was he flexible enough to accept help when it was offered? She could help him. She knew that she could. When she'd gone over his books, she'd seen the possibilities right away, and she hadn't even been thinking about a partnership between the two of them then.

That was what she wanted with a man, a true partnership, in which each of them brought unique talents and abilities to the joining that made the pair of them together stronger and more successful than either of them could be alone. The saddest part about her and Jordan and LHI was simply that if Jordan and Marshal had sat her down and explained that with her at Jordan's side, he would soon become a vice president of the company, she would have happily and proudly hotfooted it back to Dallas as the earliest opportunity. They hadn't done it that way for one reason: It had never occurred to them. It had never occurred to them to discuss that possibility with her because Jordan did not love or value her. To him, she was a means to an end and nothing more. To Dean she was a woman whom he found attractive, but was that it?

She desperately wanted to believe that Dean saw—and wanted—the real her, the whole her, but how much of that was genuine feeling and how much was simple attraction?

"He lives with his grandmother," she said, tipping her nose into the air.

"Actually," Wes drawled, pressing his head back into

his pillow, "if you want to get technical about it, she lives with him. Milburn set up a trust when he became ill, leaving everything to Dean, with Betty and her daughter, Deana Kay Wilton, as executors until Dean turned eighteen. That's how Dean was able to sell off the land to buy farming equipment and go into business for himself after Donovan was born."

"I wonder what Betty thought about him selling off the land," Ann murmured, trying to put herself in Betty Pryor's place.

"Oh, she was all for it," Wes informed Ann. "She, Deana and Dean Paul came to talk to me about it. Stuart Crowsen had offered him a loan, but I thought the terms were…dangerous."

"You advised him to sell rather than borrow."

"I did. But only after we prayed about it first."

Ann felt her chin quiver at the thought of her father and Dean, who couldn't have been more than twenty at the time, sitting down together to pray.

*I never really prayed until Donovan came into my life…now sometimes I feel like that's all I do.*

"He's younger than me," Ann pointed out softly.

Wes chuckled. "If Dean Paul Pryor isn't a man fully grown, I'd like to know what your definition for a real adult male is."

Ann had to smile. "He's stretched out on this bed here."

"Aw, sugar."

"I have to say," Ann went on carefully, "Dean measures up pretty well. And I never thought I'd say that about any man, really." She realized with a shock that she'd just accepted at some point that no man would ever measure up to her dad. She'd been wrong about that, and because she'd been wrong, she'd been willing to settle for less than she should have.

Wes's eyes filled with tears. Reaching out, he caught his hand against the back of her head and pulled her to him for a hug that set off alarms all around the room.

Laughing and dashing away her own tears, Ann settled back into her chair to await the nurses about to burst into the room.

"Well," Wes demanded, "what are you doing sitting around here? You should be back in War Bonnet."

"You know that Meredith needs my help on the trip home," Ann replied diplomatically.

"You aren't needed until then, though," Wes told her as a pair of nurses swept through the door. They fluttered around adjusting intravenous tubes and resetting machines while he argued. "The road runs both ways, you know. Go home. Come back to get us."

"I can't take Meri's car and leave her stranded," Ann protested, but she was already out of her chair and staring at the door.

"You never heard of car rental?"

Her heart beating swiftly, Ann dropped a kiss onto her father's forehead. "I love you, Dad."

"I love you, too," he rumbled, "and I'm pretty fond of that redheaded kid who keeps eating my cookies."

Laughing, Ann practically flew from the room.

Getting out of Oklahoma City took considerably more time than Ann expected, so the hour was later than she'd have liked when she pulled her sister's little car to a stop beneath the old tree behind the ranch house on Saturday evening. They'd arranged a rental for Meredith to drive, and then Ann had needed to repack, eat, find an ATM to make sure she had cash, fill up the gas tank, call Rex to let him know she was on her way home...

When she came through the back door, the house was quiet and dark except for the distant hum and flicker of the television in the living room. Aware that her little niece would be sleeping, Ann carried her suitcase through the mudroom, past the rear bath that opened into both the hall and her father's room, through the kitchen and up the back stairs. A glimpse into the living room showed her two figures sitting close together on the leather sofa.

Ann considered calling out to let her brother and sister-in-law know that she was there, but she didn't want to wake the baby. Instead, she slipped up the stairs and dropped her bags in her room then crept back down to the kitchen where she flipped on a light, went to the sink and ran a glass of water, clinking dishes and bumping into chairs. Basically, she did everything she could think of to signal her presence without waking baby Bodie.

When she walked into the living room, Rex and Callie looked over at her.

"How was your trip?" Rex asked.

"Boring," she answered drily, plopping down into her father's recliner. "I hate driving alone."

"Then why did you?" Rex asked.

"I was in the way at the hospital," she said, leaning back in the chair. "And Meri's cat's lousy company."

He rolled his eyes. "I can't stay at Meri's apartment with that cat, either."

"I thought maybe I could be of more use here." She plucked at a knotted thread in the denim of her jeans. "How's the sorghum going?"

"It's done," Rex told her easily, draping his arm

around his wife's shoulders. "Dean delivered the last of it yesterday evening."

"That's it?" she blurted, feeling stung. She'd known that it would be soon, but she'd thought it would happen Monday maybe.

Rex nodded, playing with a tendril of Callie's short, wispy hair. "Good harvest. And he did a great job with the mixing station. He actually moved the footprint slightly, but it works better this way. He would know, of course, how best to place it so you can back a pickup bed right up to the mixing pan."

Ann hummed in agreement, but all she could think was that Dean wouldn't be coming back to the ranch, not until planting time, anyway. Callie laid her head on Rex's shoulder, and he bent his head to whisper into her ear. She nodded, and they began rising from the sofa. A shaft of envy speared straight through Ann.

"Guess we'll call it a night, sis. Glad you made it home safe. See you in the morning."

Nodding, she reminded herself that they were deliriously in love and basically still honeymooning, but it did no good. As they left the room, arm in arm, she knew with sudden, shocking clarity that she wanted exactly what they had, that calm, sure, complimentary partnership underpinned with a deep abiding love, an unmistakable physical attraction and a shared, unshakeable faith. It seemed so simple, really—and all-encompassing.

Everything. It was everything.

Suddenly what she'd had—even what she'd *thought* she'd had—with Jordan seemed small, shabby and artificial. She couldn't believe that she'd been willing to settle for what he'd offered, what she'd actually thought she wanted. For the first time she realized how truly great a fool she had been.

Jordan, she realized, could not be blamed for her shallow foolishness, only for taking advantage of it. No, this was all on her. She'd let her insecurities drive her away from what was most dear in her life and had clung to her career and intellectual abilities for redemption, rather than her faith. Perhaps she'd even been angry with God for making her less than what she'd imagined she should be, when that had never been the case. She'd allowed one unimportant person's opinion to color her entire life and determine her future, even her career path, and she'd almost let it lead her to commit a great folly in marrying the wrong man.

Well, no more.

She told God how sorry she was, and then, as she turned off the TV and the lights and climbed the stairs, she began to pray for courage.

## Chapter Twelve

Dean knew the moment that Ann Billings entered the sanctuary. He'd have known even if heads hadn't turned, which had prompted his to turn, as well. Something in the air changed when Ann came around. He'd felt it long, long ago, a specific electrical charge as unique to Ann as the smell of her skin, the color of her hair, the taste of her lips. That electricity shimmered through him even as his head turned and his torso twisted, his gaze unerringly targeting the tall, elegantly beautiful woman strutting down the aisle in lemon-yellow shoes with ridiculously tall heels.

The shoes matched the tank top that she wore beneath the slender, charcoal-gray suit that screamed money and class to everyone in the room. The straight skirt stopped demurely at her knees, and the neatly tailored jacket nipped in at the waist in a decidedly feminine fashion. She'd caught her long, vibrant hair in a neat bun at the nape of her neck, allowing long tendrils to frame a face made up with the barest touch of rosy lipstick and dark mascara.

She looked like a queen, certainly not a farmer's wife.

Most especially not the wife of a farmer without a farm of his own.

He didn't have the courage to approach her, but he didn't have the strength to ignore her, either. Feeling beaten by the sheer, unreachable beauty of her, Dean turned away, pierced to the core, and prayed that she'd keep her distance. He didn't think he could bear being around her; he didn't think he could resist if she pressed.

Not a word of the service stuck in his mind. It all flowed right through his thoughts like so much flotsam in a stream. He tried to seize on the theme of the sermon, to lose himself in worship, to feel the presence of the Holy Spirit as he had so often in the past, but all he could feel, all he could think about, all he could focus upon was Ann and the deep, yawning sense of loss that he felt.

Beside him, his grandmother shifted uneasily. She had sensed that all was not well with him. He'd blamed the pending start of the school year in just three days' time, but he wasn't sure that Betty bought it. Even Donovan had felt his father's disquiet. The boy had climbed onto Dean's lap the previous evening for tickles and hugs, something he hadn't done in quite a while. He was such a big boy that he had outgrown Dean's lap, and his laughter, while bright and warming, had seemed just a little forced. Dean had felt grateful but not comforted.

He missed her. He would always miss her, but everything—including that dazzling suit she wore today—said that she didn't belong with him. Agonizing internally, he opened his Bible to Romans, his favorite book, and thumbed through the pages until his gaze fell on the second verse of the twelfth chapter.

*Do not conform to the pattern of this world, but be*

*transformed by the renewing of your mind. Then you will be able to test and approve what God's will is—His good, pleasing and perfect will.*

The pattern of the world. Did that mean Dean should disregard all these signs he thought he saw, everything that seemed to tell him that he and Ann couldn't work? Or was that so much wishful thinking on his part? He shook his head, knowing that he couldn't trust himself to divine anything correctly. His desire got in the way. So much for renewing his mind.

He flipped a few pages over and came to the eighth chapter. Verse twenty-seven said, *And He Who searches our hearts knows the mind of the Spirit, because the Spirit intercedes for God's people in accordance with the will of God.*

Dean closed his eyes and simply thought, *Intercede for me, Lord. I don't know what to say or do except... thank You.*

After the service he went straight out the side door to get Donovan. As usual, the boy bubbled over with what he'd learned that morning, waving around his coloring papers and story folder. Dean nodded and listened, half hearing as he shepherded his son back to the sanctuary. There he found his grandmother and Ann cozily chatting amongst a knot of three or four other women.

Ann's gaze zipped unerringly to meet his. Then suddenly Donovan ran across the emptying sanctuary to throw himself at her.

"Ann! You're back!"

She went down on her knees to greet him, accepting his hug with a wide smile. "Hello, Donovan!"

"You can come, then," he declared. "Dad said you

might not be back in time, but you are, so you can come for the first day of school!"

Ann glanced up at Dean then smiled apologetically at his son. "I can't promise, Donovan. I'm sorry. I may have to go back before Wednesday."

"Awwww." Donovan stepped away, slapping his hands against his thighs in disappointment.

"My father will be very ill when he gets out of the hospital," Ann explained gently. "My sister can't drive and take care of him, too. I have to go help. But it may not be on Wednesday. I just don't know yet."

"The hospital is in Oklahoma City," Dean said, gathering Donovan against him. He knew just how the boy felt, but nothing could be done about this. "You've been to the city. You remember, don't you?"

Donovan nodded. "It's a long way," he whispered huskily.

"Perhaps Ann would like to join us for Sunday dinner," Betty suggested, "just in case she's not able to be here on Wednesday."

Dean felt as if he'd received a blow to the gut, but Donovan looked up with a grin. "Okay! We got kittens in the barn."

Ann's eyebrows jumped. "Kittens?"

"Yeah, four of them," Donovan reported happily, "but we can't keep 'em all."

Ann groaned and looked at Dean. "You won't tell Meri, will you? She's insane for cats."

He couldn't help but smile. His heart was cracking into pieces, but she could still make him smile. "Not a word," he solemnly pledged.

"I have to go home and change," Ann said, cupping Donovan's chin in her hand.

Betty chuckled. "We'll see you shortly."

"Yes, and thank you."

She looked Dean straight in the eye then, as if willing him to repeat his grandmother's invitation—or rescind it. He could do nothing more than nod and usher his son up the aisle after his rapidly retreating grandmother.

He didn't have the courage to welcome Ann or the strength to rebuff her.

*Intercede for me. Intercede for me. Oh, please, Lord, intercede for me...*

Dean hadn't exactly welcomed her at church that morning. Ann had to wonder if he regretted the kisses they'd shared. Maybe he feared that she had developed expectations. She had not—unless wishes were expectations.

After changing her clothes, Ann thought about calling the Pryors to cancel, using the excuse that Callie had prepared a special dinner without her knowledge, which was true. But then every meal Callie prepared seemed to be special, and both Callie and Rex encouraged her to go. Because Rex happened to be on the phone with their father at the time, Wes got in on the act, asking to speak to Ann himself.

"So, Sunday dinner with the Pryors, huh? Well, that's a tonic to a sick man."

Now, how could she argue with that, especially as he sounded sick? She brightened her chatter, mentioning that Donovan was campaigning to get her to accompany him and his father to his first day of kindergarten on Wednesday.

"Sounds like a fine idea," Wes said. "You should go."

"I'm just not sure about the timing," Ann countered. "I want to get back to the city before you need me."

"Kindergarten's only half-day. Right?"

"Yes."

"Then I see no problem," Wes said. "Take the boy to school. Pick him up again afterward. Then head up here. We can be home before bedtime. Unless that's too much driving for you in one day."

"No, no," Ann hastened to assure him. "That's fine. If you're sure."

"Works for me," Wes told her. "Now I need a nap."

Praying for her father's recovery and thanking God for his wisdom and generosity, Ann got in the truck and drove over to the Pryor place.

The old clapboard house, with its crisp white paint and unusual rounded porch that wrapped two sides of the first floor, seemed in pristine condition. Its pale green metal roof lent an air of gentility to the place, and the guttering, railings, flower beds and brick steps and walkways showed that a great deal of time and attention had been showered on the place over the decades. Easily a hundred years old, the inner windows still bore the wavy glass of the original era. Ann saw no chimney, only a smokestack. Three black rocking chairs, painted to match the trim around the many tall, narrow windows and doors, took pride of place on the porch, pots of colorful flowers spilling over around them.

A screen door at the end of the porch banged open, and Donovan and Digger came running out to greet her. She brought the truck to a stop on a neat patch of gravel hemmed in by railroad ties next to a large, white metal barn with three garage bays and several smaller doors. At the other end of the property she saw a white chicken coop with the same pale green metal roof as the house and barn. The whole tableau made a very sweet picture, especially given the tire swing and tree house in the big hickory shading the porch.

Dean came out of a door in the barn and lifted a hand in what seemed a halfhearted greeting. Ann slid out of the truck and smiled at him.

"Good news," he announced. "The cat's moved her kittens to some unknown location."

Ann chuckled. "You'll find them."

"I'm afraid so. Just not today."

"What a lovely place," she said then, glancing around. "Neat as a pin."

"Grandma's a great believer in orderliness," he divulged, ducking his head. "There's iced tea on the porch."

"Sounds nice."

Donovan hit her with a hug just as they rounded the rear end of the truck. "Come see my tree house!"

"I saw it when I drove up. Looks cool."

"Dad and me built it. Watch how you get up."

He ran to the tree and pulled on a rope. A ramp with rails slid down, braces dropping into place to keep it steady. Donovan half crawled, half ran up it, the dog on his heels.

Ann turned a delighted smile on Dean. "Wow! Did you do that?"

"He was pretty small when we built that," Dean said. "Too small to climb a ladder. We had to come up with some other way for him to get up there."

Donovan peeked over the wall of the tree house, calling, "Come on up!"

"Is it all right?"

"Sure. Go on."

She went up the ramp, finding it solid and steady, and crept through the open doorway on her hands and knees.

Standing was possible in the center of the platform, but Dean had put a sloping roof on the thing so that it was sheltered from rain, and the outer walls were only tall enough for her if she stayed on her knees. She sat with her legs folded while Digger lolled in one corner and Donovan showed her his treasures: a huge acorn, a collection of cat-eye marbles in a tin box, several tiny cars, the skull of a squirrel and a trio of "super power" rings.

"I'm gonna sleep out here sometime," he announced, looking around with satisfaction. "Maybe this year."

She had the feeling that this event depended completely on his willingness to brave the night out-of-doors on his own.

"That sounds like fun," Ann said. "I remember the first time I slept outside. My brother and sister and I pitched a tent in our front yard and camped out. I never knew there were so many sounds outside at night."

"Dad and me, we've listened to 'em," Donovan confirmed sagely. Ann hid her smile, assuming that such listening might be the reason Donovan had not yet slept in his tree house.

The screen door on the house creaked again, and Betty appeared on the porch. "Dinner in fifteen minutes, everyone."

Ann went up on her knees and waved at Betty, calling down to her, "Anything I can do to help?"

"You and Dean can set the table, if you like," she called back, squinting up at the shadows beneath the tree.

"I'll take care of it," Dean said, starting toward the house.

Ann looked at Donovan, winked and said, "We better go."

"Come on, Digger," Donovan said, crawling to the exit. Ann followed.

It was easier to stand going down the ramp than it had been going up. She trailed Donovan across the thick grass to the brick walkway, with its lovely herringbone pattern. Dean waited for her at the top of the porch steps, a tall tumbler of cool iced tea in hand.

He nodded to Donovan, saying, "You go on in and wash up." Passing the cool glass to Ann, he added, "You just relax out here. Company shouldn't have to set the table."

"I don't mind," she told him, taking the glass.

"It's not too warm out here in the shade," he said, nodding toward one of the rocking chairs as she took a long drink of the cold, sweet tea.

"Oh, that's good," she gasped, feeling the icy coolness sweep through her. "Now, lead the way inside. I don't mind helping out at all."

Dean's jaw ground side to side, but he nodded and turned toward the door. She didn't understand the issue, unless he *really* just didn't want her here. He opened the screen and turned the brass knob on the interior door, pushing it open for her. She stepped straight into a long, narrow, pearl-gray room with a potbellied stove in the far corner.

"Does that work?" Ann asked in surprise.

"It does, but it's a replica, a pellet stove. Grandma turned the original into a planter out back. That's where she grows her herbs."

"How ingenious!"

"You'd be surprised how much heat that pellet stove puts out," Dean told her. "It really knocks down the utility bills in the winter."

"Interesting. It looks right in here, too."

He grimaced. "It's all replicas in here because that's the style Grandma likes. The dining room furniture, though, that was Grandma's great-great-grandma's, and she won't part with it, no matter how much veneer falls off it or how wobbly it gets."

"Well, I don't blame her," Ann said, walking over to look at an old portrait in an oval frame. "Surely this isn't a reproduction."

"No, no. That's Great-Great-Grandpa Hayden. I almost named my son Hayden, but I wanted him to have his mother's last name, Jessup, and one family name seemed enough for one tiny baby, so in the end I settled on Donovan."

"It's a good name, Donovan Jessup Pryor. But I like Hayden, too. Maybe you can use it for your next child."

Dean looked positively stricken for a moment. Then he lifted a hand, indicating a door at the end of the room near the stove. "Um, this way."

They walked over a rag rug atop a gleaming hardwood floor. Ann noted delicate crocheted doilies and enameled chinaware atop colonial-style tables. Somehow, the flat-screen TV atop the buffet-cum-entertainment center in front of the humpbacked sofa managed to look intrinsic and cozy in the old-fashioned room.

As they entered the dining room, Dean pointed to a chair placed against the wall and said, "Don't sit there. It's not safe. In fact, only the chairs around the table are sturdy enough to sit in."

Because there were five chairs around the table, Ann saw no problem. The size of the sideboard and china cabinet told her that the ornate, rectangular table was missing two, perhaps three, leafs. Ann went straight to the china cabinet, where Betty was setting out plates.

"What a magnificent piece of furniture."

"It's English," Betty told her proudly. "Been in my

family seven generations, eight now with Donovan. Great-Great-Grandpa Dilman Hayden bought it used for Great-Great-Grandma Rosalie at an estate sale in Boston. She gave it to her daughter, Mary Nell, who gave it to her daughter, Susanna, who gave it to her son, Arnold, who passed it down to me. Dean's mother cares nothing for it, but his aunt Deana and I agree that it ought to go to him and then, hopefully, to Donovan or another of Dean's children."

"Grandma," Dean grumbled, "Ann's not interested in our antiques or our family history."

"But I am," Ann refuted brightly. "I think it's beautiful furniture, and I love the history of it. I think you should have it completely restored."

"And how do you suggest we pay for that?" Dean snapped, his hand going to the back of his neck. "The last estimate we got was over a thousand dollars, so we'll just have to make do. Or eat in the kitchen." Betty sent him a troubled look.

Too late, Ann realized that Dean might fear she would find his home and its contents below her standards.

"We eat in the kitchen all the time," she said with a shrug, setting aside her tea to carry the stacked plates to the table, "but if we had this table, I'd insist that we eat in the dining room, even if we had to sit on benches."

Glimpsing the triumphant smile that Betty shot Dean, Ann walked around the table, setting the plates, which were painted with delicate pink peonies and drooping bluebells, onto blue place mats. Dean brought around blue cut-glass tumblers and grass-green napkins rolled neatly inside brass rings adorned with pink china peonies.

"It looks like a garden," Ann said, stepping back.

"Grandma likes her 'pretties,' as she calls them,"

Dean commented, placing a set of brass salt-and-pepper shakers in the center of the table.

"I can see that," Ann told him, walking over to finger a ruffled doily beneath an impressive soup tureen on the sideboard. "My mother would have loved this place. I can almost see her here."

"Oh?"

Ann nodded and put her back to the sideboard. "I didn't get her domestic gene, I'm afraid, but I love the history of these things and the continuity of them."

"Aunt Deana likes modern stuff," Dean said, trailing a finger along the edge of the table, "but I don't mind the old stuff, so long as it's serviceable."

"If you take care of things, then they remain serviceable," she pointed out.

"I do my best," Dean said shortly.

"I know you do."

Donovan came into the room with a basket full of hot biscuits. "Daddy, can I have a biscuit with butter? Please? It won't ruin my dinner, I promise. Grandma says for you to come get the roast."

"I'll get the roast," Dean said, looking askance at his son, "and the butter. Ann, would you see to it that he gets into his booster seat?"

"Happy to."

Donovan didn't need help. He was sitting in his booster seat with an open biscuit on his plate before she could get the chair out from under the table. She shoved it back again while he picked around the edges of the steaming bread. Dean brought in the butter dish and the pot roast then went out again to help Betty carry in the vegetables and tea. Ann buttered Donovan's biscuit and watched him quickly devour the thing, smacking his lips and closing his eyes in ecstasy. Ann had to laugh.

"He loves Grandma's biscuits even more than Callie's cookies," Dean said, placing a pitcher of tea and a bowl of ice cubes on the sideboard.

"Mmm-hmm," Donovan agreed, licking butter from his fingers.

"I don't think I've ever enjoyed anything that much," Ann said.

"Wait until she brings in the honey to go with the biscuits," Dean said, leaning close to speak softly into Ann's ear. Donovan caught the salient word, however, and crowed with delight.

"Honey!"

"*After* you eat your vegetables," Dean dictated.

Donovan wiggled excitedly in his chair and picked up his fork. Shaking his head, Dean walked around and pulled out a chair for Ann then did the same for his grandmother, who entered the room just then with a platter of vegetables to go with the pot roast. He took his own seat at the head of the table. Ann felt sure that he'd been occupying that chair since his grandfather had died. Dean had been all of, what, fifteen years of age then? As he clasped his hands together and bowed his head to pray over the meal, Ann recalled what her father had said about him.

*A man fully grown.* That was how her father had described Dean, and as usual Wes was correct. Dean had been the owner of this property since the age of fifteen, and when he'd wound up a father at the age of twenty, he'd taken responsibility for his actions, listened to wise counsel, found a solution to his problems and gone to work, surrendering himself to Christ in the process. She, on the other hand, had been a Christian almost her entire life, the product of a loving, two-parent home, raised with every advantage, and she'd let petty insecurities drive her away from her home and the people who loved her most. She felt so foolish.

There was grown, and there was mature. In some ways, Dean was much older than she was.

It was time for her to actually grow up.

## Chapter Thirteen

"Come up! Come up! Come up and see my room," Donovan urged. "I got the whole attic to myself. Don't I, Dad?"

"You do," Dean confirmed, "but you know the rules. What do we do after meals?"

"Clear the table," Donovan announced. "I get the salt and pepper. And the butter."

"Just keep your fingers out of the butter," Dean ordered with a chuckle, pushing the dish to the edge of the table so Donovan could reach it. "Then you can take the napkins to the laundry and put away the napkin rings."

Donovan ran off with the butter dish, while Dean began gathering plates and Betty started carrying leftovers to the kitchen. Ann didn't ask what she could do, just began picking up glasses and cradling them in the crook of one arm.

"You're going to get your shirt wet doing that," Dean complained. "We'll take care of this."

"It'll dry," she rebutted easily. "I want to help."

Dean frowned, but he said nothing else, just led the way into the kitchen. The large, bright room surprised

Ann. By far the most modern room in the house that she'd seen thus far, it boasted tall cabinets painted a soft yellow, mellow gold walls, brick flooring, a metal-topped island, a sweet little maple table and chairs, and white enamel stove unlike anything Ann had ever seen. It had at least three ovens and a grill and five burners. She left the glasses on the metal countertop and went straight to it.

"I have never seen such a cookstove. Mom had something similar but not so big."

Betty grinned broadly. "Amazing, isn't it? Built new in 1940. Milburn bought it used to restore, but he didn't get it finished before he died. We didn't have money for Christmas the year after he passed, but Dean managed to get this back in working order and all shined up like new for me. They don't make them like this anymore." She ran a hand lovingly over the gleaming enamel.

"Mom said the same thing," Ann told her, smiling at Dean.

"A new stove like this costs thousands and thousands of dollars," Betty said proudly.

"It's just an old stove," Dean said, shaking his head.

"It's a work of art!" Ann exclaimed. "Believe me, I've seen hotel kitchens with less."

He shook his head again, but the beginnings of a smile tugged at the corners of his lips. "I believe you're expected upstairs," he said, waving her toward a door that opened into a hallway.

"I am." She smiled at Betty. "I understand that Donovan has the attic all to himself."

The older woman chuckled. "He was promised his dad's old room when he started school. We made the move last week."

"Milestone after milestone," Ann said.

"And coming on fast," Dean grumbled, leading the way.

They passed a bedroom and a bathroom before they came to the narrow stairs. Two more rooms seemed to lay beyond, but he didn't lead her that far down the hall. Instead, they climbed the stairs. Donovan waited halfway up.

"This way! This way!" he called, as if another path might magically appear.

There was no door. The staircase, surrounded by tall railings, opened right into the middle of the long, narrow space. A desk had been placed beneath a window at the end of the room. Donovan's backpack rested atop it. A narrow bed had been tucked into the corner on one side of the railing, along with a dresser and chair. The other side of the room was basically one long wall of shelves and cubbyholes with a space at the end for a closet.

Donovan twirled in the space before the desk, his arms outstretched, and cried, "Ta-da!"

"Utterly perfect," Ann pronounced, taking it all in. She looked at Dean, who remained on the stairs, his arms braced on the railings. "This was your room?"

"Until I went to college," he confirmed. "After Donovan was born, it was easier to be downstairs with him in the room next to me."

"I'm gonna live here forever!" Donovan exclaimed.

Ann laughed. "It is a fun room."

She let the boy show her all of his most treasured possessions, including the photo album that he kept under his bed. He had photos of the mother and great-grandfather he'd never met, as well as his grandmother, Dean's mother, whom he called by her given name, Wynona. Obviously Wynona had taken after her father, Milburn in looks, and so had Dean. Sadly, she didn't seem to have inherited either of her parents' sense of responsibility. Thankfully, Dean had.

"Wynona comes around sometimes," Donovan said offhandedly, closing the album with a snap. "Mostly it just makes Grandma mad when she does, though. I wish you could come on Wednesday," he whined. "You know, just for the first time."

"Well," Ann said, wrapping her arms around him as they sat there on the edge of his bed, "it just so happens that I don't have to go to the city until Wednesday afternoon."

Catching his breath, Donovan tilted his head back and looked up at her. She winked, and he whooped.

"Yippee!" Twisting, he threw an arm around her neck, toppling her onto the bed. Suddenly he scrambled up. "Hey, now I got a dad *and* a mom to take me. Well, sort of a mom."

Ann willed back a sudden rush of tears, smiled and said, "A substitute mom. A—a stand-in."

"Yeah." He beamed. "A sustitude mom. I gotta tell Grandma!"

He tore around the end of the railing. Dean stepped up out of his way, admonishing Donovan to slow down. Ann rose from the bed to follow in the boy's happy wake, but she didn't make it past his father. Dean lifted his hands to her shoulders, where they hovered uncertainly.

"You didn't have to do that," he said softly.

"But I wanted to."

Sighing, he finally brought his hands to gently frame her face. She closed her eyes, feeling the sweetly magnetic pull that had only ever existed with this man, and willed him to kiss her. In the end, however, he kissed not her lips but her forehead. She tried not to be disappointed, tried not to fear that he had thought better of an involvement with her now that he knew she was actually available. As she walked down those stairs, however, she knew that while she might be a very welcome substitute mom to Donovan, she had absolutely no reason to hope that she might one day be a beloved wife to his father.

Substitute mother did not equal wife. Dean reminded himself of that fact over and over again throughout the coming days and nights. He kept as busy as he could, which wasn't difficult, given that he'd arranged to take off the rest of the week after school started, so he had lots to do before then. Both he and Donovan had some serious adjustments to make, and he wanted to be readily available if the school called to say that Donovan was having a difficult time. At least that was what he told himself. The truth was that he was dreading going back out into the field without his son at his side.

He remembered what it had been like when Donovan was a baby. No one could be better suited to caring for an infant than Grandma Betty, but Dean had felt an irrational fear and resentment at having to be away from his son all day. He'd made a point of returning to the house for lunch just to hold and cuddle the miraculous little bundle of humanity that had so radically changed his life. As soon as Donovan was out of diapers—and that was earlier than with many children—Dean had started taking the boy with him.

Those days were over now, and Dean felt as if his whole life had upended yet again. It was foolish to feel such emptiness just because Donovan was starting school. If he couldn't handle this, what would happen to him when Donovan actually left home?

He and Ann hadn't discussed arrangements for Donovan's first day of school. Dean had avoided doing so because he didn't want her to know what a difficult time he had talking about it. Grandma had decided that she would be better off staying home; she didn't want to cry in front of Donovan for fear he would conclude that school was a bad thing. Dean was feeling pretty emotional about it himself, though he could feign enthusiasm without tears. As for Donovan, he bubbled with excitement and at the same time felt obvious trepidation. Dean didn't know which one of them was more pleased when they walked out the front door of the house on Wednesday morning and found Ann waiting for them.

Dressed in jeans, boots and a pretty blouse, her long, straight hair hanging from a simple side part, she leaned against the fender of a white metallic BMW two-door coupe with a deep red interior.

"I hope you don't mind," she said. "I switched Donovan's safety seat from your backseat to mine."

That sleek, low, expensive automobile demonstrated the chasm between them as little else could, but Dean couldn't find it in him to protest. Ann was a successful woman. She deserved a fine car, and what could it hurt?

He lifted an eyebrow at his son. "Riding in style."

Whooping, Donovan ran for the Beemer. Dean followed more circumspectly, watching Ann help Donovan belt himself into the seat. To his surprise, as soon as he drew near, she tossed him the key fob then got into the car on the passenger side. He didn't argue, just walked around, removed his hat and dropped down behind the steering wheel.

"It's been a while since I drove a car," he admitted.

She chuckled. "Somehow I think you can manage."

He needed a little while to figure out how to start the thing. It had no key. He soon had them on the road, however. Donovan was fascinated by the video display. Used to the dually pickup truck, Dean found the interior somewhat tight, but he loved the way the vehicle handled. When they pulled into the school parking lot, Dean realized with a shock that he hadn't fretted a bit on the trip into town. He'd been too much focused on the experience of driving Ann's sweet little ride to even think about their destination. Giving her a direct look as he slapped the key fob into her palm, he silently wondered if she'd planned that.

She smiled and said, "I was enthralled for a full month after I first bought this thing."

Dean shook his head, but he was smiling, too. "You're scary, you know that?"

"I didn't think a clever woman would frighten you," she quipped, opening her door.

They all got out and headed into the building, Donovan bouncing excitedly between Dean and Ann. Fifteen or twenty other kindergarteners beat along the same path. About half seemed to be accompanied by two parents. Some were younger children ushered in by older siblings and mothers. A few had parents and some grandparents along. Clearly, Donovan would have been the only child escorted by his father only.

Donovan's teacher knew both Dean and Ann. She also clearly knew that they weren't married, but she diplomatically avoided addressing either of them in any way that called attention to that fact. If she was surprised to see them together, she hid it well.

While Dean signed a permission slip to allow Donovan to have chocolate milk that morning, Ann helped Donovan find his assigned cubby and hang up his backpack. The teacher said they would unpack their supplies later. Then it was time for hugs and goodbyes. Suddenly, Donovan turned up shy, clinging to both Dean and Ann. For the first time Dean felt tongue-tied when it came to his son. He simply did not know what to say at that moment. Ann, however, did.

She knelt and smoothed the collar of Donovan's striped knit shirt, softly saying, "Do you know, I think you're the biggest boy in the room. When I was a girl in school, I had a friend who was the biggest boy in the room. He was also the nicest boy, always smiling and sharing. He made me feel so safe. Your class is blessed to have you because you're the nicest boy I know."

Donovan beamed. The teacher astutely pointed him to an activity, asking if he knew how it worked. When he replied that he did, she suggested that he help others with it. He proudly ran off to do that. A friend from church joined him at the table, and just like that he was laughing and happy. Suddenly, Dean realized, his son was a schoolkid.

A space seemed to open inside Dean's chest. He gulped, feeling a lump in his throat and the unexpected blur of tears. Without a word he strode out into the hallway and headed for the parking lot. Ann caught up to him just as he pushed through the door. The instant it clanged shut behind him, she grabbed his hand, yanking him to a halt. Then she was on her tiptoes in front of him, her arms about his neck in a ferocious hug. He couldn't do anything except put his head on her shoulder and hug her back.

"Ridiculous," he muttered apologetically.

She shook her head. "No," she whispered. "It's wonderful." Somehow that was all he needed to regain control. Sighing, he straightened. She took him by the hand and towed him toward the car, saying, "Let's get some coffee."

That sounded very good. Dean felt strangely deflated and exhausted.

Ann drove them over to the diner. There they chose a table in the corner and settled in to nurse cups of coffee so strong that Dean almost couldn't drink it. He got enough of it down to temper the rest of it with cream. Then the waitress topped off the cup, and he was right back where he'd started. He thought a piece of pie might make the brew more palatable, and he was right, so he ate another, and all the while, Ann held his hand and he talked.

"I know it's stupid to be this broken up about my kid starting school," he admitted. "It's just that I'm so used to having him around, you know?"

"He knocks out every step you make all day, every day."

"Some folks think having him out there isn't safe, but I figure with me is the safest place he can be. I always know where he is and what he's doing."

"I realize that."

"He never gets into trouble, and he's learned a lot just being around while I work, you know?"

"No doubt about it."

"You hear about bad things happening in schools," he worried aloud.

"In War Bonnet?"

He shoved a hand through his hair. "Of course not. I'm being stupid."

"You're being a great father," she countered.

"I offered to marry his mother," Dean divulged quietly, needing Ann to know that. "She wanted no part of me. Or him. She'd have aborted or given him up for adoption if I hadn't insisted on taking custody."

"Were you in love with her?" Ann asked.

"Not at all. I met her at a party one night."

"You were young. You made a mistake," Ann said, clasping his hand, "but then you stepped up and did all the right things after."

"So far all I've had to do is love him, feed him, house him, clothe him and keep him clean." Dean chuckled. "The last has been the hardest part." His amusement dwindled. "Honestly, feeding, housing and clothing him hasn't exactly been a piece of cake."

"That was the whole point of the business plan," Ann said.

Realizing that the time had come to address that issue forthrightly, Dean sat back in his chair, pulling his hand from hers.

"Jolly, I appreciate your work on that, but I've got to tell you. That plan of yours is just so much pie in the sky." She cocked her head, staring at him solemnly. He sat forward again, folding his arms along the edge of the tabletop. "Sweetheart, I'll never have the kind of capital your plan calls for. I wouldn't borrow it even if I could, which I cannot. And I won't sell my grandmother's home out from under her. Not only did she raise me as her own, she's helping to raise my son. And you may not know this, but when my grandpa died, he left everything to me. Not to Grandma. To *me*. He trusted me to take care of her, and I'll do that to her last breath. Or mine. It's a great business plan, and I'd love to put it into effect, but

I don't see any way to make it happen. Those are just the facts. I'm sorry to disappoint you."

Ann smiled, softly, warmly. "I don't think you could disappoint me if you tried."

He took her hand again, squeezing it gently. "Thank you for that."

"What about an investor?"

Blinking at her, he needed a moment to process that idea. "An investor? Who would invest in me? Please tell me you didn't ask your dad—"

"No, no. Not with him so ill."

Dean relaxed somewhat. "Good. He's done enough for me already."

"He's quite a fan of yours," Ann said, "but this is someone who wants to invest in War Bonnet."

"Oh?"

"Someone who's been away for a while and…misses it."

"But what does that have to do with me?"

She took a deep breath, not quite meeting his gaze any longer. "Well, it's someone who's looking for something to *do* around here." She paused then softly added, "Someone who doesn't want to go back where she came from."

Dean's heart *thunked* inside his chest and then began to speed up. He flattened his hands against the tabletop.

"Where *she* came from?" he repeated. Ann nodded without looking at him. Dean could hardly speak, his heart was racing so fast. "And did *she* come from Dallas?"

Ann looked at him then, saying urgently. "I have the money, Dean."

"You have the money," he said, trying to wrap his mind around this. "Where? In, like, a retirement fund or something?"

"No! I wouldn't touch that," Ann assured him. Dean

knew that he was gaping at her, but he couldn't seem to help himself. "I have savings, investments. I've been making six figures for five years, Dean, and I don't even pay rent."

"And you want to move back to War Bonnet," he asked, thumping the tabletop with a finger for emphasis, "to invest in a custom farming business? Farming without an actual farm. Farming for other people."

She looked him straight in the eye then, and the smile she gave him both melted his insides and sent his hopes soaring.

"Sort of," she said huskily. "What I really want to invest in is *you*. I believe in you, Dean, in who and what you are."

Dumbfounded, Dean sat back in his chair, rubbed a hand over his face and silently asked God how this could possibly work.

Could he take her money, work alongside her day after day, grow his business, raise his standard of living and have a chance to make her more than a business partner? He had no doubt that she knew her stuff, that she could help him, but was it more than that? Could it be more than that?

Her heart in her throat, Ann waited for Dean's response to her proposal, but he simply stared at her.

Just then the phone behind the cash register jangled. Ann's nerve endings jangled, as well, and she glanced in that direction. Jenny, the middle-aged waitress, appeared and plucked up the receiver.

"Diner." She listened for a few moments, made a face and glanced around, her gaze alighting on Dean and Ann. "I'll see what I can do." Lowering the receiver, she called across the room. "Hey, Dean, think you could do me a favor?"

Dean twisted around on his chair. "Sure, Jenny. What's up?"

"Your bill's on the house if you can run an order over to the high school for me."

Dean looked at Ann, who shrugged. "I've got nothing going until we pick up Donovan from school at noon."

Turning back to the waitress and rising from his chair, Dean said, "We'll take that deal, Jenny."

Shooting him a thumbs-up signal, Jenny spoke into the phone. "It'll be right over." She hung up and smiled at Dean. "One second. It's waiting in the kitchen."

While Ann gathered her small handbag, dropped a tip on the table and rose, Dean strolled over to the counter. Ann arrived at almost the same moment as Jenny and the cook did. The pair of them bore a large brown paper bag stuffed to the max and a flat, rectangular cardboard box.

"This needs to go to Coach Lyons's office. They got some kind of meeting going on and some confusion about whoever was supposed to pick up the food. The school runs a tab and pays for it monthly, so you won't have to worry about collecting money."

"Okay."

"You'll want to go to the field house behind the ball field and—"

"I know where it is," Dean interrupted.

"Don't set anything on top of this box," Jenny instructed, placing the box on the countertop. "It's filled with those lemon crème pastries Coach loves."

"He's still eating those things?"

"Every chance he gets." She leaned close and muttered out of the corner of her mouth, "We buy 'em frozen and nuke 'em in the microwave, but don't tell him that."

Dean chuckled. "Your secret's safe with me."

Ann smiled, remembering with bittersweet poignancy the lemon crème pastries that she had delivered to Coach's office in the past. All the kids had known that they were his special weakness and had often plied him with lemon crèmes when begging forgiveness for some failure or misdeed. Ann had sprung for half a dozen during her sophomore year after blowing off several hours of softball camp at Oklahoma State University to run around Stillwater with her friends. They'd felt so sophisticated, hitting all the most popular college hangouts, where they went virtually unnoticed, only to return to find that they'd missed out on a meet-and-greet with the women's softball team, men's baseball team and the university athletic recruiters. Coach's disappointment had been palpable.

"Do you want a scholarship or not, Billings?" he'd demanded.

She'd privately vowed never to disappoint him again and had sincerely concentrated on her game after that. Before long he'd started giving her the extra batting practice, and then had come the nickname Jolly. She'd gotten her scholarship, and she'd thought she'd earned Coach's regard. But then she'd learned what Coach *really* thought of her, and the truth had upended her world.

Jenny patted Dean's cheek. He slid the box toward Ann and took the much heavier sack from the cook. As she turned toward the door, the thought occurred to Ann that the moment had come to face the darkest, most foolish part of her past. How could she ever truly come home if she didn't somehow put that crushing moment to rest?

As Ann drove toward the ballpark where she had spent so many hours, she wondered just how best to do that.

Should she speak to Coach, ask him about that day? From time to time she'd thought about doing just that, but what if he didn't even remember saying those things about her? What if he denied saying them?

Part of her wanted to go to her dad as she no doubt should have done in the very beginning, but the circumstances of his illness argued against that, certainly in the short-term. She could wait until he felt better, of course. He was violently ill immediately after every treatment, but then he gradually got better—better being a relative word as each treatment seemed to take more out of him than the last. Eventually the cancer would be defeated, and his body would begin to recover from the treatment. At least that was the hope.

Her gaze wandered to Dean, but the last man with whom she had shared that life-altering event had used it to pull the wool over her eyes. She had shown him her weakness, and he had used it against her. What else explained that engagement scheme? She had difficulty believing that Dean compared in any way to Jordan, but how could she trust her own judgment at this point?

Maybe if they were business partners, if Dean decided to let her invest in his business, maybe that would change everything. Maybe they would develop the kind of trust and honesty that would allow her to confide in him.

Oh, who was she kidding?

She wasn't looking for a business opportunity. She just wanted a chance for Dean to fall in love with her. The way she had fallen in love with him.

Even before she'd discovered the horrid truth about Jordan, she'd fallen in love with Dean. If she was perfectly honest with herself, she'd felt a secret sense of relief because Jordan had given her a valid excuse to break their engagement. Yes, she'd been crushed to learn that he didn't value her at all except as a means to an end. Personally she meant nothing to Jordan. She realized now, though, that she hadn't really valued Jordan as she should have, either.

His main value to her had rested simply in the supposed fact that he loved her. She hadn't loved Jordan for Jordan; she'd loved the idea that Jordan loved her. When that proved not to be true, her fragile ego had taken a definite beating, but in some ways she'd been relieved.

It stunned Ann to know that, had it been Dean whose career could be boosted through marriage to her, she'd have gone through with it simply for his sake, even knowing that he didn't love her as she loved him. The undeniable truth was that she wanted what was best for Dean and Donovan, even if it wasn't what was best for her.

So if a business partnership was all she could have with Dean, then she'd settle for that and work to make that business boom and their lives better. But she'd pray for more.

She would pray unceasingly for more.

# Chapter Fourteen

"Déjà vu all over again," Dean quipped as Ann drove around the heavy chain-link fence wrapping the spotty field. "They never could get the grass to grow properly."

"Hey, it's Oklahoma, land of three seasons," she shot back.

They said it together. "Freezing, blistering and tornado."

"With emphasis on the blistering," Dean said as she parked the car behind the long, squat building that housed the locker and weight rooms along with the coaches' offices.

Ann opened her door and got out. "Actually, it's hotter in Texas." She shook her head. "Not colder, though."

Dean followed suit, pointing out, tongue in cheek, "And we haven't had a real tornado in decades."

"There is that," she agreed, straight-faced. "Not to mention the two weeks of spring and autumn we enjoy every year."

Dean chuckled, wondering just why it was that she really wanted to come home. Did her job disappear along with her engagement? Or did she really want to be here?

"There's better weather," he said drily, "but what other place on earth has red-orange dirt?"

"So true," she agreed, playing along.

They both laughed as they gathered their packages and trudged across the graveled parking area to the entrance. Dean pulled open the metal door and stood back to let Ann enter first. The telescoping room divider that blocked off the workout room when it was in use had been pushed back, revealing an empty space. The weight benches, treadmills and other machines all stood abandoned and quiet. The showers, which opened off the workout room, were dark and silent. Both boys and girls used the facility but at different times.

Peg Amber, the girls' basketball coach, stepped out into a hallway on the right. A bright smile split her face, showing overlarge teeth and healthy pink gums.

"Dean! What are you doing here?"

"Delivering food. Coach Amber, do you know Ann Billings?"

The other woman came forward. Dressed in baggy workout clothes, her brown hair caught in a short ponytail at the back of her head, she stood almost as tall as Dean, every inch the female jock. "Don't think so." Her eyes suddenly lit as she took in Ann. "Billings," she repeated. "You wouldn't be Jolly Billings?"

Ann smiled limply. "The same."

Amber waved a hand, grinning. "You were before my day, but Lyons never stops bragging about you."

"Oh?"

"Baseball and softball are where his heart is, you know," Coach Amber said. "Most athletic directors are all football all the time with basketball coming in a distant second and everything else kind of hanging on by sheer determination. But Lyons is all about the diamond. Makes him more fair with the other sports, I think. As far as softball goes, though, there'll never be another Jolly Billings."

Ann blinked at that, though Dean couldn't imagine why she would be surprised. "I, uh, think we're supposed to leave this food in Coach Lyons's office," he quickly said.

"Actually it's the conference room next door," Peg Amber corrected, signaling them to follow her. Glancing at the box Ann carried, she asked, "Would those be lemon crèmes?"

"They would."

"Yum."

Dean traded an amused glance with Ann and followed Coach Amber down the hallway. She stopped and stuck her head into one room, calling, "Jack! Food's here."

Jack Lyons popped out into the hallway, pulling dollar bills out of his pocket. He froze when he saw Dean and Ann.

"Coach," Dean greeted the older man.

"Well, I'll be! What're you two doing here? Didn't expect a couple of my old favorites to turn up on the first day of school, delivering for the diner, of all things."

"How's it going?" Dean asked.

"Hectic as usual," came the reply. He stuffed the bills back into his pocket, took the bag from Dean and passed it to Peg, saying, "Y'all get started. I'll be there in a minute."

Nodding, she carried the bag into the next room. Ann handed the box of pastries to Lyons. "Mmm-mmm," he hummed. Winking at Dean, he said, "Not the first time this has happened, is it, Jolly?"

"No, sir," she said, smiling down at her feet.

"Now tell me. How'd the two of you wind up delivering food for the diner?"

"Well, I dropped my boy off at his first day of kindergarten this morning," Dean began.

"Is he a big boy like you?"

"He is."

"Is he going to play ball?"

Dean chuckled. "I imagine so. We'll see."

"I'll be on the lookout for him."

"Don't rush him." Dean chuckled. "I'm having enough trouble with the idea of him starting school. Ann had to take me down to the diner for a cup of consolation coffee, which is how we happened to be there when Jenny needed help."

Lyons grinned. "Oh, you single parents. They all grow up. Just look at you." He turned his attention to Ann then, asking, "How's your dad?"

"In Oklahoma City getting treatment. Should be home this evening."

"Sure hope he beats this thing," Coach said seriously.

"We're counting on it," Ann told him, "and praying that way."

Lyons nodded. "Guess you'll be heading back to Dallas soon. I saw Rex in town yesterday."

"Actually," Ann said, parking her hands at her waist, "I don't think I'll be going back, after all."

He gaped at her then looked pointedly to her hand. "So the wedding is off?"

"It's off," she confirmed, looking at Dean. "Seems that what I want is here in War Bonnet. And what he wants is someplace else."

"Well, I'll be," Lyons declared. Then he smiled

broadly. "You know what they say. There's no place like home."

Ann smiled wanly. "That is so true."

"So what are you going to do?" Coach Lyons asked. "Jobs don't exactly grow on trees around here, you know."

"I'll find something," Ann said, glancing at Dean. "Sometimes you have to make your own job, like Dean did."

"That is a true statement," Lyons said, clapping Dean on the shoulder with one hand. "He sure did do that." Lyons shook a finger at her, adding, "And if anybody else can do it, Jolly girl, you can. You were always best and brightest."

"Thank you."

"Well, I better get in there," he said, backing away. "Don't y'all be strangers now. Come on by and visit when you can."

"Sure thing," Dean said.

Coach Lyons went into the conference room, carrying his box of pastries, and closed the door behind him.

Sighing, Ann put her back to the wall and bowed her head. After a moment she said, "That's the man who drove me out of War Bonnet."

Astounded, Dean gaped at her. *"What?"*

"It happened right here," she said quietly. "In this very spot."

Dean seized her by the upper arms, appalled and suddenly frightened. What had Coach done?

"Honey, what are you talking about?" he demanded softly.

She leaned into him, tucking her head beneath his

chin and laying her face against his chest. "Dean, I'm such a fool," she whispered. "Such an idiotic fool."

More worried than ever and suddenly aware of their surroundings, Dean turned toward the exit at the far end of the hall. He walked her straight out onto the field and down into the dugout where they had spent so much of their youth. There, he gently pushed her down onto the bench, sat beside her and took her hands in his.

"Tell me. All of it. What did Lyons do to you?"

She shook her head. "Oh, it's not fair to blame him," she admitted. "It was much more me than him. He didn't even know he'd done it."

Dean edged around to more fully face her. "What are you saying?"

She waved an arm at their surroundings. "You remember how I was back then, Dean. All about the game. Taking batting practice with the boys."

"And outslugging half of them," Dean said matter-of-factly. Ann grimaced. "What? It's true," he insisted. "You're deadly with a bat."

"Mmm-hmm, as deadly as any man."

"I wouldn't go that far," he muttered, "but you could hold your own back then. That's something to be proud of."

"Is it? I thought so. Then one day I came home from college to visit, and I naturally swung by here to see Coach Lyons. It was something I did routinely."

"Yeah, I did it a few times, too," Dean commented.

"I did it *a lot*," Ann confessed. "I was so homesick. Even in my junior year at college, I still just wanted to be done with it and get back home. I thought I'd work at the bank and then maybe take over the ranch when Dad was ready to retire. Rex had gone to law school and always said he wanted no part of the ranch, so I thought, why not me?"

"What happened?" Dean asked again, squeezing her hand.

Ann sighed, staring at her lap. "Well, I stopped by as soon as school was out. I always stopped after hours. Anyway, as I walked up to Coach's office, I heard him talking to one of the teachers. About me."

Dean's brow wrinkled. "What about you?"

Ann sighed. "He called me awkward, said I was taller than half the male population, could outslug most of the teenage boys I'd worked out with and that if you cut off my hair you wouldn't be able to tell the difference between me and them."

Dean frowned. *That* was the terrible secret that had driven her away from War Bonnet? He rubbed both hands over his face then abruptly dropped them as he remembered another time she had confided in him, the questions she had asked.

*Do you think I'm feminine? What, specifically, is womanly about me?*

She'd worried that she was too tall, that her shoulders were too broad, her nose too long and her jaw too square.

Finally it all made sense. The coach she had worked so hard for, the man she'd admired and respected, had disparaged her and destroyed her self-confidence. Given his prominence in this small town, what else was she going to do but run?

"I don't know why Coach would say such a thing," Dean declared, "but it's the most absurd bunk I've ever heard. You were the hottest thing War Bonnet had ever seen! You still are!"

Ann smiled and ran her fingertips down his cheek, sucking in a shaky breath. "Caroline said—"

"Caroline Carmody?" Caroline Carmody had taught English at War Bonnet for a few years back then. She'd been a shapely blonde that all the boys had ogled.

"Yes. Caroline said that I'd probably wind up an old maid living with my parents."

"Ann," Dean said, suddenly sure what had happened, "Lyons was dating Caroline back then."

"What?"

"Everyone knew it. Everyone who was still in school. I was a senior. It was all the talk. She was probably jealous as all get-out."

"Jealous?"

"Think about it. His favorite *former* female student, a gorgeous redhead, dropping by all the time. Lyons was probably trying to soothe Caroline. That's all. He couldn't have meant those things. He's not that blind or stupid." Dean stood, pulling her up with him. "But you were."

"What?"

"Put yourself in his position, sweetheart. You were— are—gorgeous. And by then you were no longer off-limits."

"But he was my coach."

"Not anymore. You were three years out of school, babe. No wonder Caroline was nervous. The problem wasn't that you were unattractive or unfeminine. It was just the opposite."

The incredulous look on her face made Dean want to hug her.

"You think?"

"Jolly, if I'd known you were coming around to see

Lyons back then, I'd have been jealous," he confessed, smoothing her hair with his hands.

She grinned. "Really?"

Dean rolled his eyes heavenward, dropping his hands to her shoulders. "Don't you get it yet? I had the world's biggest crush on you!"

Her eyes and her mouth rounded in surprise. "I really was blind and stupid, wasn't I?" she commented, sounding stunned.

A door slammed somewhere and voices could be heard drawing closer to the dugout.

Dean grabbed Ann's hand, leading her across the dugout to the opposite end. "Come on. We're leaving."

"Okay," she agreed without hesitation. "Where are we going?"

"Someplace more private," he muttered, racking his brain for just such a spot.

"In that case," she said, dangling the Beemer's key fob in front of him, "you might need this."

He grabbed the fob with his free hand, but in his heart of hearts he knew that he already had what he needed in his *other* hand. The problem was, given the many differences still between them, he didn't quite know how to keep her.

*I had the world's biggest crush on you.* Had. That one word in an otherwise dreamy sentence needled Ann.

Well, she wanted more than a crush from him now. She wanted, oh, everything, absolutely everything. But now that he knew just how idiotic she had been all these years, could he possibly feel for her what she wanted, needed, him to feel? If he'd just agree to the business partnership, she might have a chance to show him that she'd finally wised up. She knew that she could be an asset to him when it came to the business, and if it didn't work out the way she wanted in the end, at least he and Donovan would be better off financially.

*Please, God*, she prayed as Dean drove them around, seemingly aimlessly. *I've been so foolish for so long. I know better now. It's not that I think I'm suddenly some hot number all men want. If that were true, I'd have gotten over this nonsense long ago.* But other men had shown interest in her, she realized, interest she had discouraged for fear they would discover how lacking she was in feminine attributes. *I understand now that You made me as complete as every other woman, and I let one carelessly overheard conversation shake my confidence in myself and You. That was stupid, and I'm sorry, Lord.*

Finally, Dean brought the car to a stop at the end of a shady lane near an uncharacteristically blue body of water.

"This is Clear Springs Lake."

"Can't think of a cooler spot," he said, killing the engine and rolling down the windows.

The small lake, which was fed by a spring, sat on private property, but the owners had never begrudged the public access to the site, posting numerous signs denying any responsibility for injury or loss. The local kids were known to make good use of the spot, especially at night. As a result, this place had long held a reputation as the local lovers' lane.

"Might be cooler if we get out," Dean said, opening his door.

The rear of the car was better shaded than the front, and the engine compartment was bound to be hot, so they leaned against the trunk, feet crossed at the ankles.

Ann braced her hands on the vehicle behind her. Dean folded his arms.

"I can't believe you just accepted what Lyons was saying about you as fact," Dean finally said. "I mean, you have a mirror."

"No woman trusts what she sees in the mirror," Ann muttered.

"There had to be guys buzzing around you. I went to college, you know."

"Not for me," Ann told him softly. "I wasn't raised like that. Once I let enough guys know that, they stopped *buzzing,* as you put it."

Dean smiled. "Good for you. Wish I'd been that smart. But then I wouldn't have Donovan."

"We all make mistakes," she said. "It's how you handle them that counts. I may not have handled Lyons's criticisms well, but Dean, I know what I'm doing when it comes to business."

He nodded. "I don't doubt it. What about your job, though?"

"I'm going to resign. I don't want to work for LHI anymore."

"There must be other jobs."

"There are, but I want to be here."

"And you truly have the money to invest?"

"I wouldn't lie to you."

He dropped his arms. "Well, that leaves just one problem, then."

"What's that?"

"I can't take your money. Unless you marry me."

Ann nearly fell down, too stunned to react with anything but shock. "Dean!"

He shifted, finally looking at her, the heat in his eyes

melting her heart. "I've loved you half my life already," he said softly, "literally half my life. I'll always love you. I can't work with you and pretend that I—"

She threw herself on him. "Yes! Of course I'll marry you! I'm crazy in love with you!"

He laughed, clamping one arm around her waist and pushing away from the car with the other. "I was beginning to get the idea, but you've been out of reach for so long, I—I couldn't quite convince myself it could be true."

Wrapping herself around him, she kissed him until he swept her into his arms and swung her in a circle, laughing. But then he sobered, setting her on her feet.

"Wait, wait. You need to know something. About Grandma. I promised she'd always have a home with me, and I'll never go against that. Grandpa trusted me to take care of her."

Ann kissed him into silence. "We'd starve without your grandmother in the house. I thought we'd established that I'm not exactly domestic. I mean, I'm willing to learn, but...don't get your hopes up."

Dean chuckled and put his forehead to hers. "So Grandma's safe. And there's always the diner."

"And Callie," Ann added.

"I have to think you're okay with kids because there is Donovan," Dean said.

"Would you like more children?" Ann asked carefully.

"I would," he stated, squaring his shoulders. "I like being a dad, and it would be nice to do it right."

She smiled. "I think you've done quite well, but it would be fun to do it together. I can't wait to tell Donovan!"

Dean relaxed, glancing at his watch. "Still too early."

"We could tell Rex and Callie."

"Yeah, let's do that," Dean agreed, grinning. "I feel like I'm going to bust if I don't tell someone."

"My dad's going to be so happy," Ann proclaimed. "He likes you so much."

"There's no one I respect more than your dad," Dean told her. "Oh, man, I can't believe this. Who would've thought that after all this time..." He cupped her face in his hands. "It's proof positive that God does answer prayer."

She went up on tiptoe, wrapped her arms around his neck and kissed him with all the love in her heart. Answered prayers, indeed.

## Chapter Fifteen

"What do you think?" Ann asked, showing Callie the gold satin suit. "It's not white, but I haven't worn it, and it's very expensive. Plus, I have shoes to match."

She'd brought the suit thinking that Jordan might drive down one weekend, and she'd wanted something stunning to wear to church while he was here, something that would tell everyone in War Bonnet how well she'd done, just in case Jordan hadn't impressed everyone enough. Silly, silly girl. She was so happy that she no longer thought like that. She'd never feel the need to impress anyone again. What a blessing!

"It's gorgeous," Callie told her, "and I've got something I think will make it just right for a wedding."

She hurried from the bedroom, leaving Ann to find the shoes that matched the suit. Rex was out on the range, so they'd left Dean downstairs with baby Bodie. He was an old hand with little ones, after all. Callie returned within moments, carrying a small, flat, round box. From it she drew a headband of white silk flowers with pearl centers and a face veil of wide netting that ended just below the nose. "I bought this for my own wedding, but then I found something that worked better with my dress. I meant to return it, but I'd be happy to give it to you if you think it works."

Ann tried it on, holding up the suit in front of the mirror. With her hair combed back and hanging straight, the sophisticated little veil worked very well. "I like it. Simple white bouquet, pearl earrings and I'm set."

"It's lovely," Callie agreed, hugging her. "I'm so happy for you. I think I heard Rex's truck pulling up when I was in the other room. He'll be surprised, but he really likes Dean, you know. Everyone does."

"He's so wonderful, Callie," Ann said softly.

"The man you love is always wonderful."

The two women laughed, and Ann sighed happily.

Just then, Dean called up the stairs. "Ann? Honey? Your brother's here."

"Coming!"

She laid aside the suit and the veil and hurried down the stairs, Callie on her heels. The men were standing in the foyer, staring at each other. Dean had Bodie tucked into the curve of his arm. Rex plopped his sweat-stained straw cowboy hat onto a peg on the wall and looked up the stairs, his pale blue gaze targeting Ann.

"Honey?" he echoed, eyebrows raised.

Dean cleared his throat, sending Ann a sheepish, apologetic glance. At the same time, Callie snorted behind Ann.

"Yes, well, there are things you don't know," Ann said primly, suppressing her smile as he descended the remaining stairs.

"For instance?" Rex asked, hanging an elbow on the banister at the foot of those stairs.

"For instance," Ann said, slipping past him to stand at Dean's side, "we're getting married."

Rex turned his head to glance at his wife then looked once more to Ann. "You and Dean are getting married?"

Ann grinned and threaded her arm through Dean's. "That's right. The sooner, the better."

Rex tilted his dark head. "Because?"

"Because we love each other, of course." Ann said, frowning.

"And that's the only reason?" Rex prodded.

"The *only* reason," Dean answered in a steely voice that had Bodie grabbing his shirt and crawling onto his chest.

Callie quietly came down the stairs and took her daughter in hand, shooting Ann a supportive look. "Let's sit down and discuss this like adults, everyone."

"What's to discuss?" Ann wanted to know, even as Rex followed Callie and the baby into the living room and Dean pressed his hand into the small of her back, urging her to go along.

"What's to discuss," Rex said, dropping into their father's chair, "is someone named Jordan Teel."

Ann made a show of sitting calmly on the sofa and crossing her legs. Dean came down beside her, stretching his long arm out behind her shoulders. Callie chose the rocker, nine-month-old Bodie in her lap.

"I broke it off with Jordan some time ago," Ann announced. "You weren't here so you wouldn't know." Actually no one had known except Dean and then her father.

"And you broke it off with Jordan because?"

"Don't see how that's any of your business really," Dean said lightly, and Ann fell in love with him all over again. Clearly he was trying to spare her the humiliation of revealing Jordan's treachery. She smiled and patted Dean's knee.

"He was using me to advance his career," she said bluntly. "I don't suppose I'd have minded if I'd been in love with him, but I wasn't."

Rex inclined his head in acceptance. "What about *your* career?"

"I think I'm done with hotel management. Have been for some time, really. I have other business interests now."

Her brother seemed to consider this for several moments. "That aside, have you two thought about where you'll live?"

"That's all settled," Dean said. "I do have a house."

"So you're staying in War Bonnet?" Rex asked Ann. "You really think you'll be happy here?"

"I'm sure of it."

"I don't know, sis," Rex said doubtfully, shaking his head. "Moving from the city to the country is a big adjustment. Take it from me. And what about that spectacular Dallas wedding you had your heart set on?"

"I don't want or need that anymore." She looked to Dean then, adding, "I haven't got anything to prove to anybody now." She shifted closer to him, saying to her brother, "I just want Dean and Donovan. That's all I need."

"You've only known him a few weeks," Rex pointed out.

"I've known him since he was thirteen!" Ann refuted, conveniently omitting the fact that she'd barely registered his existence for most of those years.

"Oh, yeah? What size shoe does he wear? What size ring?"

Ann felt heat stain her cheeks.

"Size twelve shoe. Size thirteen ring," Dean replied

calmly. "Callie know that stuff about you when she agreed to marry you?"

Over in the rocking chair, Callie bent her head to hide a smile. Ann ignored all of it, taking Dean's hand in both of hers.

"He's got hands like Dad," she said defiantly, "the hands of an honest, capable, hardworking man. I think I started falling in love with him the day I first saw his hands."

Dean curled his fingers through hers, smiling down at her.

"Annie, since you brought up Donovan, it has to be said," Rex went on doggedly, "your whole life I've never heard you talk about wanting to be a mother."

Truth time. Ann sucked in a deep breath. "I honestly didn't know if I wanted children," she admitted, "until Donovan. But how can you not love that kid? And Dean is such a wonderful father. Watching the two of them is amazing. Who wouldn't want more of that?"

Dean dropped his arm from the back of the sofa and drew it tightly about her, vowing, "We're getting married, and that's all there is to it."

"Well, at least give it some time," Rex pleaded. "You don't have to run right down to the county courthouse and get a license today."

"You're one to talk," Ann grumbled. "You got married in four days' time!"

"Yes, but Callie and I had known each other for a couple months," Rex pointed out. "We'd lived and worked in close proximity to one another. I'm just saying there's no reason to run right out today and get a license. Besides, you don't have time. Because you're going to Oklahoma City to pick up Dad and Meri. Right?"

A lightbulb went on in Ann's brain. "We could get a license in Oklahoma City," she said to Dean, suddenly excited. "Go with me. You're not working right now, and we'll be back tonight. Trust me when I tell you that Dad will be much more supportive than my overprotective big brother."

"Sounds like a plan," Dean agreed, smiling. He glanced at his watch, folding her close as he did so. "Hey, we'd better get going. Donovan will be out of school soon."

They got to their feet in tandem. Rex stood, too, saying, "Look, sis, I just want you to be sure about this."

"I am sure," Ann said stiffly. "I'm sure that I'm going to marry Dean at the earliest opportunity. I've already got my wedding outfit picked out. All we need now are a pair of gold wedding bands and a license."

"Are you sure that's what you want?" Dean asked softly. "Just simple gold wedding bands?"

She nodded. "Narrow, classic, modest. Everything else is superfluous."

"I sincerely hope you mean that," Rex told her. "However, Dad might be more on my side than you know."

Ann swallowed a sudden lump in her throat, beating back a surge of disappointment. She'd really expected her brother's approval. She hoped he was wrong about their father. Surely she hadn't misunderstood what Dad had meant during their talk at the hospital. On the other hand, her track record with misunderstandings was all too clear. She'd let a simple misunderstanding drive her away from home for years.

Well, she was home now, and Rex would just have to accept that she knew what she was doing. But, oh, she had so hoped that this would be a time of joy for her whole family, especially given her father's illness. At least she knew that Dean's family would take the news well.

Donovan bubbled over with tales of his first day of school. All the way home in the car he rattled on and on about story time and who couldn't stand in a straight line, write their own names or recognize certain words. Dean had fretted about preschool, but when he'd taken Donovan for evaluation, he'd discovered that his son was far more advanced academically than most other children his age, so Dean had made the decision to keep the boy with him rather than pay for preschool. After all, Donovan got classroom experience once a week at church. It seemed he'd done his son no disservice. He judged that he was about to do both himself and the boy a great boon, but it troubled Dean that his future brother-in-law was not more supportive of the idea.

When they reached the farmhouse, Ann suggested they all sit on the porch. Grandma had been waiting for their arrival, eager to hear of Donovan's day, but Dean put her off with a quiet admonition. "If you don't mind, Ann and I have an announcement to make."

"The thing is," Ann said to Donovan, reaching up from the rocking chair where she sat to lace her fingers with Dean's, "I don't want to be your substitute mom anymore."

Donovan's face fell. Dean almost laughed, but he patted the boy on the back instead, glanced at his grandmother, who occupied the other chair, and quickly said, "What Ann means is that she wants to be your real mom."

Grandma understood at once and clapped her hands together, exclaiming, "Oh, honey!"

"In other words," Ann told Donovan, reaching out to cup Donovan's drooping chin, "your dad and I are going to get married."

Predictably, Donovan's eyes rounded. Then he threw himself into Ann's lap, rocking the chair back on its runners. Laughing, Ann kissed him all over his face. Digger skittered around and wagged his tail enthusiastically.

"We have to go to Oklahoma City to get a marriage license and pick up Ann's father," Dean said, "but we'll be back in time to tuck you into bed tonight."

"Don't go yet," Grandma said, bolting up out of her chair. "Wait right here until I get back." She hurried off at a trot.

"Are you going to have a baby?" Donovan demanded as Grandma disappeared into the house.

Gaping, Ann looked at Dean. "No. Well, not right away. I mean, someday. Don't you want a baby brother or sister?"

"Lots of 'em!" Donovan proclaimed, and both Dean and Ann chuckled.

"We'll take that under advisement," Ann told him, smiling.

"Like father, like son," Dean muttered, squeezing her fingers.

Grandma returned then, something clutched in her hand. "Now, don't feel you have to wear this," she said. "It was Great-Great-Grandma Rosalie's. Milburn bought me one before he knew it existed, and of course I wasn't about to turn it down, so we put this back for our oldest child, except…we didn't trust Wynona not to pawn it, and it's not to Deana's taste. Then we figured it should go to Dean, but if you don't like it, we can always hold it for Donovan." She opened her hand to show them an unusual platinum-and-gold filigreed ring with three round diamonds, two smaller ones on either side of a significantly larger one.

"Oh, my word!" Ann breathed. "That's beautiful!"

"Grandma, I didn't know you had this," Dean said, shocked.

"Honey, don't take this the wrong way," Grandma begged, patting his cheek, "but I didn't want your mother to know about it, and later with things so tight, I—I was afraid you'd want to sell it or use it as collateral."

He hugged her then picked up the ring.

"Ann, what do you think?"

"It's the most unique, meaningful engagement ring I can imagine."

Smiling, he slid it onto her finger, feeling as if his chest might burst. It was a little large, but they could fix that. "We'll take it to a jeweler tomorrow."

"Until then," Ann asked Grandma, "do you have some bandage tape? If I wrap a little piece around the back of the ring, I can wear it now without worrying about losing it."

"I have just the thing," Grandma said.

As she hurried away, Donovan asked Ann, "Will you tuck me in at night?"

"Of course."

"And wash my hair?"

"Naturally."

"Hey, what about me?" Dean teased. He'd been doing these things for years, after all.

Without missing a beat, Donovan said, "She'll tuck you in, too. But you wash your own hair."

Ann bit her lip to keep from laughing, and Dean wondered just how soon they could arrange this small, simple wedding. He hoped Ann was right about her father. If Wes agreed with Rex, she might decide to put things off for a while—and then she might realize what a bad bargain he was.

But no, he wouldn't think like that. Ann agreeing to marry him was an answered prayer. He wouldn't believe anything else.

Grandma seemed to be taking her time finding that tape. He thought he heard the phone ring, so that might explain the delay. She eventually came with it, though, and Ann made the temporary fix. They took their leave, through many hugs and happy farewells.

Back in the car, she looked down at the ring on her finger and sighed.

"I know it's not perfect," he said, "but we'll get it fixed soon."

"It's not that," she assured him. "Really it's not. It's that I love it so much."

He hoped, prayed, that was true, and he kept up that silent prayer all the way to Oklahoma City.

It took longer to get the license than either of them expected, but when Ann called her sister to say they'd been delayed, Meredith told her not to worry. Apparently Wes was doing better than usual. Dean felt some relief that Rex had evidently not called to share their news and argue against their marriage, and he could tell that Ann was also relieved. Nevertheless, as soon as they pushed through the door of the hospital room, Wes barked at both of them.

"It's about time!"

Wes looked wan and weak sitting there in the wheel-chair. Strangely, he was dressed in a suit and tie.

"Daddy," Ann said in a confused voice, "why are you dressed like that?"

"It's a surprise!" cried a bright, familiar little voice.

"Donovan!" Dean exclaimed. "Son, what are you doing here?"

"That depends on whether or not you got the license," drawled another familiar voice.

"Rex!" Ann said.

Dean finally looked around. They were all there—almost all—Rex, Meredith, Donovan, Grandma, Wes, everyone but Callie and the baby. As if reading his mind, Rex said, "Callie and Bodie are waiting in the chapel. They wouldn't let the baby up here no matter how much we begged."

"The chapel," Ann repeated. Then she gasped. "I don't believe it!"

"Yes, sister dear, the chapel," Rex said, looking very pleased with himself. "You didn't really believe all that big brother guff back at the ranch, did you?"

"You rat!" Ann scolded, but she was laughing. Then she sobered. "My things."

"Not to worry," Rex told her. "Callie packed you a bag before we left. You have everything you need." He looked to Dean then, adding, "Your grandmother packed for you, but I tossed in a few pieces. I have a fairly extensive wardrobe that's now too large for me. The shirts and jackets ought to work well enough for you."

"I'm not sure I understand," Dean said, his brow furrowed.

"We're 'loping!" Donovan exclaimed, hopping up and down.

"We drove up with Callie and Bodie," Betty explained, grinning ear to ear.

"I came on my own to get Dad and Meri back home," Rex said. "Now, about that license…"

"The marriage license?" Dean asked, looking at Ann, who burst out laughing.

"That would be the one," Rex chortled. "Did you get it or not?"

"Yeah, we got it," Dean confirmed, still not quite with the program.

"Okay, then," Rex said. "You'll have to change in the men's room downstairs. Annie, you can use this room. When you're ready, Meri will show you where the chapel is."

Dean looked at Ann, who finally confirmed it all for him. "They're throwing us a wedding, darling."

"We're not about to let her kick you to the curb," Rex said happily. "Brothers-in-law with working combines and hay-balers don't come along every day."

Ann put her head back and laughed at that. Wes dug into his coat pocket, producing a small, velvet-covered box. "Here. You're going to need these. My gift to the two of you."

Dean just stood there, so dumbfounded that Ann had to prompt him to take the box. He popped open the hinged lid. Two narrow gold bands nestled inside.

"Perfect," Ann pronounced, a catch in her throat. "It'll go well with my engagement ring." She took a moment to show that off, Callie and Meredith oohing and aahing appropriately while Dean wrapped his mind around the fact that he was about to get married. Married!

"And this is my gift," Meredith said, bringing out a bouquet of mixed white flowers tied with gold ribbon.

"They're exactly right," Ann said, hugging her sister, tears in her eyes.

"My gift," Rex announced, "mine and Callie's, is a suite at the Luxury Hotel here in the city through Friday evening."

"Convenient," Ann said, grinning. "That's an LHI hotel. I'll be able to tender my resignation right after we check in."

"Let's move, people," Wes ordered in a husky voice, "before my meds wear off. That chaplain's not going to wait forever."

"Believe it or not, he said he's done this kind of thing before," Meredith told them.

"Donovan, come with Grandpa." Wes beckoned. Beaming, Donovan ran to clasp onto Wes's chair. Dean saw that his son wore his best dress pants and a white shirt. A necktie had been tucked into his back pocket.

Married! He was about to get married! And have Ann all to himself until Saturday morning.

Laughing, Dean caught the suitcase Rex shoved at him.

Dean shook his head and winked at Ann, smiling. "Just so you know, I love you enough to completely overlook your crazy family." She laughed, beaming. "And just so *you* know," he said to the grinning about-to-be brother-in-law at his side, "harvesting and hay-baling don't come free. I'm running a business here, and I have a growing family to support."

Rex laughed, shoving him through the door. "We'll negotiate."

"We will," Dean allowed. "And family does get discounts."

What, after all, was business between brothers?

Especially to a man whose every dream had been fulfilled and every prayer answered?

## *Epilogue*

It was a wedding like no other Wes had ever attended. The tiny chapel with its backlit stained glass and few pews contained no altar or dais, only a simple cross upon the wall. No music played. No guests other than the immediate family attended. Then again, his daughter made a bride like no other.

Dressed in shiny gold and white, she looked like a million bucks. Meredith acted as bridesmaid. Rex pushed Wes in his chair at Ann's side then moved to stand next to Dean and Donovan, who held the rings and could barely contain his excitement. Dean wore almost exactly what Rex had worn for his wedding, dark jeans, black boots, white shirt, black jacket and a string tie. He looked more prone to tears than the bride.

The chaplain kept it simple, leading them both through their vows. Within very few minutes, they were at the point of pronouncement, when Dean suddenly lifted a hand as if to bring a halt to the whole proceeding.

"Oh, my word, Jolly!" he said, clapping his hand to his face, the newly installed gold ring on his fourth finger gleaming in the canned light. "I just realized. Sweetheart, you weren't being stupid. You did just what you were supposed to. Think about it. You are a beautiful, talented, intelligent, loving woman. It was a plan to keep some guy from snapping you up while God worked on me. He put you in a safe place and kept you there until the time was right. Until now. For me. For us."

Wes had no idea what that was all about, but Ann certainly did. Lifting her hands to Dean's shoulders, she sniffed back tears and tremulously said, "That's the most beautiful thing I've ever heard."

"What a gift!" Dean exclaimed, pulling her close, his big hands at her trim waist. "I'll never deserve it, but I'll always be thankful for it, and I'll love you until my dying breath."

If Wes had had any doubts about this marriage, they would have vanished on the spot.

Ann wrapped her arms around Dean's neck and went up on tiptoe to kiss him.

The chaplain chuckled and said, "A little premature, but appropriate. I now pronounce you husband and wife."

Everyone applauded and wiped at their tears. Wes gulped down the nausea rising within him and tried not to shiver. Meredith noticed, however, and hurried to hand Ann her bouquet and come for him, picking up a blanket from the front pew as she did so. A blanket in the middle of August. Wes wanted to rage as Meri draped it about his shoulders, but then Donovan grinned at him and waved, posing with his parents as cell phone photos were snapped, and the rage dissipated beneath the weight of his blessings.

Not long ago Wes had feared that he might not live long enough to be a grandpa; now he had two grandchildren, and two of his children had come home to stay. God was good.

For a while now, Wes had wondered why he labored so at Straight Arrow Ranch. For what? For whom? With Gloria gone and his children uninterested in the family concern, the years had begun to seem pointless, but even if God chose not to heal him from this cancer, Wes would forever be thankful that he had lived long enough to see the plan that God had set into motion for his family.

Was it selfish and foolish of him to hope that his youngest child, the one with whom he had the least in common, might also find her way home to stay? She deserved to have more in her life than a spoiled cat.

He told himself that he would be thankful for the time that he and Meredith had together. He would be thankful, but he would also pray. It was a father's privilege and responsibility to pray for his child.

And prayer, as he knew well, availed a man much.

So very much.

\* \* \* \* \*

## WE HOPE YOU ENJOYED
## THIS BOOK FROM

# LOVE INSPIRED
## INSPIRATIONAL ROMANCE

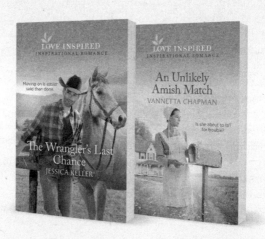

*Uplifting stories of faith, forgiveness and hope.*

Fall in love with stories where faith helps
guide you through life's challenges, and discover
the promise of a new beginning.

**6 NEW BOOKS AVAILABLE EVERY MONTH!**

# SPECIAL EXCERPT FROM

*Love Inspired*

*Could this bad-boy newcomer spell trouble for an Amish
spinster...or be the answer to her prayers?*

*Read on for a sneak preview of
An Unlikely Amish Match,
the next book in Vannetta Chapman's miniseries
Indiana Amish Brides.*

The sun was low in the western sky by the time Micah Fisher
hitched a ride to the edge of town. The driver let him out at a dirt
road that led to several Amish farms. He'd never been to visit
his grandparents in Indiana before. They always came to Maine.
But he had no trouble finding their place.

As he drew close to the lane that led to the farmhouse, he
noticed a young woman standing by the mailbox. A little girl was
holding her hand and another was hopping up and down. They
were all staring at him.

"Howdy," he said.

The woman only nodded, but the two girls whispered, "Hello."

"Can we help you?" the woman asked. "Are you...lost?"

"*Nein.* At least I don't think I am."

"You must be if you're here. This is the end of the road."

Micah pointed to the farm next door. "Abigail and John Fisher
live there?"

"They do."

"Then I'm not lost." He snatched off his baseball cap, rubbed
the top of his head and then yanked the cap back on.

Micah stepped forward and held out his hand. "I'm Micah—
Micah Fisher. Pleased to meet you."

"You're not *Englisch*?"

"Of course I'm not."

"So you're Amish?" She stared pointedly at his clothing—tennis shoes, blue jeans, T-shirt and baseball cap. Pretty much what he wore every day.

"I'm as Plain and simple as they come."

"I somehow doubt that."

"Since we're going to be neighbors, I suppose I should know your name."

"Neighbors?"

"*Ja.* I've come to live with my *daddi* and *mammi*—at least for a few months. My parents think it will straighten me out." He peered down the lane. "I thought the bishop lived next door."

"He does."

"Oh. You're the bishop's *doschder*?"

"We all are," the little girl with freckles cried. "I'm Sharon and that's Shiloh and that is Susannah."

"Nice to meet you, Sharon and Shiloh and Susannah."

Sharon lost interest and squatted to pick up some of the rocks. Shiloh hid behind her *schweschder*'s skirt, and Susannah scowled at him.

"I knew the bishop lived next door, but no one told me he had such pretty *doschdern*."

Susannah's eyes widened even more, but it was Shiloh who said, "He just called you pretty."

"Actually I called you all pretty."

Shiloh ducked back behind Susannah.

Susannah narrowed her eyes as if she was squinting into the sun, only she wasn't. "Do you talk to every girl you meet that way?"

"Not all of them—no."

*Don't miss*
An Unlikely Amish Match *by Vannetta Chapman,*
*available February 2020 wherever*
*Love Inspired*® *books and ebooks are sold.*

LoveInspired.com

Looking for inspiration in tales
of hope, faith and heartfelt romance?

Check out **Love Inspired**® and
**Love Inspired**® **Suspense** books!

**New books available every month!**

---

*Clang, clang, clang.*

The hammering outside her new schoolhouse grew
louder. Eva Coblentz moved to the window to locate
the source of the clatter. Across the road she saw a man
pounding on an ancient-looking piece of machinery with
steel wheels and a scoop-like nose on the front end.

When he had the sheet of metal shaped to fit the front
of the machine, he stood back to assess his work. He
knelt and hammered on the shovel-like nose three more
times. Satisfied, he gathered up his tools and started in
her direction.

She stepped back from the window. Was he coming to
the school? Why? Had he noticed her gawking? Perhaps
he only wanted to welcome the new teacher, although his
lack of a beard said he wasn't married.

She glanced around the room. Should she meet him
by the door? That seemed too eager. Her eyes settled on
the large desk at the front of the classroom. She should
look as if she was ready for the school year to start. A
professional attitude would put off any suggestion that
she was interested in meeting single men.

Eva hurried to the desk, pulled out the chair and sat down as the outside door opened. The chair tipped over backward, sending her flailing. Her head hit the wall with a painful thud as she slid to the floor. Stunned, she slowly opened her eyes to see the man leaning over the desk.

He had the most beautiful gray eyes she'd ever beheld. They were rimmed with thick, dark lashes in stark contrast to the mop of curly, dark red hair springing out from beneath his straw hat. Tiny sparks of light whirled around him.

"I'm Willis Gingrich. Local blacksmith." He squatted beside her. "Can you tell me your name?"

The warmth and strength of his hand on her skin sent a sizzle of awareness along her nerve endings. "I'm Eva Coblentz. I am the new teacher and I'm fine now."

*Don't miss*
The Amish Teacher's Dilemma
*by* USA TODAY *bestselling author Patricia Davids,*
*available March 2020 wherever*
*Love Inspired books and ebooks are sold.*

LoveInspired.com

# LOVE INSPIRED

INSPIRATIONAL ROMANCE

## UPLIFTING STORIES OF FAITH, FORGIVENESS AND HOPE.

---

Join our social communities to connect with other readers who share your love!

Sign up for the Love Inspired newsletter at **LoveInspired.com** to be the first to find out about upcoming titles, special promotions and exclusive content.

---

### CONNECT WITH US AT:

Facebook.com/LoveInspiredBooks

Twitter.com/LoveInspiredBks

Facebook.com/groups/HarlequinConnection